PEN
SECON

Shobhaa Dé's eighteen books include the bestsellers *Socialite Evenings*, *Starry Nights*, *Spouse* and *Superstar India*. Her latest book is *Sethji*. A widely read columnist in leading publications, she is known for her outspoken views, making her one of India's most respected opinion shapers. Dé lives in Mumbai with her family.

Also by the author

Fiction

Sisters

Socialite Evenings

Starry Nights

Strange Obsession

Sultry Days

Snapshots

Non-fiction

Speedpost

Surviving Men

Selective Memory

Spouse

Superstar India

SHOBHAA DÉ

SECOND THOUGHTS

PENGUIN BOOKS

PENGUIN BOOKS
Published by the Penguin Group
Penguin Books India Pvt. Ltd, 11 Community Centre, Panchsheel Park,
New Delhi 110 017, India
Penguin Group (USA) Inc., 375 Hudson Street, New York,
New York 10014, USA
Penguin Group (Canada), 90 Eglinton Avenue East, Suite 700, Toronto,
Ontario, M4P 2Y3, Canada (a division of Pearson Penguin Canada Inc.)
Penguin Books Ltd, 80 Strand, London WC2R 0RL, England
Penguin Ireland, 25 St Stephen's Green, Dublin 2, Ireland (a division of
Penguin Books Ltd)
Penguin Group (Australia), 707 Collins Street, Melbourne, Victoria 3008,
Australia (a division of Pearson Australia Group Pty Ltd)
Penguin Group (NZ), 67 Apollo Drive, Rosedale, Auckland 0632,
New Zealand (a division of Pearson New Zealand Ltd)
Penguin Books (South Africa) (Pty) Ltd, Block D, Rosebank Office Park,
181 Jan Smuts Avenue, Parktown North, Johannesburg 2193, South Africa

Penguin Books Ltd, Registered Offices: 80 Strand, London WC2R 0RL, England

First published by Penguin Books India 1996
This edition published 2013

ISBN 9780143422228

Typeset in Sabon by CyberMedia Services Ltd, Gurgaon
Printed at Gopsons Papers Ltd, Noida

For my husband Dilip,
with whom I hope to
co-author a marriage manual
someday

Prologue

It was on a sultry May evening in Bombay that Maya met Ranjan, her future husband.

She had arrived from Calcutta earlier in the day to meet her in-laws-to-be. It was Maya's first visit to the city she had heard so much about. Unfortunately, her first impressions were far from favourable. As she alighted from her cool, air-conditioned compartment onto a broad wet platform at the famed Victoria Terminus, her senses quickly took in a few things about the metropolis the rest of India held in such fascination.

Bombay smelt. Well, so did Calcutta, but it was a different smell. Besides, she was used to that particular stench. Bombay smelt of desperation and deceit. Or maybe that was what rotting fish did to the fumes that seemed to cling permanently to the city. Maya tweaked her nostrils and took a deep breath—just to make sure. Maybe she had made a mistake about the stench. Maybe it wasn't Bombay that exuded it but just this dirty, overcrowded platform.

Maya took a few tentative steps forward and recoiled in horror. She had almost tripped over a figure lying prone on the platform. She looked down to see it was a man, and he was dead. None of the thousands of people nonchalantly walking past the

1

corpse so much as paused. Maya watched in utter disbelief as coolies in tattered red shirts crossed deftly over the body, their eyes bulging with the strain of carrying two or three overstuffed suitcases on their heads. She tried to draw her mother's attention to the man, but Chitra was far too preoccupied with counting their luggage to bother with the still figure lying on the grimy platform.

Maya edged closer to the corpse and noticed a small trickle of vomit flowing out of the wide-open mouth. The dead man's eyes weren't closed either. They seemed to be staring fixedly at the pigeons dancing on the rafters. The youngish man—no more than thirty, she reckoned—was clad in loose-fitting pajamas and a stained kurta. He looked like a 'grassroots' politician, thought Maya, the sort she often spotted in televised rallies. His hair was long, matted and unruly. His footwear, torn and shabby. One hand rested on his heart. The other was stretched out, clutching a rag. His features were regular and he was clean-shaven. Maya couldn't take her eyes off him—he was the first dead person she had ever seen, and he seemed almost alive with those staring eyes.

But more than anything else, Maya wondered why nobody else was bothered by his presence on that stuffy, slimy platform. Had it been a platform in Calcutta, it would have been difficult to even get out of the compartment. There would have been a thick, over-helpful crowd converged around the corpse with everybody talking simultaneously, excitedly and demanding immediate answers. There would have been a couple of railway policemen trying unsuccessfully to keep the crowds at bay, plus a doctor or two eager to offer opinions on the possible cause of death. The word 'murder' would most certainly have cropped up with speculations galore about the victim's identity and the murderer's motive.

It was just the sort of situation that newspapers loved to describe as a 'heinous' crime. But here in Bombay, it was business as usual as people with troubled, distant gazes rushed around barely noticing one another or the dead man in their midst.

Maya shuddered as she finally tore her eyes off the corpse and looked around her. Just then, Chitra tugged at Maya's bright purple dupatta and gesticulated in the direction of the exit.

'Look, do you see him? It's Prodipda . . . there . . . that one in the blue checked shirt. He has put on weight.'

Maya smiled before correcting her mother. 'You mean—more weight.'

She waved enthusiastically. She liked her mother's good-natured pumpkin of a brother. It was at his urging that she and her mother had decided to come to Bombay and meet Ranjan Malik and his mother.

*

'An arranged marriage? For me? Don't be ridiculous. Besides, I have one more year to go before I finish college,' Maya remembered protesting just two months earlier.

'So? Who says you can't finish college and then get married?' her mother had argued.

'Then why do we have to go to Bombay now?' Maya had sulked.

'Because boys like Ranjan get snapped up before you and I can blink our eyes—that's why. Besides, he's available for only two weeks. Something about a big assignment he has to do. His family wants to finalize everything before then. Prodipda was very keen on our meeting the Maliks. Ranjan is quite a catch. Who knows, by the time we get to Bombay, some other lucky girl might have grabbed him. Don't think there are no pretty

Bengali girls in that city. Bombay is full of them, I'm told there are thousands and thousands of good Bengali families there,' Chitra had commented in her characteristic agitated fashion.

'Calm down, Ma. It's not as if whoever-he-is is the last eligible bachelor left on earth. And neither am I a hundred-year-old spinster. Frankly, I'm just dying to go to Bombay . . . whether we meet Ranjan Malik or not.' Maya had said this in her usual off-hand manner that so annoyed her mother.

'Your father is not a millionaire who can afford to send us to Bombay for mere sightseeing. Remember that. I have had to beg him to sanction our train fares and give me a little extra for two nice sarees—one for you and one for me. You look pretty in yellow. Fairer. I've already spotted a lovely yellow tangail at Aanchal,' Chitra had announced resolutely. 'And I need a new saree anyway. I've told your father I won't pester him for another one till Puja.'

'I hate yellow, Ma,' Maya had groaned. 'You know I do. Who cares if it makes me look fairer? In any case, what do you mean "fairer"? I'm not fair to begin with.'

'Oh yes, you are,' Chitra had swiftly interjected, 'don't even say such a thing. If you think of yourself as a dark-complexioned person you'll actually start looking dark. I've told you that hundreds of times. Think fair and you'll look fair. Wear yellow for the meeting. Prodipda has told me the Maliks are all very fair. They certainly wouldn't want a dark daughter-in-law.'

*

Maya pulled a face at the memory of that conversation. She caught sight of her reflection in a cracked mirror atop a rusty weighing machine on the platform. Fair! What was Ma talking about. She wasn't fair at all.

But Maya liked her skin-tone—a warm, rich golden brown, like sunlight dancing on the Hooghly, that offset her gleaming jet-black hair and large, dark eyes to advantage. Maya straightened up, threw back her head and concluded that by any standards she was an attractive young lady—and never mind the complexion. A few shades here or there didn't make any difference, not to her.

Oh, but to her mother . . . that was another matter. Chitra had an elaborate system worked out. Women were not merely 'fair' or 'dark'. Within those two broad categories there were several sub-divisions. Complexions ranged from 'pinkish fair', 'yellowish fair', 'milky fair', 'brownish fair', 'milk-and-alta fair', 'fine-skinned fair', to just plain 'pale'. Shades other than these did not count. Her daughter's complexion, for example, was a source of great concern to her.

As she explained time and again, 'It's not as if I'm colour-conscious or anything. But it's true that fair skin denotes prosperity. Class. Upbringing. Background. Position. A dark person rarely looks wealthy. Well-fed. Happy. To be born dark is to be condemned for life!'

Maya would shrug exasperatedly and snap, 'Okay, in that case I'm condemned for life. And it isn't my fault.'

Chitra would look further dejected before muttering, 'Too bad you had to take after Baba's side of the family. Look at our side—not a single dark family member. I should have married a West Bengali—one of us. But your Baba's family was so keen on me. Naturally, they realized how difficult it would be to get a fair bride for Baba. East Bengalis, as you know, are much darker. They even speak differently from us.'

Maya had never understood her mother's countless hang-ups. And neither had she figured out what she was supposed to be—an East or West Bengali. Given her in-between complexion, she guessed she didn't belong to either side. And that was fine by her too. Maya had inherited her father's tall, lithe frame, long, tapered fingers and a full generous mouth. From her mother she had acquired her thick, glossy hair and luminous dark eyes. She was perfectly happy at the manner in which the Maker had so evenly distributed the physical assets of her parents. All right, her nose could have been less flat and her cheekbones slightly more prominent, but the total picture was that of a high-spirited, energetic, bouncy young girl ready to meet life's several challenges head-on. Ranjan was just one of them.

*

Maya had never seen her mother more nervous. They'd set out for the Malik residence a good hour before the appointed time. Prodipda had tried to calm his sister down by jesting about the evening.

'I am told by my neighbours that the Maliks have interviewed ninety-nine girls and rejected all of them. The boy wants to set a record, it seems, and score a century, like Sachin Tendulkar.'

Maya's mother had slapped her brother's wrist and urged him to be quiet. 'Are you sure you have the correct address? Did you cross-check it?' she asked casting quick, anxious glances in Maya's direction. 'Oh God, your kaajal, quick, give me a handkerchief, it's looking terrible. So black and thick. As if you have not slept peacefully for ten years. Dark, dark rings. What will they think?' And she wet a corner of Maya's brand new kerchief with her spit to wipe off a small speck of smeared kaajal while Maya winced. 'Ma—be careful. That hurts. And, ugh, don't use your spit. Let me use my own.'

They had arrived fifteen minutes too early. Prodipda had consulted his old trusted Favre Leuba stainless steel watch and declared, 'We will tell the taxiwallah to circle round the colony. We can't go to their house just yet.'

Chitra had looked at the taxi meter with growing alarm. 'You want to pay your entire month's salary for this one trip or what? Do you realize the cost?'

Prodipda had chuckled. 'For my Bulbul, I don't mind going without fresh prawns for a month. Only, don't let my wife know.'

One slow circle around the sprawling maidan had taken care of the extra time. Maya, her mother and uncle had rung the doorbell smartly while the clock chimed five inside the Malik residence. Chitra clutched her daughter's warm hand and hissed, 'My God. Are you ill? Why is your hand so hot? Just my bad luck that my child gets high fever on the one day she has to look her best.'

Maya had smiled, pinched her mother's dry-as-a-bone cheek and said, 'Ma—you know my hands are always warm. I don't have fever. Don't worry. I'm fine. Now, please, Ma, smile, relax. Everything will go off just fine.'

Chitra had managed a tight little smile—more for Maya's sake than anything else—and stiffened at the sound of approaching footsteps. An urgent whisper had warned Maya to straighten her back. 'Don't slouch,' were her mother's final words of advice before Maya found herself looking directly into a pair of very dark, very interested eyes—Ranjan's.

*

The Malik household wasn't all that different from her own Calcutta home, Maya concluded with relief as she took a quick look around the neat living room. She couldn't spot an air-conditioner. The furniture too was sturdy and old-fashioned. The curtains? Clean but not of the heavy, expensive variety.

There were lots of old books covered carefully with brown paper. The day's newspaper lay on the round centre table. Bengali literary journals in the walnut-wood carved book-rack. A large divan with embroidered cushions strewn on it. An ancient china chest in one corner. A showcase filled with porcelain figurines and Japanese painted fans. A modest-sized television set that was at least ten years old. Three Jamini Roy prints framed and hung up on one wall. And Orissa applique-worked bolsters all over.

There was just one corner that stuck out in the entire area. A sophisticated sound system occupied pride of place there. Standing beside the tape-deck and smart Bose speakers was a black metal tree stacked with CDs. Within minutes of Maya sitting down on a stuffed sofa, Mrs Malik pointed to the corner and announced, 'That's my Ranjan's system. He brought it back from America. He loves music. We all do. Music is . . . is . . .' she searched for the right word before exclaiming triumphantly, 'inspiring. Yes, very inspiring. Don't you think so?'

Chitra nodded a bit too enthusiastically, while Maya and Prodipda smiled in a manner that indicated they were in perfect agreement with the sentiment.

Maya glanced sideways at a garlanded photograph of Mr Malik on the beige wall in front of her. Prodipda had informed Chitra about Mr Malik's demise two years earlier, adding that the death of Ranjan's father was one of the main reasons why he had opted to return to India and remain by his widowed mother's side.

'What a dutiful son,' Chitra had commented while reading this vital tid-bit aloud from her brother's letter.

Mr Malik. He looked a lot like her own father, Maya realized with a start. It wasn't as if their features matched or anything. Rather, it was his personality. He seemed equally remote and disconnected. He also seemed like the kind of man who was used to being ignored and preferred it that way.

Ranjan had his father's slightly hooded eyes but their respective expressions were different. Ranjan darted quick looks around the room while Mrs Malik spoke in a ringing, strident, assertive voice barely pausing for breath between pronouncements. Maya saw her future mother-in-law sizing her up. She couldn't really tell from Mrs Malik's expression whether or not she'd passed the test. She only knew that she'd felt her heart sinking when she had awkwardly offered to help Mrs Malik serve tea only to be told rather brusquely, 'No thank you. We have servants to do that for us.'

Ranjan, Maya noted, had remained rudely seated through the small ritual, not even bothering to rise to his feet to pass on a cup of readymade tea to her mother. Leaf tea served out of elegant but chipped English crockery. And piping hot, home-made samosas neatly arranged in a stainless steel tray. The obligatory 'misthi' was ceremoniously presented with a lofty remark from Mrs Malik. 'Well, living in Bombay we have to compromise, you know. It's not possible to get Ganguram's kalajam here. One has to make do with this . . .' and she'd pointed at the rosogullas, adding, 'From Calcutta, of course. But tinned.'

Maya had been surprised and disappointed by Ranjan's lack of common courtesy and commented on it to Chitra on their way home. Chitra had explained hastily, 'Don't misunderstand him. Boys from that sort of a background are not supposed to participate in such matters. If Ranjan had helped the servants, he'd have been thought of as a sissy. Men do not undertake housework—especially foreign-returned men. It's not done. It would embarrass his family. There is a certain way to deal with servants—no familiarity whatsoever. Did you notice Mrs Malik's expression and tone when she asked for tea?'

9

Maya nodded, 'It was scary. Why does anybody have to sound so rude?'

Chitra smiled, 'She wasn't being rude. She was merely asserting her position as the mistress of the house. Servants are funny creatures. Treat them nicely—like human beings—and they sit on your head. Take advantage of you. If this alliance works out, you'll learn how to deal with them soon enough from your mother-in-law. Besides, Bombay servants are different from Calcutta ones. There we pay them next-to-nothing, throw stale food in their direction, give them discarded rags to wear, and they're happy. Nobody complains. But look at the specimens in the Malik household—just look at them. They were better dressed than we were!'

Maya looked pityingly at her mother raving on in a star-struck fashion about how grand everything was at the Malik's. Was Chitra really all that easy to impress? Or was she trying a bit too hard to sell the Maliks to her? Maya wanted to tell her mother to save herself the effort in case it was the latter. Ranjan had seemed fairly impressive to her as he chatted smoothly about overseas' life as a student as compared to overseas' life as a careerist in the fast track.

'The entire picture changes once you start pulling in the big bucks,' he said with a wave of his hand.

His mother had gazed at him proudly and said with a forced, light laugh, 'Maybe. But why don't you be honest and admit that you hated coming home from work and cooking?'

Then, turning to Maya she added significantly, 'Our Indian boys are so spoilt, you know. They always expect their mothers . . . and later, their wives, to slog for them.'

Maya had stolen a glance in Ranjan's direction to see his reaction. He was leaning back, arms outstretched along the back of the stuffed sofa, a smug smile creasing his face. Mrs Malik's remark had promptly started Chitra off. 'Don't I know it! It's the same story in our house. Maya's father acts like an absolute lord at home. So does his brother—and mind you, he's younger. Don't worry, Maya is used to housework—on weekends she refuses to let me enter the kitchen. "Ma, you rest," she says. "I'll do everything."'

Maya had winced at the overkill. Ranjan's eyes were on her, studying her carefully. She fidgeted with her saree and thought about his smart blue shirt. American, no doubt.

When they left the Malik home, Chitra had begun a virtual non-stop rave about their recent hosts. 'Did you notice Ranjan's watch? Must have been imported. His mother's too. Maybe he bought it for his mother from the USA. I'm told he is a very loving person.'

Maya had noticed Ranjan's solicitous attitude towards his mother—the way he sprang to his feet and held onto her elbow when she rose to say goodbye or the quick eye-contact the two of them made when Chitra dropped a broad hint that Maya was keen on pursuing a career 'later in life'. Maya had blushed at that point and looked beseechingly towards Prodipmama.

'Career?' Mrs Malik had raised one eyebrow, 'What kind of a career?'

Chitra had fumbled a little before saying, 'Oh, nothing special. That is, she is a trained textile designer. Good with her hands. Maybe she'd like to work with a big textile mill in Bombay. We were told there were good opportunities here. Good pay. These days both people have to work if they want to live well—isn't it?'

Ranjan had taken over from his mother and declared, 'True, that is the modern trend. But in my case, I am earning well enough to support a wife and family. I believe it is a woman's duty to run a good home.' And then, turning directly to Maya, he had asked in a challenging sort of voice, 'Would you agree with that?'

Taken off guard, Maya had nodded dumbly while everybody waited to hear her well-considered views. Finally, it was her uncle who'd intervened to say with a laugh, 'Our Maya is very talented. Always getting high marks in school and college. She can always use her training to do something from the house itself. Design and sell sarees, for example. After all, modern girls also need to express themselves. In a small way, of course. Nothing that might interfere with their household duties. In any Indian family, the husband's comforts always come first. Everything else follows. But it's good for young girls to have a hobby. Keeps them busy also.'

Ranjan had maintained a non-committal silence while his mother had busied herself issuing rapid-fire instructions to her cowering servants.

As they spotted a taxi, and headed towards it, Chitra returned to the theme of servants. 'Mrs Malik has a pucca Bombay attitude. Maya . . . I hope you were observing her closely. Dealing with servants is a real art. These Bombay people have mastered it. No insolence to be tolerated. Did you notice her expression when she scolded them for not handling the tea-tray properly? She looked like a queen.'

Maya felt slightly sorry for her mother. Why was she getting such a complex? How was it that that overbearing lady had managed to diminish her usual self-confidence? Was it Mrs Malik or Bombay that made her mother feel inadequate? Or both?

There was no doubt about how overwhelming Bombay appeared to visitors. But it wasn't as if her mother had never travelled out of Calcutta. She had even been to Bombay twice, visiting her brother and his family. But that was suburban

Bombay—a different world from what Maya could gauge. Suburban living is suburban living no matter where it is. South Bombay was different—glittering, menacingly intimidating. Fortunately, it had had an entirely different effect on Maya. As the three of them climbed into a taxi which had a car-stereo belting out '*Bholi bhali ladki*'—the latest Hindi film hit—Maya found herself falling inexorably in love with this Bombay. Marrying Ranjan would make her a part of it immediately. If she were lucky enough to become the other Mrs Malik, Maya knew she'd be bonded with Bombay forever.

*

Prodipda was uncharacteristically quiet as the taxi negotiated its way past hand-carts, buses, pedestrians and cows.

'Every year more crowds, more cars,' he grumbled, holding a kerchief to his nose in a vain effort to keep the exhaust fumes from gagging him.

Chitra turned to her brother before asking Maya, 'So, what do you think? How did it go? Do you think they liked us?'

Prodipda's voice was muffled as he spoke through his makeshift mask, 'I don't know whether they liked *us*,' he said, 'but Ranjan seemed to have liked Maya all right.'

'Really? How could you tell? I couldn't make out a thing,' Chitra exclaimed. 'Could you?' she asked her daughter, her brows creased with deep lines of anxiety.

Maya nodded, with a small smile playing around her mouth. Chitra wasn't satisfied. 'Tell me, please. How could you tell? He hardly said anything. I mean, he didn't speak directly to you, Maya.'

Prodipda chuckled, 'I am a man—ask me. He employed the far more romantic language of the eyes. Didn't you notice?'

Maya was busy staring at the fleeting images of Bombay as the taxi whizzed through streets overflowing with people. 'Where are they going?' She asked her uncle.

He looked up, a little puzzled by the question. 'Who? Where? What? I don't know. Maybe to work. People in Bombay are always going somewhere. The city is never still.'

Maya continued to look out of the car window. 'Doesn't all this movement make you dizzy?' she asked.

Prodipda replied, 'Not at all. I'm used to it. Once you start living here, you'll get used to it too. Become a part of it. See that man with a briefcase darting across the street? He must be spending at least fourteen hours outside his home in constant motion. That's what makes Bombay interesting.'

Chitra asked irritably, 'What? Motion? How absurd. You people are wasting time talking nonsense. I'm so tense. When do you think they'll let us know their verdict?'

Maya turned around to look at her mother, 'Verdict? Ma, how can you use that word? I'm not on trial, you know.'

Flustered and taken off guard, Chitra stuttered, 'Okay. All right. So what if I used the wrong word? Big crime, is it? Remember, I'm not an English professor at Loreto House.'

Prodipda patted his sister's hand, 'Calm down. I'm telling you all has gone well. Maya was looking exceptionally pretty. Ranjan kept staring at her.'

Maya interrupted. 'How could they tell me not to work after marriage? Do any educated, trained girls stay at home these days? I didn't like that remark.'

Chitra broke in sharply, 'All these matters can be sorted out later. Let them first say "yes". Then we can bring it up. And now stop chattering uselessly. I'm praying to Kali Ma. If she heeds my prayers, we'll get an answer by tomorrow evening. After all, we can't hang around in Bombay indefinitely.'

Maya's attention turned to a group of young girls chatting animatedly at a bus-stop. 'Look, Prodipmama—look at those girls. Aren't their skirts a bit too short and tight? Nobody would dare to dress like that in Calcutta. Aren't these people afraid?'

Prodipda smiled, 'These girls? Afraid? My dear, you don't know them. They are typical Bombaywalis. Nobody can dare try any funny tricks with them—nobody. They are as tough as any male. In fact, the boys are scared of them—what a hammering they can give.'

Chitra fidgeted with her saree. 'I should have worn something else. Something more fashionable—don't you think? I thought since we are all Bengalis, a good silk tangail would have been appropriate. But Mrs Malik was wearing a Bombay-type saree—chiffon, wasn't it?'

Maya put an affectionate arm around her mother. 'Relax Ma, what difference does it make? Besides, you are far better looking than Ranjan's mother. I bet she was jealous of you.'

Chitra shook her head vehemently, 'At our age, women look at each other's sarees, jewellery, not faces. I saw the way she stared pointedly at my appearance—it must have looked very shabby to her. But at least you were looking good.'

Maya laughed, 'I was looking great. And you know why? Because I felt great being in Bombay.'

Her uncle teased, 'Not meeting Ranjan?'

'That too. I liked his eyes. And his height. Not bad on the whole? Maybe he plays cricket. Or badminton. His wrists look strong. His chest is broad. Teeth? White enough. He needs a hair cut. And his shoes, some polish. The mole underneath his left ear is cute. So are his extra-long eyelashes. And I definitely liked his voice—if not his words.'

Chitra looked triumphantly at Prodipda who was travelling in the front seat of the taxi. 'My, my—did you hear that? Our Maya has fallen head over heels in love with the boy.'

Maya blushed and said nothing at all. She was far too busy looking at the neon-lit shop-fronts along the road and wondering when she would become a part of the city whose spell she had fallen under so quickly. Too quickly. Especially since her first impressions had been so entirely different. Practically hostile. As the taxi swung around a gigantic football field and stopped at the entrance of her uncle's house, Maya alighted with a light step and an even lighter heart. She knew intuitively that the Malik answer would be a 'yes'. And that Bombay would most definitely become her eventual home. Maya was here to stay.

One

'Don't you ever get out of the house?' Nikhil asked in passing as he rushed past me carrying a roomy sportsbag and tennis racket. Nikhil Verma, my fourth floor neighbour.

I was at the door negotiating the price of floor mops. The salesman was both persistent and persuasive. 'The best quality,' he assured me, flicking one open with a quick twist of his wrist.

I was watching Nikhil. Through the windows on the landing, I followed his progress as he raced nimbly across the small lane adjoining our building, jumped over a ditch and onto his motor-bike. I wondered which college he was studying in, what it was like, how far he had to ride each morning and whether his classes were co-ed. I tried to visualize him walking into the lecture hall a few minutes late, his professor reprimanding him and other students greeting the man who quite possibly was the class hero. Had he been a student in my own college days, he would most definitely have been, I concluded, as I absently fingered the rough texture of the 'best floor mops in Bombay'.

*

Nikhil wasn't like the rest of his family. Certainly nothing like Pushpa, his overbearing mother. I smiled wryly at the thought.

17

'Pushy Pushpa', as I mentally referred to her, had been my first 'official' friend in Bombay. Friend and neighbour. Ranjan, my husband, and Dipankar, Nikhil's father, were colleagues at the bank, and Pushpa had decided to take me under her wing. Adopt me, as it were.

'You are new to Bombay. I've lived here all my life. Born, studied, married,' she had told me when she invited me up for coffee the day after I'd moved into the building. 'I'll show you around. Bombay is not like Calcutta. People are very different, you'll see. It's nice that the bank has given Ranjan the adjacent flat. Thank God it wasn't allotted to Mr and Mrs Dadlani. They are simply horrible. Especially Kamli. You'll meet her, of course. You know how it is in bank jobs—parties, parties, parties. Don't worry, you'll get used to it.'

At that precise moment, Nikhil had walked into the crammed-with-knicknacks drawing room and asked for twenty rupees.

'Beta, come and meet our new neighbour, Mrs Malik. Mrs Ranjan Malik. Papa and Mr Malik are colleagues at the bank. Mrs Malik . . . Maya Malik, is from Calcutta. She doesn't know Bombay at all, poor thing. I've told her to relax. I'm there, after all. What are neighbours for if they can't help each other, no?'

I had looked curiously at Nikhil. My first impression was a slightly bland 'Nice'. How old could he be? No more than eighteen or nineteen. I recalled the moment with some amusement. 'Nice'. What a weak sound it had. You could describe an inoffensive water-colour as 'nice'. Or a piece of cheap, pretty porcelain. But a young man?

Perhaps what I meant was that Nikhil didn't resemble or reflect his mother (I had yet to meet his father). While Pushpa was rotund, Nikhil was rangy. His narrow thickly-lashed brown eyes weren't anything like Pushpa's round, greedy ones. His body language was different too—he moved quickly, like an animal in a hurry. He wore his hair just slightly longer than convention dictated while his clothes were nondescript though neat. Very neat. Clean sneakers, clean socks, clean hands with neatly-clipped nails and an overall air of a fastidious person who valued himself and his appearance. Nothing flashy. Nothing loud. Nothing exceptional. Except perhaps his mouth and smile. A smile so unexpected and so completely disarming when it was flashed that it transformed his features almost miraculously and made him look like a warrior leading a victory parade.

I had noticed a gold chain gleaming against his practically hairless chest. It had a small pendant dangling from it—a charm of some sort. Or a talisman. Pushpa had caught me staring and explained, 'Oh . . . you're looking at the lucky pendant. You see, Dipankar and I wanted a son so badly, so badly we were praying night and day. Tell me, which woman does not want a boy? That too after two daughters. Not that I don't love my girls. My! I adore them. But whatever people might say, a boy is a boy. After a lot of pujas and all that, we finally got our Nikhil. I put the chain round his neck at his naming ceremony. Do you know, he has never taken it off? He's like that only, my Nikhil. So sentimental, you won't believe it. Birthdays, anniversaries, everyone else might forget—but not Nikhil.'

'Twenty rupees.'

I had started when I heard his voice. Too deep. Too adult. Too firm. It had been a command more than a request. Pushpa had waddled off to a steel cupboard. Carefully, she had picked the right key from the heavy bunch tucked at her waist.

'Money, money, money,' she had repeated indulgently. 'These days that's all that children want—more and more money.'

Nikhil had tapped a tattoo on the floor with his sneakers, looking impatient.

'Here,' Pushpa said thrusting a fifty rupee note at him. 'Take fifty, beta.'

'Twenty,' Nikhil had repeated. 'I need twenty . . . to pay for the cab.'

Pushpa had shaken her head in mock anger. 'Cabs! At your age, we used to travel by bus. Or train. We didn't mind walking. What is all this cab business?'

Nikhil had snapped, 'Hurry up . . . the meter's running. And the driver won't have change. Twenty rupees.'

I had opened my purse hastily, fished out the money and thrust it into Nikhil's hand. 'Here . . . twenty rupees. Take it.'

That had been the first moment Nikhil had looked straight at me, into my eyes . . . and smiled. His fingers had touched my palm briefly and lingered there for just a few extra seconds more than they needed to.

'Thanks,' he had said charmingly, and hesitated. 'Should I say "thanks, aunty"?'

I had blushed and shaken my head. It was Pushpa who had interjected swiftly, 'Of course you must address Mrs Malik as "aunty". So what if she is young? She's a married woman, your father's colleague's wife. She is not of your age group that you can act familiar with her. Learn to show proper respect, beta. This is India, not America, remember. I always tell you that.'

Flustered, I had risen to my feet. 'It's all right. Really, it's perfectly all right. I don't mind if he calls me by my first name. Or addresses me as Mrs Malik. But please, none of this aunty business. I feel very embarrassed.'

Nikhil had sprinted out nimbly to pay the cab driver while Pushpa had turned to me. 'We must not encourage youngsters to flout our tradition. See how some of the other children in this complex behave—no values. No manners. No culture. I tell you, it is disgraceful. In our house, both of us are very particular.

Elders must be shown proper respect, don't you agree? Or else these children start sitting on our heads.'

I had smiled. 'It's true what you're saying. But basically, I don't feel like an "elder". Nikhil must be just five or six years younger than me.'

Pushpa had mulled over that and a few minutes later, her face had brightened. 'Okay. All right. I have found a solution. Let Nikhil call you "didi" in that case. That is all right, I think. You are like an elder sister to him. My daughter is your age. I'll tell him . . . don't worry. That will solve the problem.'

*

The salesman was showing his impatience. Following my gaze, he watched Nikhil roar off, leaving a trail of exhaust in his wake.

'Fourth floor boy . . . Mrs Verma's son. A little hot-headed . . . but who can blame him with a mother like that?'

My voice was sharper than I intended. 'How would you know?'

The salesman folded the mops he had spread out on my doorstep. '*Arre baba,* I've been coming to this building for more than ten years. Everybody knows me and I know everybody. I've seen that boy grow up. A real shaitan when he was young. What beatings he got from his father when he was fifteen-sixteen.'

Before I could stop myself, I asked, 'Why? What did he do?'

The salesman shook his head disapprovingly. 'What do boys his age do? Get mixed up with girls, of course. That Nalini Mehta . . . ground floor . . . what a tamasha that was, don't ask. The whole locality was talking about it. Now, how many mops shall I give you? Take six. Special discount for you. Trust me. You won't get them cheaper anywhere in Bombay. That's my challenge to you.'

I went to the bedroom to fetch the money. As I slowly counted out the exact amount, I found my fingers trembling. Nalini Mehta . . . which one was she? The girl with the long flowing hair and impertinent light eyes? Or the plumper, shorter one with a bouncy walk and braids? Which one was more Nikhil's type?

I looked up to see my own face in the mirror fixed to the wardrobe. A worried frown had creased my forehead and my eyes looked wild and distracted. This was ridiculous, I told myself as I recounted the twenty-four rupees. Why should it make any difference to me what Nikhil did, who he was interested in and which of the two girls was more his type?

And yet an irrational jealousy temporarily paralyzed me. My breath became shorter as hot tears rolled down my cheeks. I tucked the notes into my saree blouse and rushed to the bathroom to wash my face. I didn't want the salesman to see me like this. Even that thought confused me. Who the hell did the salesman think he was . . . the presumptuousness of it all, walking into my home and gossiping irresponsibly about the neighbours. I'd give him a piece of my mind.

When I returned to the door, I found the salesman in animated conversation with the next door neighbour's man servant. They broke off abruptly when they saw me.

'Here,' I said, holding the money out. The salesman cleared his throat.

'Don't mind, memsaab,' he said slowly, 'but you really should go out a little. There is so much to see in this city, so much. It is an entire world in itself. And yet you stay cooped up at home all the time. Are you missing Calcutta?'

How dare he! How dare this complete stranger—a door-to-door salesman at that, talk to me about my life, advise me—the audacity of it all! I was about to raise my voice and express my indignation at his effrontery, then thought better of it.

'Here's your money,' I said curtly, a cutting edge to my voice. He took it casually and waited with an expectant air for me to say something. When I didn't, he took his time tying his bundle of mops together. I couldn't shut the door with his foot placed squarely inside the threshold. I could sense he was in the mood for a chat when he further delayed his departure.

'Water,' he said, jerking his fat thumb into his open mouth. I clicked my tongue disapprovingly against my teeth and went in to look for a stainless steel glass—the one reserved for servants and other menials. Instead of opening the fridge and pouring cold water for him, I deliberately filled the glass with tepid tap water. He didn't deserve anything better.

When I went back to the door, he was leaning against the wall, leaving large sweat stains on it. With an impatient twist of my wrist, I indicated that he should stand straight. A little surprised, he moved away and hunkered down to drink thirstily from the glass, sitting as though he was in a village and drinking from a brass lota.

Feeling slightly guilty about my earlier meanness, I asked indifferently, 'Where are you from?'

He named an obscure town.

'Where's that?' I asked without really wanting to know.

The man wiggled his eyebrows. 'Bihar, memsaab, Bihar. Do you know where that is?'

Was I imagining it or was he being sarcastic? I looked at him witheringly and nodded. He still showed no signs of leaving. 'Do you have any of saab's old clothes?' he asked, wiping the sweat off his face with the end of his filthy turban.

'I'll check,' I said exasperatedly, adding, 'next time.'

He stared up at the moulded ceiling of the landing. 'Next time. Who can say about the next time? There is no next time, memsaab. Only today. Only now.'

23

I burst out laughing. 'Where did you pick up all this wisdom?'

He pointed skywards. 'Knowledge comes from God . . . only God. Books provide you with facts, they teach you nothing else.'

I stared at his threadbare dhoti, his stained shirt. 'Why did you come to Bombay?' I asked him.

'Why does anybody come to Bombay? To live. To survive. To fill my belly.' And then he paused before adding slyly, '. . . and to enjoy life. Bombay is the only place worth livng in in India, memsaab, you will agree, I know.'

I smiled. 'How can you say that? It's overcrowded, filthy, harsh.'

He lit a beedi. 'Yes. But it is also human and compassionate. People don't kick you here when you are sleeping on the pavement. A man like me who is willing to work hard, work at anything, does not have to starve here. Nobody cares, true. But nobody harms you either. I live my life as I want to . . . as I choose to. No questions asked. But back home in my village? A man cannot go to the field to relieve himself without the entire population finding out—that is the difference.'

He gave back the stainless steel glass and folded his hands in gratitude. Suddenly I felt wretched, petty, mean and small.

'Wait,' I said, 'Perhaps I can find an old shirt for you.'

He remained silent, a grave expression on his face. His voice followed me as I went back into the flat to look for one of Ranjan's discarded shirts. 'That boy Nikhil . . . his line is bad.'

I stopped and turned around. 'What do you mean, "his line is bad"?' I demanded, and then realized what a fool I was making of myself.

It was too late. The man looked around as if to ensure there weren't any eavesdroppers lurking in the shadows and whispered, 'He has two bad habits . . . liquor . . . and . . .' he stopped, as if too embarrassed to carry on. He glanced over his shoulder and picked up his bundle. 'Ram, Ram, memsaab,' he muttered as he turned to go.

'What about the old clothes?' I asked, a desperate edge to my voice. I had to know. I just had to. What was Nikhil's other bad habit? How could this man leave a half-finished sentence dangling so mercilessly between us and walk away? Perhaps I'd never see him again . . . in which case I'd never know.

I ran after him as he went down the staircase shunning the service lift. In my frenzy, I was prepared to grab him by the shoulders and drag him back into the house to complete the sentence.

I would have done it too, had Nikhil's mother not blocked my way. In my confusion, I blurted out stupidly, 'What are you doing here?'

She gave me an odd look. 'Why? Is there a new law in the building that gives different timings to different people? What do you mean by asking me such a question? This is a public area, not your father's property. Really, I'm surprised at your behaviour, Mrs Malik. I don't know how neighbours behave in Calcutta, but in Bombay we show better manners.'

I'd asked for it. I knew I had. Mortified, I said, 'Oh, Mrs Verma . . . I didn't mean that, I'm sorry. I was slightly preoccupied, you see . . . busy . . . besides, it's so hot, I can't think straight.'

She continued to look at me strangely. 'Nonsense,' she snorted, 'utter nonsense. Hot! As if Calcutta is Iceland. I tell you . . . I don't know what happens to these out-of-town women when they come to Bombay. They seem to lose their heads completely.'

Unknowingly, of course, she had put her finger right on it. I had lost my head. And a bit of my heart too.

Two

Ranjan came home early that evening, complaining of a 'sinus headache'. In the few months that we'd been married, I had grown used to his periodic depressions which he preferred to call by assorted names—'gas' or 'joint pains' or 'muscular cramps' or 'blurred vision'. I could usually sense their onset by the little tell-tale signs that heralded their arrival.

Ranjan would wake up even earlier than usual, sometimes as early as 4.30 a.m. and start rifling through the medicine chest after switching on every single light in the room. That would be my cue to leap out of bed, don a solicitous expression and ask softly, 'Not feeling well?'

To that, he'd screw up his eyes tightly, shake his head from side to side and start groaning, clutching whichever part of his anatomy was meant to be bothering him. I would then go to the kitchen and fetch a glass of unchilled water and wait around till Ranjan had located the right pill to pop.

There was no question of going back to bed after that. Ranjan would pace the room restlessly, looking agonized, and keep drawing back the curtains as if by so doing he could hasten the process of the sun heaving itself up over the horizon.

I would urge him to lie down which he would stubbornly refuse to do, saying shortly, 'Please . . . if I lie down the pain will only get worse. I need a doctor.'

As the first cheerful rays of the sun hit our bedroom window, Ranjan would point weakly at the telephone. 'Call him . . . tell him it's very bad this time . . . very bad.'

Dutifully, I would dial Dr Goel's number and describe Ranjan's symptoms. After making sure to cover the mouthpiece, I'd consult Ranjan. 'He wants to know whether a house visit is necessary.'

Ranjan would moan like a man on his deathbed and nod in slow motion. As if even that slight movement was causing him agonizing pain. An hour later, Dr Goel would arrive and march straight into the bathroom to wash his hands. Ranjan would be lying back against the pillows, his eyes shut, his mouth puckered and his breathing alarmingly shallow.

Dr Goel would examine him efficiently while cooing soothing words of reassurance. 'Relax,' he'd say, pummeling Ranjan's stomach. Even the lightest touch would evoke sharp yelps from Ranjan, accompanied by exaggerated writhing.

Dr Goel would treat me like a badly-trained nurse and issue staccato commands like 'towels', 'ice cubes', 'thermometer', 'cotton wool'. I'd scurry around nervously and invariably drop a few things en route to the 'patient'. Ranjan would cast a long-suffering glance in my direction and mutter something about 'clumsy butterfingers'.

Strangely enough, I found him rather endearing in these grouchy moods. After Dr Goel's departure, I'd find myself in an unusually loving frame of mind, clucking sympathetically, fluffing up the pillows and switching channels obligingly since Ranjan preferred to remain motionless, too fatigued to move his finger over the remote control.

*

In his own way, Ranjan could be demonstrative and charming. But I soon realized that any open show of affection made him uncomfortable. He knew, for instance, that I enjoyed wearing flowers in my hair, and that this was a recently acquired fancy. Women didn't embellish their nape buns or braids with strung flowers in Bengal . . . respectable women, that is. It was seen as the exclusive prerogative of 'baijis'—courtesans. Women who enticed other people's husbands with fragrances and perfumes, flowers and kaajal.

In Bombay, gajras and venis were worn with a naturalness that was charming and disarmingly feminine, young girls, brides, even toothless old crones not yet widowed adorned their hair with summer blossoms. Unlike in the north where gajras were invariably neatly strung from white, star-like flowers that bloomed late in the evening on untidy bushes, Bombay's venis were varied and colourful. One could quite easily distinguish between communities by looking at the flowers in a woman's hair. The kolis, for example, preferred elaborate arrangements inclusive of leaves and tinsel. High-caste brahmins chose seasonal flowers threaded in simple single strings. The lower castes went in for showy venis which were stiffer than gajras and used multi-coloured flowers in geometrical patterns. All this I'd observed on my few outings to the vegetable market where the flower sellers squatted right outside a row of ancient temples.

The first time I had come home with a gajra of mogras coiled in my hair, Ranjan had sniffed the air suspiciously. 'What's that peculiar smell? A new scent?' he had asked with a small frown. I whirled around to show him the flowers.

'Oh,' he said, 'I didn't know you liked those.'

I had smiled and walked up and down the room jauntily. 'I didn't know either, until now,' I said.

Ranjan had looked a trifle unsure, as if debating in his mind whether or not to 'approve'. Finally, he had decided to let it pass and had gone back to his evening papers.

*

That evening, he immersed himself in his paper again as soon as I gave him a cup of tea. 'Did you know the crime rate has gone up by 3.5 per cent in Bombay?' he asked me. 'It's terrible, you know. It used to be a pretty safe city in the old days. My mother used to travel alone, and she never felt scared. These days, I don't allow her to go anywhere unescorted.'

Then, turning to me, he said somewhat sharply, 'You . . . I hope you aren't gallivanting around during the day. As it is, you don't know the roads or anything. This isn't Calcutta. I suggest you stay at home. If you want to go anywhere, ask my mother to accompany you.'

I busied myself in the kitchen and maintained a non-committal silence. Somehow, the thought of discovering Bombay through my mother-in-law's eyes didn't appeal to me.

Timidly, I asked, 'Why can't we go out together? Not on weekdays, I know how tired you are. But at least on weekends. How will I ever explore Bombay otherwise?'

Ranjan looked up from his paper. 'Sometimes, you talk like such a kid. Life isn't a picnic, you know. And you aren't in Bombay on a holiday. As a married woman, you have to learn to deal with responsibilities.'

Seeing my whipped expression, he added more kindly, 'Cheer up . . . anyway, there is the Sinha dinner to go to next week. They live way out at Juhu. You can see something of the city then, it's a long drive there.'

I wanted to tell Ranjan that that wasn't my idea of discovering a city. That's not how I wanted Bombay to happen to me. I wasn't interested in taking in the sights. I didn't want to attend a son-et-lumière show at Rajabai Towers or go for a harbour cruise. Neither did I feel like an obligatory, voyeuristic visit to a film studio or a drink at a five-star bar. Rather, I wanted the city to seep into me slowly. I wanted to absorb it, digest it, make it a part of my system. I wanted desperately to become a Bombaywali. I wanted to belong. But I said nothing at all.

Instead, I allowed the rice to remain on a high flame a little longer than I ought to have. Ranjan detected my folly immediately. I heard him as he entered the kitchen, sniffing exaggeratedly and saying, 'Burnt rice! There's nothing worse than burnt rice. You'll have to throw the lot away. Don't try and serve me the top layers because it doesn't help. Once the bottom gets singed, that's it. My mother doesn't keep such rice even for the servants—she always gets rid of it.'

Ranjan had uttered a magic word. Servants. But as usual, my timing was wrong. I looked at him brightly and announced, 'I think I may have found a good cook—part-time, of course.'

Ranjan looked even more displeased. 'A cook? Just for the two of us? And I don't even come home for lunch. That's absurd. We don't need one. If we do get someone, what work would that leave you?'

While I washed and drained another cup of rice, I asked, 'Do I have to work? I mean, do I have to do housework? I could always find a job. I do have a degree in textile designing, after all.'

Ranjan snorted dismissively. 'A job? In Bombay? Maya, you don't know what you're talking about. Bombay is not Calcutta, where just about anybody can walk into an office and get a job. Bombay is like New York. Or London. Tough. Competitive. You have to be good . . . great . . . brilliant . . . to get a job here. People don't waste time on nobodies.'

My head was beginning to hang lower and lower. 'I may not be great or brilliant,' I muttered meekly, 'but I'm quite good at what I do. At least that's what they used to tell me in Calcutta. I could at least try and find something to keep me busy.'

Ranjan stopped opening and closing assorted spice jars to say abruptly, 'But Mummy won't like it.'

I turned my back to the gas range and looked at him in absolute puzzlement. 'Why not? Why won't Mummy like my working somewhere? I'd make sure it's a decent place. I'm not a fool.'

Ranjan began popping roasted peanuts into his mouth one by one. He'd assumed his evasive expression. 'In our families the only sort of work ladies do is social work. Our relatives might criticize us if you suddenly take up a job. It's not done. They might think I don't earn enough. Or that I'm forcing you to contribute towards household expenses.'

And then suddenly Ranjan stiffened. 'The rice,' he bellowed, 'check the rice. It's burning again.'

*

I confess it wasn't a very successful dinner. I was sullen and tearful while Ranjan studiously avoided eating the rice (which had been saved in the nick of time) concentrating instead on breaking off pieces of bread in a careless gesture that signified his complete lack of interest and satisfaction in the meal.

I ought to have remained silent but didn't. Foolishly, I decided to make small talk. I launched into the story of the floor mop salesman and our conversation. Ranjan threw down a half-eaten slice of bread onto his plate. 'Now you've started chatting with useless ruffians.'

A little fool inside my head began heatedly to defend my new acquaintance. 'He's not a ruffian,' I shot back. 'Besides, he's been coming to this building for years. Everybody knows him.'

Ranjan had a triumphant gleam in his eye as he roared. 'That's just my point. Everybody knows him. It is precisely that which makes him doubly dangerous. Women like you—gullible outsiders—are so easily tricked. Today he is chatting, tomorrow he'll rob and rape. Then where will you go crying? I keep telling you—grow up. Remember, this is Bombay. B-O-M-B-A-Y. You can't trust anybody. Nobody at all. Understand?'

I began to blubber. 'But . . . but, I have nobody else to talk to all day. I'm so lonely.'

Ranjan pushed his plate away angrily. 'That's enough, Maya. No more nonsense. I don't believe I'm listening to an educated woman's conversation. Lonely? How can any intelligent person be lonely? In a city like Bombay at that? There's music. Television. You can read, clean the house, write to your parents. Do something constructive. What's the point of complaining all the time?'

I tried to eat another mouthful of rice and dal but it stuck in my throat, making me gag. At the sound of my choking, Ranjan left the table in disgust.

'A man comes home to relax after slogging all day. He looks forward to a hot bath, a hot meal, soothing conversation. Not this rubbish.'

I started to clear the table. I heard the smart click of the television. It was the BBC World Report with Niki Marx talking crisply about various killings in various places around the world. I could hear parallel news bulletins from different networks emanating out of neighbouring flats. Soon everybody would switch, as if on command, to another programme—a film music countdown. Ranjan would complain about the jarring sound and wonder aloud how civilized people actually spent God's precious time watching such 'nonsense'.

It amused me each time Ranjan used that word—'nonsense'. In Bombay, 'nonsense' was just, well, nonsense. Not so in Calcutta. 'Nonsense' was a serious abuse, the ultimate insult, at par with 'bastard', 'son of a bitch' or 'swine'. A putdown to beat all putdowns. It was used only under extreme provocation and as a noun. For example, if a woman wanted to verbally wound a man in public, all she had to do was look witheringly and spit, 'You are a nonsense.' If that didn't crush him effectively enough, he was no man at all. Only the hardened, insensitive, shameless person survived the brutality of a 'nonsense' hurled at him or her. I must have fallen in that category.

*

That night, I crept into bed as quietly as possible. Ranjan seemed to be in deep sleep. I dared not switch on the bedside lamp and flick through the magazines he'd brought back from his office pool. I lay awake wondering how to induce sleep—a lack of physical exercise combined with mental lethargy had dulled my senses to a point where I felt dopey and drowsy even when I was awake. A condition, I believe, known as terminal boredom. And yet sleep, good sleep, eluded me.

I lay in the darkness gazing at the dimly-lit ceiling. A bright halogen street lamp on the adjoining road enveloped our room in a strange, sci-fi glow. I expected E.T. to crawl in through the window. Or the entire Star Trek team to march in. I tried humming old film songs in my mind. Or going over the day's non-events. I even tried resorting to pleasantly distorted memories of my college days, lacing them with wild exaggerations and silly fantasies.

Nothing worked. Till Nikhil crept into my consciousness.

*

The day after I had had coffee with Pushpa, Nikhil had rung my doorbell at noon. I was expecting someone from Ranjan's office. A handyman who was going to come over and help me with the fixtures. I was dressed in a maxi-length skirt and one of Ranjan's T shirts—the kind that are distributed free as promotional gimmicks. Nikhil was wearing jeans too. And a similar giveaway T-shirt. We had looked at each other and burst out laughing.

'Hi,' Nikhil had said, 'I've come to return your twenty bucks.'

I had taken the neatly folded notes from his hand and said, 'There was no hurry, really. It's not as if I wouldn't be seeing you again. We are neighbours now.'

Nikhil had ignored the remark as he strode into the flat. With his back to me, he had said, 'My mother wants me to call you "didi". I think that's crazy. Don't you?'

I had remained silent for a moment, then said, 'What's crazy about that? I am your sister's age . . . besides, if that's what your mother would like . . .'

Nikhil had whirled around. 'But what would you like? Do you really want me to call you "didi"?'

I had turned away and crossed over to the telephone. 'Please—I have to speak to my husband about the carpenter,' I said abruptly.

Nikhil had watched me dial, and repeated the question. 'Should I call you "didi"? I'm waiting for an answer.'

I had put down the phone and said softly, 'Call me by my name . . . it's short enough. Call me whatever you feel comfortable with.'

'Thank you. I was hoping you'd say that . . . Maya,' Nikhil had replied before striding out briskly.

I had remained sitting by the phone without redialling. I could always deal with the carpenter the next day.

*

This boy . . . this man . . . irritated me with his nonchalant manner. While I couldn't accurately describe his behaviour as being rude, I still found it insulting. And a bit too familiar. But what annoyed me even more was the effect it had on me I felt strangely flattered. I hated myself for that. Flattered? By an arrogant college boy's careless attention? It was true. Nikhil noticed me, that was enough. His eyes registered interest—there was no mistaking that. I didn't at that point stop to ask myself whether mine did the same. But Nikhil most definitely affected me and one part of me didn't 'approve'. This was ridiculous—a newly married woman day-dreaming about a neighbour's young son. Disgusting. And shameful.

I reasoned (unconvincingly) that Nikhil intrigued me only because I had never known boys like him while I was in college. Nikhil was all that I'd imagined Bombay's young men to be—good-looking, confident, sporty, cocky, flirtatious, lazy, spoilt and quite, quite irresistible. Damn. In any case what real yardsticks did I have—the only other 'men' I'd encountered in this city thus far had been door-to-door salesmen, sweepers, drivers, watchmen, domestics and dhobis. Nikhil really didn't have much competition. On the other hand, if I had to have a student as a neighbour why not someone as fascinating as Nikhil?

*

As Nikhil's image formed in my mind (it took a while forming since I was busy chasing it away), I felt a strange relaxation come over me. I stopped trying to resist the melting ache that was flowing through my rigid body. Gradually, my limbs loosened up and my eyelids stopped flickering. I could feel my shoulders unlock and my knees straighten up. At first, Nikhil's features were indistinct, hazy. Only his outline looked sharp and well-defined. Gradually, I could see his eyes, mouth, the funny angle at which he held his left shoulder, the scanty hair on his chest.

Initially his image remained unmoving and static like a polaroid print. It took me some time to get it to blink . . . smile . . . relax. And talk to me playfully. Our 'conversation' was really quite silly, consisting as it did of corny jokes and childish digs. But the important thing was that it made me laugh. In fact, I laughed so much, my body shook with unleashed, unexpected, unfamiliar mirth. I was half-afraid my secret and silent enjoyment would disturb Ranjan's sleep. It didn't. It never did.

Three

My mother had taken to writing long, dull letters full of motherly advice. She would clip out recipes from *Sunanda,* the popular Bengali magazine for women, and mail them, along with 'Household Tips' from various weekend supplements. Occasionally, she would ask me how I was keeping, whether or not I liked my new environment and if I had lost weight. I couldn't figure out the last query. Did my mother think I was fat? Was she trying to tell me something? Or was it her oblique way of finding out whether or not I was pregnant?

I realized that must have been it. Just to be contrary and keep her guessing, I wrote back mysterious letters describing assorted symptoms—some of them culled from an old *Reader's Digest* I'd found amongst Ranjan's books. I'd improvise as I went along, describing the state of my health in baffling terms.

My mother was not a stupid woman. She saw through my game and promptly wrote back an aggrieved letter telling me she didn't appreciate this sort of humour and that as a newly-married daughter I had no business misleading her. Funny how my mother and I rarely laughed at the same things. Not that I found my non-pregnancy particularly amusing (as a matter of fact, it worried me).

Yet, I couldn't resist the impulse to needle my mother a bit about 'the issue'. Everything was an 'issue' to her. She often began her conversation with an assertive 'The issue is . . .' Perhaps the strident tone she employed even in normal, everyday exchanges had something to do with her days as a college lecturer (a 'junior lecturer', my father never failed to underline with just that little hint of malice).

I couldn't help feeling sorry for 'Chitra' as she preferred to be called by everybody except me, and perhaps if I had switched to addressing her by her first name after I grew up, she'd have secretly liked it. Only I didn't dare. It's not as if Chitra was overbearing or formidable. But her manner or rather her voice, conveyed precisely that impression. It sounded like a slightly scratchy 45 r.p.m. record and it had the same effect on people as nails scraping across a blackboard.

While it was true that Chitra loved lecturing, beneath the abrasive exterior hid a perennially nervous, overly anxious mother hen who lived in a permanent state of mild agitation. Her gestures were jerky and stiff. She clasped and unclasped her hands constantly and her eyes were rarely still. Her body, wiry as it was, was rigid and hard, even to the touch.

As a young girl (strictly a pre-pubescent), I was occasionally allowed into her room while she dressed after her quick, efficient bath. She would cast darting glances in my direction, embarrassed by my openly curious stare and say, 'The issue is water preservation. You must remember that water is the world's most precious commodity. Without water, there'd be no prosperity. When you take a bath, refrain from splashing more water than you actually need to take the soap off your body. That goes for when you are brushing your teeth as well—turn on the tap when you're gargling but remember not to let the water run. Such a waste, I tell you. But we Indians will never learn. These are simple, practical habits. If you follow them during childhood, you'll stick to them throughout your life.'

I knew this speech only too well. In any case, my attention was invariably elsewhere. I'd wait for that one careless moment when she would allow the pleats of her cotton saree to slip from between her fingers. For some reason, my mother rarely wore undergarments (except when she was menstruating, when she'd wear thick, white cotton panties plus a white bra to support her tense little breasts).

So, if she draped her saree carelessly, I'd get a glimpse of her pubes and feel inexplicably afraid. For years, I couldn't figure out what that dark shadow between her thighs actually was. Once or twice, I'd tried to climb up on a wooden stool and peep through the tiny cracks of the bathroom window. But the angle had been wrong and my efforts entirely wasted. I'd only succeeded in seeing her narrow, thin buttocks with their sad droopy cheeks, her long back with the bones of her spinal column jutting out prominently and the nape of her neck with tendrils of wet hair clinging to it.

On hot summer days, my mother would spend the long afternoons lying on a high, four-poster bed and reading Bengali novels. Sometimes she would invite me to lie beside her. I enjoyed the closeness of those moments and I think she did too, awkward though we both were about touching one another. When she thought I was asleep, she'd prop her knees up unselfconsciously and continue reading. That was when I would slide down unobtrusively to try and look up her legs at the darkness between. I never succeeded. Perhaps my wiggling alerted her, or may be she was fully aware of my curiosity for I'd soon find a damp, hard hand reaching down and pulling me up on the pillow.

*

My parents had always slept in different rooms. I didn't think there was anything unusual about the arrangement. My father's room was at the far end of our home—a crumbling 'mansion' in urgent need of repairs. The small bungalow had belonged to my grandfather who had died at the age of forty-two, leaving a son and daughter behind. My father had inherited not just the bungalow but a cantankerous tenant as well—a distant cousin who lived on the ground floor with his family.

To get to our house, we had to go past their kitchen and up a wooden staircase. As a child, the tenant's home and family fascinated me, mainly because I was strictly forbidden from having anything to do with them even though they had young children as well.

'The issue is,' my mother would rasp, 'these people are not good people. They occupy our place. It does not belong to them. It's ours, all ours. They are uncouth and ill-mannered. No refinement whatsoever. I don't want you to mix with those awful children or else you'll grow up like them—rowdy and disgusting.'

Partho and his sister Bubli didn't seem in the least bit disgusting to me. I'd watch them play in the tiny patch of shrubs and weeds my mother grandly referred to as 'our garden', and long to join them. They seemed to be having so much fun as they swung from an improvised rope ladder suspended from an old champak tree. Watching them, I'd wonder why their parents slept together on a large double bed and how come the children often slept with them or on mattresses spread on the floor.

I had once asked my mother the question and she had stared at me in a distracted sort of way. 'The issue is . . .' she had begun vaguely and then allowed the sentence to hang mid-air.

Impertinently, I'd teased her. 'What is the issue, Ma? Tell me. Why don't you and Baba sleep on the same bed? And why can't I sleep between the two of you?'

She patted me on the head as though I were a friendly pup. 'I need time to think . . . on my own,' she had finally said lamely.

I ought to have kept quiet at that point, but didn't. 'If Baba is on the same bed sleeping quietly, how would that disturb you? I'd also sleep very quietly.'

Chitra had turned away and whispered, 'I need to be alone to think. I can't think when there are people around.'

I bit my lip (a habit I still had) and said petulantly, 'We aren't "people". Besides, what is it that you need to think about all the time?'

My mother wrung her hands nervously. I had half-expected her to launch into another round of 'the issue is'. Instead, I thought I saw tears brimming up. It made me feel awful. Like a pesky interloper.

I left her room in a hurry and went to hang around the large open window in the sitting room. I could hear Partho and Bubli chattering noisily downstairs. I could smell kitchen aromas wafting up from their home. Aromas far different from the ones that emanated from our kitchen. I wondered why. They were Bengalis like us. How was it their food smelt different?

It wasn't the right time to ask my mother. So I decided to ask my father instead. He looked up from his crossword puzzle (he was addicted to puzzles of all kinds) and said briefly, 'Their food is not the same as our food. Is that clear?'

Of course it wasn't clear at all. But what could I say without sounding like a pest? So I wandered back to the large window and strained my ears to catch a few snatches of happy conversation.

Four

When we had been married almost a year, I said to Ranjan one day, 'Let's talk.'

He seemed stunned at the suggestion. 'Talk?' he asked suspiciously. 'What about?'

I replied brightly, 'Oh . . . anything . . . something.'

A guarded look came into his eyes and I could see his shoulders bunching up. His voice changed as well, becoming thicker and slower. I paced up and down the room on my toes like a dancer practising her steps.

'Stop walking around like that,' Ranjan said sharply, 'you look so ridiculous. Why can't you be still. You know? Just still. You are always so restless, it's tiring to watch.'

I whirled around mischievously and chirped, 'Hey! You're talking. What fun. See, we're actually having a conversation.'

Ranjan stood up and glared. 'Is that meant to be funny? If so, I'm not in the least bit amused. Wives should realize that when a man comes home dead tired, he needs a little peace in the house. Not poor jokes.'

For once, his attitude and more importantly, his tone, didn't crush me. Normally, I would have promptly clammed up and gone to the kitchen to sulk. Somehow, the kitchen had become symbolic of my refuge. I never felt wanted or welcomed in the bedroom. That remained Ranjan's room, his domain. Whereas the kitchen was an area that belonged exclusively to me.

Well . . . almost. Like most Bengali men, Ranjan was a good cook. A far better one than I was which created its own set of problems. I could never fob off a mediocre preparation by giving it some exotic-sounding name. Ranjan recognized the difference instantly. At such times, he would pick up the offending dish and sniff it mockingly. He could tell by its appearance and aroma exactly which ingredient I had forgotten to add. I'd hold my breath and wait for the verdict. It would come swiftly and harshly. 'No jeera. Too much haldi,' Ranjan would declare, holding it at arm's length. I would look at my effort miserably and timidly slide another mediocre culinary effort in his direction. Often Ranjan would refuse to glance at it, preferring to stride masterfully into the kitchen and take over my precious space.

*

Late one evening while I was struggling to keep mustard seeds in hot oil from spluttering into my nervous eyes, I heard the doorbell. Cursing under my breath, I rushed to see who it was. I saw just an extended arm, checked shirt sleeve carelessly rolled up to reveal a cheap plastic watch on a broad, strong wrist. Of course I knew immediately who the wrist belonged to.

'Greetings, memsaab,' Nikhil sang out, 'I come bearing a priceless gift for you . . . from my priceless mother.'

'My dish is burning,' I cried out as a sharp hiss from the kitchen told me the oil had spilled over and ruined my 'bagaar.'

'No problem ma'am . . . give the master of the house these outstanding, exquisite, superb, delicious dahi-wadas instead,' Nikhil crooned.

From behind his back, he produced a covered glass bowl. 'Compliments of Mrs Verma—the world's best dahi-wada maker,' he laughed.

I took the dish from his hand gratefully—Ranjan loved dahi-wadas, and I had failed his test the last time I'd tried making them.

'From a packet?' Ranjan had asked suspiciously. 'Instant? Don't tell me.'

I had hotly denied resorting to 'instant' anything and gone into a long explanation, a step-by-step one, to prove to my husband that I had taken a great deal of trouble to prepare his favourite dish.

'Too lumpy,' he had snorted, before pushing it away. 'Thanks . . . I mean, say "thank you" to your mother,' I stammered now to Nikhil.

'What about a tip for the delivery boy?' Nikhil teased.

'What shall I give you . . . wait . . . I think I have some chocolates in the fridge,' I continued wildly.

'Another time,' Nikhil grinned. 'And remember—I won't settle for chocolates.'

He was gone, leaving me feeling foolish. I didn't know what sort of conversation to make with this chap. He was too smart for me. And far too sure himself. Besides the only kind of conversation I'd ever had with males my age had been restricted to curriculum talk, classes, skipped notes, likely questions in the exams or puja plans. I wasn't accustomed to these kind of very casual exchanges. Was I supposed to laugh at Nikhil's jokes? Would that encourage him to go a little further the next time? Would it have been better to ignore him? Or maybe tell him frankly that my husband would not appreciate or tolerate his attitude? I was puzzled and angry. Maybe this was the way Bombay boys spoke to friends of their parents. In Calcutta such presumption would never be forgiven. Children—even adult children—knew their place in the social hierarchy, and generally kept to it. I resolved to give Nikhil a small lecture when I next met him. I hoped it would be soon—and that hope itself made me feel diminished.

*

Ranjan baffled me. He was someone who was so completely self-absorbed that I often wondered whether he had actually ever seen me. Really seen me. Sure, he looked at me hard and critically before taking me to an office party. But that was more like a car check. You know, the way men behave with their automobiles—windshield wipers functioning, tyres washed and gleaming, no chips, no dents. That sort of thing.

Ranjan's observant eye missed nothing. A mismatched saree blouse, bindi slightly askew, bra strap showing, scuffed heels, unblotted lipstick, untidy hair—he took it all in quickly and efficiently. But that was not the same thing as seeing.

I can say quite truthfully that I saw Ranjan. I recognized things about him that he probably had never even thought of. For instance, I knew he was self-conscious about nostril hairs and removed them surreptitiously once a week. Or that he picked the mole on his neck while concentrating. Or the small vanity he displayed about his well-shaped feet ('no bunions' he'd state, proudly examining his big toe).

I also saw his competitive streak that made him push himself aggressively at the office. He would often grumble in frustration, 'It's a pity we Bengalis lack the killer instinct. Imagine, had I had it, I would have become the vice-president of my company by now instead of that pushy Punjabi fellow. I tell you, those men have mastered the art of boot-licking the boss. Whenever I look at him, he's busy buttering up someone or the other. And when our foreign bosses arrive—oh my God! It's sickening to watch. No self-respect.'

That would be my cue to say something mild and positive about Bengali pride. I'd murmur, 'Let the Tulis of the world get ahead. At least we have a moral backbone. It's better not to compromise than grovel at someone's feet. But don't worry— eventually talent and hard work do pay. It's only a matter of time.'

Ranjan would be half-listening, his attention focused on the moral battle ahead. Then he would shake his head regretfully and say, 'It's a good thing I went to America. If there's one thing those Americans know, it's aggression. They don't care. They simply don't care. Ruthless bastards. Each one for himself. Had I not had that exposure, I wouldn't even have got this far.'

I understood Ranjan's frustrations. I had seen Tuli operating and I knew Ranjan was not exaggerating. Tuli's blatant sycophancy was disgusting, almost embarrassing to watch. It began with his phoney smile and extra-friendly greetings. He had a ready compliment for everyone with a super heavy dose reserved for the bosses and their wives. There wasn't a birthday or anniversary that Tuli forgot—not even the children's. Cakes, pastries, toys, flowers, perfumes, he'd shower the lot.

Resentful colleagues hated his oily charm. But far more than that, they felt intensely annoyed to see it work. As Ranjan would explode, 'Can't they see through the bloody bugger? Don't they know he's only flattering them?' I'd place a restraining hand over his and calm him down by promptly switching on the sports channel. Ranjan was (or rather, had been) a keen sportsman. He diligently practised cricket strokes in the living room even though he hadn't played the game in over ten years. One shelf of the showcase in our living room was reserved for Ranjan's cricketing trophies. There were standing instructions that these were to be polished and replaced in a particular order once every fortnight. He was proud of his college boy successes on the sportsfield and still dreamt of staging a 'comeback' as he called it (without specifying in which particular sport or how).

I enjoyed polishing Ranjan's trophies (he noticed if I delayed the chore even by a day) as it gave me something to do. I had started enjoying mindless, mechanical activity more and more. Like ironing. I could spend four blissful hours carefully ironing every piece of ironable fabric in the house—towels, bedsheets, tablecloths, dust jackets. Once I'd even pulled down all the curtains and ironed each one lovingly.

I had discovered that by concentrating my full attention on the job, not only did I stop worrying about what to do with my hands and limbs, but my mind too switched off completely. I would switch on the radio (but not the TV), spray a little starch powder over whatever lay obediently on the ironing board and iron away, taking my time over collars, cuffs and sundry creases. It was strangely satisfying plus it took care of all those hours.

I could have ventured out, of course. Ranjan hadn't exactly forbidden me from going anywhere. But I knew my little adventures made him uneasy. Once, when I'd got back late after jumping onto a bus and heading for Juhu Beach, I had found Ranjan sitting sternly near the entrance to our flat. I half-expected to see a cane across his knees. I looked contrite and apologized hastily, pretending I'd had a pretty rotten time on my own anyway.

But my shining eyes and flushed cheeks must have given the game away for Ranjan stared hard at my windblown appearance and said caustically, 'The sea breeze seems to have done you a great deal of good. But Bombay's beaches aren't at all safe. Forget women—strangers to the city at that. Even men have been attacked in broad daylight. Don't you read the newspapers? At least two rapes a day in Juhu alone. And a dozen robberies.'

I said animatedly, 'Really? But I didn't see a thing. In fact, there was hardly anybody around.'

Ranjan followed me into the bedroom. 'What do you mean? Was the beach deserted in that case? That makes it doubly dangerous. Anybody could have slashed your throat and nobody would have even heard you crying for help. Really! I'm amazed at your irresponsibility. You behave like a silly child sometimes. If my mother finds out . . .'

The threat was left hanging, open to interpretation. As I guiltily washed my face, I saw my image in the mirror over the wash basin. My hair was a mess of tangles. I stuck out my tongue and licked the corner of my lips. The salt was still there. It was encrusted in my hair, too, and on the skin of my arms. It had got under my fingernails, and was clinging to my clothes.

Suddenly, I imagined Nikhil tasting me and a small secret smile danced around my mouth.

*

I crossed over to my cupboard to get a clean saree—the sturdy wooden cupboard from Calcutta that had arrived at my husband's home in a truck along with a few other pieces of furniture. Chitra had decided Bombay lacked well-made furniture. The quality of wood was no good, the workmanship poor and the design decidedly nouveau riche. Calcutta still boasted of a few, fine old furniture showrooms on Park Street— Burma teak, rosewood, even mahogany if you looked hard enough. Wonderful examples of colonial furniture often sold for a pittance by the original owners while changing homes or emigrating. Chitra imagined she had an eye for a good bargain. My bedroom had been furnished with an odd but compatible collection of second-hand furniture. And it was the handsome teak armoire that had followed me to Bombay and my new home.

As I idly fingered my collection of sarees (all from Calcutta, delivered by obliging friends and relatives visiting Bombay or by Prodipda after his annual visit home, for I had never taken to anonymous 'Bombay' sarees) my fingers stopped at a parrot green one with a narrow black woven border. I traced the elegant pattern with its flowering creepers as I remembered Nikhil's comment when he had seen me in it a few weeks ago.

'You look like a beautiful garden today,' he had said approvingly, catching sight of me in the tiny foyer as I left for my daily visit to the nearby fish market.

I had stopped in my tracks and smiled warmly at him while he tried to kick start his battered motorcycle. Just then his mother's harsh voice had disturbed the charm of the moment with its strident tone.

'Ni-khi-l . . . don't waste time. Hurry up or you'll be late for college.'

Nikhil had whispered, 'Ignore her. She's always nagging.'

But I had rushed off to the market, flushed and confused. That morning, my mind hadn't been on the fish I was buying, and Ranjan had noticed the difference. He'd poked a stubby finger into the too-soft flesh and snorted his disapproval.

'Look . . .' he had demonstrated, 'it's stale. Fresh fish is firm to the touch and happy-looking. I've told you many times, leave the fish-buying to me.'

I had been overcome by remorse and said penitently, 'But . . . but where do you have the time to buy fish? You're so busy always.'

Ranjan had snapped, 'That may be. But it's better than wasting hard-earned money on rotten fish.'

Sheepishly, I had removed the offending fish from the table. God was punishing me for smiling at Nikhil's careless compliment and feeling pleased by it. Ranjan was still scowling about the mushy fish when I returned to the table with a crisply baked papad. He had continued to look irritable throughout the rest of his meal.

The fried fish had been stone cold and even more limp by the time I had begun my own meal. I had eaten it with deliberation. Eaten all four pieces to prove to my husband that I was a frugal housewife who didn't waste food. With each mouthful, my throat muscles had tightened as I tried to gulp my dinner down.

Ranjan had waited with a long-suffering, annoyed expression. I had looked up to tell him not to bother to stay at the table but to go ahead and wash his hands.

'It's all right. Take your time,' he had replied, adding, 'I simply can't understand how you've been eating that rotten fish. I hope it doesn't give you an upset tummy. One has to be extra careful during this season. As it is, the waters around Bombay are horribly polluted. Combine that with bad weather and you get disease-carrying fish in the market. Dangerous. Very dangerous. Don't force yourself to eat more. Give it to the servant tomorrow.'

'And what if she falls sick? Who'll clean the house, wash the clothes, and scrub the cooking pots?'

Ranjan had leaned back in his chair, thrust his chin out and asked, 'Didn't you do housework at your mother's house? Don't tell me you've forgotten already.'

I had bitten my tongue in dismay. I had wanted to say that I had worked in Calcutta, done household chores, but I had never been made to feel like a servant. A menial. I didn't have a problem about doing my own housework. It was Ranjan's attitude that hurt me. The bank provided him a fairly generous allowance and we could well have afforded full-time help. But Ranjan was adamant.

'Since you are not a career woman, there's no reason why you shouldn't keep yourself busy looking after the house. It's not as if you have to go somewhere. You don't have any appointments to keep, like our neighbour, the Verma woman. She is a professional lady, a beautician. I wouldn't be surprised if she earns more than her husband. We don't need full-time domestics. Manage with part-timers.'

And he would often point out to me, 'When I was living in the States, I did all my work myself. Yes, imagine, me. A man who hadn't had to pick up his own glass and put it back in the kitchen. I was washing my own clothes, tidying my room, even cooking.'

I would smile indulgently and obediently as if to convey my awe. Ranjan and housework! Amazing.

*

When I went back to the bathroom with a fresh set of clothes, I noticed Ranjan's reflection in the mirror. He'd crept up silently from the back and was watching me thoughtfully. He had his rare 'lovemaking' expression in his eyes—there was no mistaking it. I stiffened and moved abruptly away from the basin, trying to push past him to tie on my saree. Ranjan blocked my path and reached out for me.

I would be lying if I said his unpredictably amorous moods didn't flatter me. Oh yes, they did. But the lovemaking that followed was always a let-down. Initially, I had blamed myself for it. Perhaps I was too inhibited, too inexperienced, too uptight. And then I discovered something that rather surprised me. It was Ranjan who was all of that.

When I recognized the fact, it endeared Ranjan to me. Here I was at twenty-three with only one 'kissing boyfriend' behind me. And there was the foreign-educated, modern, confident Bombay boy of twenty-eight who had never known another woman. I'd married a virgin.

Ranjan had revealed this to me two weeks after our four-day, clumsy-sex honeymoon at a depressing hotel in Mahabaleshwar, a hill resort near Bombay. I was expecting my period and didn't know how to break it to my brand-new husband. My breasts were swollen and sore, my skin had broken out and my insides felt strangely constricted and dry. What was I supposed to say? Or do? Resort to coy euphemisms such as 'It's that time of the month . . . I hope you understand?' Or just let him find out for himself and may be jump back in horror or disgust?

Ranjan made it easy for me. He pulled out his planner crammed with neat entries. He studied it carefully and announced, 'Hmmm, according to my calculations, you should start menstruating any day. Is there something I could get for you from the chemist?'

I didn't know what to say. Embarrassed and confused, I stuttered, 'It's . . . it's okay. I mean, I'll manage.'

Later that night I asked him shyly how he had known. Ranjan said his mother had told him to maintain a monthly guide for future medical reference. And how had she known my dates? Ranjan looked at me in surprise.

'Oh, obviously, that area was covered before fixing the marriage date. Your mother informed my mother and we decided to keep the ceremony exactly five days after your fourth day, that's how its done. Surely you know Hindu women don't participate in any religious ceremony during their menses. These things are discussed well in advance with the family priest.'

The family priest? Good heavens. I hid my face in the corner of my saree and burst into tears. 'How could anybody discuss such a personal matter with a complete stranger—some man paid to come to the ceremony and chant a few mechanical mantras? I'm so embarrassed, I could die.'

Ranjan awkwardly placed an arm around me. It was an almost brotherly gesture. He seemed to sympathize as he said softly, 'It's all right. Please stop crying. That's the way it's done for everyone. That's tradition. The priest hears the same thing five times a day. It doesn't matter to him.'

I burst out, 'But it does matter to me—don't you see? I've never talked about it to anybody, not even to my mother. I mean, never directly, of course she *knew*—but it wasn't something we actually discussed or anything.'

Ranjan looked miserable. 'Look,' he said, 'unless those four days are known, no auspicious function involving a menstruating woman can be scheduled. This is the law laid down in our shastras. I can't change it. And you shouldn't argue with it. Besides, it's behind us now. So . . . go wash your face. Let's watch the World Report on the BBC. May be they'll show Winnie Mandela. Or Leeson, or O.J. Simpson.'

And that's when I'd brought it up. I reached across the bed to hold my husband's hand (my own was trembling).

'Tell me,' I started, my voice soft, 'have you known lots and lots of girls before me?'

Ranjan stiffened. I could feel his fingers under mine, holding onto the bedcover. 'Sure,' he said, 'a few.'

'How well did you know them? A little or very intimately?' I probed.

Ranjan hesitated. 'Well . . . I knew a few better than I knew the others . . . that's all.'

I paused. He withdrew his hand and reached for the remote control. Our channel-surfing half-hour was about to begin. I jumped to my feet and ran in front of the TV set, blocking his vision. Ranjan looked distinctly annoyed.

'Hey . . . I can't see anything. What are you doing, standing in front of my TV?'

I squared my shoulders, searched frantically for my voice and finally found it. 'Ranjan . . . please . . . it's important to me to finish this conversation. I want to know about your life before you met me. Just a little. I don't know a thing. And then, I want you to ask me about mine—not that there's anything much to tell. Don't you think we should discuss such things?'

Ranjan looked exasperated. 'Why do women always insist on this silly exercise?' he complained. 'What's the point in asking all these silly, meaningless questions? Does it really make the slightest difference? What will you get by finding out about my past, or I by digging into yours? Forget it, Maya. Let's begin with a clean slate.'

I came up to him and caught his shoulders. I was almost pleading. 'Please . . . just this once. I swear I'll never ask you again. I want to know.'

Ranjan stepped back. He seemed a little repulsed by me, by my nearness. He looked skywards and stared thoughtfully at the door as if contemplating an instant escape. He began pacing the floor with a fierce frown of concentration between his brows. He suddenly looked so agitated that I found myself feeling sorry for him and for what I was putting him through.

My shoulders slumped and I sat down heavily on a stuffed chair in the corner of our bedroom. I could hear one of those giddy new Veejays prattling on about a 'Countdown'. Ironically, I was counting down too. Mentally, I'd given Ranjan two more seconds to make up his mind—to confess or not to confess.

The absurd lyrics of the latest film hit came floating in through the window. The words made no sense at all. *Ruk-Ruk. Tuk-Tuk. Oh no. Oh no. Love ho gaya.* I was ready to give up on Ranjan when he whirled around abruptly and said in a strange, high voice, 'It's not that I don't like women or anything . . . don't misunderstand me. It's just that I've never felt very comfortable with them. They're . . . they're different. I never know what's going on in their heads. I've tried to make friends with them . . . but it has never worked.'

I listened sympathetically, my mind distracted by the mindless yet hypnotic Hindi songs playing on my neighbours' TV set. This was new to me. In Calcutta, I had hardly ever watched any Hindi programmes, not even those on the entertainment channel. I barely spoke Hindi myself other than a very functional variety used mainly to issue instructions to Bihari servants.

Bombay's brand of Hindi was entirely different and very addictive—like the city itself. I strained my ears to catch the words and marvelled at the magic of the slang. It was amusing, eccentric and wicked. I felt terrible about not paying attention to Ranjan but at that moment I was enchanted by the stream of silly songs. I couldn't help thinking to myself that I'd missed out on all the fun for so many years.

I heard Ranjan say in a broken voice, 'It's been difficult for me to get into a relationship with any woman. Very difficult. But I've tried.'

Mechanically, I asked, 'Wasn't it easier when you were in America? I mean, the girls there are so free, that's what everybody says.'

Ranjan shook his head. 'It's not true. It's nonsense. Girls there are like girls anywhere. I did get to know a few but they didn't remain friends for long.'

I wondered why. Ranjan wasn't bad looking. As a matter of fact, there was something positively attractive about his smile (lovely white, even teeth), his thick dark hair and the intense, large eyes that regarded the world solemnly. His body may not have been perfectly proportioned (he was short in the legs) but his chest and shoulders were strong and broad, plus he didn't have a belly or a jiggly bottom. He was self-conscious about his thick waist but I didn't find it offensive. He projected an easy manner (that is, when he wasn't preoccupied with some office problem) and I could sense that other women found him attractive.

This could have been because he was reticent in their presence, unlike other men who tended to come on a bit too strong or who went overboard in the 'I'm-so-charming' department. Ranjan preferred to stick with the men, rarely going beyond a stiff greeting during the introductions. Ranjan did have his own brand of humour but because of his heavy Bengali accent (with its well-rounded vowels) tinged with an overlay of Americanisms, people in Bombay found it hard to catch every word he uttered especially since his voice level was naturally low and soft.

I would have thought someone like him would have been vastly successful in the West. He looked 'Oriental' all right, with his heavy-lidded, tip-tilted eyes (a little like Chinese ones), and he was unfailingly polite to strangers.

Ranjan continued to talk about his experiences (or rather his lack of them) with co-students on the campus. But I noted he had scrupulously avoided answering the one, crucial question I had wanted to be enlightened on. Had he slept with anyone before he'd married me?

Ranjan looked trapped. Then he mumbled evasively, 'What does it matter?'

'I want to know,' I maintained stubbornly. 'Isn't it a wife's prerogative to ask that question?'

Ranjan went and stood by the window, his shoulders slumped over. And then he spoke in a voice that was barely audible over the raucous film songs choking the atmosphere with their blatant vulgarity.

'I tried,' he said miserably. And repeated it again, 'I tried, Maya. But it didn't work.'

I guess I'd figured that out. I was willing to leave it there. But obviously Ranjan wasn't. It must have been painful for him to discuss his failures with the six girls he'd tried to make love to. 'Somehow, nothing happened. I must have done or said something wrong because . . . because . . .' and he couldn't get himself to complete the sentence.

I waited for my husband to compose himself. He was weeping, his face turned away from me. After a while, I said gently, 'Maybe something was wrong with them. Maybe they weren't the right women. Maybe you didn't love them.'

Ranjan whirled around, and I could see the gratitude on his face. 'That's right,' he exclaimed, 'You've hit the nail on the head. I didn't love them. And they didn't love me. I should never have bothered.'

Tentatively, I began stroking his broad back. It wasn't at all a sexual overture. Not at a moment like this. But Ranjan misread it. He turned towards me eagerly. 'Maya, tell me frankly . . . did you find anything wrong? I mean, was I all right? Are you happy with . . . with . . . things?'

His arms were around me. I could feel the wetness of his cheeks dampen the top of my head. I snuggled close to him, resting my face against his chest. I recognized all the mixed fragrances—Mysore sandalwood soap (Ranjan's favourite), Pond's Dreamflower Talc (his mother's favourite) and Yardley's

English Blazer aftershave (my favourite). He was stroking my hair thoughtfully and then letting his fingers travel down my back. One hand was caressing my bare waist. And one leg had casually swung across my lap.

It was getting uncomfortable in that awkward clinch and I shifted my weight accordingly. By doing that, my breasts pressed against him. Ranjan pushed me down on the bed gently and started undressing me. It was something he'd never done before, preferring to lie on the bed staring fixedly ahead of him while I clumsily fumbled with my saree blouse and petticoat.

Encouraged by his gesture, I reached for his shirt buttons and started to undo them. Ranjan held both my hands in his and stopped me.

'Wait,' he said urgently.

Taken aback by the abruptness of his command, I tried to sit up.

'Why not?'

Ranjan rolled off me and leaned on his elbows. 'I'm not ready yet,' he said slowly. 'Maya . . . you'll have to be patient. It's going to take time. I can't. I just can't.'

I was more puzzled than hurt. Ranjan needed time. So did I. So did I.

Five

As the first year of our marriage drew to a close, my life began to fall into a routine of sorts. I had discovered FM Radio. And television. When I wasn't listening to Rajesh sending UB2 requests for Anoushka or a sloppy DJ trying desperately to sound American, I was glued to the colour set in our bedroom looking for the big answers from Donahue and Winfrey.

Every once in a while, I would receive sugary phonecalls from the 'office wives' as we were referred to, enquiring after my well-being and issuing invitations to various saree sales in the city. I would have thought these extended hands of friendship from within the fold would please or at least flatter Ranjan. To my surprise, they didn't. He was instantly suspicious when I mentioned Vimla Rangani's call.

'Stay away from that woman,' he said sharply.

'Why? Is she not nice?' I asked innocently as I folded his underwear (always white, never high-cut).

'These Bombay women are different. Why do you think my mother chose a girl from Calcutta for me?' he said as though he was discussing a third person and not me.

I started sorting out his socks (steel grey, navy blue, black, no patterns). 'In what way are Bombay women different?' I asked.

Ranjan went to the dressing table and poured a palmful of hair oil into his thick hair. 'They have no morals,' he announced flatly.

'Is Vimla immoral?' I persisted.

Ranjan stopped massaging his head and glared at me. 'Why do you keep arguing? Just accept what I'm saying. After all, I live here. I know how these women are. They'll have a bad influence on you. Just stay away from all of them, okay?'

Petulantly, I muttered, 'As if I'm a kid who can be so easily influenced. As if I don't have a mind of my own. As if I lack any sense of judgement.'

Ranjan sat down heavily on the bed. 'As if, as if, as if. You know, you have a very bad habit of arguing. I am your husband. What I tell you is for your own good. How much experience do you have in such matters? You are still a baby in a lot of ways. Bombay is not Calcutta. I don't want you to get wrong impressions or you'll go astray.'

I pulled out the ironing board. It had a large tear on the surface out of which the stuffing was falling. Ranjan came up and stuck a finger in the tear.

'What is this?' he asked, like a stern schoolmaster.

'It was like that from the beginning,' I said sullenly.

Ranjan tore a larger hole with his finger. 'Are you telling me my mother bought a torn board from the shop?'

I was close to tears. 'I didn't say that,' I replied hotly, 'all I'm saying is that this was its condition from the day your mother gave it to us. I haven't torn it—it was already torn.'

Ranjan regarded his image in the wardrobe mirror. 'This is exactly what I mean. You are becoming like these lazy, spoilt Bombay women who spend all their time shopping or eating— unconcerned about their domestic life.'

I picked up a pillow cover and placed it over the tear. 'There . . . it's okay now,' I said defiantly.

Ranjan's voice assumed a low, long-suffering tone. 'It's not okay. Please. If you have a problem understanding things, just ask me. And I'll ask my mother since you seem to have some sort of an allergy when it comes to picking up the phone to consult her. I will find out for you where and how we can get this board repaired. Concentrate on keeping your house neat instead of gallivanting with these useless women.'

Chastened, I began ironing his office shirts (blue, white, grey to match the socks). After he was through with the BBC news bulletin, I foolishly went back to the subject of Vimla and the other office wives.

'I must make some friends in Bombay,' I whined. 'How else will I spend my spare time? You are far too busy during the week. And then you're too tired by the weekend. I also need an outing. Is that unreasonable?'

Ranjan paused as if he was considering my request with the seriousness it deserved. 'If you need company, call my mother. She knows Bombay inside out. She has lived here for over twenty-five years. Whenever she can spare the time, she'll let you accompany her to the market—that's the best way for you to get used to Bombay. Don't try going to these places on your own, they'll cheat you. Even haggling is done differently here. Besides, your Hindi isn't all that good.'

Before I could stop myself, I snapped, 'It's better than your mother's—or yours for that matter.'

Ranjan got up and raised both his hands. He sighed deeply and pretended to count. 'Look, Maya . . . I've had a hard day at the office. I'm not in a mood to talk rubbish with you. I have some papers to read. I suggest you go over our conversation carefully. I'm sure it will make sense to you when you think about it. You will realize on your own that a housewife's duty is to stay at home and make sure everything is tip-top. That is where her true happiness lies. You've seen my mother's house—learn from her.'

I wanted to ask but didn't—'If your mother is all that happy, how come she always has such a sour expression on her face?'

*

Ranjan's relationship with his mother was clear enough—he adored her and she adored him. But what about his father? I was curious about my late father-in-law, Amartya Malik. For all practical purposes, he remained a ghost. A non-person in their lives.

Why did Ranjan avoid speaking about him? Had he been an ogre of some sort? Once or twice when I had tried asking him some questions, he would shut me up by saying stiffly, 'I don't really remember.' I would notice his expression changing as well.

I had tried asking Prodipmama about Mr Malik too and drawn a blank. 'He was a good man—respectable. A gentleman. Highly cultured,' was all he had said.

Some time ago, I had come across an old photograph of his with Ranjan and asked him lightly about their relationship. Ranjan had assumed his irritable expression (forehead creased, nose twitching, lips pulled back over his teeth). 'What do you want to know? There is nothing to know. He was okay. Quiet. Studious. That's all.'

Ranjan had started flicking the pages of some company's annual report rapidly. Stubbornly, I had persisted, 'When he died . . . how did you feel? How did Ma feel? Was it sudden?'

He had pretended he hadn't heard and simply asked me to fetch him a glass of water ('no ice, please,' he had added, as though he was instructing a waitress in a diner). I had gone scurrying into the kitchen and come back with 'his' glass delicately balanced on a plate. Quite soon after our wedding, I had made the mistake of handing him an ordinary glass (the kind I used for myself) without placing a saucer under it. Ranjan had slapped his forehead impatiently and scolded, 'My God! Maya—is that the way to serve water? Thank God my mother isn't here. This is how we give tumblers of tea to servants and sweepers. Please understand . . . I don't mean to nag you. But there has to be some grace.'

I had understood. But now I wanted to understand something else, someone else—a man who was no more. Perhaps, by knowing a little about him, I would find the key to unlocking whatever it was that Ranjan guarded so fiercely inside his heart and mind.

So, I had tried once again. Gently, I asked, 'Was your Baba something like my Baba?'

Ranjan had pulled out a calculator and started punching the buttons furiously. I had wondered what it was that he was adding up. 'See, Maya, since I barely know your father, I cannot comment on the comparison. In any case, fathers are fathers,' he mumbled.

I had smiled and asked slyly, 'And mothers?'

Ranjan had flung the calculator on the bed. 'You know, I can't understand you at all. You really ask very silly questions sometimes. My father was like any father. I didn't spend that much time with him anyway. He did his work and I did mine. Any other question?'

I had felt rather sorry for poor Mr Amartya Malik. His son had not been able to come up with anything more than a

63

bald line to sum up his life. How very sad. I had stared hard at the black and white photograph. 'Where was this taken?' I had asked Ranjan.

He had looked up sharply and grabbed the photograph from my hand. 'Give that to me. Where did you find it? Honestly, Maya, when will you learn to leave things alone? Tell me, does it really matter to you where this was taken? If I said "Tokyo" or "Timbuctoo" would it make any difference?'

I had shaken my head. Ranjan had exclaimed triumphantly, 'Then, why ask?'

I should have kept quiet at that point but I couldn't stop myself from saying softly, 'All I was trying to do was . . .'

Ranjan had held up his hand. 'Enough. There is nothing to know about my father. And there is no need for you to poke your nose into matters that do not concern you. He isn't alive. Heart failure. You don't have to deal with him. You concentrate on getting to know Ma—that should be your job.'

Job? Was that what it was? Well, there was no point in pursuing the subject. The secret Ranjan was trying to protect would remain with him (and his mother). I only hoped for Mr Malik's sake that it wasn't something humiliating that would damage his frayed dignity. I had liked the little glimpse I had had of him through his portrait on the wall and now this photograph. Irrationally, perhaps, I had decided that Mr Malik was the wronged party even though nobody had really framed any charges against him.

My mother-in-law's attitude was calculatingly vague. She let drop a few casual remarks just to show that there had been a father in Ranjan's life. A father who was someone 'important'. That was what counted. His designation, his job, his income and their social status thanks to his position—whatever that was. Had he been a weak figure like my own father? Had Ranjan ever been close to him? Why was the subject taboo? Questions whose answers I would never be given.

*

As I reflected on Ranjan's relationship with his parents, I began to compare Ranjan's mother with my own.

My own home wasn't a messy one. My mother was a frugal housewife who prided herself on 'managing'. I would often overhear her saying with ill-disguised glee, 'No matter what it is, I manage.'

I couldn't remember whether or not the ironing board had tears in it, but I did remember other details of our home. My mother's meticulously maintained diary, for instance. At the beginning of every year, my father would bring home at least four or five large diaries with plastic covers.

The two of them would debate their respective merits for over an hour. Were the printed dates prominent enough? Were Sundays and Saturdays marked in red? What about the pages—two days to a page or one? Lined or unlined? Vertical or horizontal? A separate section indicating bank holidays was vital. Plus two pages devoted to the previous year's calendar plus the coming year's. A poetic 'thought for the day' was a bonus but not essential. The important thing was a sturdy cover and extra sheets at the back of the diary.

'The issue is, one always exceeds the space. So much happens in one day—one needs more pages to jot down important things.'

These 'important things' were life insurance policy numbers, gas registration certificates, ration card details, electricity metre codes, bank locker numbers, bank account numbers plus phone numbers of all the relatives and emergency services. The question of discarding last year's diary while replacing it with the current year's did not arise. My mother had a special shelf where she kept all her old diaries. These were taken down and dusted on alternate Sundays. Once, I had asked her why she kept them, considering there was nothing more filling the pages than the day's accounts.

My mother had looked hurt and shocked. She had thought about my question deeply before replying, 'You see Maya, these diaries are an important record. If I want to know exactly how much a two-litre bottle of cooking oil cost five years ago, I don't have to guess—I can find the answer in one minute.'

The answer hadn't satisfied me. 'Why would you want to know the price of cooking oil five years ago?' I had asked.

My mother had looked even more shocked. 'How else can your father and I monitor inflation? The issue is—if oil today costs five times as much, are we earning more in the same proportion? And if not, how do we balance our accounts? Should we cut back on deep-fried items such as fish and loochis? Or should we give up something else? This is how a housewife manages her expenses.'

My mother had optimistically and thoughtfully included a shiny green diary in my trunks when she'd packed all the belongings that were to accompany me to Bombay. I had looked at it sitting atop my small pile of new sarees and smiled. I was never going to maintain a diary. Not for accounts at any rate.

*

The green diary had not been discarded. It had just been put to an entirely different use. I'd started recording my impressions of Bombay in it. And I realized that far too many of the entries concerned Nikhil. Was I really that bored? That frustrated?

No, no, no. I was being unfair to Nikhil. There was something undeniably attractive about him. Perhaps it was the boundless energy he exuded. And the look of genuine interest in his eyes when he interacted with just about anybody. He was good-looking too but not especially so. Average height, athletic build, tanned skin, nice hands, nice eyes, nice smile. That made him sound like a college girl's dreamboat, and perhaps that's exactly what he was. And perhaps I was regressing and carrying on like a lovestruck teenager.

At the time that he made his first sly entry into my diary, though, I hadn't as much as acknowledged my feelings. What were they anyway? Careless curiosity about a young, sporty male neighbour, nothing more. Or so I told myself.

The very fact that his existence made even a marginal difference to my monotonous life, underlined the state that I had allowed myself to slide into. My entire being was sensitized to the sound of his impatient footsteps on the staircase outside my closed door. How did I know it belonged to his feet and nobody else's? I just did. Nikhil didn't keep to a schedule and yet, even as I lay down on my bed for the daily afternoon siesta, my drowsiness would disappear temporarily at the unmistakable thud-thud of his heavy boots charging past my entrance. I'd rouse myself and rush to the window only to see his lithe leap over the low wall, and the quick kick to the motorbike before he disappeared entirely from view.

Even that all-too-brief image began to assume an exaggerated crazy importance in my dull schedule. I asked myself what it was about Nikhil that I was reacting to so strongly. And whether I'd feel this way if I had more to do during the long, eventless hours that stretched like a blank, white sheet in front of my listless gaze. Occasionally, I caught sight of myself and was startled by the permanently glazed expression in my eyes.

*

Once, when I was rummaging through my cupboard, I had come across a blue saree with a tiny white peacock motif. Nikhil had complimented me on it in his characteristic off-hand way.

'Hmmm, blue. Blue for a lady with the blues. You are wearing a mood saree—how come? Not happy to see me?'

When had that exchange taken place? Six months ago, or earlier? I reached under the neatly ironed heap of saree petticoats and located die green diary. The legend on its shiny rexine cover read 'Indian Cold Extrusion Industry'. I flipped open the pages with damp, nervous fingers. I knew exactly which entry I was looking for. After a few quick flicks of the pages, I replaced the diary tiredly. There was someone at the door—the idli seller, perhaps.

Idlis. The Tuesday idlis. Every Tuesday, Vishwanath brought a batch of fluffy, white idlis steamed by his wife, to the building and went from flat to flat asking the housewives if they wanted to buy some. To me, idlis were an alien taste. I'd hardly ever eaten them in Calcutta. It was Vishwanath who had introduced me to the pleasure of eating a well-made idli dipped in the special sambar whose secret only his wife knew.

'Taste it, memsaab, taste it. Nobody in Bombay can give you this flavour,' he would boast, spooning it out carefully into the stainless steel container I had provided. He would generously throw in a dollop of coconut chutney swimming in yoghurt, accept a couple of rupees with grace and leave, jauntily swinging his idli-container.

One afternoon, as I was standing at the door debating whether or not to buy six idlis to serve Ranjan as a tea-time snack, I heard Nikhil leaving his house, banging the door noisily behind him as he came hurtling down the staircase whistling. My instinct was to dart back into my own flat—I hadn't bathed or combed my hair, and last night's kaajal was smudged around my eyes. But how could I do that with Vishwanath wedged in the doorway?

It was too late, anyway. 'Hi, Maya,' Nikhil stopped to greet me. My one hand flew to neaten the stray strands of hair while the other clutched onto my caftan as though I was about to brave the flood waters.

'Off to college?' I asked, as cheerfully as I could muster, stricken with embarrassment at being caught in this dishevelled condition.

'Hey, you're looking . . . you're looking different,' Nikhil commented, staring at me with open curiousity.

'Yes . . . I haven't had the time to take a bath this morning,' I mumbled.

Nikhil laughed. 'That's what I call stating the obvious. But, don't worry . . . you're looking good anyway.'

I leaned against the door frame, feeling shabby and entirely unattractive. 'Like some idlis?' I asked, unsure of what to say or do next.

Nikhil came forward confidently. 'Sure, love them. I don't know why but my mother never gets any for us.'

I held out the stainless steel container. 'Go ahead, take two or three. I only need some for my husband.'

Nikhil helped himself to one, dipped it in chutney and stuck the whole idli into his mouth.

I burst out laughing. 'Is that how you generally eat idlis?'

'Not generally. Just today. I'm in a hurry . . . late for lectures,' Nikhil mouthed through the idli.

I stood there holding out the sambar container and stared fascinatedly at Nikhil's rapidly moving jaws. Three idlis disappeared down his gullet within seconds.

I couldn't stop myself from teasing, 'Don't you get enough to eat at home?'

Nikhil shook his head. 'What exactly is your definition of "enough"? Let's put it this way, I'm always hungry. Always.'

He looked at me enquiringly for a moment, as if searching for some mysterious clue. Then he said, 'I didn't know Bongs ate idlis. That's funny. But then . . . you are funny too.'

By the time I'd manage to call out, 'What do you mean?' after his retreating figure, he had jumped over the low compound wall and onto his motorbike, leaving Vishwanath and me to stare after him.

I turned to Vishwanath with a start. I had completely forgotten about him. Strange, it was as if he'd suddenly turned invisible. Disappeared altogether. And there he was once again, standing two feet away from me, patiently waiting for his money, and looking at me in a manner he hadn't previously.

'Those people never buy my idlis,' he said abruptly. 'That woman—that boy's mother—is a rude person. I don't force anyone to buy anything. She can just say "no". Where is the need to shout and abuse? I'm not begging for alms.'

I didn't want to discuss Nikhil's mother with a vendor. I handed him the money and turned to go, but he lingered on. 'That boy is all right. Nice fellow. Always cheerful. It's his mother who is not good.'

I refused to comment or change my expression. Vishwanath took his time to retrieve his container. With it still wedged in my doorway, I couldn't shut the door. Vishwanath sighed. 'Modern life is so lonely. So lonely. Nobody to talk to. Nobody to share anything with. Isn't that right?'

I smiled non-commitally. 'See you next Tuesday,' Vishwanath said before resuming his idli rounds.

*

And Tuesdays acquired a new meaning for me. Shared idlis at the doorstep with Nikhil. I started to wake up early in order to finish bathing, brushing my hair and applying a neat line of sindhoor in its parting. I chose my sarees with care, going to the extent of ironing them. I had a special lot of old, worn sarees that I wore at home. These were never ironed, merely folded neatly and piled up. My 'good' sarees were on another shelf lying carefully wrapped in layers of muslin.

On Tuesday mornings, I would examine my 'home saree' collection and pick one with care. Ever since Nikhil had noticed the blue one, I'd separated the other blues and kept them aside. Tuesdays became my 'blue' days. Even Ranjan noticed that.

'You're wearing so many blue sarees suddenly. I thought you didn't like blue. You've always told me that blue doesn't suit you because of your dusky complexion. Though if you ask me, I think you are quite fair . . . compared to your father, for example,' he remarked one day.

I winced at the comment. Not that Ranjan was being insulting—just straightforward. In any case, why be so touchy about the family? Smiling weakly, I said, 'I don't know what's got into me—may be like Picasso, this is my blue period.'

It was a joke that was entirely lost on my husband. 'I don't understand all this Picasso-Wicasso business,' he said mildly. 'I only know what I see, which is another blue saree.'

I went into the small kitchen to get a fresh batch of hot chapattis. Ranjan grumbled, 'Sit here, for God's sake—don't keep running away. I don't mind eating cold chapattis . . . though I must say in my mother's house I never as much as tasted one that wasn't straight off the fire. God knows how she did it—but the entire family was served hot chapattis meal after meal without her once leaving the dining table. Mummy is a very good housekeeper and home-maker. When I was working in New York, I really used to miss her cooking. I'd come home for my holidays and go back with my suitcases crammed with all sorts of goodies—home-made papads, snacks, pickles. She's amazing. Maybe you should train with her instead of doodling away your time at a drawing board.'

I was tempted to defend myself but refrained. So, that's what Ranjan thought of my tentative freelancing efforts—doodling. I sighed deeply as I gave him another helping of his favourite vegetable—diced potatoes with poppy seeds.

Ranjan beamed. 'Well . . . aloo poshto is one dish you cook almost like my mother. She adds green chillies split down the middle which give her poshto an extra kick. Maybe you should do that next time.'

I stared at the pallu of my pale blue saree and said nothing.

Six

I was often tempted to pick up the phone and speak to my mother or an old schoolfriend called Aarti, in Calcutta. But I couldn't do that on two counts: I didn't dare make long-distance calls without seeking Ranjan's permission. And I didn't know the code that would unlock the phone line for STD calls.

Soon after our marriage, Ranjan had given me a guided tour of the flat and had pointed to the phone. He had said sternly, 'Only for emergencies, not for idle chit-chat.' He'd also made it clear that the phone bills were not picked up by the company and that each time I dialled, it cost him over a rupee for the first five minutes. And that was for local calls.

I hadn't minded his little lecture on economy since it had reminded me of my own father's attitude. My father would often tell my talkative mother to keep a stop-watch near the phone and time her calls.

'Five minutes are sufficient to convey anything to anyone,' he'd grumble while my mother launched into another one of her 'the issue is . . .' rebuttals. The 'issue' was really quite simple. My mother talked compulsively. My father hated to pay for it.

I wasn't much of a talker. In many ways, I was more like my father, an observer, not a participant. He would tell me quietly, 'Our side of the family is philosophical and poetic. We are thinkers. But your mother's! Try interrupting her when she's talking to Prodip. I have never seen a brother and sister duo who have so much to say to one another.'

It rather amused me to realize that my father saw himself as a poet, philosopher and thinker. I suppose it was a common Bengali trait. He'd forgotten to add 'revolutionary'. Yet in his own gentle way, my father influenced the way I conducted myself in the world. Like him, I was non-aggressive and withdrawn. Like him, I found absurdity in most everyday situations. Like him, I enjoyed the unpredictable beauty of a monsoon evening. Or the taste of piping hot, deep-fried snacks with a cup of strong tea.

My mother scoffed at all this. She, I was sure, would have preferred a more dynamic man as her partner in life. Her deep sense of disappointment at my father's lack of ambition manifested itself in the strident high-pitched tone she employed to 'put things in perspective'. If he minded her frequent and pointed attacks, he didn't show it, preferring to withdraw into his room and immerse himself in Tagore.

It was my mother who made all the decisions—big and small. It was she who ran the house, managed the finances and planned for the future. Had it not been for her initiative, I would never have married Ranjan. My father's views on the subject weren't sought and his participation in the wedding had been marginal. Between my mother and her brother, they had managed it all—the presents and arrangements, the accommodation for close relatives, the exact sequence of various ceremonies, even the purchasing of my trousseau.

My father had gone along obediently, almost meekly, offering not a single suggestion, nor interfering in any way. It was Chitradi and Prodipda's show, and perhaps it was better that way.

My uncle had inexplicably disappeared from the scene once I was married. Perhaps he felt he had discharged his duty and there was nothing further to be done. I had hoped he would be around to hold my hand during the first few months—my ally in an alien city. I had tried to phone him a few times but he had been remote and vague. I wondered about his abrupt withdrawal from my life.

I had mentioned it to my mother in a letter and she had written back promptly, 'The issue is, you are a married woman now. You belong to your husband's family. In traditional families such as ours, it is simply not done for the bride's relatives—male ones in particular—to maintain frequent and close contact with her. That prevents the girl from integrating into her husband's family. Besides, it may also lead to misunderstandings between the couple. Advice can also be seen as interference no matter how well-meant it is. Take my word for it, it is far better this way.

'This does not mean that your uncle doesn't love you. Only that he is being wise and discreet. By leaving you alone, he is encouraging you to become a part of jamaibabu's family. Besides, we don't know how they'll react to your mamu visiting you. Or even phoning frequently. After you settle down a little, the picture will automatically change. Don't worry. Of course, if you do need something urgently, he's always there.

'The issue is, you have to get to know your new family and become one of them as quickly as possible. It is for your own good, for your sake, that mamu is leaving you alone. Don't misunderstand that. Girls who cling on to their own family for too long never succeed in adjusting to their husband's people. We don't want that to happen to you. I'm sure you'll understand. Don't forget to take extra iron and calcium—just in case.'

Trust my mother to be subtle. Not that I resented her advice. My mother and I had a strange relationship. We were wary of each other most of the time. I could never tell what she actually felt towards me apart from a strong sense of duty. While I could rarely cross over to her side and demonstrate warmer sentiments. If she was inhibited, so was I. As for my father, it was even harder to figure out what he truly made of either of us. He left my mother strictly alone, preferring to lead a quiet, pensive, secluded existence in his side of the home.

With me, he was affectionate in a detached sort of way. Far too shy to ever hold me close or kiss me, he would sometimes pat my head stiffly while passing, nothing beyond that. If I ever ran into his room unannounced, he'd all but jump out of his skin and look so startled, I'd feel like an absolute intruder. Climbing onto his bed and stretching out by his side was unthinkable. Nor could I initiate a touch by reaching out for his hand or clinging onto his arm. Not that he ever told me anything—it was implicitly understood. He shrank away from physical contact so visibly, it would have been the worst sort of imposition to force the issue.

*

Since my parents hardly ever talked to each other, quarrels or heated arguments were out of the question. If they disagreed at all, it was indicated through disapproving glances and impatient gestures which I soon taught myself to both intercept and interpret.

My father's closest ally was a college friend of his—a bachelor who worshipped Nirad Chaudhuri and Bankim Chandra and could quote Keats and Shakespeare verbatim. Ashishda would arrive at our home around tea-time clutching a small box of sandesh in one hand and his dusty dhoti in the other. Over three (always three) cups of tea, my father and his friend would spend two companionable hours debating burning issues of the day (pollution, prices, politics) in voices that rose and fell with the level of the tea in their cups. These were the only times I saw my father animated, argumentative, voluble and involved.

Of course, it was understood that Ashishda wasn't supposed to make a habit of it, or else my mother's tolerance would wear thin. Ashishda was sensitive enough to recognize the signals—my father's edginess, his frequent, darting glances in the direction of my mother's room, his shifting positions from the armchair to the bed. His references to the hour of the day ('Oh . . . I see it's now five-thirty—it gets dark so quickly these days').

My mother would pace on the small balcony overlooking the courtyard, unable to conceal her impatience. I never did understand her annoyance at these visits. It wasn't as if she was waiting to talk to my father or that the phone was in his room thereby denying her privacy while making calls, or even that the TV set was positioned there.

Maybe it was access to the toilet in that case, I concluded. While there were two other bathrooms, those were strictly for bathing and washing one's hands. The toilet could only be reached through my father's room. My mother, a creature of well-regulated habits, only used it once every morning at precisely 7.30 a.m. right after she'd consumed her second cup of tea for the morning. She strongly disapproved of anybody who needed to go more than once every day.

'What exactly is the matter with your bowels?' she'd demand glaring aggressively if she ever caught me sneaking into the toilet at mid-day. At times I would lie and say, 'I didn't do anything, promise.'

To which she would stare suspiciously to see whether my hands were wet and then say, 'If you didn't do anything, why did you go there at all?'

I suspected her pacing in the balcony was her way of discouraging Ashishda from using our toilet. I'd overheard her once grumbling to a neighbour, 'These outsiders have no consideration. They barge into your home and head straight for the toilet. It's not done, I tell you. It's simply not done. The issue is, they bring in all sorts of germs with them . . . infections . . . dirt. Can't they wait till they get back to their own homes?'

It was true that Ashishda spent nearly twenty minutes out of the two and a half hours he spent with my father, locked in the toilet. I couldn't figure out what he did in there for that long. I tried asking my father one day, but he was evasive. It was my mother who provided the answer.

'Piles,' she proclaimed, 'he has piles. Don't think I don't know.'

She looked significantly at my father as if challenging him to deny this awful fact. He looked sheepishly at his toes while I waited for a confirmation.

'Does he, Baba?' I asked finally.

My father didn't reply but my mother did. 'The issue is, these people have no concept. They do not realize that reading Shakespeare in the toilet leads to constipation. Chronic constipation leads to piles. No matter how educated and erudite that man may be, when it comes to simple things, he knows nothing. That's why he is a bachelor. If he can't look after his own bowels, how can he look after a wife, tell me?'

I didn't quite see the connection, but I noticed my father's crestfallen face and his narrow shoulders slumping more than usual. Instinctively, I felt the need to take sides and show clearly where my sympathies lay.

I said to nobody in particular, 'I like Ashishda very much. He is kind and sweet. So what if he has piles because of Shakespeare? At least he doesn't shout at children and act mean.'

My mother turned around and left the room, shooting me a dirty look. I was alone with my father. He was very still and quiet. After a few minutes, without looking at me, he gestured to me to come near him. He reached under his armchair and produced Ashishda's little box of freshly squeezed sandesh and offered it to me. There were precisely two pieces inside. I took one and he took the other. We ate the sandesh in silence. In that act of sharing, I recognized and understood my father's mutiny, his defiance, his defence. It couldn't have been easy living with my mother.

Seven

As I went about my morning chores, I often wondered idly how Nikhil spent his day. I hadn't seen him for days except for a brief glimpse as he ran through the June rain and jumped into a waiting car. I'd seen his mother a few times as she tripped gingerly over puddles, holding up her saree so high I could see her hairy legs right up to her fleshy knees. Where did he roar off every morning? What was his college like? Did he attend classes regularly? Which subjects appealed to him—if any did? Did he have one girlfriend or several? Was he a campus heart-throb? A sportsman? A hero?

Did his awful mother give him pocket money to buy all those tight jeans and khadi shirts? What exactly did his father do at the bank? What did his room look like—had his mother furnished it for him with her awful, vulgar taste, or had he imposed his own more subdued one? Which room was his? The one that overlooked the crammed parking lot or the other one that had a slightly better view of the busy main road? Was it neat? Did it have posters on the wall, and loud music blaring? How much time did he spend in it?

What did he wear when he was at home—pajamas, or a lungi? I found that out soon enough. It was around seven one evening. There was a strange light in the sky that day, as though God couldn't quite make up his mind about how to paint his palette at that moment, which shade to employ—a lurid orange, a dull gold, a boring grey or all three.

I was in the kitchen preparing Ranjan's tea tray. It was a ritual he was always very particular about. On the third day after we returned home from our honeymoon, he'd told me, 'My mother is very particular about everything. I am used to a certain way of life, a pattern. Evening tea has to be served correctly. The tray must have a lace tray cloth covering it. The tea—yes, I like leaf tea. It's expensive, far-more expensive than the CTC brands, but I've grown up on it. My mother generally prepares a snack or two. If there is a deep-fried savoury, then a sweetmeat is also served to balance the taste. If, on the other hand, there is a pastry, nothing else is required unless of course cheese sandwiches have been made. If you do make sandwiches at home, please remember that I like them to be cut diagonally with the crusts removed. Remember to place a glass of cold water and a clean napkin. And please, no tea should spill from the cup onto the saucer. If it does, mop it up immediately.'

I'd been singularly unsuccessful in my attempts to create the perfect tea tray so far. That evening, distracted by the sky, I'd dropped a blob of thick red tomato ketchup onto the lace tray cloth. The other one had yet to come back from the dhobi. I tried desperately to wash off the ketchup stain and pat it dry before Ranjan's arrival. I even considered ironing the wet patch.

A spectacular rainbow was readying itself to stretch languorously across the sky. I thought of how the beach (it wasn't all that far from our home) must look, bathed in its eerie glow. I pictured myself running in the sand alongside the colourful pony-carts filled with excited children. I wanted to get wet in the waves like those curvaceous heroines in Hindi films;

I wanted to laugh as I shot all the coloured balloons with an air rifle and the audience cheered. I wanted my insides to perform a wild dance while a mangy camel sauntered down the beach carrying me atop. I wanted my fortune told by parakeets . . .oh God, I don't know what I wanted. Maybe just to be free and alive and reckless and mad.

I heard the doorbell ring. It couldn't have been Ranjan. That wasn't his sound. I checked my watch—well, it could have been him running seventeen minutes ahead of schedule. I guiltily covered up the stain with a napkin, straightened my saree, took a quick look at my untidy hair and smoothed it over with a wet hand. There, presentable enough for Ranjan. I crossed my fingers. His critical eye made me nervous. Each evening, he surveyed my appearance and made a telling comment ('blouse doesn't match', 'saree petticoat showing', 'complexion looking greasy', 'kaajal smeared').

Oh well, he'd caught me off-guard today, there was nothing I could do to improve things. I rushed to the door. And there stood Nikhil. I must have looked a little stupid with my rehearsed-for-Ranjan smile freezing at the sight of him.

'What are you doing right at this precise minute?' Nikhil asked cheerfully.

'Waiting for my husband,' I replied, noticing his batik lungi (so . . . that's what he wore at home). 'Why?' I continued, flustered and fumbling for words. Damn. He must think me utterly stupid.

'I was wondering whether I could come in and play something on your cassette recorder,' Nikhil said, holding out a tape.

I hesitated. 'What's wrong with your player?' I asked, making sure to step outside my door just so as if Ranjan came up, he'd see that I wasn't inviting strange men in.

'Nothing wrong with mine. I just felt like listening to this with you,' Nikhil smiled.

I stared miserably at my toes and wiggled them. 'It's . . . it's . . . not possible,' I finally heard a small voice emerging from my throat. I held my hand out. 'Leave it with me . . . whatever it is . . . and I'll listen to it later . . . tomorrow,' I muttered, my eyes fixed on an ugly brown flower on his hideous orange lungi.

Nikhil shrugged. 'Okay. But I really would have liked to listen to this together.'

I refused to meet his eyes. My feet were stepping back already. Nikhil paused. 'The thing is—it's my tape. I've written the songs. I've recorded the music. And I've sung everything.'

I looked up and beamed. 'Really? That's fantastic. I mean it. I didn't know you could . . .'

He didn't let me finish the sentence. 'I can,' he said quietly, a hint of mischief in his voice. 'Trust me.'

He turned to leave. I wanted to tug his lungi and drag him back. I stood there with what must have been a dumbstruck look on my face, not expecting him to turn around and catch it. He did just that.

'Listen to the fourth song on Side B,' he drawled. 'It's about you.'

And Nikhil was gone.

*

I stood there transfixed, clutching the tape tightly. I must have resembled a child playing 'statue'—too scared to move ever since the leader had thundered 'Freeze'. And that's exactly how Ranjan found me minutes later when he huffed and puffed up the stairs, sweating profusely. He wiggled his eyebrows quizzically with a 'what's up?' expression and promptly broke the spell.

I smiled my best benign smile (I used to rehearse it often enough in front of the mirror) and said, 'Nothing, really. I'm feeling happy, that's all.'

Ranjan pushed past me and threw his briefcase down on the chair closest to the door. 'That's good to hear for a change. I was beginning to believe you were feeling . . . what is the word—homesick? I was going to tell my mother to come and spend a few days with us. These distances in Bombay—I tell you. And the traffic. It's like we may as well have been staying in two different towns. Poor Ma, her asthma really suffers. Total setback when she has to travel all the way here.'

I nodded brightly but I wasn't really listening. I could hear all the familiar sounds of Ranjan chucking his office clothes in the direction of the laundry basket. I heard the dull thud of his shoes as he flung them to the floor. I could visualize him now, walking around the room in his underwear, getting ready to have a quick wash, collect all the evening papers and wait for his tea tray.

Normally, I would have been nervous about the stains and the colour of the tea (too dark? too light?), but not today. Ranjan hadn't noticed the tape in my hand. I didn't want him to find it. Ranjan's powers of observation were erratic—sometimes he took in everything instantly, at other times I didn't exist. I opened the drawer where I kept extra spoons, knives, can openers and screwdrivers, placed the tape carefully at the back and shut the drawer.

The earliest I'd be able to listen to it would be the next morning. Wait a minute. Tomorrow was a Saturday—Ranjan would be home. My heart sank. Two whole days would be wasted. What a pity Nikhil hadn't turned up earlier, even twenty minutes earlier. My mind started working on getting rid of Ranjan for at least a couple of hours. I could suggest an outing.

Or better still, I could offer to cook a dish especially for his mother and request him to deliver it.

Cheered by the prospect, I walked in briskly with the tea tray. Ranjan was humming a tune as he brushed his hair and stared at a blackhead on his forehead with utmost concentration. I announced, a little too loudly, 'Tomorrow is Saturday.'

Ranjan replied without turning around, 'Yes, I know it's Saturday.'

'Why don't I cook something for your mother?'

Ranjan turned to look at me with undisguised delight. 'What a superb idea. Yes, let's invite her to lunch. No, that might be a little tiring. I'll ask her to come and spend the day here. But please . . . don't make her work in the kitchen. She needs to rest, relax.'

My heart was thudding as I interjected softly, 'Oh . . . that's not what I meant. Why make her come all the way, just to sample one dish? Won't it be better if you take it across? I'll get up early and keep it ready by ten.'

Ranjan shook his head. 'That won't be possible. I have a lot of paperwork to attend to. I can't get out of the house for even a minute.'

My heart sank. I felt it fall heavily on to my toes. How could Ranjan be so unreasonable? All I wanted was for him to be out of the house for just one hour—I was even willing to settle for half. And here he was blithely sipping his tea, completely unaware of my turmoil.

To make things worse, I'd put my foot into it about his mother. Now I was stuck with both of them. Plus, I'd have to slave over preparing an elaborate lunch in a hotter than hell kitchen.

Ranjan sipped his tea suspiciously. I waited for his usual comments. But he decided to spare me for once, for he gulped it down quickly and settled back against the pillows to watch BBC. I was free to brood on my own. Feeling intensely sorry for myself, I went into the kitchen, opened the drawer and touched the tape.

Intentionally, I hadn't switched on the light. As I groped for the slim black cassette in the dark and curled my fingers around its hard edges, I felt strangely comforted. A song about me. Nikhil had actually written a song about me.

What could possibly have inspired it? And just as suddenly as my euphoria had soared, it came crashing down. Melancholy. That was it. Nikhil had noticed my melancholia and decided to write a sad, sad song about a lonely, lonely lady. A pathetic little anthem. Perhaps it was better not to hear it. Perhaps the right thing to do was to send it back with the mop man or the idli-seller. Why depress myself further? Why inflict avoidable punishment?

I heard Ranjan's voice calling out to me, 'What are you doing in that dark kitchen? Come and see something quickly. It's about India—fast, or it will end.'

I hastily shut the drawer and went back into the bedroom. Ranjan extended his hand and reached for me affectionately. His voice was tender as he stroked my hair and asked, 'Maya, tell me truthfully, are you missing your mother?'

And I answered truthfully that I was not. He nodded, satisfied by my answer. I saw him reach for the remote. It was time to channel-surf. I picked my feet off the ground and swung them over the bed. I closed my eyes and thought of my brief encounter with Nikhil. As I dozed off lightly, the ghastly flowers from his lungi leapt out at me and started a crazy dance. I could hear yet another Top Ten countdown overlapping the drone of a BBC news commentator.

It would be two days before I'd get to hear Nikhil's version of my life. I reconciled myself to the thought with a reminder that at least there was something to look forward to at the end of the weekend. A song. A man. In whichever context. And no matter how cruel the final judgement.

*

As it turned out, my wait and anxiety were short-circuited at 10.30 the next morning when a smart knock (not the doorbell) made me drop the kitchen knife noisily on the counter and rush to the door. It was Nikhil, dressed in dirty jeans and a white khadi kurta.

'Well?' he demanded, standing with his legs apart, arms akimbo. Noticing the stricken look on my face, he altered his tone and posture. Without saying a word, he raised his eyebrows, gestured with his hands as if to ask, 'Is your husband at home?'

I nodded, my eyes conveying the panic I was experiencing. He raised the first two fingers of his left hand and waved, mouthing the words, 'See you on Monday.'

I didn't dare react. Instead, I raised my voice unnaturally and said, 'No thank you, I don't need any.'

Nikhil became his usual blur as I quickly shut the door on him. Ranjan was shaving with the bathroom door wide open. It was a sight that always irritated me. My father had always had a fairly elaborate shaving ritual but it was conducted in privacy, behind closed doors. Neither my mother nor I ever saw him with his face all lathered over. I had always thought men looked comical when they were covered with shaving cream. Like circus clowns out of costume.

Ranjan looked even more so as he preferred to shave clad just in his underpants. I'd catch sight of him concentrating on his upper lip, his mouth tightly puckered in, his eyes straining to see the last errant hair, and I'd look away. The white underpants, the white on his face, the hairy belly jiggling with each movement—no, I didn't like it at all. Sometimes, I'd surreptitiously shut the door as I walked past the bathroom. But most times, I couldn't since the TV would be blaring the latest baseball scores.

Why baseball scores interested Ranjan, I never could figure out. May be it was a throwback to the years spent in the United States. It had to be. In his happiest state of mind, Ranjan's accent would change, and I'd discern an American drawl, along with stray American expressions (outdated though they usually were).

This morning, the bathroom door was indeed open, but the TV was off. Ranjan called out, 'Who was that?'

I trilled, 'No one.'

'But I heard you talking to someone. In English.'

I tried to sound casual. 'Oh . . . it was one of the neighbours.'

'Which one?' Ranjan persisted. I was surprised by his interest.

'The upstairs person,' I said, without defining the sex or identity.

'We have three flats above us—who was it?'

I hesitated. 'Nobody really . . . that young Verma boy.'

Ranjan had emerged from the bathroom and was standing at the bedroom door, about three feet away from where I was in the kitchen. 'That Verma boy. What was he doing here? And did you describe him as "young"?'

I nodded, busying myself with Ranjan's mother's lunch. She'd be here in another twenty minutes. 'Isn't he young? A college boy—right?'

Ranjan started wiping his face with a hand towel. 'That worthless, no-good loafer . . . it's a wonder he hasn't been thrown out of whichever college he claims to be in. Huh! It's people like him who are going to pull India down. What is his contribution to society? Zero. Parasite, that's what he is. And you call him a "boy"? That fellow is well into his twenties. At his age, I'd started earning my own living. I wasn't mooching off my parents. Shameless lout. In any case, how dare he come here? Besides, I didn't hear anybody ring the doorbell.'

I started to stir the fish (bought by Ranjan, not me) in a shallow pan. The entire house was filled with the sharp smell of mustard oil. My eyes were smarting. Bubbles of hot oil were bursting around my wrists.

'He knocked,' I murmured.

Ranjan had come into the kitchen by now and was at my elbow, carefully monitoring my clumsy culinary efforts. 'Turn it over carefully . . . watch it, the fish might break. Are you sure the oil was hot enough before you put the pieces in?'

I nodded miserably. It was hopeless, I knew it. The lunch was going to be a disaster. Everything was going horribly wrong. And now the skin of the fish was spluttering angrily and threatening to tear. Ranjan drew even closer.

'Does he always knock?'

Flustered, I replied, 'No he rings the bell.'

Ranjan held my arm tightly (the same one I was using to stir the fish). 'So, he's a regular visitor in that case? Why haven't you told me?'

I tried to free myself from his grip. Hotly, a bit too hotly, I said in a voice that was dripping self-righteousness, 'Of course not. How could you think such a thing? He'd come once before to return something his mother had borrowed, that's all.'

Ranjan was standing uncomfortably close to me. I started to feel suffocated with the hot oil burning my face. Ranjan seemed to be thinking deeply. 'What on earth could Mrs Verma borrow from you . . . from this house?'

I said shortly, 'Sugar? Tea? Dahi? Matches? Onions? Neighbours do borrow from each other. Not that I ever do. And not that I encourage such a thing.'

Ranjan refused to budge even when I sighed in an exaggerated way and started to mop my brow irritatedly. 'I've been living here for quite some time now and nobody has ever knocked on the door to ask for something. Suddenly, you arrive and every young man in the locality is turning up to borrow things. Don't you find that peculiar?'

I removed the fish from the pan and placed it on a brown paper bag (my mother's advice—the bag soaked up all the excess oil). 'I don't know why you are making such a big thing out of a small incident,' I said, my voice low and sulky. 'I can't help it if his mother didn't come herself. It's not as if I invited him over.'

Ranjan moved away a little and stood leaning against the refrigerator. 'I've been watching that boy. He is no good. A loafer. Bad character. Maybe a drug runner—everybody in this city has something or other to do with drugs. How else can people survive with all the expenses? I tell you, Tokyo is cheaper—and that's supposed to be the most expensive city in the world.'

I kept quiet and started dicing potatoes (I was planning to attempt a speciality that involved a coating of poppy seeds). Ranjan continued to talk.

'That fellow is far too cocky. No guidance. I've noticed his mother. Slovenly woman with hairy arms. Imagine—hairy arms and she is a beautician. What does that boy do? Has he even finished school? I doubt it. I wouldn't employ him as even a doorman in my company. You should feel ashamed of yourself for hobnobbing with trash like him. If your mother is told about this incident, she'll be shocked, very shocked. I just hope my mother keeps quiet about it.'

I slit six green chillies down the middle. 'Don't tell me you are planning to tell her?' I mocked.

'What do you mean? I tell my mother everything. She has a right to know. After all, it was she who brought me into this world.' (Like she did it all on her own.)

I left the chillies to splutter in a tiny pool of oil. Ranjan wasn't finished yet. 'Maybe you should discuss this matter with my mother. You are not from Bombay, after all. It's different here. Young married women do not invite loafers into their homes when the husband is away. In Calcutta, possibly, nobody misunderstands. But here! Even without doing anything at all, people gossip. And this is truly the limit. Your mother will also agree. I may have full faith in you (he sounded as though he didn't have even a shred) but what about people? How can you face them?

'And our good name? My reputation? I'm disappointed in you, Maya. You have probably heard all sorts of stories about Bombay. That it is this and it is that. Let me tell you, life is not a Hindi movie. That is the problem with outsiders. They only believe what they read in all those film rags. They only pay attention to the cheap gossip. You are not Monisha Koirala, understand? This is a respectable house. There are certain rules. You have to abide by them whether you like it or not.'

The chillies burnt to a brown—I'd forgotten to turn down the flame. Ranjan was seized by a fit of coughing. And then he began sneezing uncontrollably, tears streaming down his face. I left the chillies to burn some more as I rushed to fetch water. I could hear Ranjan gagging. His face was red and puffy.

'My mother . . . she'll be here any minute. And what are you going to serve her? Charred chillies? Oh God! This is terrible. She will be so upset.'

I opened the garbage pail and chucked the chillies into it. Calmly and slowly, I reassured Ranjan that I'd get things under control, but for that he'd have to step out of my way and let me get on with it.

'Please,' I pleaded, 'we'll discuss everything later. But first, let me finish cooking before she arrives.'

Ranjan grabbed a kitchen towel, pressed it to his nose and fled. The doorbell rang precisely twenty minutes later. By then I was ready to receive my beloved mother-in-law. My secret remained hidden where it was, tucked away with the knives and forks.

Eight

Ranjan did not raise the topic of Nikhil again that weekend and I was truly grateful. Perhaps he felt he'd said his piece and if I had the slightest bit of sense, I'd pay attention to it and change my ways.

That night, as I wrote in my diary, I was truly penitent. Maybe Ranjan was right. Maybe I really did not understand Bombay and Bombay people. Maybe they thought and behaved differently from people in Calcutta, or Delhi, or Indore or Ranchi or wherever. Maybe I was being a monumental fool, and Nikhil was actually insulting me by being so daringly familiar. Maybe the song he'd written was also nothing more than an insult.

How could I have been presumptuous enough to think I had become a Bombay person just because I now lived in this city? Ranjan was absolutely correct in his assessment. I was making a fool of myself. An absolute fool. Bombay people were smart and shrewd and sophisticated. How could someone like me fit in—me with my Calcutta upbringing and hangups? What did I know about the ways of the world?

Still, Ranjan had been a little unfair when he'd said that life was not a Hindi movie. As if I didn't know that. I wasn't that dumb. Besides, I didn't even like Hindi films. In my life, I'd seen maybe ten of them altogether. As for Hindi film magazines, the only ones I'd flipped through were during our train journey to Bombay. I'd borrowed them from a fellow traveller after finishing my collected short stories. Unlike some of the other Calcuttans, I was indifferent to and unmoved by the film business.

Of course, there was no escaping the onslaught. Bombay was defined by its film culture—it was evident in everyone and everything. People even spoke like heroes and heroines, mouthing dramatic dialogues instead of standard conversation.

It amused and fascinated me, especially when I heard snatches of the latest hit songs being sung by everyone from the bank manager downstairs to the teaboy who sold his brew in tiny, chipped cups which he filled from a gigantic aluminium kettle, which in turn rested in an iron bucket. I'd stand by the window and listen to scraps of conversation from the busy street below—taxi drivers, vendors, urchins, eunuchs, beggars, students, office-goers and sundry idlers. All of them sounded like caricatural Hindi movie characters. Some of them even looked the role, dressed in absurd polyester, their hairstyles and mannerisms a peculiar parody of the images projected by their favourite screen idols.

There was so much energy and innocence on the streets of Bombay (at least the one I could observe) that it was hard to believe all those horror stories I'd grown up on in Calcutta ('*Hey maa* . . . don't even think of walking alone in Bombay—not even in daylight. The people are such hardcore goondas. They can't help it. Unless you are a crook, you cannot survive in that city').

I thought of Ranjan and Nikhil. They didn't look like crooks to me. And yet, they were surviving all right. Bombay inspired as much respect as fear in people's hearts, and looking out of my window, I could understand why. Nearly every day I'd witness something that would open my eyes wider.

I could spend hours watching a banana-seller with her toddler. Each morning she'd arrive at her 'spot' (amazingly enough, nobody thought of usurping it. Obviously, each vendor had a clearly demarcated territory). She would arrive, baby on hip, bananas on head, and sweep the tiny square of pavement with a small broom she kept hidden in the branches of the tree under which she had set up shop. The semi-naked infant would crawl around near her feet, happily picking up things from the filthy road and sticking them into his mouth (he was a boy-child and she was proud of it—he rarely wore even a rag around his waist, his genitals exposed, while the torso and head remained scrupulously covered).

From time to time, the mother would grab her son and stick an elongated, dark brown nipple into his hungry mouth. She rarely bothered to cover her naked breast. I'd watch them between chores and think how lucky she was to be outside in the midst of people, earning for herself and nurturing another life.

At such moments, I wouldn't see the comedy of reducing my own life to such a simplistic comparison. I'd only see the closed door of my house and the iron bars on the windows ('Bombay is so unsafe, you never know who might come in through the window'). I wanted to flirt with the 'other Bombay'—the one I read about in the lively city papers and saw in Hindi films. Living away from India's showbiz capital, I had grown up with all sorts of bizarre images of the world the filmstars lived in. My mother had even warned me against being sucked into it.

'You are young and quite good-looking,' she had told me seriously. 'I've read there are touts on the look-out everywhere. They can tell very easily if you're an outsider to the city. And that's when they pounce. Be on your guard. These people can trick you . . . deceive you. The issue is, nobody is safe in Bombay.'

From my kitchen window, I'd wonder which of the men loitering under the large, shady silk-cotton tree was a tout and who he was preying on. It was true that there were always dozens of seemingly idle men standing around listlessly. Sometimes, they would buy a banana from the woman, follow that up with a cigarette or paan and then lean against a parked car and wait.

Who or what were they waiting for? I'd asked Ranjan, only to be told, 'Why are you staring at strange men in the first place? They could be pimps or thieves on the look-out for an opportunity. Remember, there are millions of unemployed people in this city. They are armed and highly treacherous. One wrong move and they pull out knives. I've seen people—innocent people—being stabbed in broad daylight. Or they could be drug dealers luring children with lollipops. Yes, these same men you spend hours staring at, could be the ones who knock on the door with chloroform to rape and rob housewives like you. I can give you any number of stories. It happened to my colleague's neighbour's wife last year. Poor woman—through no fault of hers. And she wasn't even looking at them, the way you do. Don't blame me if anything happens to you. Remember, I've warned you.'

I remembered. And laughed a little. The laugh wasn't entirely free from anxiety. Ranjan couldn't have been bluffing, he had lived here all his life. And yet, while he uttered all those well-meaning words of caution, he looked and sounded so ridiculous.

Once I'd asked him playfully whether he had ever done anything wicked in his life, something he regretted, that had gotten him into trouble. Ranjan had looked at me suspiciously and then snorted, 'Are you crazy? Do I look the type?'

That was true enough. But even Ranjan-types occasionally slipped up and redeemed themselves. Not him. He had given me a lecture on 'right upbringing' and 'sound value systems'. I had successfully stifled a yawn. The next day, Ranjan had presented me with a copy of Swami Vivekananda's life, adding, 'This helped me a lot when I was in America with daily temptations to distract me. May be it will help you too.'

I'd thanked him humbly and promised to read it.

*

Looking out of my window one afternoon, I'd noticed my banana woman wasn't at her usual spot. I had waited for her, feeling restless and distracted. Finally, I'd picked up the house key and gone down after making sure I'd shut the main door carefully.

Out on the busy street, I had felt disoriented and lost. Besides, I hadn't really known what to do next. Ask one of the regular idlers who was standing there smoking vacantly, or just go right back to my home and forget the whole thing?

The man selling luridly coloured sherbet from a handcart had called out, 'Looking for something? How about a kala-khatta gola to quench your thirst?' He had spoken in a heavy Bihari accent.

I had shaken my head and stood around feeling stupid. That's when Nikhil had spotted me and walked up briskly. 'What's the matter, Maya?' he'd asked with obvious curiousity.

Mutely, I had pointed to the empty spot on the pavement. 'Lost your purse?' he had enquired helpfully.

Then I had blurted out, 'The woman—she isn' t there.'

'Which woman?' he had asked, looking at me quizzically.

'That woman, the one who's always here with a baby. She sells bananas.'

Nikhil had gazed at me with open amusement. 'Are you hungry? Want an orange instead?' And he had reached inside his satchel.

'No, no, no. I'm . . . I'm wondering why she hasn't come today . . . I'm worried,' I said, the words coming out clumsily.

Nikhil had laughed carelessly. 'Oh, don't worry about her. She's probably been beaten black and blue by her husband. Maybe he broke a few limbs this time. It happens.'

I stared at him, my eyes wide with alarm. He had laughed again. 'These women are used to it. Don't react like that. It's a routine thing in their lives.'

I had continued to stand rooted to the spot, unsure of what my next move should be. 'Come on, I'll treat you to some bhel,' Nikhil had urged, taking me lightly by the elbow.

I had pulled away quickly with a, 'No-o-o. I have to go back.'

Nikhil had blocked my path, crossed his arms over his chest and asked in a genuinely puzzled voice, 'Go back? What for? I mean, you don't have guests in the house or anything, right? Let's go . . . I have to run an errand for my mother. The world's best bhelpuriwallah is right on the way.'

To make me feel more confident about the little adventure, Nikhil had pointed out the vendor of that perfectly evil snack. 'There, see him? Just there. It will take a minute. And our grocer is right round the corner too. I have to pick up some washing machine powder for my mother's latest toy—our wonderful washing machine. She prays to it every morning, she's so proud of it.'

Blankly, I'd asked him, 'Is it very efficient?'

Nikhil had burst out laughing. 'I don't know. But Mrs Bajaj across the landing has one. So does the Malhotra family downstairs. That was enough for my poor mother to start having sleepless nights till my father bought one for us on an instalment basis.'

He had started walking in the direction of the bhelpuri man leaving me standing at the same spot. '*Chalo*, I have to get back in a hurry. If you haven't tasted this bhel, you haven't tasted anything.'

I still didn't—couldn't—move. Finally, in my smallest, silliest voice, I had whispered, 'I . . . I can't. My husband won't like it.'

Nikhil had exploded, 'What? I don't believe it. Are you saying your husband has forbidden you from eating bhel?

I had been far too embarrassed to explain. Without another word, I had turned around and run back into the building. My hair, suddenly freed from its constricting topknot, flew wildly behind me.

Nine

The long wait to hear Nikhil's tape ended at 9.47 a.m. on Monday. Ranjan left the house exactly twelve minutes later than usual. He had made a fetish out of punctuality all his life. He would often tell me that a person who couldn't stick to a given time could never be trusted with anything.

'Take my mother's example,' Ranjan told me after I'd kept him waiting outside his office for eight whole minutes. 'In all these years, she has never been late.'

I could believe that, all right. In fact, I could imagine her timing herself in the bathroom every morning. Two minutes and fifteen seconds brushing her teeth. Six minutes on the toilet. Eleven having a bath (eighteen, if washing her hair). Thirteen for wearing her saree, fixing her coiffure, dusting talcum powder on her feet and creaming her elbows. Not a second more, not a second less.

Such precision frightened me, And yet, I rather welcomed it each morning. I knew exactly when Ranjan would pick up his office bag, take a quick look around the house (to spot cobwebs, dust particles and stains) before saying a shy, 'See you in the evening' and leaving.

His exit always generated a sense of exhilaration—not because I didn't want him around (I didn't really, but if he did linger, it didn't exactly hurt). But I felt free to breathe normally. With him around, I seemed to hold my breath and walk around on tiptoes trying to appear as invisible as I possibly could. Ranjan was a nervous, tense dresser who could rarely see or find things even if they happened to be under his nose.

'My socks,' he would exclaim. 'Where's my belt?' and I'd scamper off nervously to hand them to him from where they would be lying all along, on the bed.

He took a long time grooming his hair and saying his prayers. I found that rather touching. Ranjan was a deeply religious man with a high moral sense of righteousness and truth. In some ways, he reminded me of my father—a more aggressive version.

Ranjan was also surprisingly old-fashioned about several things. He never walked shirtless around the house, for example, just in case the part-time maid was in the vicinity. Bodily functions embarrassed him to the extent that he preferred me to wait in the living room each morning while he finished off all his 'jobs' (as he called his daily routine).

But today Ranjan had encountered a major disaster—he had misplaced his handkerchief, the one with a grey border. I'd offered him another one, plain white. But he had pushed it away impatiently with an irritable, 'For God's sake, Maya. I need the grey-bordered one. It's Monday, remember? The plain white one is for Wednesday.'

We had launched into a frantic hunt for the missing kerchief, with Ranjan cursing the maid for not putting it back in the right place. 'Didn't she wash it?' he asked, stopping dead in his tracks and looking at me with open accusation.

I shrugged non-committally, more to protect her than anything else. 'I'll go and check the bathroom,' I said calmly.

'You should know. A housewife should know what is washed and what isn't. There should be some sort of a system, a method. This woman may be a thief. She could be stealing our clothes without your even knowing about the theft.'

I scampered out of the room and began searching in the wash basket. I could hear the kitchen clock ticking away . . . The sound so exaggerated, it could have been a sonic boom. Ranjan was flinging bedclothes around the room and looking under the dressing table while I emptied out his trouser pockets with trembling fingers, worried that the errant handkerchief would jump out at me, leading to another lecture (it was my job to make sure Ranjan's shirt and trouser pockets were cross-checked before sending them either to the laundry or the wash basket).

Then, eventually, I heard an enormous sigh of relief coupled with an indulgent chuckle. 'Maya . . . it's all right. Don't bother. I've found it.'

I ran back into the room. My heart, which had been thudding against my rib-cage, went back gratefully to its familiar rhythm. 'Where was it?' I asked.

'Oh, right here,' Ranjan patted the bed. 'God knows how I didn't see it. Anyway, it's found. That's good.'

Then his eyes moved to his wristwatch (the one he hadn't changed since his college days because he felt sentimental about a gift given by his mother on his eighteenth birthday).

'I'm late,' he said, his voice a discordant squeak. A minute later and Ranjan had become a grey blob dashing across the compound. And me, an excited schoolgirl clutching her crumpled nightie and rushing to the kitchen shelf to retrieve the hidden tape.

It took me a while to locate the song. Nikhil had said it was number four on Side B but I had never been smart with gadgets, not even the simplest ones. Nor had I ever been able to play the right side of a cassette at first shot.

And this wasn't just another cassette. First, I dropped the tape a couple of times. Then I forgot to plug in the player. When I finally got it going, it was the wrong song, something do with Bombay trains and commuters with bad breath.

I thrilled at the sound of Nikhil's voice. It didn't matter at all that his song, *Lonely Lady*, was utterly banal and definitely off-key. All this I could recognize in retrospect. But at that moment, when I heard the opening bars and Nikhil's voice humming along, I couldn't stop myself from shivering. The thought that a man—not any man, Nikhil—had been inspired enough by me—me—to write a song, strum a guitar and present me with a copy of the cassette was more flattering than anything I had ever experienced.

I must have heard *Lonely Lady* twenty times in a row, savouring each plaintive note, each soulful line. When I felt I'd fully absorbed it into my system and the song was coursing through my bloodstream, I switched off my tinny two-in-one and sat down for a good cry.

I hadn't wept so much in years. I sat crouched on the kitchen stool and wept my heart out. I might have wept till evening had the telephone not rung. It was Ranjan. He was speaking in his 'office voice'—very businesslike and abrupt.

'Listen,' he started off without a greeting or a pause. 'I hope you remember we are going to the Mathur's tonight. Mrs Mathur delivered a son last month. It's the boy's naming ceremony. We'll have to give them a gift. And cash will not look proper. Go to the Dadar market and get a good baba suit. Nothing very expensive, mind you.'

I didn't utter a sound, I was so busy stifling my sobs. 'Hello . . . hello . . . listen, are you there?'

I nodded and then remembered to speak. 'I heard you,' I stammered.

There was a pause. 'Listen . . . are you all right?'

I said a brief 'yes'. Ranjan rarely phoned, and when he did it was usually to issue instructions. This time he seemed unsure. He hesitated and cleared his throat.

'Hello? Maya—if you're not feeling well, don't worry. Phone my mother. She'll know what to do.'

I sniffed loudly and managed a weak, 'It's okay. I'm fine.'

Another pause. 'Sure?'

'Sure,' I repeated.

Ranjan waited awkwardly. I could tell he was debating what to say or do. 'Listen, wear that nice yellow saree tonight, all right? The one with the red border. It suits you. Know which one I'm talking about? The silk one. And yes, iron my blue shirt. The American one. Bye.'

I replaced the receiver feeling more sorry for Ranjan than I was for myself. He was so innocent. And so sweet. He liked the yellow saree because it belonged to his mother, not because it suited me. I had lots of her hand-me-downs. Not that I minded, but there was no occasion to wear them. I was rather surprised that she had parted with the sarees in the first place since they were in pretty good condition.

I had written to my mother about these gifts and she had replied, 'The issue is, she is your mother-in-law and as such she is entitled to pass on her sarees to you. Be gracious and grateful. But you are under no compulsion to wear them unless of course you like them.'

So I'd dutifully stored my mother-in-law's sarees away, making sure not to mix them up with my own. There was 'her' pile and my pile in the old cupboard. Ranjan had noticed and commented, 'How come you never wear those sarees?' as he fingered the fine silks.

I had been tempted to say, 'Where do I go wearing such expensive clothes? We hardly have any occasions.'

Instead, I had smiled sweetly and said, 'They're so beautiful. It was really sweet of Ma to give them to me.'

That had been explanation enough. But today, the thought of wearing that ghastly yellow saree seemed doubly irritating. Imagine a woman for whom a song had been composed by a very attractive young man that very morning, going out to a boring function clad in her mother-in-law's discarded yellow saree. Nothing could have been more irksome. The lonely lady.

Ten

The idea of going to the Mathurs would have made me hit an instant low on other days. But nothing could affect my spirits now. I was soaring on Nikhil's voice and words. The melody, such as it was, provided background music for my little expedition to the market on Mission Baba Suit.

The banana seller was still missing but today was not the day to worry about her. Today was reserved for me and my little secret. Feeling wildly adventurous, I wore a pale pink Lucknowi chikan kurta, grabbed a bright blue plastic shopping bag and danced out of the flat whistling—yes, whistling.

I ran straight into Nikhil's mother. She glared at me in a way that suggested she thoroughly disapproved of me, my clothes, my whistling, my very existence.

'Well, well, well, you are seeming very happy today. Like a schoolgirl or should I say schoolboy? Something special? Good news?' And she gazed pointedly at my belly.

Blithely, I sang out, 'Yes, good news. But not what you are thinking. Today, I feel like singing. I'm very happy.'

Her disapproval turned to disgust. I noticed the large, discoloured sweat stains under her armpits and held my breath to protect myself from the rancid b.o. that was hitting me in waves. She was dressed in a shiny, synthetic salwar kameez, studded with rhinestones. The grey roots of her hair were visible where the henna had outgrown them, her lipstick looked like smeared raspberry jam. Her eyebags hung over her rouged cheeks like discoloured awnings.

More than any of this, it was her expression I found scary. Her eyes glinted with malice. Her body language indicated her readiness to spring into a boxing ring to slug it out with Mike Tyson. I ran.

The baba suit seller was from Bangladesh. I recognized his Sialti accent immediately, just as he recognised my West Bengali lilt. He offered me tea and a snack. I sat down on the precarious stool and chatted companionably. It was comforting to talk to someone who was as much of an alien in Bombay as I was.

We discussed life in this unsettling city like two conspirators, in low, hushed voices, almost as if we were afraid to be overheard. And yet, when I asked him if he planned to go back, he shook his head vehemently.

'This is the place,' he said, patting his little 'shop', such as it was. Mentally, I agreed with him. This was the place. If only I was free to discover it on my own. Or even with Ranjan. If only he'd be more enthusiastic about sharing his city with me. I used to devour the two evening papers he brought home every day. And read all the weekend papers from cover to cover. There were obviously so many exciting things happening out there, just a little beyond my circumscribed existence.

Why didn't we ever go to watch a silly play (the 'hit and hot' comedies that were so popular, going by the announcements of '100 house full shows'). Why didn't we step into one of the lively pubs playing jazz? Not to get drunk but just to sway to the music, watch all the people present and lose ourselves a little in its carefree atmosphere?

Why didn't we stroll along any one of the many beaches, eat a roadside snack, stride into a gaudy shop or just pound the dirty, overcrowded pavements not doing anything in particular?

I had suggested it to Ranjan once or twice and he had said in his usual, slightly irritated-with-frivolity tone, 'We can, we can. But shouldn't there be an agenda? Let me know exactly what you intend doing and I'll consider your request.'

I didn't quite know exactly what I wanted to do. But as I lingered in the Bangladeshi's shop, I felt my entire body de-tensing. I could have stayed on for hours, doing nothing at all, without a single point on my agenda. Just looking.

The one thing I did notice was that Bombay didn't have Bombay people the way Calcutta had Calcutta people. It was impossible to tell who belonged and who didn't. In that vast sea of faces rushing past me, I would try and pick one or two who might be the true residents of the city. But I also knew I'd be proved wrong. The only people who walked around as though they owned the city were the tireless, voluptuous fisherwomen, clad in flimsy sarees wrapped tightly around their well-muscled buttocks, laden with gold jewellery, their oiled nape buns adorned with the season's brightest flowers, the catch for the day balanced gracefully in large baskets held at their waists or balanced on their heads.

It was these women who exuded a formidable sense of purpose. Sitting in the Bangladeshi's shop, I watched one of them quarreling with a man who had accidentally bumped into her, sending tiny silvery fish gliding across the glistening asphalt of the street. She had grabbed the hapless man by the shoulders and cursed seven generations of his family before giving him an aggressive shove and sending him on his way. Nobody had bothered to pause, much less intervene.

Catching my curious expression, the Bangladeshi explained, 'This is Bombay. No time. No feelings. Everybody saving his own skin. You fight, you shout, you scream. You die. Others will step over your corpse and carry on.'

I shook my head. 'And yet you want to stay here?'

He looked at me with genuine surprise. 'Is there any other city in India for people like us?'

And when he said 'us' he indicated with a gesture that he included me. I felt flattered. 'But I hear the police are creating a lot of trouble. Is that true?'

He smiled knowingly. 'True. That is for Bangladeshis without proper papers. Me? I've managed everything. Took two years and eight thousand rupees. But now nobody can throw me out. Look . . .' he picked up his shabby, smelly shirt and patted a sheaf of important-looking papers sticking out of a roomy pocket in his grubby vest. 'Passport, ration card, domicile certificate, everything.'

'You're lucky,' I said admiringly.

'Lucky? No, I wouldn't say that. I'm smart. Within two weeks of getting here, I made friends with the slum lord. I gave him my wife's gold bangle with promises of more. He provided me with a corner in a cramped room shared by eight other migrants. At least I knew nobody would harm me or report me to the police.

'I got employment sorting out rags the next morning with the understanding that I'd give the man a hefty cut from my earnings. No problem, I said. It was still worth it. What had I to lose? Sister . . . that's how it began. Today, I have permanent quarters in a slum that has been recognized by the government. There is running water, electricity, everything. I'm buying a TV next year. I already have a cycle. My wife and two children live with me. God has been kind.'

He stared at a gigantic water tanker groaning through the narrow street. He turned to me and asked with some concern, 'And you?'

I smiled and shook my head. 'It's good,' I lied, 'I like it here.'

I think he guessed I was fibbing. We exchanged a silent message. I picked up my packet and started my longish walk back home.

*

I found Nikhil's hastily scribbled note under the door as I let myself in.

'Liked it?' were the only two words on the small slip of paper. I stared at his writing as though hypnotized by the patterns it had created, scanning those two perfectly legible, perfectly simple words for some hidden meaning, wondering whether there was some secret message encoded in them.

Nikhil had been careful enough to avoid names. He hadn't even initialled the paper. I wondered cynically whether he made a habit of this sort of thing. Perhaps there were dozens of 'lonely ladies' scattered around Bombay. Perhaps each one of them was clutching a similar note and searching for some hidden message in it.

I crushed the piece of paper angrily, and then unclenched my fist to see what I'd done. It looked so miserable lying in my palm that I placed it on the kitchen platform and tried to iron out the creases with the flat of my hand. It didn't work. I pulled out the chapatti rolling pin and tried again. There was only a marginal difference.

I sat down heavily, my eyes smarting with tears. I could hear the phone ringing outside. Defiantly, I decided to let it go on ringing. It had to be Ranjan checking on whether I had run the assigned errands successfully. I heard him ring off finally and felt triumphant, as though I had defied his edict and got away with my little rebellion.

*

My throat was parched, my clothes soaked with sweat. Even though Calcutta summers were hellish in their intensity, Bombay's mugginess was getting to me. Rivulets of sweat would course down the length of my inner arms right after a cool bath. Ranjan had installed a second-hand air-conditioner in our bedroom but there was a tacit understanding regarding its use. It was to be switched on after dinner and kept on only till such time as the room cooled down sufficiently.

Hot weekday afternoons were to be suffered silently and stoically with just the whirr of a noisy ceiling fan to stir the warm air around the room. I would lie on the large bed with the rough texture of our hand-woven bedcover (a wedding gift) burning against my raw skin. I dared not switch on the machine for fear that Ranjan would question me about its use and deliver a lecture on economics. Of course, it was fine to have it on over the weekend when Ranjan was also occupying the room.

All this was never articulated. I didn't have to be told, I knew. And I didn't mind. Ranjan worked very hard. And life in Bombay wasn't cheap. Each evening, he'd ask me to produce the diary in which I scrupulously maintained accounts. There was a little ritual involved, and a specific time set aside for it. After touching his toes exactly seventy-five times, Ranjan would step into the bathroom for approximately four minutes ('I have to wet my hair'). He would emerge with a towel around his waist, say a quick prayer, pick up his glasses and sit down on his reclining chair.

'Bring the book,' he'd say, calculator in one hand, pen in the other. I'd hand over the diary to him nervously. Invariably, it was a tense moment and I always felt inexplicably guilty, like a petty thief who had been caught fudging the figures.

Ranjan would go over the expenses minutely and question me later. 'You've bought expensive Basmati rice for daily consumption. That is an extravagance, Maya. I don't mean to insult your family, but I'm sure you didn't grow up eating this quality every day. I'm afraid I cannot afford this luxury. Kindly scale down. Find out from my mother where she gets her supplies and buy the same brand.'

I'd nod my head obediently and make notes in a special rough book he'd brought back for the purpose from his office. 'Ladies' fingers? At twenty rupees a kilo? Why do we have to eat ladies' fingers at a price like that? I'm not that fond of eating them—are you? I mean, is it that your meal is incomplete without ladies' fingers? I'm quite happy avoiding the vegetable, even though it is excellent for bowel movements. Wait till the prices come down, all right?

'Next . . . fish. Now I know Bombay doesn't have the same variety and range as your Calcutta bazaar. Even so, if you look around carefully, you'll be able to find reasonably priced fish which can be served crisp-fried. That way it doesn't matter whether or not it's a sweet water kind.'

He would peer, while I wrote down his remarks. Often I would feel tempted to doodle or scribble. Worse, I'd even considered writing something rude and nasty about Ranjan even as he lectured me on the virtues of eating leafy greens ('far cheaper, far healthier') and the sins of over-indulgence.

At precisely 9.45 p.m. each night, Ranjan's mother would call and ask to speak to her son if I happened to pick up the phone. I knew my presence in the same room made Ranjan slightly uncomfortable at these times. So, I'd take myself off to the kitchen and potter around making sure to create just enough noise for Ranjan to feel reassured that I couldn't hear the conversation. Sometimes, he would raise the volume of the news on TV before going into a huddle over the phone.

I often wondered what the two of them discussed so intensely every night. Once or twice, unable to resist the impulse, I had walked boldly into the room as if looking for an errant hand-towel. I could only catch a few glum 'umms' and Ranjan's furtive glances in my direction. It gave me a perverse thrill to realize I'd ruined his concentration.

I had even asked him a couple of times to tell me the contents of his nightly calls. 'Oh . . . nothing. Just routine enquiries,' he had answered airily.

'What kind of enquiries?' I'd persisted.

'You know how mothers are about their children.'

I had choked on that. Children? I'd looked innocently at Ranjan, my expression displaying total ignorance in that area. He'd evaded my eyes and mumbled, 'She phones to ask about my general health and welfare . . . you know . . . what I've eaten for dinner, my digestion problem, domestic problems.'

I had folded his shirts carefully before asking, 'What digestion problems? What domestic problems? I didn't know you had any. Why haven't you told me?'

Ranjan had stared fixedly at a tea company's plush annual report. 'I don't like to bother you.'

I had fetched a bottle of cold water from the fridge for the night before continuing, 'But . . . what did Ma do when you were away in America? I mean, she couldn't have phoned you every day, right?'

Ranjan had had the grace to look embarrassed. 'No. But we did write to each other every day. I still have all the letters.'

'Did you ever write to your father?' I had asked.

'What for?' was Ranjan's short reply. After thinking about it, he had changed his tone and said, 'There was no need, you see. Ma conveyed everything to him anyway. Why write separate letters? Besides, postage is so expensive.'

*

The phone was ringing again. This time, I couldn't avoid it. I put on my 'wife voice' (low, controlled, friendly) and answered it.

'So . . . liked it?'

It was Nikhil. I drew in my breath sharply, audibly.

'Scared you?' He was obviously laughing at me.

Hastily, I said, 'No,' my attention distracted by my reflection in a distant mirror. My kurta was crumpled, my hair was a mess and my forehead was dotted with clusters of sweat-beads. I saw myself as I would have appeared to Nikhil at that very moment, and shuddered.

'Why aren't you telling me your reaction? Was it that lousy, my song? I did write it for you, you know. For you.'

I kept quiet for a moment. Then, instead of answering him directly, I said 'How did you get my number?'

I couldn't think of anything beyond that. And to tell the truth, I was alarmed since I knew we weren't listed in the phone directory.

Nikhil laughed. 'Is that all you're going to say—"how did you get my phone number"? Come on Maya, grow up. Get real. It's not on the high security list exactly, is it? Besides, I have contacts in high places. Like the little telephone man who comes to our building to fix defective lines. Does that answer you? Now . . . are you going to tell me about my song—your song—or not?'

114

I was still too flustered to put my thoughts together coherently. Besides, the doorbell was ringing. It was the part-time maid and she was the kind who wouldn't wait an extra minute (she worked in five other residences and had her schedule worked out to the last micro-second).

'Someone's at the door,' I told Nikhil.

'And it isn't me,' he mocked, 'so don't bother to open it.'

I stuttered, 'Nikhil, please excuse me . . . I'll be back in a second. If I don't answer the ring, the bai will go away and I'll have to wash the clothes myself. Plus, all the dirty dishes.'

Without waiting for his response, I placed the receiver on the table and rushed to the door. It wasn't the bai but her son.

'Vatsala bai is not coming today,' he informed me sullenly, 'she's sent me to tell all the memsaabs.'

I panicked at that and pleaded, 'Why couldn't she send a replacement? Why couldn't her daughter come?'

The son stared at me as though I was an imbecile. 'That's not possible. My sister is in hospital, that's why my mother isn't here—she is taking care of her there.'

My mind wasn't on the boy's words. My entire being was focussed on the phone and the thought that Nikhil would get impatient and hang up.

'Okay . . . okay . . .' I told him. 'What about tomorrow? Will she come tomorrow at least?'

He shrugged indifferently. 'Depends on my sister's condition.'

My voice was rising to a hysterical pitch. 'Wait here,' I instructed. 'I have to answer the phone.'

He shook his head. 'I also have work to do. My mother has told me to go to all the memsaabs and inform them.'

'Go then,' I said impatiently and closed the door on his face.

I flew back to the phone, certain Nikhil would have disconnected. But he was still there. Still laughing at me.

'I heard the whole conversation, memsaab,' he jeered, 'and you sound just like my mother.'

I was about to start wailing. It was oppressively hot, I hadn't even begun to think of cooking—and even if I did start right that minute, I had nothing in which to cook. The prospect of washing a large bucketful of soaked clothes plus scrubbing a sinkful of last night's utensils made me feel faint and teary.

'Need some help, ma'am?' Nikhil continued. 'I'm pretty good around the house. My place is totally disorganized. No servant—part-time or fulltime is willing to stay for more than a few hours at a time. My mother is a nag, a tyrant, a horror. So . . . you get the picture. No servant round the year and obliging Nikhil to do the dirty work. If I can do it at my own home, I can do it at yours. No problem. Swear to you.'

I thought it was the sweetest offer anybody had ever made me. And Nikhil sounded obviously sincere about it.

'It's all right, I'll . . . I'll manage,' I said awkwardly.

'Yeah? Like how? Like you manage everything else? In silent suffering? Come off it, Maya. Act real. Get real. It's no big deal to ask someone for help, you know. It's not considered shameful.'

Nikhil's language stumped me. I wasn't used to his kind of English. I didn't know what this brand was called. It was a mixture of film dialogues, MTV slang and Hollywood movies. It sounded far too smart for someone like me, who'd been indoctrinated into using a strictly conventional idiom, the sort of English our teachers in Calcutta expected students in England to use—formal, grammatical and somehow lifeless.

I liked the way Nikhil spoke and I enjoyed his uncultivated accent. It wasn't exactly crude, just charming in its lack of

116

contrivance. Nikhil didn't speak for effect. He spoke naturally, adopting a rhythm that was entirely his own.

'So—listen? Do you want me to come over or not? It's no hassle. I can skip the next two lectures without a problem.'

For one wild moment I was exceedingly tempted to invite him into my home. I could picture the two of us washing dirty dishes and rinsing out clothes companionably, happily (excluding my underthings which I kept scrupulously out of sight of Ranjan as well). But I heard myself saying lamely, 'It's fine—really. I must go now. I have a lot of work to do.'

My voice was tight and strangled. Nikhil remained silent. I could sense his disappointment. 'Okay, cool. Fine. By the way, did you hear the tape? Or didn't you? Were you too busy even for that?'

I found his petulance heart-breakingly endearing. 'I loved it,' I whispered, my own voice far from steady.

'And your song?' he asked anxiously.

'It made me sad. Very sad,' I confessed reluctantly.

'Oh,' was Nikhil's short response, followed by 'I'm sorry that's how it made you feel. I didn't mean to hurt you. Anyway, I must disconnect. I'm calling from a public phone booth and there are people waiting.'

'Nikhil . . . I . . . I would like to talk to you again,' I stammered, panic-stricken at the thought that he would hang up and never phone me again.

'Right,' Nikhil said abruptly. 'Well, bye. See you.'

And I heard the sharp click as he replaced the receiver heavily. I cursed myself as I sat motionless on the sofa, staring blankly ahead of me. I must have sounded so cold and unfeeling. What must he have thought of me? Would he ever bother to look in my direction again?

I'd ruined our relationship for good, I was sure of that. And now it was back to my mundane, eventless predictable existence. I stormed into the kitchen and took it out on the pots and pans. I started chopping up vegetables with swift savage swings of the sharp, long knife.

I must have been so preoccupied in my chores that I didn't hear the postman at the door at the first ring. When I finally answered, a visibly annoyed man, drenched in sweat, was leaning against the doorpost and complaining loudly in exasperated tones, 'I was about to leave. Three times I have rung the bell. You people have no consideration for us. Half the buildings don't have lifts. It is required by the authorities to instal letterboxes on the landing, but who has done so? And then there are people like you who enjoy keeping us waiting in the heat while they watch television.'

The man had caught me at the wrong moment. It wasn't his day, just as it hadn't been mine. I waved the kitchen knife in his face and said, 'Look here, I'm not one of your Bombay memsaabs who can afford to sit watching television all day. As you can see, I was working in the kitchen.'

The postman's stare was insolent. 'So what? All wives work in kitchens, including mine. Does that make them deaf? Couldn't you hear me? If you couldn't, you should have your ears cleaned.'

I bristled at his rudeness. 'How dare you speak to me like that? Why couldn't you just slip the letter under the door like other postmen do? Why do you disturb people and harass them?'

The postman waved an envelope in my face. 'This is a registered letter, madam. If you don't want to sign for it, that's all right by me. I'll take it back.'

I lunged forward and grabbed the letter from his hand. In the process, the knife clattered to the floor, making me utter a soft Bengali epithet under my breath. The postman took advantage of my distraction to grab the envelope right back and shout, 'Now you are cursing me. You think I don't understand your language. But I do. And I know what you just called me. I will have to report this matter to the supervisor and we will stop delivery to your house.'

I picked up the knife and held it close to my body. It had suddenly occurred to me that the letter could be an important document—an official letter for Ranjan. And here I was fighting with the man who had come to deliver it. I changed my stand and assumed a humble expression.

'Please . . . the letter may be important. Please give it to me.'

The postman straightened up. 'Now you are talking a different language. Come to your senses, have you? First you curse, then you beg. I've seen women like you—Bombay is full of them. Rude, ill-tempered women. It's a wonder your husband hasn't left you.'

I bit my lip and willed myself into silence. I needed that document. 'Wait,' I told him, 'I'll be back in a minute.'

I ran into my bedroom and opened the top drawer of the small dressing table where I kept a little house money. I picked up a ten-rupee note and returned, holding it out gingerly.

'Here—please accept this for all your trouble.'

The postman stared greedily at the note but something made him spurn my offer. Pride or cussedness, I didn't know.

'Huh!' he mocked, 'Now you want to bribe me with ten rupees. This is Bombay, madam, not Calcutta. You can't get a shoeshine boy to polish your shoes for ten rupees. Forget it. Besides, insults are expensive. *Yeh sab nahi chalega* with me. Won't work, understand.'

For the second time that morning, I felt tears pricking my eyes and I hated myself for it. 'Please . . . I'm requesting you . . . please. If my husband gets to know . . . please hand me the letter.'

My attention was so focussed on the elusive envelope in the postman's hands that I didn't notice Nikhil standing quietly near the staircase and watching the scene with a puzzled look on his face.

'Any problems?' he asked, coming upto the postman and towering over him.

'Yes . . . I mean no . . . that is . . . they've been sorted out. It's okay, he's just leaving,' I replied, conscious of how unkempt I must be looking with my crumpled, sweaty kurta and unwashed face. I hadn't even bothered to run a comb through my hair after the baba suit expedition. I'd planned to have a bath later and freshen up after completing the cooking.

Nikhil smiled at my obvious embarrassment and said reassuringly, 'Don't worry, Maya. It's okay. My mother looks far worse in the mornings. Besides, your hair looks great even when you haven't combed it.'

And then he turned to the postman. '*Kyon? Takleef hai?* Give the lady her letter and disappear. You are a real trouble-maker. I've seen you doing this earlier to the woman on the second floor. One more time and your bones will be crushed. Understand?'

Sullenly, the man handed me a delivery form to sign but refused to lend his own pen. Nikhil reached for his shirt pocket and handed me a ball-point. The letter was finally in my hands. I looked at it carefully. I didn't know what it was I had expected, but it turned out to be nothing more important than a fixed deposit receipt from a textile mill that was clearly dying.

'So much nonsense for this,' I fumed.

Nikhil smiled indulgently. 'Relax, Maya,' he said and touched my cheek playfully. I stepped back and stiffened. Nikhil followed me and stood inches away, his face close to mine.

'I said relax, Maya. I don't bite. And I'm not going to hurt you. It's all right. And the offer to help with the housework still stands.'

He began to roll up his shirt sleeves with a determined purposeful air. 'Move,' he added, pushing past me and heading for the kitchen.

I ran behind him, saying, 'Don't be ridiculous, Nikhil. Please leave now. I can do this on my own. I'm an able-bodied woman.'

He whirled around. 'And what if I refuse to go? Will you call that lazy, decrepit watchman and ask him to remove me from your precious flat? Really, Maya, you have far too many hang ups. I told you, I have no problems about washing, cleaning, dusting, polishing. I used to be a boy scout at school—okay? Now, let's get to work.'

There was nothing I could say. I watched him as he attacked the pots in the sink energetically. I felt suddenly useless, standing around doing nothing. It was a very small kitchen. Now there was just room for Nikhil.

He turned around and grinned over his shoulder, 'Play some music or just put up your feet and read a magazine. You deserve a rest, you're looking exhausted.'

I glanced at the front door furtively—I had left it open deliberately. He caught my glance and laughed out loud. 'Is this an old Calcutta habit? Don't people shut their doors there? Maya, you really are so strange, so funny. So . . . different from Bombay women.'

I sighed and remained silent. I was too scared to relax, worried sick that at any moment some vendor or the other would appear. Or worse, a nosy neighbour sensing scandal.

More than anything else, I was worried about Ranjan. What if he suddenly took ill and decided to come home? How could I possibly explain Nikhil's presence in our kitchen?

Unable to contain my tension, I blurted out, 'Nikhil, I feel scared with you in the house like this. If my husband ever finds out, he'll kill me. And you.'

Nikhil held up a gleaming frying pan and said brightly, 'I'm willing to take my chances. But it's up to you. If you are really scared of the guy finding out, which he won't, I'll leave immediately.'

I nodded, vastly relieved that the message had got home so quickly. 'Please. I hope you don't misunderstand. I appreciate your help. But it's just not done for a . . . for a young man to be alone like this with a married woman.'

I expected Nikhil to laugh at my comment. He didn't. He dried his hands on a handy kitchen towel, straightened his shoulders and walked briskly to the door.

'Maya, I'm not angry. In fact, I'm a little pleased. I won't tell you why. Don't worry. I don't want to complicate your life. Or make you unhappy. I would have liked to listen to my tape with you. Maybe some other time.'

He was about to leave when I rushed up to him and touched his arm hesitantly. 'I loved your song. I want you to know that,' I managed to say.

'Thanks,' he responded softly. Then he turned and ran up the stairs to his flat two at a time.

Eleven

That year, I experienced my first Bombay monsoon and enjoyed it. Far from depressing me, I had actually surrendered to the monsoon's many moods. From my window, I would watch the rain coming in over the tree tops and wait for it to invade my bedroom. I liked the little puddles it formed on my window sill (which now bore tiny potted plants, some of which were in flower).

The room smelled slightly musty because of the constant and all-pervading dampness. It also looked rather dingy unless I switched on the lights. Even so, I didn't feel melancholic as I gazed at the glistening street downstairs, emptied of the usual people.

The banana seller showed up on the comparatively dry days. The other vendors were more irregular. Occasionally, a passing car splashed the banana seller and her child with dirty rain water, but nothing bothered her. She would dry herself with a rag and huddle under a broken-ribbed umbrella, waiting patiently for the skies to clear and for customers to buy her fruit.

In contrast, the rains put Ranjan in a bad mood. He hated to step out in the morning and get his clothes wet. More than his clothes, he loathed raindrops ruining his hair. He would leave home in a foul temper and return in the evening earlier than usual, still cursing. My cheerfulness would irritate him further.

'How can you tolerate this horrible weather?' he would grumble, as he sipped his tea.

I would say, 'Calcutta has far more rain storms than Bombay. I'm used to it.'

Ranjan would stare angrily at his raincoat dripping in the corner of the bathroom and mutter, 'If only Bombay could change its weather, everybody would be happier.'

Each evening his mother would call to ask him, always in the same order, 'Are you wet? Have you changed into dry clothes? Did you catch a chill? Are you sure you don't have fever?'

His answers were invariably the same each day. But just to highlight his miserable condition, he made sure to sneeze and sniffle a few times or blow his nose noisily. His mother would then ring off after issuing a few instructions.

'Make sure you dry your feet thoroughly. That's where a cold generally starts. Don't sleep directly under a fan with wet hair. Don't wear damp clothes to bed. Make Maya re-iron them in case they aren't completely dry.'

Ranjan would say, '*Theek hai, achcha*, Ma,' half a dozen times before ringing off.

*

Ranjan was due for a promotion later in the year. It was obviously weighing on his mind. Especially since he had now acquired a new boss, an American whiz, all of twenty-nine.

'How can Tom handle India?' Ranjan would say. 'What does he know about how things function around here? He's trying to introduce American systems without realizing that we are years behind that level of business sophistication.'

Sometimes, I would prod him with a comment or two. 'But I thought with the new liberalization policy, the business climate is rapidly changing. That's what everybody is saying—at least on TV.'

Ranjan would shoot me an impatient look and ask witheringly, 'Who is everybody? And which TV programme are you referring to?'

I'd say, 'Oh . . . the BBC, and some of our local Doordarshan panel discussions.'

Ranjan would snap, 'I didn't know you listened to any of those. Every time I come home, I hear Hindi film songs, or some stupid countdown or other.'

I'd defend myself in a mild sort of way. 'I also enjoy those. And the Oprah Winfrey show—do you know what she was saying the other day about men who murder their wives and marry their mistresses?'

Ranjan would hold up his hand and say, 'Please,' which was a polite way to shut me up.

I would try my best to take his mind off Thomas Becker Jr. But Ranjan was getting to be obsessive about him. 'What the hell does he think? Just a fancy Yale degree is not enough. You have to know the environment from within. This is his first foreign posting. I don't know why they send novices to India. Maybe they think they can use Third World countries as cheap training grounds. We are nothing better than guinea pigs, I tell you. Back home in his own country, Tom wouldn' t stand a chance.'

I'd bait him just a little more, not to hurt his feelings but more to amuse myself a bit. 'I was reading a *Time* magazine cover story about current CEOs in America. They say if a man hasn't made it by thirty, he can forget it. Tom has another year to go to prove himself. Maybe this is his big assignment. He can't be all that dumb.'

Ranjan would raise his voice and say impatiently, 'You know something, Maya—it's better for women not to make immature, ignorant comments on subjects they know nothing about. You've never worked in a large multinational organization. I have. I know how things operate. Tom will not last—take it from me. He won't be able to stand the pressure.'

I would nod and pretend I had switched off before adding, 'But surely, he must have learnt something at the World Bank. Isn't that his background?'

Ranjan would finally explode, 'World Bank—huh! As if that's some great achievement. I could have got into the World Bank too. Only, I didn't want to sell my soul. I believed in commitment to my country. I wanted to serve our economy. And contribute my bit. I had fantastic offers to stay back. So many big corporations were wooing me. But I said "no". It's India for me.'

I'd smile at his passionate declarations. Ranjan was so transparently earnest about his goals. And me? From where had I acquired this wicked, almost sadistic streak? Or was it the dog-eat-dog atmosphere of Bombay that was doing this to me?

Each day, Ranjan would come back with more stories about the American brat who was now his boss. I could sense his frustration and sympathize upto a point. Tom Becker Jr. sounded pretty obnoxious.

'What does he look like?' I asked Ranjan as I ladled out steaming hot rice one night.

'Oh, him? He looks like an American,' he answered dismissively.

'And what do Americans look like?' I persisted.

'They all look the same to me,' Ranjan snapped, adding, 'just like we all look alike to them. It's true. They can't tell one Asian from the other. Pakistanis and Indians fall under a single category. Koreans, Japanese, Chinese and South East Asians in another. That simple. Well, if you ask me, all whites are identical. So are all blacks.'

I was slightly taken aback by the vehemence of his words. I knew Bengalis were very colour conscious, but Ranjan's remarks bordered on the racist.

'Why don't you invite him home to dinner?' I suggested mildly. 'Perhaps if you get to know him better in an informal sort of way, he'll be easier to get along with at work.'

Ranjan thought about it as he helped himself to ghanto, his favourite mixed vegetable dish. 'Not a bad idea,' he mused. 'He has been talking about sampling an authentic Indian meal.'

I laughed at that. 'He's probably looking for a curry dinner—whatever that is.'

Ranjan stared at me in surprise. 'Where did you get to hear that expression?'

I felt embarrassed and precocious all of a sudden. 'I watch BBC's Food File. They have some excellent cookery programmes. I've seen Madhur Jaffrey's show too. Each time there is a reference to Indian food, the presenter talks about curries and more curries—as if there's nothing more to our food than that. Let's call Tom over for a Bengali curry—the one that doesn't exist in Bengal.'

Ranjan looked vaguely impressed. Perhaps he felt slightly more confident about inviting his American boss home knowing his Calcutta wife wasn't entirely ignorant about things around the world. All these months since our marriage I had got the feeling that Ranjan felt a little ashamed of me. After all, I wasn't a Bombay girl.

It used to hurt me sometimes and make me wonder why he hadn't picked someone—even a Bengali—from this city. There was a large congregation of Bengalis in Bombay—some of them three and four generations old. They had their localities where they celebrated Durga Puja, Saraswati Puja, Poila Baishakh and all the other Bengali festivals with great gusto and zest.

In fact, my mother-in-law was on two important puja committees and had been telling me about the celebrations with tremendous enthusiasm. It was obvious from the tone of her voice that her position on the committee ('Honorary Secretary: Fund Raising and Evening Programmes') meant a great deal to her. Surely, she could have screened eligible girls during the annual ten-day festival and found a worthy bride for her son? Someone born in Bombay, educated in Bombay and comfortable in Bombay.

I'd asked Ranjan about it once. He had replied shortly, 'Oh no, no. These Bombay Bengalis are different. They've lost their cultural identity. Their roots are not in our tradition. They are all mixed up—neither here nor there. My mother wouldn't have been able to adjust to someone like that.'

'But what about you?' I'd asked.

Ranjan had stared into his business paper and said, 'Me? I'd left all this to my mother. It was up to her. And frankly, I wouldn't have adjusted either.'

But why, I had demanded, unwilling to let it go that easily.

'You know . . . these Bombay girls are used to a very fast way of life. Their morals are no good. They don't speak proper Bengali. They don't know the rituals connected with our pujas. They wear all sorts of funny clothes, they refuse to oil their hair. They cannot cook our preparations. They don't know Bengali songs or dances. All they can do is eat roadside food and dream of going to bars and discos. Such girls do not make good wives. Not at all.'

Idly, I wondered if Nikhil knew 'such girls'. I wanted to meet a few myself—not because I was keen on joining their tribe but they seemed to live such a different life from the one I knew. I'd read about girls like that in popular women's magazines. They often featured on the cover and were interviewed inside talking about their *'bindaas'* lifestyles. That word itself fascinated me. What exactly did *'bindaas'* mean? Reckless? Carefree? Defiant? Liberated? Who could I possibly ask to interpret this tantalizing word for me?

And the Bombay Bengalis Ranjan damned so easily, how different were they from me? I sometimes had the feeling he was a little scared of them. What was he afraid of? And my mother-in-law, with her superior airs—did these girls intimidate her as well? Or was she shrewd enough to realize that perhaps her son wasn't the ideal partner for them? Had she tried and failed to find a Bombay bride for him?

I would never know. My mamu would never tell me (that is, if he was aware of it). And in any case, after the wedding, we'd hardly met or spoken, even on the phone. Our timings didn't match. He preferred to call on Sunday when Ranjan was at home. Somehow, I always felt inhibited talking to anybody from 'my side' in his presence. Not that he actively objected. But his expression invariably altered. He would look slightly irritated and impatient and if the conversation exceeded five minutes, he would interrupt me to say he was expecting an 'important call'—a call that never materialized. My uncle was discreet—and sensitive—enough to get the message. His calls tapered off and on one level it was a relief.

*

I made a mental note to ask Nikhil in our next conversation on the landing if he knew any *'bindaas'* Bombay girls. And may be, if he did, whether he would be willing to introduce me to them.

But meanwhile, I had to concentrate on a 'sensible' menu for Ranjan's American boss.

'Shall we call someone else? What about the Mathurs?' I suggested. A wild expression came into Ranjan's eyes, as though I had suggested something totally preposterous.

'The Mathurs? Are you crazy? You know how these people from Uttar Pradesh are—pushy, aggressive, shameless. If they even find out that I'm planning to invite Becker, they will fill his ears with all kinds of stories. And before we know it, they will get him over to their side. No, no. Nobody must know about this dinner. The only other person I've talked to is my mother. She has also advised me not to invite the Mathurs. You are very innocent, Maya. Our office is so competitive, people like Mathur would do anything to keep me down.'

He paused to chew a mouthful of food, and then continued. 'That's the trouble with Bengalis. See how other communities help their own people—Mathur must have brought dozens of relatives to Bombay and given them jobs. But ask a Bengali for help—even the smallest thing, and he will snub you. Jealousy— that is our problem. We don't like our own people to come up and prosper. That's why my mother tells me to keep everything absolutely quiet. You have to be secretive or else you are finished. Take yourself—you have a bad habit of talking too much. Don't deny it—I have noticed it. It's important to keep one's mouth shut. Who knows who the enemy is?'

I felt strangely hurt by that last remark and sulked for the rest of the evening, barely conversing and staying deliberately out of Ranjan's way.

It was while I was defrosting the fridge and mopping up all the water that had drained out that Ranjan walked in looking for something cold to drink. Once again, I was caught on the wrong foot. I mumbled apologetically that there weren't any ice cubes and even the drinking water was lukewarm.

Ranjan shook his head in disgust. 'What is this? A man comes back from work dehydrated and exhausted, and there is no cold water in the house. Is this the time to clean the fridge?'

He stared pointedly at his wrist-watch and then, as though unable to believe what he was seeing, he consulted the kitchen clock. 'Have you seen the time?' he asked in horror.

'Yes—it's nearly nine o'clock,' I replied evenly, wiping the shelves clean.

'And no ice cubes till tomorrow morning, I suppose.'

'That's right,' I said, washing the stainless steel tray at the sink.

'You expect me to drink warm water on a hot night like this? I won't be able to sleep tonight, you know. And I have a very busy day ahead of me tomorrow—including a meeting with Becker. How will I face it with a parched throat and a throbbing headache?'

I put the mop down and said, 'I'll borrow some ice cubes from the neighbours. It will only take a couple of minutes, okay?'

Ranjan rolled his eyes heavenwards. 'Borrow? And from the neighbours? That's a very bad policy, if you must know. Very bad. Today, you ask them for ice cubes, tomorrow they'll walk in and demand a cake. That's how the world is. My mother had vowed that in our home we would do without something but not approach a neighbour. These people misunderstand. They take it as a signal that you wish to establish intimacy with them. They'll begin to get over-familiar. From tomorrow you'll have them sitting on your sofas drinking tea and coffee and asking for tomatoes and what not. These people cannot be trusted at all.

'Go ahead . . . go and beg for ice, if you want to . . . but remember, you'll be lowering yourself in their eyes. They will say, "see, what a bad housewife she is—she doesn't even have ice cubes in her home on a hot day like this". And then they'll start speculating about other things.'

'Like what?' I asked, a slight edge to my voice.

'Oh, you know . . . things which aren't their business at all. Personal things. They'll wonder how our marriage is working out and all that.'

'Only because I'm defrosting the fridge? Is that really how people's minds work here?' I challenged, looking Ranjan straight in the eye.

'Maya . . . you will take some time to get adjusted to Bombay. It's not your fault. In Calcutta even neighbourliness works differently. In Bombay, the way people think is blunt and harsh. No time to waste. Their first worry is, "what does he or she want from me?" And if you want ice cubes, they will say "aah—today she feels free enough to ask for ice cubes. Tomorrow she will ask for something bigger." Now . . . if they think they can also get something from you in return, they will smile and give you not just the ice but some ice-cream as well. And after a few days they'll knock on your door to borrow money—small amounts first, bigger amounts later. This money you will never get back. That's how it starts. Ask me.'

I was breathing hard as I asked, 'Has it ever actually happened to you?'

Ranjan snorted, 'Everything doesn't have to happen to everyone. Does a woman wait to be raped before she avoids dangerous places? Talk sense, Maya. You are being absurd.'

I repeated my question slowly. 'Tell me—has it ever happened to you? Have your neighbours taken advantage of you? Have they barged into the house and asked for money?'

Ranjan shrugged, 'I still think you are being obstinate and foolish.'

I kept quiet while Ranjan paced around restlessly.

'Do you know there's a heat wave on. Anything can happen. I might get dehydrated at night. One has to drink a lot of water, especially since the humidity levels in Bombay are so high. See how much I'm sweating?' He pointed to the large, damp stains of perspiration on his night shirt.

I said, 'Look, I'm really sorry about the ice cubes, but there is nothing I can do about it right now, and since you don't want me to go to the neighbours', I suppose we'll both have to do with lukewarm drinking water tonight.'

Ranjan stopped pacing and stared at me, his eyes bulging out of their sockets even more than usual.

'You are sounding more and more like those rude Bombay girls we were talking about earlier. The ones I didn't marry. Do you know when your maternal uncle heard that I was back in India and open to the idea of settling down, he rang up my mother no less than five times to tell her about you. I'm not saying I regret what happened, but my mother was a little taken aback. Five phone calls.

'Of course, she was receiving several similar calls from other parties. But because you were from Calcutta, she said "yes". The reason was simple—we didn't want to get involved with Bengali families from this environment. We believed our cultural roots would remain strong and our traditions would be respected if we picked a girl from your sort of background. And now, you are behaving like this?'

I reasoned with myself that Ranjan was feeling drained and tired. It had been an extraordinarily hot day. The leaves of my potted plants were droopy and wilting. I didn't wish to aggravate the situation by either arguing or defending myself.

So I tactfully suggested that he cool off in the bedroom and get sufficient rest before the big meeting while I completed the few remaining kitchen chores.

Fortunately for me, Ranjan went off quietly and shut the door. I heard the whir of the bulky, rusting air-conditioner as it groaned to life. We had bought it at an auction for a pittance and spent more on repairing it than a new one would have cost.

*

I surveyed my small kitchen. It smelt of stale food. With the mercury soaring, nearly everything began to spoil if left outside the fridge for even half an hour. I looked at the neatly stacked dishes, the ceramic mugs and the rack containing spoons and ladles of varying sizes. It was a neat and organized sight.

It ought to have given me a sense of accomplishment. But, like my own mother, I had never seen any particular virtue in housework. By temperament, I wasn't cut out for domesticity. If I took the trouble to keep my home tidy, it was more because I had nothing else to do, not a single other diversion. If I didn't obsessively dust and clean, how would the hours pass?

Of course, with the part-time servants to help me, I could have performed a supervisory role and not done very much. I'd tried that too. But I found I couldn't concentrate on either reading or watching television if there was another person hard at work around the place. That induced some silly guilt in me ('how can I sit around flipping through a magazine while that poor woman is scrubbing my floors?'). To make myself feel better, I would start cleaning my cupboards mechanically or rearrange books while the woman went about her fixed routine.

I had found that most of the bais lead frenzied professional lives. They didn't have the time or desire to chat. I had tried it on a few occasions and come up against monosyllabic replies.

I had thought at first that it was a language barrier that was creating the problem. (My Hindi was functional and accented.) But then I realized most of the women were not from Bombay themselves.

The one who worked at my house was from Andhra Pradesh—a swarthy, well-built handsome woman with gold gleaming all over and around her face. Since she commuted from quite a distance, she had a schedule she had to stick to with clockwork precision. I tried once in a while to get her to share a cup of mid-morning tea with me. Even that fractured interaction would seem desirable compared to the nasal twang of a music video Veejay from Hong Kong playing vintage requests from Indian teenagers called Ashish or Monisha. But no, Savitri would politely decline my invitation and rush off, her gold gleaming in the strong sunlight.

I knew I needed to work on my Hindi. Not that Bombay Hindi was refined. People from Delhi openly mocked the way people here misused and distorted the language. Since to me it was an alien tongue, I struggled to master even this bastardized version so as to make myself better understood while dealing with vendors, liftmen, milkmen and others. I did feel ashamed when I made obvious mistakes but then I reasoned that Hindi was neither my mother tongue nor did I accept it as the national language. Nobody did in Calcutta, they didn't need to.

Ranjan's Hindi was equally disgraceful. So was his mother's, though she chose to speak it in a peculiar, chi-chi lilting accent that I found unbearable and put on, like practically everything else about her. I also disliked her 'memsaab' voice—the special tone she reserved for servants and underlings—high, cold and distant. She changed her posture accordingly too, with her chin tilted back and arms crossed at the waist.

Ranjan would comment admiringly, 'My mother really knows how to handle servants. See how she keeps them all in their place? You don't know these Bombay servants. They think they're doing you a big favour by working in your house. If you're good to them, they take full advantage of you. Have you seen the ayahs in this building? Even film stars aren't this fashionable—lipstick, nail polish and what not. My mother does not tolerate all that rubbish. She is strict, very strict.

'You are far too lenient with these people—if you don't watch out, they'll be behaving like queens around the house. I've been noticing how they take advantage of you. Shameless creatures. And remember, no loans. The minute you give someone money, finished. That's the last you'll see of it or the person. Disappear—that's what these rascals do as soon as they've got your notes in their pocket.'

I paid close attention to Ranjan's lecture. About a few things, he was perfectly right. I had experienced ingratitude, even theft during my first week as a housewife. Foolishly, I'd 'loaned' the brand new recruit fifty rupees from 'my' money. (I had received a small sum from my mother right after the wedding. She had pressed a few hundred rupees into my hand and whispered, 'Keep it. Buy some small things for yourself.')

I had wondered if I was supposed to inform my in-laws about this tiny gift. Ranjan had told me, 'Now that you are my wife, no secrets. I want to know everything, and I will tell you everything.'

Would my mother's little present qualify as a 'secret'? Was I meant to hand over the amount to my husband? Would I then have to ask him to give me some from it as and when I needed it? I thought not. This was my money, to be used at my discretion.

Which was why I felt upset when Ranjan took me to task for granting the loan. He had immediately thought I had doled out 'his' money. When I clarified that it was mine, he seemed stumped.

'What do you mean it's yours? Where did you get it from?'

So I mentioned casually that my mother had given it to me. Ranjan had thought for a while before saying, 'Please do not encourage your mother to spoil you like this. I know I'm not a rich man but I earn enough for both of us to live comfortably. A good wife has to learn to adjust and sacrifice. I hope you do not have foolish extravagant habits. Because if you do, then sorry but I won't be able to meet your demands.'

That night, I had surrendered four hundred and fifty rupees to Ranjan. And, of course, I had never seen them again. I don't think he used the money for himself, and chances were it was still there, somewhere. But what use was it to me? I didn't have access to it. I didn't even know where he had hidden it. I had learned a valuable lesson and I vowed never to disclose the existence of 'my' money in future (that is, if I ever got any again) and never to trust thieving servants.

It was different in Calcutta. Servants didn't have to be shown their place, they knew it. Most of them were from the bustees on the fringes of the city. They lived a sub-human existence well below the poverty line. Unlike the well-fed, well-dressed Bombay servants, these creatures looked like beggars and had a disposition to match. Clad in filthy rags, the women often blouseless, they would be willing to work for two pathetic meals a day and a meagre salary.

Some of them were refugees who lived in constant fear of deportation. They were the worst specimens, dressed in tatters, their eyes hollow with hunger and fear. Housewives grabbed them eagerly since they demanded nothing more than one dirty corner of a staircase to sleep on. For as little as forty or fifty rupees, these migrants would surrender their lives to their employers and work a twenty-four hour day without regular rest, wages or food.

Compared to them, their Bombay counterparts were a pampered, arrogant lot. Tough, talkative, ambitious and mobile, they made it clear that the arrangement worked two ways. The employer needed them as much as they needed their salaries. No favours. No concessions.

Often, it was they who set the pace for the relationship by setting out a detailed charter of demands which clearly stated their rights. In some residential areas, domestics had already unionized the work force, making it virtually impossible for a dissatisfied employer to sack anyone.

Ranjan would shake his head disbelievingly and say, 'Look at these servants. We are at their mercy now. What do they think of themselves. I have never heard of such nonsense. Servants are servants, why can't they understand that? They're trying to behave like pampered factory workers. I tell you, if all this nonsense doesn't stop, Bombay will become unlivable. A city that can't control its servants will never be able to control anybody else, mark my words.'

Twelve

I was expecting to meet an albino monkey or at least some sort of monster. Tom Becker turned out to be just another very pink, very tall white man with watery blue eyes, blond eyelashes and bad teeth.

When the doorbell rang at precisely 8.30 p.m., Ranjan took one quick look at himself in the mirror, adjusted his new tie, frowned at me to release my saree pallu (which I had tucked in at the waist for convenience), straightened his shoulders and opened the door with an extra cheery 'Hi there!'

Ranjan had a peculiar way of talking to and greeting foreigners. I had noticed it at our wedding reception to which Ranjan's mother had invited the few English people she knew from the old days when she worked for various charities in the fund-raising committee. I had observed Ranjan as he stiffened, assumed an expression unfamiliar to me, altered his accent (even his posture) and lapsed into a strange and dated slang ('Howdy? How ya' doin'?').

Years spent at an American university had tinged Ranjan's basic Bombay English with a peculiar twang that was neither here nor there. Ranjan's use of the language was forced at the best of times—he spoke it as if it was a strain to translate his thoughts from Bengali to English. I found this rather hard to understand since Ranjan had gone to an English-medium suburban school that had laid great emphasis on mastering the English language, both spoken and written. His mother had told me with some pride that Ranjan had always scored very high marks in 'English composition' and maths. She had also mentioned that she had made it a point to talk to her son exclusively in English since she wanted him to be very fluent ('We always knew he'd be going abroad for further studies—better to start with an advantage').

And yet, there were times when Ranjan made the most basic of errors, grammatical and phonetical. I had tried to correct him gently, once or twice, only to be told that his was the right way of phrasing, spelling and speaking.

'Maybe in Calcutta they teach you a different sort of English,' Ranjan had scoffed, 'but this is how we speak it in Bombay. Besides, as you well know, I had no language problems in America, no problems at all.'

Tom was casually dressed in jeans and an open-necked T-shirt. He punched Ranjan playfully in the ribs and joked, 'Hey, what's this? I thought you said this was going to be an informal evening?'

Ranjan's false smile stretched even further as he laughed exaggeratedly and pulled funny faces. Tom turned to me, hand outstretched and said, 'Hi, my name's Tom.'

I was wondering whether to shake his hand or greet him with a traditional namaste, when Ranjan nudged me and whispered urgently, 'Handshake, handshake.'

Tom looked me up and down appreciatively and said, 'Nice saree. Lovely colour—Bengali, right?' He pronounced 'Bengali' to rhyme with 'Svengali'.

I blushed and looked at Ranjan, who said, 'Sit, sit—come on in. Make yourself comfortable.'

Tom continued standing. 'Mind if I look around a bit first? I just love folk art.'

Ranjan shrugged and looked slightly puzzled. Tom stared intently at a crudely crafted set of brass rice measures.

'Beautiful. Just look at the intricate work on that—wow.'

I felt secretly pleased to hear him praise the rice bowls. They had been given by my paternal uncle as a wedding gift. It was just one of the several gifts Ranjan's mother had sniffed at disdainfully and suggested, 'Why don't you leave it packed in its original carton. It will be easier to pass it on to someone later. I always keep useless gifts in their original boxes. It saves so much time when you are in a hurry.'

I had felt particularly hurt by that comment. For one, I was very fond of my Kaku. For another, I was the one who had asked for the rice bowls when he had given me the choice to pick a gift. I had seen them in our relatives' homes as a child and been fascinated by their unusual shape and structure. Nearly every Bengali home in our locality had a set of these rice measures. I had asked my mother if we could buy a set, but she had refused, saying caustically, 'Frankly, there is just no place in the house for them. And, who is going to polish them? The issue is, it's all very well for people to ask for this and that—but who is willing to take care of such things?'

I had been disappointed then and vowed that one day when I had a home of my own, I would acquire a set of rice bowls and polish them lovingly, and leave them to gleam proudly near the entrance. And that was exactly where Tom had discovered them. I shot Ranjan a triumphant look. Suddenly, I felt vindicated. As though I had won a small victory over his mother and her ideas of tasteful home decor.

Tom walked around slowly, staring at some of the inexpensive wall hangings and bell-metal figurines I had brought from Calcutta. Ranjan walked self-consciously behind him, offering small, inaccurate descriptions about the pieces, shooting me a look that said, 'don't you dare contradict what I'm saying.'

'Nice place you have here,' Tom said, addressing the remark to me. His voice was friendly, his manner, open. Before I could say a polite, 'Thank you', Ranjan did, adding, 'My mother, you see, she is a very artistic lady. That is, she is not actually an artist as such, but she has a liking for artistic things.'

Tom raised his eyebrows and said, 'Oh, is that right? Well, in that case your wife has certainly put them all together very well. It's a cozy home you run here, ma'am.'

I smiled uncertainly, wondering whether Ranjan would once again interject and say his mother had arranged every piece of furniture according to her taste. Instead, Ranjan rubbed his hands vigorously and asked, 'A drink for you? Beer? Not Indian—I have managed to get hold of some foreign stuff. A few cans only, but it's good—Carlsberg, you know.'

Tom nodded and said, 'Sure. But I'd have been equally happy with Indian beer. It's pretty good—in fact, I've been drinking it regularly. Becoming something of an addict—can't seem to get enough.'

Ranjan smiled a broader than necessary smile. 'It's not too bad, actually, if you don't mind the glycerine in it.'

Tom turned to me with an expression that said, 'So . . . what are you all about?'

I had noticed that expression before. I supposed it happened when people worked together in offices and wondered about the sort of people their colleagues were married to. And the first time they encountered the spouses, a certain recognition registered—either the spouse conformed to the preconceived image or came as a surprise package ('That man/woman married to this person? Unbelievable').

I couldn't quite decipher Tom's expression but since it was pleasant enough, I smiled back and offered him some toasted peanuts. He waved them away and mouthed, 'High in cholesterol.'

I nodded and offered them to Ranjan. Tom grinned. 'If it's bad for me, it's bad for him too.'

Ranjan looked at us suspiciously as if we'd shared some significant secret and conspired to leave him out of it. Switching to Bengali, he told me to go and check on the dinner. I rushed to the kitchen and promptly started opening the lids of the pots and pans on the stove. Ranjan had instructed me to produce bland, spice-free dishes with plenty of cheese. No chapattis, he'd said, only bread and butter. One meat dish, one chicken dish, one baked dish, one green salad, two desserts—preferably caramel custard and jelly with ice-cream. I'd tried. Now I could only hope the food was edible.

I could hear the two men talking shop outside—technical matters that didn't make too much sense to me. The phone rang and I knew it was Ranjan's mother. He excused himself and took the call. I overheard him giving her a brief description of the menu and adding that he was a little nervous about the dinner. Just then, Tom wandered into the kitchen. I found him standing awkwardly at the entrance.

'Yes?' I said, whirling around, conscious of the fact that I had tucked in my saree pallu at the waist again.

'Water? I'm looking for some drinking water. Do you have mineral water . . . if not, I'm easy.'

'No mineral water,' I said, 'but I boil and filter all the drinking water. It's quite safe. And much better than the water in Calcutta.'

Tom smiled. 'Are you from Calcutta? And is the saree you're wearing typical of that region?'

I looked down at my white and blue tangail (it was one of the wedding sarees) and said, 'Yes. It's typically Bengali. We call it tangail.' And I spelt out the word carefully.

Tom listened keenly, as though he was genuinely interested. 'I'm fascinated by Indian textiles,' he said, 'in fact I'm reading a great book on the subject right now. I could lend it to you if you are interested.'

I nodded and opened another lid.

'Smells good. We are eating Indian, I hope. I so rarely get to eat the genuine thing in an Indian home. I'm sick of all those five star curries. They all taste the same.'

I must have looked embarrassed because Tom leaned forward and asked, 'Something wrong?'

I smiled weakly and said, 'Oh no . . . nothing really, it's just that my husband was sure you wouldn't like our spices, so . . . so . . .'

Tom completed the sentence for me, '. . . so you've made some baked food with lots of cheese, right?'

I burst out laughing.

'Don't worry about it—there will always be a next time, I hope. And then you can introduce me to Bengali food properly. How about that?'

Ranjan walked in just then with a slightly nervous expression. 'Everything all right, I hope? No problem?'

Tom swung around. 'No problem, just sharing a joke with your charming wife.'

Ranjan darted a quick glance in my direction and gestured to Tom to follow him into the sitting room. I busied myself with warming the food. Tom seemed like a pleasant enough person. It was hard to connect him with the image Ranjan had conveyed. But of course Ranjan knew better since they worked together.

As I stirred the gooey-looking baked fish lightly (I didn't want to disturb the browned top layer), it occurred to me that Tom was the first foreigner I had actually spoken to. Of course, in Calcutta I had attended a few lectures at the Max Mueller complex and met visiting professors at our college. But I had not had the opportunity to chat casually with a white man. In my mind, I had decided that such an encounter would be far from easy, and that I would become tongue-tied. Instead, Tom had made me feel so totally relaxed, it was as if we had known each other previously.

I heard him tell Ranjan to ask me to rejoin them. And I heard Ranjan politely dismissing the request with a brief explanation ('She's needed in the kitchen. You see, we don't believe in keeping full-time servants. It's too dangerous in Bombay').

The dinner that followed was dominated by Ranjan. He wasn't about to miss this opportunity to hog his boss' time and discuss 'pending matters'. Tom ate his food sportingly and even complimented me on it. It appeared to me that he was only half-listening to Ranjan. I tried to keep out of their conversation since it was obvious Ranjan wanted to use the occasion to air his views on company policy. It sounded suspiciously as though he had prepared his speech, for he seemed to have a specific agenda which he rattled off at great speed.

From time to time, Tom caught my eye and smiled. I wasn't sure whether or not to return his smile, since it felt a little like disloyalty to Ranjan. When it was time to clear the table, Tom sprang to his feet and said, 'Here. . . I'll get that.'

Ranjan grabbed his elbow and said, 'Oh no, no, no. She'll do it. No problem. In India, we don't allow our guests to lift a finger.'

Tom got to his feet anyway and shrugged. 'Well, Ranjan, I'm not Indian. And back home, this is how we do it.'

Ranjan giggled and pulled funny faces. He didn't get up. Tom followed me into the kitchen and said generously, 'Excellent dinner.'

I muttered 'Liar,' under my breath, half-hoping he wouldn't hear me.

'I heard that,' Tom laughed, 'and I'm not lying. However, next time I want the real thing, okay? It's a deal.'

He extended his hand and shook mine warmly. I could hear Ranjan humming a Simon and Garfunkel number outside. I tried, foolishly, I know, to imagine Nikhil in his place. It was heart-wrenching to do so, and completely futile. Nikhil was probably out with his college friends, drinking frothy beer in a lively pub somewhere. Or maybe he was composing music and strumming his guitar.

I tried to imagine how he would have responded to Tom even though it was an unfair comparison as far as Ranjan was concerned. I concluded that the main difference would have lain in his complete naturalness, as opposed to Ranjan's stiff self-consciousness. Ranjan was trying far too hard to make a 'good' impression on his boss. A little like an eager student trying desperately to impress his class teacher.

Fortunately, Tom was not a nasty man. I saw sympathy and kindness in his eyes as he listened attentively to Ranjan's string of complaints (along with a few practical suggestions). He didn't belittle Ranjan's opinions. Nor did he snub him by looking bored or disinterested. I was happy for Ranjan. I realized that, funnily enough, it would have hurt me had Tom dealt harshly with Ranjan. I knew Ranjan would have been unspeakably wounded and unable to figure out Tom's reasons for doing so.

*

Later, after Tom had left and Ranjan had stripped down to his underwear, he asked me thoughtfully how I had assessed the evening.

'Did he like your dinner?' (Not 'the dinner' or 'our dinner').

I nodded non-committally.

'Did he tell you he liked it or are you just guessing?'

'He told me he liked it.'

'What exactly did he say?'

I started to oil and plait my hair for the night.

'Well, he said the dinner was excellent but that the next time he wanted to sample proper Indian food.'

Ranjan stopped cleaning his ears with a tightly rolled up corner of the pillow-cover and asked excitedly, 'He really said that? Did he actually use the words "next time"?'

I nodded impassively. Ranjan broke into a broad grin. 'That's great. Really great. It means he wants to meet me again—informally, casually, at my home. Good, good, good.'

I noted his words a little sadly. 'Me', 'my home'. As if I had nothing to do with the success of the evening. I could have been a resident cook, or a hired caterer.

I thought of pointing that out but changed my mind. Ranjan was so obviously delighted with the news, he kept repeating it to himself.

'Excellent. That's good. He liked everything.'

A thought came unbidden to my mind. I was scared to even think it, but in my heart of hearts, I knew Tom had actually liked me. And perhaps felt a little sorry about the dismissive way in which Ranjan kept talking to me. I had sensed it strongly—Tom's embarrassment at Ranjan's attitude, not just once but at several points during the evening.

He had also succeeded in catching my eye. I had immediately averted my gaze and feigned non-awareness. And it wasn't out of fear. I knew that had Ranjan even succeeded in intercepting those few looks, he wouldn't have been able to decode them. Ranjan was far too full of his own anxieties and preoccupations to notice what transpired between other people. Just as well.

And now he was busy exulting, his voice high-pitched and choked with excitement. 'I must call Ma first thing in the morning and let her know. She was so worried, so worried. She kept doubting, you know, doubting. I told her to relax. I said it was all right. Every wife is not an expert cook. Besides, he is a foreigner. Even if one or two of the dishes weren't good, there would be something for him to eat. That's why I'd insisted on the baked dish. These people simply love cheese. See how they gobble up pizzas and all that? I tell you, I used to hate junk food when I was there. Just hate it. But no choice. Ma used to send me a few dry snacks through relatives, but how long did they last?

'Anyway, I'm glad Tom said he wanted to come back. It's a good sign. He's giving me a green signal for my other work. I will definitely follow it up in the office tomorrow. These people don't understand our systems, the pace at which everything happens in India. They expect computer precision for things. Impossible, I say. "Make it possible", Tom insists. But how? My hands are tied. After today, no problem. The ice is broken. Very good. Very good. Now everybody in the office will get damn jealous. You mark my words, damn jealous.'

I said my prayers while Ranjan continued to talk with a ring of childish animation in his voice. As if he had won a medal for speech day.

'Tomorrow everybody in the office will know that Tom has been to my home for dinner—just see how their attitude will change now. That's the whole problem here—everybody is busy doing chamchagiri to the bosses. Not me. My invitation was straight—no buttering up. Just straight. Please come over to my home for dinner, that was all. And Tom immediately accepted. No fuss. It shows the high regard he holds me in. Other people have also tried to call him home. Do you know something? He has refused. Yes, just like that. Said, "Sorry, maybe another time".'

I half-listened as Ranjan spoke on. In any case, he wasn't really talking to me. He was reassuring himself. I was happy for him. It obviously mattered a great deal that Tom had honoured us with a home visit. Now it was upto Ranjan to maintain the cordiality and informality that had been established over the evening.

In any event, Tom didn't seem like a typical overbearing white boss to me. The stories I'd heard from my father about English bosses in Calcutta tea companies had led me to believe that white people in power were the worst sort of tyrants—petty bullies who preyed on the insecurities of the locals. My father used to describe them as boorish, arrogant, rude and altogether despicable. He had narrated enough stories about his own humiliation at their hands. Slights small and big that he had never forgotten nor forgiven.

My mother would sniff, 'Snobs. That's what the angrez really are. The world's worst snobs. The issue is, why we as a people don't have more pride, more self-respect? Haven't you seen the way our people behave in the presence of white men? Go to any Calcutta club and you'll see these fellows lording it over us while we stand with our heads bowed, ready to swallow any and every insult. It you ask me, we deserve the way they treat us.'

But Tom didn't seem to be anything like that. He was so natural and so polite, he made Ranjan appear boorish and insensitive. But then, I'd heard that Americans were different.

They believed in equality. They treated colleagues as colleagues, not as bonded labourers or slaves.

Tom was young—just a year older than Ranjan. I wondered about his family life—what were his parents like? And his home? It was difficult to tell from his dress whether he came from an affluent background. My father had told me that with Britishers you didn't scrutinize their clothes ('always shabby') but their accents. The way a man spoke indicated his status in life. And after years of working with them, my father's ears had learnt to distinguish between upper, middle and lower class accents. He considered himself something of an expert. My mother too had taught herself to sift out the trash from the aristocrats (not that Calcutta attracted aristocrats in droves).

With Americans, class distinctions merged into a generalized blue denim blur. Jeans had turned out to be the great levellers.

*

'So . . . impressing the boss-man last night, were you?'

Nikhil was at the door holding out an envelope, a mocking smile on his face. For a change, I didn't feel defensive (maybe I too had been affected by the dinner's success like Ranjan).

'Why not? Do you think it's your parents' monopoly?' I answered, my expression arranged carefully to match his insolent one.

'Relax, Maya. I'm glad for you. Good. Good. I thought only my mother played these silly one upmanship games. I guess you aren't all that different. Office-politics, chamchagiri, sucking up to the white man . . . All part of the game, huh? Well . . . I hope you didn't burn the food as usual.'

I bristled at that (like a fool). 'How dare you make such a comment? And how would you know about my cooking ability anyway?'

Nikhil stretched out his hand to give me the envelope he was holding. 'Invitation. To my mother's beauty workshop. Seven hundred bucks. Two days. Lunch and tea included. You must attend it . . . and get that moustache bleached.'

My fingers flew to my upper lip (he'd done it again).

'I don't have a moustache,' I half-screamed.

'That's not what your mirror will tell you—if you ever looked into one, that is,' Nikhil taunted.

I tried changing the subject by asking irritably, 'Who told you about our dinner, anyway? Nobody at the office knew about it.'

Nikhil laughed uproariously, 'Maya, Maya, Maya. Don't they teach you anything in Calcutta? Nothing remains a secret in Bombay. Nothing. In any case by now you should know how the building grapevine works. It's not everyday that a white saab looks for parking space downstairs and then asks for directions to the Maliks' flat, geddit dumb-dumb?'

He turned on his heel smartly, blew me a kiss and left. I cursed myself for having fallen for his bait. Again. I stared hostilely at Pushy Pushpa's invitation in my hand and flung it away. That angry action took care of the beauty workshop. That left Nikhil to deal with. I vowed to myself I would handle his unannounced intrusions into my life more competently in future. I would prove to him what 'Maya from Calcutta' was capable of if she really set her mind to it. I'd wipe that smirk off his face. I would . . . I would . . . kiss him.

Thirteen

I awoke on a late November morning and discovered a sharp, pleasant nip in the air. At first, I thought I was imagining it. Perhaps Ranjan had left the air-conditioner on longer than usual. But no, he had switched it off the moment he'd woken up, a habit I had grown used to. Like everything else in the house, the air-conditioner too was exclusively his, to be switched on and off at his convenience.

So, if it wasn't the air-conditioner, what was it? I rushed to the balcony and took a few rapid deep breaths. Something had changed. The air smelled different, and there was a thin grey veil draped over the city. Could it really be the onset of 'winter' in Bombay? I hadn't known it had one, and even now I wasn't sure.

I turned back into the bedroom excitedly to check with Ranjan. He had finished his bath and was struggling with a knot in his shoelaces preparatory to putting on his shoes. It was a pretty comical sight—Ranjan clad in just his underpants and socks, grappling with a pair of highly polished (by me) shoes and cursing under his breath.

'Ranjan . . . I think it's winter. Did you look outside? It's beautiful and misty.'

Ranjan snorted. 'That's pollution, not mist,' he explained and cursed again.

'Don't say that,' I moaned, 'it always gets this way in Calcutta at around this time of year. And then the Ghariahat market overflows with superb vegetables and fish.'

Ranjan was now standing in front of the mirror, combing his hair carefully. 'Bombay is not Calcutta,' he said in a preoccupied way, as he examined the slightly thinning patch on his crown. 'In Bombay we don't have mists and all that—just a fog of foul air. By tomorrow, you'll be coughing and coughing. Your lungs will be choked.'

I continued to stare out of the window. 'But won't it get cooler? I can already feel it.'

Ranjan said, 'That's your imagination. In Bombay, we only have two basic seasons—hot and wet. That's all.'

Suddenly, without a preamble, I blurted it out. 'Ranjan, I've decided to join a few classes. Pottery and things like that.'

Ranjan stopped the close examination of his scalp and stared at me suspiciously.

'What?' he said, his eyes wide with disbelief. 'Classes? What sort of classes? That's nonsense.'

I pretended to fold already folded washing and continued mildly, 'I have so much free time, you know, after my housework is finished. I thought I should do something good . . . constructive . . . You know, learn something. Why waste time?'

Ranjan sat down heavily on the edge of the bed.

'Learn? Time? I don't know what you're talking about, Maya. Housewives don't have extra time—there's so much to be done around the home. What extra time are you talking about? Take Ma's example. She is busy round the clock. She has never gone to some useless classes. What will you do learning pottery or whatever that nonsense is?'

I placed the clothes on the ironing board.

'I've always been interested in pottery. In fact, I was very keen to go to Shantiniketan after finishing college. I also wanted to learn painting and batik. I'd love to take some basic lessons—and then, of course, I'll do it from home.'

Ranjan put on his favourite blue shirt as he stared into the mirror. 'You have to give me a shock early in the morning. Just when I was preparing myself for an important meeting. I tell you, all a husband expects is a little consideration before he leaves for the office, not these sort of threats.'

I stopped what I was doing and turned around in amazement. 'Threats? Have I threatened you? How can you say that, Ranjan? All I want is to learn pottery. It's only a matter of two hours twice a week, that's all. It won't interfere with my household duties, I promise you.'

'Is all this necessary? What will you do with pots?' Ranjan grumbled.

'Don't call them "pots" like that. Pottery can be so artistic and beautiful. I used to love looking at photographs of Mohenjodaro samples when I was a child,' I said, trying to keep the edge out of my voice.

'See, Maya, in Bombay it may be considered very fashionable for housewives to take all these meaningless classes. But how does it actually help you? Or us? And besides, they cost quite a bit, don't they?'

I started tidying the room nervously even though it was perfectly neat.

'I'll have to find out the exact fee, but I know it isn't too much since the man who's conducting these classes teaches from his flat and the raw material is cheap—just clay to start with.'

Ranjan stiffened, suddenly alert. 'Man? Which man? You didn't tell me the classes were run by a man. My God, Maya, don't you think about these things? Do you know what you could be getting into? These so-called classes are often nothing but recruitment places.'

I was genuinely puzzled. 'Recruitment for what?' I asked, plumping up a pillow.

Ranjan struck his head noisily with the palm of his hand. Since he was sweating, it made a flat 'thwack' sound. 'For prostitution, what else? Bombay is the country's biggest recruitment centre. And to think my wife was going to walk straight into a trap like that. Imagine the embarrassment I would have suffered. And my family, of course. Once you are in, there is no way out. Finished. Your life is over. These sort of men are high-powered pimps who prey on women like you. Strangers to the city. Women who don't know enough about the world. First they tempt you with all sorts of flattery, next they make you their slaves—then there is no choice left. You understand?'

Even as I listened to Ranjan, my mind was wandering off in a crazy direction. I felt strangely flattered to think that my husband imagined a sharp-eyed pimp would be impressed enough by me to lure me into his den using pottery classes as a bait. How incredible it sounded! And how amusing, really.

In the background, I could hear Niki Marx talking about the Oklahoma bombings with a short report on the O.J. Simpson trial. Ranjan had turned down the volume when I began the conversation and now he was far too agitated to pay attention to Niki. This was again quite flattering, since I was sure he had a crush on her. At any rate, he did admire Niki tremendously, often commenting on her clothes and hairstyle ('Red really suits her. See how smart she's looking today. But this hairstyle needs to be changed a little—what do you think?').

I admired Niki too and often fantasized about her life. How exciting it seemed. How challenging too. Something dramatic, something new happening everyday. During my college years, I used to dream about becoming a journalist and changing the world. My parents took their newspapers very seriously. While my father read the *Ananda Bazar Patrika* diligently (holding die paper inches away from his face), my mother preferred *The Telegraph*. As she would explain, 'The issue is, news presented in the old dull way is no longer news. In order to attract readers, one has to move with the times. I grew up on *The Statesman*. But then, that was before *The Telegraph* was started. Now, if you ask me, this is the paper to read.'

At that point, my father would snort into his fifth cup of tea for the morning and mutter dourly, 'What news? Only gossip and photographs.'

I had to admit I didn't read either. And yet, the thought of taking up journalism as a career excited me. Each time my tram trundled past Writer's Building or the offices of *The Statesman*, I would imagine myself working there, reporting on world events, interviewing prime ministers and presidents, attending important press conferences and being taken seriously, very seriously, by everybody.

But I was far too lazy to try my hand at freelance writing. My mother would urge me, 'Why be afraid to speak your mind? If you have something to say, put it down on paper. That's the way to self-discipline. Look at me—till today, I note down everything, including my thoughts.'

Yes, I had seen my mother's 'thoughts' as she put it. Unlike my father, who meticulously copied down reams of romantic poetry in English and Bengali, my mother hunted out and noted down the darkest quotes and the most depressing comments. I don't know where she found them. But each time I would flip idly through her 'thought book', I would feel low and morose, as I read the extended passages dealing with suicides, death and reincarnation.

*

I was quite young when I first noticed my mother's morbid preoccupation with violent and unnatural ways of ending life and felt slightly disturbed by the obsession. I had also noticed that my mother would always be most animated when discussing, for example, a stranger's gruesome accident, lingering over the smallest, goriest detail. It was only during these conversations which she sometimes had with my father that I would see my mother's eyes light up with excitement and her voice go up by a few decibels.

On his part, my father would grunt occasionally to indicate that he was listening. But that half-hour session really belonged to my mother. She would recreate the incident and invest it with imaginary characters who harboured malevolent motives. I wondered why she hadn't tried her hand at crime fiction since she seemed so clever at inventing complicated plots.

This in itself was not worrying—after all, some people were excited by football scores, others by suicides. It was when I would chance upon her talking softly to herself that I would freeze. When I was much younger, I would tiptoe around her at such times to retrieve a toy or cross into the adjoining room. If she noticed my presence at all, she didn't bother to interrupt her monologue with the phantom figure. She would glance in my direction in an absent sort of way and continue talking without the slightest self-consciousness.

Later, perhaps afraid of my reaction, she would stop abruptly, hold her breath, glare pointedly and wait for me to leave. I would feel guilty too, as though I had trespassed during a secret rite. Once or twice I had hidden behind a door and tried to overhear her communion with whoever or whatever it was she needed to share her thoughts with.

I was almost certain she was addressing her dead sister—an aunt I remembered only hazily since she had passed away when I was only seven years old. I had been told by my grandmother that the two sisters had been inseparable. And that when Amritamashi had died suddenly of typhoid, my mother had lapsed into a prolonged depression, often refusing to get out of bed. Inconsolable and grief-stricken, she had also stopped talking to people—my father included.

Initially, the two families—my maternal and paternal grand-parents—had thought this was a natural reaction to the loss of a sibling separated in age by just one year. But after six months of non-communication, they had jointly decided to summon a witch doctor from the famous Kalighat temple. My father had been the only one to strenuously oppose the move, registering his protest vociferously in his feeble, high-pitched voice. Nobody had paid the slightest attention to his objections. Nobody ever did.

And so, a wild-eyed, wild-maned scrawny man was produced at dawn and led to my mother, who had stared at him unseeingly before falling into a swoon. The relatives had exchanged significant looks, while an aunt said, 'See, she has fainted. That confirms it. Poor Chitra is possessed. Let's get everything ready for the rite.'

I had been at home when it happened, and it was an event I could never forget. I had cowered near the door, terrified by the dark stranger clad in a flimsy loincloth which clearly outlined his genitals. He had begun to sway rhythmically while chanting mantras that sounded suspiciously like nonsense rhymes.

My mother had continued to lie lifelessly on the cold ceramic-tiled floor. I remember feeling embarrassed for her since her saree had climbed up well above her knees. I was seeing my mother's taut, hairless thighs for the first time. I had seen my uncles staring curiously at them too, while my father had kept his eyes carefully averted, making it clear that he was certainly not a party to what was going on.

By then, the aunts had got busy lighting agarbattis and oil lamps in preparation of the ceremony to follow. Someone whispered, 'Will a chicken be killed . . . or a goat?'

The witch doctor had begun rolling his eyes and flagellating himself with a light jhadu. I had seen his genitals moving obscenely as he spread his legs and leaned back, his matted hair sweeping the floor behind him. He had demanded some water in a copper vessel and peacock feathers if they were available. An aunt had rushed to the downstairs neighbour's house and come back waving the graceful tail feathers of the national bird. My mother hated them and refused to keep them in the house like most families did ('to scare the lizards away', as one of my uncles had explained).

The witch doctor had sprinkled water on my mother's face and stroked her body with the feathers. She continued to remain motionless. His chanting had become louder and more aggressive as he danced around her form, genitals jumping jerkily under the loincloth. Still, nothing had happened. The witch doctor had reached inside a tattered cloth bag he had brought with him and triumphantly produced a skull.

There had been an audible gasp in the room as the relatives stepped back reverentially for the finale.

'It's the dance of death,' my aunt had whispered, as my father shrank further into a corner and I held my breath. I had expected something dramatic to happen though I wasn't sure what that would be. Maybe, I thought, my mother would suddenly leap up and join the crazed-looking man in a macabre *pas-de-deux*.

The witch doctor had carried on vigorously with his skull dance, leaping around my mother and letting out banshee-like screams that scared the sparrows off the window sill. Finally, drained by the effort, he had collapsed in a heap, sweating and panting in exhaustion.

Everything and everybody had suddenly been very still, as if awaiting a miracle. I could see my mother's right leg begin to twitch and then the movement continued all the way upto her arm. Soon her entire body was convulsing spasmodically, as if a strong electric current was being passed through it. One of the aunts had started to wail while a low moan escaped from my mother's firmly clamped mouth.

The witch doctor had raised his head and motioned for everybody to be quiet.

'The spirit has been awakened,' he had intoned. 'Let it speak.'

Minutes later, my mother had opened her eyes and risen slowly to her feet, but it was obvious she couldn't really see. There had been no signs of recognition, only deadness. The witch doctor had commanded her to speak. She had swallowed, raised her head and spoken.

It hadn't been her voice at all. Nor was it her natural language. An aunt had hissed, 'It's her sister talking—of course it is. I recognize Mita's voice. That's exactly how she used to speak.'

The witch doctor had shut his eyes and held his palm up. It was hard for me to tell what exactly it was that my mother was saying, since the shock of her changed voice was troubling me. I had looked for my father and seen him near the window with his eyes tightly screwed up and his hands over his ears. I had wanted to go and stand as close to him as possible since I had suddenly felt cold and my teeth had begun to chatter. But to do that I would have had to cut across the room and make my way past all those people. The prospect had terrified me. So, I had continued to stand near the door and shiver while my mother had spoken to the assembled gathering.

The tone of her voice was calm. And her body was still. I noticed she had altered her posture. The characteristic stoop was missing and she was holding herself very straight and tall. I had recalled seeing poorly taken black and white photographs of my aunt and her in which Mitamashi had always seemed to tower over my mother only because she didn't slouch, not because she was taller.

The witch doctor had placed his hands over my mother's head and recited a long prayer. The relatives had stood with bowed heads and folded hands. Except for my father who had looked utterly disgusted and faintly annoyed.

The prayers had continued for a while as my mother's dialogue began to peter out, finally becoming an incoherent unintelligible mumble. The witch doctor had pranced around the room excitedly, sprinkling 'holy water' on everybody and chanting 'Shanti, shanti, shanti' repeatedly. All the aunts had looked pleased while my father had left the room abruptly, his disgust apparent to all.

I had been far too confused to know what I was supposed to do. But I recall cringing when the witch doctor had come up to me to anoint my head with the holy water. I couldn't really see beyond his outsized genitals which were at eye-level, making them appear even more menacing than they were before. And my mother? She had had a strange calm about her as she straightened her saree and smiled benignly at everyone.

Unfortunately, the so-called exorcism had not freed her of her sister's ghost. On the contrary, her conversations with Mitamashi had increased in their frequency, the only difference being that these lonely encounters were no longer furtive. Whenever I came home from school and heard my mother's animated voice, I knew she was in communion with her dead sister.

If these prolonged sessions bothered my father in any manner, he never showed it, preferring to listen raptly to his radio or read and re-read the day's newspaper. Eventually, I began to take my mother's morbidity for granted, even inventing gory stories for her benefit and then laughing in private over her searching questions. Her suicide fixation too stopped upsetting me. I dismissed it as yet another quirk, a spillover from her sister's premature death.

Instead, I became a willing accomplice, often drawing her attention to violent deaths and bloody accidents. It became something of a game—and my mother conveniently forgot to draw it to a close.

Fourteen

The first time Ranjan went out of town on business, I was tempted to take the next train back to Calcutta. In plain words, I was terrified at the thought of being alone in an impersonal Bombay flat. I could have moved in with my mother-in-law or my maternal uncle. But that would have been just the sort of cowardly act that would have instantly elicited a mocking sneer and an uncharitable comment from Ranjan.

'Will you be able to manage?' he had asked, as he threw open his cupboard and started selecting appropriate shirts and ties for the trip.

'Of course,' I replied even as my heart fluttered violently.

'Sure?' he asked again, this time examining his neat pile of well-ironed handkerchiefs.

'Sure,' I assured him as I pulled down a heavy suitcase from an overhead loft.

'You can always stay with my mother,' he half-challenged, waiting for me to contradict him.

I shook my head firmly and stuck to the 'I'll manage' line.

'Or,' Ranjan paused, 'you could ask your dear mother to come here for a few days. That might be a good change for her.'

It was obvious he was baiting me. 'She's busy these days,' I said quickly, adding, 'In any case, I've no problems.'

He stared thoughtfully at his image in the mirror.

'As such this is a pretty safe building. Plus, your good friend Pushpa is there to take care of you . . . in case there's some emergency. The neighbours are all helpful—don't you think so? Just make sure you keep the latch on at all times. Don't let strangers into the house. And sleep with a light on.'

The last instruction amused me hugely, since it was Ranjan who hated the dark and insisted on keeping a night lamp glowing through the night.

'Don't worry about me,' I said softly.

He chuckled at that. 'Funny . . . but I do worry about you. I don't think you've ever been entirely on your own before, have you? It can be a frightening experience.'

I guessed from the way he spoke that he was referring to his own fears when he first went to study in America. I said cautiously, 'The first night may be a little frightening. After that, I'll get used to it. I did go on a college trip once but that was different since there were three other girls in my room.'

Ranjan asked for a duster. I scampered off to get it.

'When do you leave—tomorrow?' I said as I examined his shoes. He nodded and jerked his head in the direction of the suitcase.

'So much dust in this house, my God. Clean that first—especially from the inside, or else my shirts and underwear will get dirty. And after that, find me matching socks. Check whether the shoes are properly polished. I won't have time to clean them there.'

I got down to the job immediately. 'Where's there?' I asked.

'What?' Ranjan said irritably. I repeated my question.

'Half the time I can't figure out what you're saying. Your way of speaking is quite strange. And very abrupt. If you're asking where I'm going, the short answer is—on tour. And before you want to know my precise travel plans, here they are—Delhi, Bangalore, Cochin, Calcutta and back. Five star all the way.'

I tried to look impressed.

'Jealous?' he teased.

'Very,' I responded.

'Well, well, well . . .' Ranjan smirked, 'these are the perks of a job like mine. Work hard, play hard, as the Yanks say. That's my philosophy.'

He checked the bag carefully, especially the crevices. 'My mother always stored the bags in muslin or plastic covers. That way, they stayed clean. I think you should do the same in future.'

I nodded passively. 'How long?' I asked.

'How long, what?' Ranjan countered, his eyebrows knotted, his lips curling up.

'How long will you be away?' I enunciated.

Ranjan threw up his hands. 'Why can't you speak normally and ask normal questions like everybody else? Why do you speak in short-hand? It drives me crazy. Didn't they teach you to speak properly in your school or college? Our teachers in Bombay were very strict about such nonsense.'

I stared at him with mild amusement before asking, 'Dinner?'

Ranjan exploded. 'There—you're doing it deliberately. I know it. You want to annoy me—why? Speak like I do, for God's sake. What the hell do you mean by saying "dinner"? What am I supposed to understand from that?'

I said calmly, 'I'm sure you got what I was saying. It was my way of asking when you want to have your meal—now or later. There was a question mark at the end of the word. Didn't you notice?'

Ranjan shrugged exasperatedly. 'Notice what? How does a man "notice" a question mark in a conversation? I think you're going mad. It's either the Bombay weather or Bombay itself. Maybe you should go back to Calcutta for a month or two. You obviously need a change.'

'Sick of me?' I asked, my voice half-serious.

Ranjan chuckled. 'How can you say such a thing, madam? You are my wife.'

I continued to look for his missing prey socks.

'Men do get sick of their wives,' I said a little sadly.

Ranjan scratched his ear thoughtfully. 'That's true. But not this soon. Let's see . . . how long have we been married—do you remember?'

I refused to answer. Ranjan came close to me and pulled my hair playfully. 'You are getting too serious . . . too intense . . . like all Bengali women. My mother always says, "Be careful with Bengali ladies, they are the most hysterical women in the world".' He seemed immensely pleased with that comment.

'Does she include herself?' I asked, trying to keep my voice even.

'You shouldn't be asking such a question. She was referring to girls your age, of course.'

'Am I hysterical? Do you find me unstable?' I demanded. I must have looked rather silly, standing as I was with two different coloured socks dangling from my hands.

Ranjan shook his head fondly. 'Don't worry, my dear,' he assured me, 'you are too sweet. Besides, I like it when you get a little angry. Not too angry, mind you.'

I smiled to myself. Ranjan was in good spirits at the prospect of a five star, ten-day trip. In his place, I would have felt the same way. He was escaping the turgid monotony of our daily life. I would have given anything to jump on that plane and fly away. It wasn't Calcutta I longed to go to but some distant, unknown destination. Each time I would see glossy pictures of an exotic resort in a magazine, I would shut my eyes and place myself in the azure blue of the pool or on the inviting slopes of a mountain.

Invariably, I would be alone and in search of adventure. The daydream would exhilarate me and for those all too brief moments that I fantasized, I would be filled with a strange hope.

One afternoon as I lay on my bed flicking channels and wondering what to do next—tackle Ranjan's socks' and underpants' drawer or water my thirsty plants, I saw a rivetting image on the screen. A man and a woman were swimming like playful dolphins in an azure lagoon, their bodies moving gracefully through what looked like coral reefs. As if unaware of their presence, schools of iridescent fish darted past them while dappled sunlight created magical patterns over their taut limbs. I found my cheeks wet with tears. How beautiful the image was. And how blissful, the couple.

I became the woman in the orange bikini, and Nikhil, my underwater companion. Like innocent children, we swam holding each other's hands trustingly. The azure lagoon became our home and we, the only occupants of that amazing world. I visualized us emerging from the water onto an island filled with tropical birds of incredible hues. Nikhil would dry my wet body with a bright yellow towel and lead me to our shack in the middle of a rain forest. And there we would remain—me with a hibiscus in my hair, swaying in a hammock strung between fruit-bearing trees. And Nikhil close by chasing exotic butterflies across a waterfall.

My sporadic longings induced an unbearable sadness in me. Of course I knew none of this would ever happen. Not with Ranjan. And certainly not with Nikhil. I would never see a rainbow arching over a distant mountain. It was foolish of me to dream. I switched channels abruptly to break the spell. Strange how my fantasies rarely went beyond the travel-brochure level. Why didn't I for instance, have the courage to take them further—from a deserted beach to a secluded bedroom? I simply didn't. Even the thought was threatening. Nikhil never appeared naked in my dreams. And I of course always remained chastely covered.

Not that it mattered. These little breaks, even though they left me feeling immeasurably depressed, served as safety valves. It was easier to attack Ranjan's cupboard and rearrange it enthusiastically after a precious reverie . . . even if Ranjan never figured in it, Nikhil invariably did.

Now, as I went into the bathroom to look for Ranjan's shaving kit, I felt slightly jealous and resentful that it was he who was going somewhere—anywhere—and me who would be left all alone in a flat I didn't feel at home in at all. It was also the first time in my life that I would be on my own. The dark had never held any fear for me, even in Calcutta. I wasn't afraid of spirits or ghosts, but of intruders. Ranjan seemed to have a great deal of faith in the security system in our apartment block, but I had none. Even during the daytime I would find all sorts of strange characters strolling in and out of the building with great nonchalance. Who were these people? And why didn't anybody stop and question them?

The Nepali nightwatchman was usually sleeping on the job and the Bihari day fellow indulged in some nifty moonlighting, running small errands for servantless residents. Even though our flat was secured with heavy bolts, the windows could be opened with a light push and the ledge outside our bathroom—with conveniently placed pipes next to it—seemed far too inviting for a cat burglar not to want to scale it. There were grills, of course, but that would hardly stop a slick city burglar in his tracks.

I swallowed rapidly a few times and tried to distract myself. The BBC woman was going on about Bosnia (again) and Ranjan was listening in rapt attention. It always annoyed me to see him so preoccupied with countries, people and situations that had so little to do with us. I had asked him about it once and he had answered shortly, 'In this age of globalization, it is important to know what's going on in the world. You should also pay attention sometimes or else you'll make a fool of yourself at our bank parties. Wives of promising officers are expected to be well-informed.'

'Is that upstairs woman—the stupid beautician—well-informed?' I had asked cattily.

Ranjan had wiped shaving foam off his face and said, 'Nobody expects her to know anything about Bosnia.'

'Why?'

'Oh—because she's a beautician. She has a profession. She earns her own livelihood. She makes money—see? You don't. People would wonder what you do all day since you aren't really occupied. You don't want them to think you spend all your time watching Hindi movies, do you?'

I had started to fling bedsheets and pillow covers angrily into, a heap for washing before saying in a raised voice, 'I don't care what your bank people think of me. Let them say I'm retarded, dumb, stupid, useless. Let them imagine me watching Hindi films all day. What does it matter. Or do you want me to tell them the truth—huh?'

Ranjan had glowered. 'And what is the truth?'

Heatedly, I had shot back, 'The truth, dear Mr Malik, is that you have me here as a fulltime, domestic servant without pay. Shall I tell your colleagues that? And also tell them that you've forbidden me from pursuing a career—even a part-time one. And in any case, does your promotion depend on whether I know who's bombing whom in Bosnia?'

Ranjan had looked very taken aback and finally stumped. He had glared at me for a second or two in stupefied silence and then retreated abruptly into the bathroom. I had bitten my tongue, regretting the outburst, and made a vow never to discuss BBC or CNN with my husband.

*

A couple of days after that conversation, Ranjan had come home and tossed casually, 'Maybe you should look out for something to do in the afternoons—you know—to further your hobby.'

I had smiled to myself at his choice of words. By reducing my textile designer's degree to a 'hobby' he had indicated just exactly how much he valued it. I had avoided a response by nodding my head vaguely and saying, 'Not now. There are too many things to do around the house. Maybe later . . . next year.'

Even though I couldn't see Ranjan's face at that moment, I knew it must have registered great relief. I wasn't being contrary when I said what I did. At that point I didn't at all feel like scouting around for some measly freelance assignments. To begin with, my self-confidence needed bolstering. Acquiring a degree in Calcutta was not the same thing as proving myself in Bombay.

Yes, had I been in my home town, I would have known how to go about getting a break. I would have enlisted the help of my professors and made use of the meagre contacts my parents had. But here in this ferociously competitive city, I didn't know the first thing about job hunting. From what I could gather through Ranjan's conversations, one needed to be mega-influential to get a toehold anywhere. And who did I know in Bombay? Only sweet old Prodipmama. And who did Prodipmama know in Bombay—other middle-level Bengali executives.

The feeling of inadequacy and failure was leading upto resignation and defeat. I had given up any hopes of ever getting a job in Bombay. I knew that Ranjan's mother could have helped me if she wanted to since she did deal with people associated with the arts in the course of her various charity works. But I was far too intimidated by her to make the request. Just as I couldn't approach Ranjan for help. Pride? Could be. Or it could have been the fear of scorn and rejection.

I had begun to trivialize my chosen vocation even to myself. I had taken to being slightly apologetic whenever people asked me what I did.

'Well . . . I've trained as a textile designer . . .' I would say with an embarrassed little laugh and then shrug, to suggest it wasn't something I took very seriously. In any case, at that point most people would lose interest and turn to someone who had more to say or looked more important.

The same sentence evoked very different reactions in Calcutta. Eyebrows would go up and I would be asked what made me choose that particular line and whether I had always been interested in textiles.

I had noticed that in Bombay people didn't really listen closely to anything or anyone. And people were not interested in nobodies (like me). I had known of course that this was a very success-oriented city (Ranjan and my mother-in-law couldn't emphasize the fact enough) but it continued to amaze me as to how easily a person could be dismissed and marginalized for not being a big-shot—someone known and influential.

To the people I met through Ranjan, I was a non-person—just another housewife from Calcutta. An alien being who did not speak with the right Bombay accent and wasn't in tune with the city. Very often, colleagues of his didn't even bother to be polite. After a cursory greeting, they would turn their attention to other matters, leaving me to amuse myself. Ranjan too would abandon me with a clump of gossiping women and rush off to 'circulate' (his favourite word in social situations). The 'bank wives' couldn't have been less interested in me since I didn't shop at the same places or watch the same television programmes. The few professional ladies with jobs of their own preferred to spend the evening with the men making it very clear they weren't there to waste precious time with mere housewives with nothing to do but talk about promotions and office politics.

I was a complete misfit whichever way I looked at it. Often, I would spend the entire evening with a strained smile and anxious eyes that tracked Ranjan's progress around the room. Even though Ranjan tried to project himself as something of a loner, parties always brought out a charming, sparkling side of him. Unlike his colleagues who tended to drink too much and eventually make fools of themselves, Ranjan scrupulously stuck to two small whiskies which he nursed right through the tedious (for me) evening. Whisky made him garrulous in a lovable way. He laughed much more and conversed with easy informality. He even ventured into mildly flirtatious quips with the women, complimenting them on their choice of sarees, accessories and make-up.

This was a completely different Ranjan from the one I knew. And I felt very attracted to him. Unfortunately, his party mood ended abruptly the moment we got into the car for the drive home. He would assume his characteristic scowl and glum expression. If I tried to make light conversation, often apeing the women at the party, he would turn to me with puzzled eyes which said, 'What's wrong with you now?'

I could never be light-hearted with Ranjan. It was sad, because I longed to giggle and joke and be foolish occasionally. But Ranjan firmly discouraged such conduct. It was as if he had a certain mental picture of a 'wife' and I had to conform to it—no lapses permitted.

On a couple of occasions, the 'bank wives' had told me what they thought of Ranjan. 'We call him either "Bengali babu" or "Babumoshai",' one of them had simpered, casting sidelong glances in his direction.

That was another thing about Bombay—instant slotting. Every community had its stereotypes and despite its cosmopolitan boasting, Bombay only reinforced these caricatures. People from the south were 'Madrasis', even when they were from other regions. Gujaratis were 'Gujjus', Maharashtrians were 'Ghatis', Bengalis were 'Bongs' and Punjabis were 'Punjus'.

In the beginning, I had resented this 'Bong' business. The first time I was asked 'Don't tell me you're a Bong', I had been stupefied. The woman had laughed and placed a conciliatory hand on my arm. 'I hope you didn't mind that remark—but in Bombay that's what we call Bengalis.'

I had smiled weakly, swallowed and turned away. That night, as I lay in bed with Ranjan breathing heavily next to me (not out of passion—he just happened to be a very noisy breather), I asked him how he felt about such derogatory terms.

Ranjan had put down the business paper he was reading and said, 'Look, it has stopped bothering me. And it shouldn't bother you either. People don't mean it negatively. That's how everybody talks in this city. Why be so sensitive to it? There's nothing wrong in being a Bong! It's not an abuse or something. Forget it.'

So, I forgot it. Once or twice, I even pre-empted the remark by announcing brightly, 'Hello, my name is Maya . . . and I'm a Bong.' No one found it funny. The more I interacted with people, the stronger I felt about our differences.

'You are too damn intense,' Nikhil had once told me, 'Stop looking for hidden meanings in everything—okay? Be normal. Act normal. You get worked up about the smallest things. Remember people here are far too busy with their own lives to bother about hurting your precious feelings. It sounds very cruel—but nobody gives a shit. You live. You die. Bombay ticks on. People make money, people lose money. Who cares? Nobody.'

As always, our meeting had been an impromptu one. I was busy haggling over five rupees with a mosambi-seller and he was rushing off to wherever it was he was always rushing off to (I never asked).

'Stressed out?' he'd teased in an off-hand way.

'Don't make a joke of everything,' I'd snapped irritably. And that's when he had launched into his little lecture on my 'intensity'.

I had felt slighted and small. Here was a younger person—a mere college student—giving me advice, when it ought to have been the other way around. I realized only later that it was a basic survival lesson that Nikhil had given me. He was being a friend when he advocated toughening up.

He was also very right about my thin skin. I hadn't been so touchy in Calcutta. But then I hadn't been so miserable either. My vague depression (a constant) had to do with loneliness. Crippling loneliness. There was nobody, but nobody I could talk to, turn to, in Bombay.

It wasn't as if I had had hundreds of friends in Calcutta or that I was an extrovert there. But there was always someone I could call, someone I could spend a few minutes with, someone who spoke the same language—my language. Bengali.

That was another thing about Bombay—people didn't converse in their respective mother tongues. They preferred a strange brand of English or mangled Hindi. It was a rough, crude dialect picked off the streets which people spoke out of necessity. It hurt my ears, it jarred with its harsh cadences, its hard emphasis. I was repulsed by its basic, functional rhythms. Where was the poetry, the subtlety, the romance of Bengali? Bombayese sounded abusive even if it wasn't. It was vulgar and offensive.

Nikhil had corrected me when eventually I voiced these sentiments to him. 'Expressive. That's what it is Maya. People use it because they get understood. Nobody wastes any time. Where is the need to go into flowery speeches? And who the hell has the time for them anyway?'

He was right, of course. Nikhil was right about a lot of things. But the short-hand adopted by Bombay people was an assault on the ears and I doubted whether I would ever get accustomed to it or even less likely, start speaking like that myself.

Fifteen

With Ranjan gone, I experienced a strange emptiness. At first, I thought I was bored and lonely. But it was much more than that. Bombay was experiencing its annual ten-day 'winter'. Compared to Calcutta's two-month long high season, Bombay's ten cool days were something of a joke—but an eagerly awaited one, nonetheless.

I sat by the window after Ranjan had left for the airport at dawn and watched the sky grow gradually lighter. The morning star was glowing brightly on the eastern horizon which had taken on the colour of pale pink flamingo feathers. I thought of my mother as I stared at the luminous star and wondered how she was—she no longer wrote regularly, and the news I got about her from Prodipmama was sporadic and sketchy.

I felt uneasy about it. My uncle wasn't the kind to be evasive or off-hand. Was he trying to hide something from me? Was my mother ill? When eventually I had confronted him with the question, he had rung off abruptly, insisting that there was a visitor at the door. Ranjan, of course, had locked the out-station phone facility before leaving, saying, 'You won't be needing it—so why not take the elementary precaution of locking? I hear there is a lot of misuse these days. And God knows our bills are high enough.'

Ranjan was obsessed with bills—all bills. Not a day passed when I didn't receive an extended lecture on curtailing expenses. 'My mother is not an economist,' he would remind me, 'but look at how well she manages.'

Well, my mother was a frugal housewife too, but then, she wasn't married to a bank officer on a generous salary. What did Ranjan do with his money? Why was he so mean with it? It was far too sensitive a topic and he hated any references to it. The few times that I had dared to raisé it, he had regarded me coldly and asked, 'Are you having any particular problems? Is there a shortage in the house of anything? Are we not comfortable enough—or is there anything you require?'

I had retreated quietly and never brought up the subject again. Before giving me a brotherly peck on the cheek, picking up his battered briefcase, shrugging into his jacket, and checking his image in the mirror, Ranjan had carefully counted out a thousand rupees—a hundred for each day of his absence from Bombay.

'I'm leaving a great deal of money with you,' he had observed. 'I expect you to be careful with it. Just because you have a thousand rupees in your hand does not mean you can blow it all up on some rubbish. Try and live within fifty rupees a day. In case there is an emergency, you can always contact my mother. But don't bother her unnecessarily. She'll get alarmed.'

I had accepted the proffered notes gratefully. It *was* a great deal of money compared to the twenty and thirty rupees he normally left for daily expenses in a special box on my dressing table. My first thought was, 'Oh good, I can buy myself a one-way train ticket to Calcutta and never come back.'

But that was only a childish impulse. Who or what awaited me in Calcutta? Even the thought filled me with some dread—would I go there only to find my mother on her deathbed? My dreams had been forewarning me about such an eventuality but I dared not find out for myself.

I sat around dully, unsure of what to do with myself next. This was ridiculous. Ranjan being out of town on a weekday morning was no different from Ranjan being away at the office. And yet, I felt abandoned and horribly isolated. There was nobody I could phone for a chat. Nobody I could call over to keep me company. Nobody for me to visit. And nothing for me to do.

The waves of self-righteousness and self-pity were making me teary and I disliked that. I found tears unattractive and almost revolting, as did my mother. She had always discouraged weepy breakdowns all through my childhood with a lofty, 'Stop that tap flowing—there's no shortage of water in this house.'

My father had been only slightly more sympathetic. His way of dealing with my crying spells was to gently march me into the bathroom and wash my face. It was as tender a gesture as he was capable of. And I particularly liked it when he dried my sore eyes with a lightly-woven cotton napkin that he always hung over his left shoulder. It had a special smell—my father's smell. A very specific combination of Brahmi hair oil, Lifebuoy soap, mustard oil and Himalayan Bouquet talcum powder.

He was very particular about changing his napkin twice a day. It was one of the few things that he fastidiously adhered to, explaining to my bored mother that it was a matter of 'personal hygiene' since he wiped his mouth with it after all those cups of tea throughout the day. He kept his napkins in a neat pile by the side of his armchair—six crisply ironed ones at a time. And he deeply resented it if, occasionally, my mother forgot to replace the soiled ones.

That morning, I thought of my father's napkins and broke down. What was I doing here in a city that wasn't my own and with a man for whom I didn't feel very much except a feeble affection? Ranjan was my husband. I was supposed to love him, respect him, miss him. And all I was feeling at that moment was relief at his absence. So many contradictory emotions to deal with. While I hated the thought that I'd be alone in our home, I also felt free of pressure, free of approval-seeking, free of being judged, watched, corrected, scolded, nagged, pushed, instructed. The guilt this induced in me was horrible. Was I really such an uncaring, cold and selfish person? Why was I not longing for my husband's return like a loyal, loving wife? Why was I, instead, all but revelling at the prospect of ten days on my own? Ten days of insecurity and vague fears, no doubt. But ten precious days to myself, nevertheless being my own person?

The truth was, Ranjan made me tense. Ranjan also made me self-conscious. I never felt free to be myself when he was around. Was it his smugness that froze me? Or his judgemental, supercilious attitude that conveyed superiority over me? In my generous moments, I did recognize some of Ranjan's better qualities. But that didn't stop me from feeling resentful most of the time. It was no use telling myself that I was lucky compared to women married to alcoholics or wife-beaters. Ranjan had his faults, but he was not an evil man and I knew in my heart of hearts that he wished me well. He was generally kind to me, but his kindness was the sort people reserved for the physically handicapped or the abject poor.

Didn't he ever wonder what went on in my head all day? What bothered me, affected me, depressed me, made me happy? Why was there no curiousity, no questions other than those related to domestic matters?. Why did he never notice the changing expressions on my face? Or ask me, even once, whether or not I was happy being married to him?

The clock was making a racket or so it seemed in the silence of my small, neat, soulless flat. I couldn't bear its incessant ticking and rushed into the kitchen to glare at it angrily. If the doorbell hadn't rung just then, it was more than possible I would have hurled a frying pan at it and broken its ugly glass face in a rage.

I went out onto the balcony to get some fresh air. The sky was overcast with dark clouds. It did nothing to lift my spirits. Suddenly, there was an ominous rumble and a few drops of rain splashed against my cheek.

I went back into the kitchen. I thought about my collection of indoor plants which I had placed so carefully in the balcony for a little sunshine between showers. Normally, I would have rushed back and brought them in. Today, I felt drained of the energy to make the effort. I gazed at them sadly as the water level inside the glazed ceramic containers rose steadily and overflowed. The roots were sure to rot. It was only a matter of time before the lush, lovely leaves would drop off. Too bad. I would have to start on a new collection all over again—that is, if I wanted to replace my dying plants. They had been with me from the time I had come to Bombay—one or two had accompanied me from Calcutta—the ficus and the dresinia. During their first few months in their new environment, they had drooped and nearly withered away, discouraging me from acquiring new ones. But soon I had understood their redefined needs and made the necessary adjustments. Less watering, more sun and lots of fresh air.

My breath was coming in short, sharp, shallow gasps as if someone was choking me. My forehead was covered with beads of perspiration. I steadied myself against the refrigerator and took a few deep breaths. I was going crazy—that was the first thought that crossed my mind. Never before in my life had I experienced such despair. I didn't feel like answering the door—or dealing with anybody or anything that day. I told myself I would skip lunch and forget about having a bath. What difference would it make?

*

The bell rang once again, followed by a knock. Reluctantly, I walked in slow motion towards the door and opened it without taking the precaution to secure the safety chain in place. And there, standing silhouetted against a backlit door frame, was Nikhil, whistling tunelessly.

'Where the hell were you?' he asked aggressively.

I didn't bother to be polite. 'How does that concern you?' I asked, sounding equally aggressive.

Nikhil walked past me and sat down heavily in the nearest chair. 'Shit!' he exclaimed.

I continued to wait by the door. Even he hadn't noticed me or my state. At my heightened level of persecution, I placed Nikhil in the same category as Ranjan and felt an upsurge of utter contempt as I watched him sitting inelegantly in the chair, cursing God knows whom or what under his breath.

Finally, when there was a slight pause, I said coldly, 'And now, if you've finished, please leave. I'm in no mood to listen to your abuses.'

That's when he whirled around to look at me. 'God,' Nikhil snorted, 'what's the matter with you?' He got up from the chair and came up to me.

I was quivering with anger while waves of helplessness swept over me. I knew I was a minute away from a flood of hostile tears. Nikhil gripped my shoulder and shook me.

'You're looking awful. Go wash your face quickly. Are you ill? Jesus—I thought only my mother behaved like this.'

I pushed his arms away. I could smell him clearly and see the stubble on his cheeks as if I were peering through a magnifying glass—each hair breaking through the glistening skin. I could tell by his breath on my face that he had just stubbed out his cigarette before entering my home. And that he had eaten eggs for breakfast before that. The overly-spicy fragrance of his after-shave made me slightly giddy. And all I really wanted was for him to get out that instant and leave me alone to wallow in my misery.

The front door was still open and I pointed to it, saying shortly, 'Please . . . I don't feel like talking to you.'

Nikhil followed my eyes, went upto the door and shut it firmly. He strode back, his eyes questioning and a little hurt. 'Have I said something to upset you? Did I do anything wrong? What's the matter? Are you tense because your husband isn't in town?'

I was startled when he said that. 'How do you know that?' I demanded, my voice strident and unattractive.

Nikhil shrugged and said with utmost naturalness, 'I was up early . . . I saw him get into a cab with his bags, that's how I know, okay? Don't worry. I'm not spying on you. It's just a bloody coincidence.'

I hadn't moved at all. My voice was cracking as I said, 'Just because you saw my husband leaving town does not give you the right to barge into my house. Where were you all these days, anyway?'

I realized how foolish I sounded the moment I had uttered the words. Nikhil burst out laughing—he threw his head back and roared. I didn't know then what he had found so funny even though I did feel instinctively that I had made a mistake.

'So, that's what all this dramabazi is about. Why didn't you just say that you missed me? And that you are angry and hurt—huh? So much simpler to be direct . . . honest . . . like I am.'

I started to shake my head vehemently. 'That's not at all what I meant,' I protested. 'It's just that I'm feeling a little scared in this place all by myself. And I'm annoyed that you've turned up after disappearing for so many days.'

Nikhil pulled out a pack of cigarettes. 'Even if you do mind, I'm going to smoke,' he announced lighting one. 'Exams,' he explained. 'I was busy with my finals. And my results arrived today. They weren't very good. My mother is going to be angry.'

I nodded without really caring whether he had failed or passed.

He went on, 'No—I didn't flunk. But my grades aren't good enough to get me into an engineering college. So that's it. I'll have to stick around and rot here. I missed the required aggregate by just two per cent. Imagine. Two per cent can change the course of a person's life. Now I'm screwed. I'll have to think of what to do with my life. Any ideas?'

'You could join films. Or television,' I said dully.

'I take it you are paying me a compliment. So . . . you do find me good-looking. I knew it.'

Nikhil was beginning to get on my nerves with his self-assured swagger that didn't go with my flat. 'You could become a pop singer and appear on all those crazy TV channels,' I carried on, my mind filled with images of Nikhil jumping up and down on a trampoline for some odd reason.

He stubbed out his cigarette on a porcelain dish that didn't double as an ash tray and abruptly went into my bedroom. I stood rivetted to the spot, my heart pounding. I couldn't figure out what he was upto and I certainly didn't know how to deal with it—whatever it was. Feeling unsure and foolish, I wondered whether to follow him in and once again urge him to leave or wait for him to emerge.

I decided on doing the latter. Five minutes or so later, Nikhil came back into the living room, zipping up his fly. 'Had to go—sorry,' he said cheerfully.

I stared at him disbelievingly. 'I hate your attitude. You really have no manners whatsoever. How can you just land up at my home like this and loll around as if you are in your own bedroom? I'm not used to such rude behaviour. I have never met anybody who dares to act like this.'

Nikhil looked unperturbed. 'How about a cold coffee—with lots of crushed ice? Come on, relax, Maya. You are so uptight. What great sin have I committed? I felt like seeing you, and I'm here. It's true I turned up knowing your husband is out of town, but that makes sense, doesn't it? Be honest. You don't really expect me to visit you when he's around. You'd be embarrassed, he'd be angry and I'd be uncomfortable—right? This is cool.'

He shot me a look. 'Why don't you stop behaving like some silly Bengali film heroine and just calm down? I'm not going to rape you or anything. I won't even touch you, if that makes you feel better, okay? Let's just chat and laugh and listen to some music. I'm feeling awful today. So are you. I need cheering up. So do you. Now, off you go—cold coffees for two. Got it?'

Numbly, I went into the kitchen and reached for the coffee jar. I realized I was doing things automatically, like a programmed robot. Nikhil was fiddling around with Ranjan's stereo and my mind was completely blank. I didn't want to look at the clock and wonder what time the woman who did the dishes would turn up. All I knew was that Nikhil's presence had started to lift up my spirits ridiculously. I didn't care who saw him there or what the consequences would be for me later. I didn't care if at that very moment Ranjan had walked into the house saying his flight had been cancelled.

I didn't even care if my mother-in-law herself chose to arrive right then. I would deal with it. But first, I would jerk my neglected mixi to life and get it going. The last time I had made cold coffee for anyone had been years ago. I had almost forgotten how much pleasure it was to get a frothy moustache and coffee stains on one's pallu.

*

Nikhil was staring moodily out of the window when I went back into the room with the coffees neatly arranged on a small tray. I watched his back and became acutely conscious of my own shabby appearance. How must I have looked through his critical eyes? Like a slothful, neglected housewife with uncombed hair and an oily face—my permanent state, I reflected a trifle sadly.

If Nikhil did notice my self-consciousness, he let it go. Perhaps he was far too preoccupied with his own poor results.

'Cheers,' he said cheerlessly, holding up the heavy ceramic mug.

'Does your mother know?' I asked.

'Know what? That I'm here with you or that I've flunked my chances of becoming an engineer?'

'Both,' I replied.

Nikhil swung his legs over the arm of the chair. His sneakers were muddy and splitting at the seams. That was something new.

'No,' he said, 'no to both your questions. I'll tell her later. About my percentage, nothing else. She doesn't have to know every goddamned thing about my life. Where I go, who I meet, what I do. She's not my personal policewoman. I'm old enough to decide such stuff.'

'But if she did find out that you were here, would she mind? I'm sure it would upset her,' I said.

'I'm sure too. But that's really her problem, not mine. Let her deal with it.'

I sipped the coffee nervously. 'Your father would be furious too, right? He'd speak to my husband about it. And then, he'd get furious. And we'd both be in trouble. Big trouble.'

Nikhil grinned. 'Right. Absolutely right. Does that make you scared?'

I nodded. It was true. I was terrified, and I couldn't pretend to the contrary.

Nikhil smiled carelessly. 'You are so sweet and innocent. Honestly. It's such a change. I mean . . . the sort of girls I meet— you know—the typical Bombay girls—God, even twelve-year-olds are bolder than you.'

I blushed, unsure whether the comment was meant as a compliment.

'Listen, Nikhil . . . whether it's in Calcutta or Bombay, a married woman is not supposed to meet other men. That's all.'

Nikhil shrugged. 'Supposed to, not supposed to. I don't believe in such rules. Each person should be free to do whatever he or she wants to, that's it. And I know you want me to be here with you. Besides, we aren't doing anything wrong, just chatting like two normal human beings. So forget it. Forget all those "supposed to's".'

I wished I could. I wished my conversation was different. I wanted more than anything else to laugh and converse freely and ask Nikhil a thousand questions. Instead, I said stiffly, 'Do you do this often—visit married women after making sure their husbands aren't in town?'

Nikhil laughed lightly. 'All the time. My diary is crammed with the travel schedules of various husbands. In fact (he glanced at his watch), I'm due at Peddar Road in another twenty minutes. There's another bored housewife waiting for me there.'

I found myself laughing and feeling very foolish.

'What do you mean, "another bored housewife"? I'm not bored, for your information. Don't presume so many things—okay?'

Nikhil threw up his hands. 'Let's get out of here. Come on. Be daring. Do something spontaneous for once in your life. Put on a pair of jeans and let's go. I'll show you some interesting places . . . even buy you lunch. Stop thinking, Maya. Hurry up or else it will get too hot.'

I half considered Nikhil's suggestion. 'I don't own a pair of jeans,' I said lamely.

'That's all right. Think of a better excuse. Change your saree, in that case. I can't take you out in a crumpled one—my image will be ruined.'

I looked shamefacedly at the creases in my saree. I had slept in it and it showed. Nikhil gave me a light push in the direction of the bedroom.

'Go,' he commanded. 'I don't have all morning.'

I remained rooted to the spot. 'What about your mother? What if someone sees us? What about the watchmen and servants?'

Nikhil got up and went towards the door. 'Listen, all this is very tiring and stupid. If you are going to think like this, we'll never get out of here. By the way, your flat is most depressing. And dingy. Why don't you get some air and light into it? How do you breathe in here? Or think. Or relax. Phew! I'd die of suffocation. No wonder your husband has left town—which man can bear to live in such surroundings. And I used to think all Bengalis were *maha* creative. I expected your home to look like a Satyajit Ray movie set—not an antiseptic hospital room.'

Nikhil's cool arrogance suddenly got to me and I flared up. 'How dare you walk in here uninvited and start criticizing my life, my house and everything? Who has given you the right—huh? I'm quite happy with the way things are. And I don't care what you think. Now please leave.'

Nikhil regarded me coolly, a small smile on his face.

'Relax, Maya. Cool it. Don't get so hyper—even though you look very cute when you're angry. Listen . . . lighten up. Don't behave like an ordinary housewife, because you aren't one. Stop pretending to be someone you want the world to believe you really are. I'm only being a friend. You think I have nothing better to do with my time? I could be loafing around, swimming, at the gym or playing tennis. Why am I here? Because I like you. I genuinely do. And I've liked you since the day we first met—satisfied? Now . . . you are free to do what you want. Stay home and suffer. Go nuts for all I care. Or come for a ride with me—it's up to you.'

As I stood there uncertainly, I felt utterly low and miserable. At that moment, just about everything seemed wrong with my life—all the choices I'd ever made. My marriage, my decision to move to Bombay, my cowardice at not asserting myself vis-à-vis Ranjan, my giving up a career—even my standing there and allowing a younger man to talk to me like this. I felt it was wrong—completely wrong. I felt I was being disloyal to Ranjan, to my parents, to all that I had grown up believing in. I wanted Nikhil to go away.

And yet, there was the other pull tugging me in the opposite direction. With just a little encouragement from him, I was ready to jump on Nikhil's motorbike and say 'goodbye' to my uninspiring life without the slightest regret. The choice was frighteningly mine.

Without a word to Nikhil, I went into my bedroom, found a fresh saree, locked myself in the bathroom and changed into it. I wasn't sure whether Nikhil would still be outside when I emerged. But it didn't matter. I was determined to get out of the house anyway and find out if I was still in love with Bombay, or if even that had died within me.

*

The heat was far less oppressive riding on the pillion of Nikhil's motorbike. If I licked my lips with the tip of my tongue, I could taste salt brought in by the strong sea breeze.

'The tide is coming in—look,' said Nikhil, pointing to the bay, as he wove his way nimbly through the mid-morning traffic. I looked, but moving my head at that awkward angle gave me a crick in the neck.

'Next time, don't wear a saree,' Nikhil advised. 'Invest in jeans and sit astride. You'll feel safer and be able to see much more.'

I nodded obediently. The way I was perched so precariously behind him was making me decidedly nervous. First, there was the obvious awkwardness to deal with. I didn't want to touch Nikhil. Which meant I couldn't hold onto his shoulders or waist as I could observe other pillion riders doing. I had to cling to a handle positioned behind the seat with my other hand resting on the luggage rack. My feet were left to dangle, often touching the asphalt of the highway clumsily. My entire concentration was on maintaining my balance as Nikhil negotiated his way past monstrous goods lorries, vagabond taxis and behemoth buses.

Nikhil rode his bike with authority and obvious enjoyment. I was the one feeling awkward and as though everybody was staring at me.

'Where are we going?' I asked Nikhil loudly, since I didn't want to lean too close and have my breasts brush past his back.

'No idea,' he said cheerfully, 'but we'll soon find out.'

I smiled at that—it was a typical comment that wasn't meant to be taken seriously. It was remarks like this that made me wonder whether Nikhil took anything seriously at all. And if he was indeed this lighthearted, what he found in a boring person like me. Me with all my anxieties and fears.

He stopped on the top of Malabar Hill. 'This is it. This is where I wanted to bring you. This is Bombay at its prettiest, especially now while the gulmohurs are in bloom.'

I clambered off the bike and stood by him quietly. It was undeniably an impressive sight and I couldn't imagine anybody remaining unaffected by it. From that vantage point, it was possible to survey the dramatic sweep of the entire city with its erratic topography. It was equally easy to ignore the blanket of smog hanging over it and concentrate on the seascape and high rises sticking out of the skyline like metallic fingers.

'Beautiful, isn't it?' Nikhil asked.

Visibly moved by the view, I nodded silently.

'Do you come here often?' I asked.

'Very,' he answered, 'nearly every day. I never tire of the sight. In any case, it changes depending on the time of day and the season. I'll bring you to watch an October sunset from this spot. Now that's something. I don't know what happens to the environment in that month but the sky looks spectacular with fascinating cloud formations. Sometimes, if you're lucky, you get twilight and this entire garden is bathed in a golden glow. I've . . . I've written a song about it. Maybe I'll sing it for you later.'

After parking his bike, Nikhil and I walked upto the famous garden constructed over an enormous water tank. As we walked, we crushed hundreds of gulmohur blossoms that had drifted down from the graceful boughs, creating a mottled orange carpet on the sidewalk beneath our feet.

Nikhil was withdrawn and thoughtful. I imagined him composing a fresh song about his favourite spot in Bombay and didn't want to disturb his concentration.

'Feel like a beer?' he asked after we had walked for ten minutes.

'Beer?' I said, my eyes betraying my momentary shock.

'Why not?' Nikhil continued, 'I'm thirsty. Aren't you?'

'Yes . . . I am, but beer? I don't drink. I mean . . . I haven't . . . that is, I'm not accustomed to anything alcoholic'

Nikhil smiled a devilish smile. 'Good—great. Now is the time to begin. Why waste another moment. To sip a perfectly chilled glass of beer on a hot day like this is to experience the true meaning of life. Come on, try it. God will forgive you. Promise.'

I was tempted to sulk, something I would have done with someone else. Instead, I asked petulantly, 'Do you always make fun of people like this?'

Nikhil grinned. 'Always. But Maya . . . you aren't "people". You are Maya. And I'm not making fun of you. Don't get so bloody serious about everything. I'm only asking you to take a few sips of beer—it's an innocent enough suggestion. You can refuse if you don't want to. But why make such a production out of it?'

Nikhil was right. What he probably didn't know then (and nor did I, for that matter) was that it was my utter lack of experience with men that was showing. I didn't know how to speak to them, deal with them, behave with them or react to them. And because of my natural inhibitions, I ended up being snappy and curt.

I apologized to Nikhil, who shrugged and led the way to a place called Naaz Cafe. As we climbed up the narrow staircase to another level, I felt that everybody was staring at us and commenting on the incongruous sight—Nikhil, so obviously a younger, college student, and me, so obviously a married woman with bright red sindhoor in the parting of my hair.

I wondered whether he too felt conscious about being seen with me. After all, I wasn't one of the countless Bombay women—trendy, carefree, bold and couldn't-care-less. I had 'married' stamped all over me. And, with all that vermillion in my hair, it would have been easy enough for anybody to even identify which part of the country I was from.

Suddenly, I felt shabby, dowdy and ugly. Ashamed to be so out of sync with this glamorous city where every woman felt obliged to make her presence felt by taking the trouble to dress up. And here I was looking so drab, so frumpy, with a younger man clad in torn jeans and scruffy sneakers—symbols of his generation that were quite alien to me, who was only a few years removed from it myself.

'People are staring at us,' I whispered to Nikhil nervously.

'Don't be silly, Maya. This isn't Calcutta. Nobody stares at anybody here. People don't give a damn. They're far too busy with their own worries. Just relax.'

I wished I could. It had been hard enough leaving our building. I had refused to prance out with Nikhil and insisted on his getting out of the flat first (after carefully checking through the peephole that nobody was around). I followed a safe five minutes later with 'guilt' written across my face. Nikhil was waiting for me at a crossroad, a short distance away and I was certain nobody, but nobody, had seen me. Even so, I had felt the world's eyes boring holes in my back and I had climbed onto the bike in such an agitated state, I had nearly displaced Nikhil from his seat.

We found a table near the edge of the large balcony. Nikhil had obviously been to this unpretentious cafe before since he greeted one of the waiters by name and was hailed in return like a familiar friend. The beer arrived promptly along with two thick, chipped and decidedly dirty glasses. Nikhil poured carefully, making sure not to spill anything. I stopped him from giving me more than a few sips, and he didn't argue.

Raising his glass, he said a trifle too dramatically, 'To sunsets . . . to Maya . . . to new dawns.'

I must have looked exceptionally pleased for he leaned over, looked intently at me and said softly, 'That's nice. You are smiling with your eyes. It suits you, Maya . . . you're beautiful. Believe it.'

Immediately, I shrank back into my chair and stiffened. 'Please don't say such things. I feel very embarrassed.'

Nikhil caught his ears in both hands and said, 'Okay. Sorry. No more compliments. So . . . what shall we talk about—the Enron project, Mani Ratnam or Medha Patkar?'

I was only half-listening to his easy banter. The view was distracting me far too much. I was equally curious about the people at the other tables—were there others like us, mismatched in every respect?

I looked around cautiously. Nearly every chair was occupied but it was hard to tell whether those people were from Bombay or tourists who had come to look at the Old Woman's Shoe in the adjoining park. Not that it mattered. It felt so good to be out of my house, out of that locality, just out.

Surprisingly, I was no longer weighed down with guilt, nor did I want to think about the consequences. I wasn't even sure what those might be. For all I knew, Ranjan would ignore my 'confession' (if I ever dared to make it) and start questioning me about some undusted piece of furniture or a missing shirt button. And as I reasoned with myself, I wasn't doing anything sinful or wrong. It just so happened I was married.

That didn't prevent me from longing for an innocent outing like this and grabbing the opportunity to enjoy it when it presented itself. Nikhil was a younger man and I was acutely conscious of the fact. He was being nice to me—that's all, since he seemed to have recognized my loneliness and claustrophobia.

I gazed at the slow moving cars along Marine Drive and nearly missed Nikhil's next remark which was, 'How do you like Bombay now—without your husband in it? Is it better or worse?'

I was confused by the question. I didn't know what the implication was. Nikhil's intention to provoke me was clear enough but I didn't have a good enough answer ready. I tried being evasive and ended up sounding dishonest.

'My husband has nothing to do with what I feel about Bombay,' I said loftily, my accent echoing the one I had left behind in Calcutta.

'No?' Nikhil mocked. 'Who do you think you're kidding?'

'Let's change the subject please,' I suggested, gulping my beer a little too noisily.

'Fine,' Nikhil said mildly, 'I don't want to ruin our outing. My reason is selfish. If you have a lousy time today, you won't come out with me in future.'

I smiled weakly and asked, 'You must know hundreds of girls . . . girls of your own age, from your own background. Why are you bothering to waste your time on someone like me? We have absolutely nothing in common. In fact, I'm sure you find me a big bore—don't you?'

Nikhil nodded his head vigorously. 'That's the first smart thing you've said. You are dead right—I find you a big bore. But, like that TV ad goes—"What to do? I'm like this only". I happen to enjoy being with bores. Satisfied? Really Maya . . . you are so full of complexes. I wish I'd met you earlier. Haven't you had a good friend in your life? Someone sensible who would tell you a few things about yourself? Each time I meet you, I feel like I'm standing in front of the Narmada Dam and that any moment the flood waters could gush out and drown me. I actually feel nervous thinking about what could happen to you if you opened up the sluice gates of your heart.'

My fingers gripped the beer glass so tightly, I could see the knuckles turning white. Nikhil reached across the stained tablecloth and touched them lightly, saying, 'It's okay. I don't want to push you into saying or doing anything you don't want to. I have absolutely no right to probe into your life. And you are not obliged to listen to me . . . or my cheeky questions. Maybe your husband is a great guy. That's your good fortune. But I can't help it if I just cannot imagine you married to him.'

I looked up, my eyes filled with tears, and said an almost inaudible 'Don't.'

Nikhil looked away quickly and started whistling tunelessly. It was getting oppressively hot. Even the proud gulmohurs were beginning to wilt. I thought about what I would have been doing on an average day had Ranjan been in Bombay. Looking at my watch, I realized it was close to lunch time and I hadn't even bathed—just jumped into a fresh saree at Nikhil's bidding and rushed out of the house blindly. What if my mother-in-law had phoned and found me missing? What if Nikhil's mother had put two and two together and figured out that we were with each other? What if Ranjan's flight was cancelled and he had come back home to leave his bags? What if my uncle had phoned to convey some bad news from Calcutta?

With an effort, I dismissed all the 'ifs'. And then I remembered—I had completely forgotten about all the bais who must have arrived on schedule, found the flat locked and rushed off to their next jobs. That meant I would have to go back to a pile of unwashed clothes, dirty dishes and an unswept house.

The prospect filled me with dread. Then I told myself firmly that I wasn't going to bother—let everything remain where it was, as it was. My fastidious husband was not going to be around to nag me. I was free of housewifely duties for the next ten days. And it was time to enjoy this short-term liberty before it was snatched away.

Of course, I may not be able to sleep that night in a filthy house without waking up with nightmares. But I didn't want to ruin this moment by allowing my mind to crowd itself with these petty anxieties. I knew I was being selfish, horribly so. But this was just the outing I had been craving for ever since the day I had stepped off the train and felt Bombay under my eager feet. Feet that wanted to run from one end of the city to the other and explore every square inch of it. I refused to deny myself this simple right.

Sixteen

Nikhil was uncharacteristically quiet on the way home. When we approached our building, he asked me somewhat rudely, 'Where do you want to get off?'

I had been away from home for over four hours. I knew nobody was around waiting to clock me in and yet I felt uneasy about sneaking in. If Nikhil sensed my feelings, he chose to ignore them. I was hoping he would offer to visit me later or at least ask me my plans for the next day (knowing fully well that I didn't have any).

I hopped off the bike about half a kilometre from my house. He didn't turn around to look at me. I heard him ask disinterestedly, 'Are you sure you'll find your way back from here?'

I answered 'yes' in a hoarse whisper. He roared off seconds later, leaving me standing on a busy street looking completely-devastated. Nobody paid the slightest attention to me. My distraught appearance was lost on all the busy people rushing past me with ferociously preoccupied frowns. What were they thinking about so intensely? Why did everybody in Bombay look so worried? Was it the mugginess? The all-pervasive stench? The impossibly high cost of living?

I trudged back home with a heart heavier than my tread. I was hating the aftertaste of beer in my mouth and wanted to gargle. I needed a long bath and some sleep. Also, I didn't want to run into anybody who might connect my movements to Nikhil's.

As I entered the compound, the watchman told me conversationally that there had been several people looking for me. He himself had walked upto the flat and rung the doorbell several times.

I stared coldly at the man. I didn't like his monkey-like eyes at all. 'If there was no response, obviously there was nobody at home. Why the panic?'

He stared back shamelessly and said, 'But memsaab, you are always at home. You never go anywhere. And saab is also not in town. So naturally we became a little worried. Anything can happen in a city like Bombay. And that too, to an outsider. Who can trust anybody these days? When a woman is all alone in the house . . .'

I cut him short. 'None of this is your business,' I said curtly.

He shrugged and began picking his discoloured teeth with a twig. 'I am only trying to do my job and protect you. If you would rather handle problems on your own, suit yourself. But don't complain later that I didn't warn you.'

I patted my leather handbag (one of the better gifts I had received at the wedding) to make sure my house keys were in there. In my flustered state, I could so easily have forgotten to take them along. And then, I would have been forced to swallow my pride and approach the same swinish watchman for help. In all likelihood, he would have taken his revenge and refused to cooperate. In which case I would have had to go in search of a locksmith in the neighbourhood. I had absolutely no idea what Bombay locksmiths looked like or where I'd be able to find one.

Which would have meant phoning my mother-in-law from a public call booth.

And that would have led to a dozen embarrassing questions like, 'How is it you left your flat at this hour without anybody in it?' (Like who could possibly be in it if I was out of it?) 'What were you doing gallivanting around when your husband is not in town? Don't you know how risky that is?' (Yes, I do. And that's precisely why I was gallivanting.) 'What will Ranjan say when he hears about this?' (Like I care.) 'It was highly irresponsible of you.' (I should do it more often in that case.)

No. That would have been just too awful for words. As I slipped the key into its hole, I heard a female voice behind me.

'Oh, Mrs Malik, I came to your flat four or five times since morning. You see, I was told you know something about textiles—and my daughter is very keen on holding an exhibition-cum-sale to earn some pocket money. I was told by everybody that you're always in the house. Funny, I said to myself. Just the day I go and visit her, she's out. I also knew that Mr Malik has left for the airport early this morning—the boy who cleans your car and mine, told me so when he came to return the keys. That's when I decided to trouble you a little. You know how it is when husbands go out of town—we women feel so free. Our time becomes our own. We can relax, chat, enjoy a cup of tea with our neighbours. You don't mind, do you?'

I was still standing with my hand on the door knob. The woman hadn't given me a chance to open my mouth. Tiredly, I said, 'Come in,' hoping she would sense my lack of enthusiasm and say, 'Another time. You look a little unwell.'

Instead, she all but pushed past me in her hurry to get a foot into the flat. Before I could put my bag down or kick off my sandals, she had started walking around the living room, making small, throaty gurgling sounds.

I felt embarrassed to ask her name—I was probably spposed to know it, just as she knew mine. While I was wondering how I could ask her to identify herself, she announced shrilly, 'By the way, I'm Leena. Leena Mehta from the ground floor—flat number three. You know, the one with the bright curtains and lots of plants. I just love plants, don't you? In fact, I conduct ikebana classes from home. Bonsai too. I'm planning to open a small plant boutique. People keep telling me to do up their farm houses—landscaping, gardens, flower arrangements. But where is the time?

'I also do weddings—I mean, I arrange all the nice-nice things at the marriage hall. They say I'm a little expensive—but when you want something top quality, you have to pay for it. My wedding decorations are exclusive. Very exclusive. And different. I don't use the same old roses and lilies. Oh no. I go in for unusual materials, fantastic items.'

Disinterestedly, I asked, 'Like?'

She hesitated. 'Oh, like coconut husk, jute, handmade paper, shells, rocks—everything natural, you understand.'

I nodded listlessly. Inwardly, I was saying a little prayer, begging God to drive this irritating woman out of my house that very instant. I watched warily as she picked up the few brass objects I had around the house.

'Very pretty. Nice,' she said, not meaning a word. 'Must be from Bengal, no? That way you Bengalis really love your own things too much, I would say. Your culture, language, sarees and all that. Even gold jewellery. Being a Gujarati, I of course like my own type of gold work. But I have one Bengali kada also. Big. Not solid. You people make light, hollow jewellery, right? That is also good. People think it is more expensive than the actual price. Showy. And the polish of the gold is also different. Too shiny and reddish. We people prefer more yellow—like good gold is.

'Anyway, it's nice to have your own taste. Take your mustard oil. My God, everything has mustard oil, mustard oil, mustard oil. I know when you are cooking for your husband. The whole building knows, I suppose. What a smell. And your fish. I must tell you, Mrs Malik, that the fish smell comes down upto my flat level and my children complain. I tell them, "What to do? Neighbours are neighbours. Can I tell Mr and Mrs Malik what to eat and what not to eat? Will they listen?"

'Oh—I also have a beautiful saree from Bengal—not like the one you are wearing just now, of course. Mine is simply beautiful. It is called Tangail or something. So expensive—that too for a cotton saree. I can get five from Gujarat for the same price. But my daughters say "Mummy, you must have at least one Bengali saree like the film people." Young girls are like that only.'

I thought to myself how easily she had slotted me with her age group even though I was closer to her children's. Women did that constantly. Married women. It was as if by being someone's wife you automatically acquired a life membership to a club you had no real desire to join. Married women of all ages gravitated towards each other even though they had nothing at all in common apart from their marital vows.

This woman made me feel hostile. I felt like calling her 'aunty' just to make her aware of our age difference. But I held back my words just like I was holding back my tears. I wanted to be alone. I wanted to relive the morning, to reconstruct our conversation, to recreate the precious moments Nikhil and I had shared so recently. At this moment, I had no idea whether we would ever be able to meet again in this fashion, with the same spirit of adventure and the sort of recklessness that only desperation creates.

Foolishly, I had risked everything during the outing, Nikhil nothing at all besides a certain embarrassment at being seen with an older, married women—his mother's 'friend'. I felt irritated by that. What did I have in common with Nikhil's mother or this loud, obnoxious woman who was examining every nook and cranny of my home.

I heard her ask, 'And your mister—he's in a bank job, that much we all know. But why does he not mix? We are not all that bad, you know. My mister would like to get to know him—after all men prefer each other's company. They get bored with our talk, talk, talk. But I'm thinking your husband is on the reserved side. May be all Bengalis are like that. We Gujaratis—my God— two things we are very good at—talking and eating. We can do both without getting tired.

'Tell me, do you like Gujarati food? I can send you to sample—but please, don't mix up my dishes with yours, we are strict vegetarians. I was thinking for some time of sending you dhokla or something. Then I stopped. Frankly, I was scared. What if by mistake you put mutton or chicken or fish on my plate? Finished. Okay, do one thing—you send your plate to me. Much better idea. That way, no problem. No headache. Today only I'll send you something tasty. Hope you like it—no mustard oil. We only use til. Better for health.

'Now that I know you, we can meet often. Then, our misters can also meet. Mine is a businessman. We are traders, you know. Aluminium rods, pipes, all that. Maybe your husband can guide him. Bankers are very smart people—like that upstairs man, Mr Verma. Same bank, I think. But look at their show and look at yours. You people are simple. Their house—my God—so many imported things. Big, big TV, fridge, CD, everything. Nothing Indian. And the number of servants. Of course, Mrs Verma is a beauty woman. Where does she have the time to look after her house and family? Not like us, no? Fulltime housewives. I'm told she earns very well. And hardly any taxes. Everything in cash. These people have that knack, I must say. She gives facials at home also. Waxing, threading, everything. Have you tried?'

I shook my head miserably. Mrs Mehta stared worriedly. 'You are not looking well. See, all perspiration on your face. Sit down, sit down. I'll get you cold water.'

I snapped, 'It's all right. I'm fine. There's nothing wrong with me.'

Mrs Mehta called out from the kitchen, 'Oh my—obviously your maid didn't come today. Just look at the dirty dishes. Shall I send you my woman? For a few extra rupees, she'll do the work. But you'll have to watch her like anything—she steals whatever she can. Sugar, matchboxes, empty cartons, old newspaper, plastic bags, string. And money, of course.'

She returned with a glass of water. 'Here. Drink, drink.'

She was watching my face closely. And then her eyes brightened up.

'Now I've understood. You were feeling shy, no? There seems to be good news. We were all wondering—when will Mrs Malik start her family. Looks like it has happened. Don't deny it. Don't confirm it. I understand. I also used to be very superstitious and suspicious in this condition. Everybody's eyes are not the same. The world is a jealous place. Today I'm saying congratulations to you. Tomorrow I may curse you. What to do? Can anybody peep into someone's heart and see the truth?

'But I'm telling you frankly—I am not that type. God has been kind to me. I have children. Healthy children. One son. Two daughters. Why should I be jealous of you? By God's grace, my husband is doing well. We may not be wealthy but we have enough. Everybody is not like me. This building is full of jealous people. Someone gets a new car and people say they've used

Shobhaa Dé

influence. A man gets promoted and they say he has bribed his
senior. A girl gets engaged and the women insist she's already
pregnant. Very horrible, this building. The worst people are the
servants, watchmen and drivers. Take my advice and tell nobody.
You and I may not believe in the evil eye or black magic but I know
cases where women have aborted because of all that business.'

I didn't have the energy to correct her. Let her think whatever
she wants to, I thought to myself as I drank down large gulps of
water. I wished Nikhil was here. I wouldn't have cared about the
mess in my house or even my own grubby appearance. I would
have made him a cup of tea, a nimbu paani for myself and sat
around chatting companionably.

That was when it occurred to me that in all my longings
for Nikhil, not once had I imagined myself having a sexual
relationship with him. Then what was the attraction? Surely
not brotherly love? Even my acknowledging the lack of passion
in our relationship didn't make me want him less. Nor did it
confuse or bother me. I liked having Nikhil around. I felt good
with him. That was it.

It could have been a need for companionship, nothing
more, for I was desperately lonely. But why did Nikhil seek me
out? I was sure he had several friends and opportunities. I often
heard sounds of laughter as he and his college mates rushed
down the stairs. Or sometimes, late in the night, I would hear
the dying splutters of Nikhil's motorbike as he parked in his
father's garage and ran up.

Reluctantly, I turned my attention back to Mrs Mehta.
She had forgotten all about my state of health and was busy
examining a few photo frames propped on a Kashmiri rosewood
side table (Which my mother had insisted I take with me).

'Wedding pictures?' she asked cheerfully, when it was
obvious they couldn't be anything else.

I nodded dully. 'Nice, you look quite good here all dressed up,' she admitted, unable to keep a note of surprise out of her voice. 'Dressed up nicely also. Typical Bengali bride.'

She held the frame closer to her eyes and looked keenly at my jewellery. 'Gold, no?' she enquired.

'Yes,' I answered as shortly as possible.

'They gave or Mummy? Means, from your side or theirs?' Mrs Mehta continued her scruitiny.

'Does it matter?' I asked.

'Of course, my dear—what are you saying? That way, we also don't believe in dowry-showry and all that. But some amount of giving-taking, what we call *lena dena,* is still there—no? How I am planning for my daughter's trousseau from now only? Everything is organized, sarees, jewellery, even panties and bras from London. Top quality. Your mother must have also given you quite a lot. Only child or what?'

I got up abruptly and said, 'Mrs Mehta, I am sorry. I have got a lot of work to do. Plus, I have a headache. I will call you some other time, okay?'

She put down the frames with great reluctance.

'Fine, fine, fine. Next time I want to see your wedding video and all the albums, promise?'

I nearly pushed her towards the door. 'I don't have a video. We didn't take one,' I said abruptly.

She stoppecd dead in her tracks, whirled around and asked accusingly, 'Why? This is very great. These days everybody has a wedding video—even maidservants and drivers. Last month only the third floor driver got engaged. Two thousand five hundred rupees—only on the video. Music, titles, everything proper. Just like a professional film. I thought I was actually watching that hit, *Hum Aapke Hain Kaun.* Seen it?'

I confessed I hadn't. She circled her thumb and forefinger.

'Too good. Simply too good. I have seen thrice. With my family. And how much I cried.'

'Is it a very sad film?' I asked indifferently.

'No, no, no. It is not sad but touching,' Mrs Mehta said triumphantly, obviously proud of herself for making such a distinction. With that she was gone, leaving me to feel intensely sorry for myself and the mess everything was in.

*

Ranjan phoned from Delhi that night. He sounded so happy, I very nearly didn't recognize his voice. It was high-pitched, and he sounded terribly excited about something.

'Are you okay?' he asked. 'Or should I phone Mummy?'

I was tempted to say, 'No, I'm not at all okay. In fact, I'm thinking of killing myself right after I put down the phone.'

I didn't say that, of course. Instead, I mumbled something—anything. Wifely sounds. He wasn't listening anyway.

'I'm fine, just fine,' Ranjan continued, 'good flight, great room. Flowers, fruits and chocolates. All complimentary, of course.'

I smiled at that. Ranjan was really quite easy to please. Why didn't I make more of an effort to do so, in that case? All I would have to lay out were a few roses, a bar of chocolate, and ripe bananas.

'How did you spend your day?' he enquired, and then carried on about his own without waiting for an answer.

I half-heard him. For one, I was sleepy. For another, hungry. I hadn't eaten anything the whole day. It was some sort of silly penance. I was punishing myself for God knows what. My head was spinning and my eyes shutting. I'd kept every single light on and the TV was blaring film music.

Ranjan paused. 'I can hear a lot of noise. What's happening?' he asked, a worried note coming into his voice.

'The TV is on,' I replied.

'Lower the volume, I can hear everything clearly in Delhi,' he commanded.

Weakly, I whispered, 'I'm scared Ranjan. I'm really very scared.'

He didn't hear me. I heard an electronic beep indicating three minutes were up. And then the phone went dead. I cradled the receiver close to my cheek and drenched it in a flood of tears. An actress was gyrating wildly on the small screen and urging viewers to help her discover what exactly lay behind her skimpy blouse. It was an old song, and it reminded me of happier times.

I didn't know how I would be able to survive the night. I wanted to call my mother in Calcutta. Not that she would have understood my anxieties, but at least I could have sought some comfort in hearing her familiar voice saying sternly, 'The issue is, you must grow up. You are no longer a baby. Husbands travel. It's part of their work. You'll have to get used to it. Or else, convince jamaibabu to employ a fulltime maid. If he doesn't agree, pay your part-time woman a little extra while he is away and request her to keep you company at night. That is the only solution. And another thing—don't panic. Panic is the worst thing. You can't think straight if you panic, remember that. I hope you know how to dial the police number. Where is the nearest police station? Close, I hope. It's also good to keep other emergency numbers—the fire brigade and ambulance. Nothing is going to happen to you, but just in case.'

Yes, just in case. Paralyzed with fear, my head crammed with all kinds of absurd images, I sat on my bed, clutching a pillow and staring with terror-stricken eyes at the menacing shadows cast by the looming branches of the neem tree outside my window. I didn't dare move, not even to switch on the fan. The question of having the air-conditioner on in Ranjan's absence did not arise, of course.

Ruby, the bubbly Veejay hosting a popular music video programme, was about to barge into a stranger's home and ask the servant boy there whether he would like to marry her. I couldn't concentrate on her either—and she was my favourite. Whenever Ranjan allowed me to watch her, that is.

I'd read somewhere that she was more or less the same age as I—and yet, her life was so totally different. I felt a pang of jealousy. She looked as though she was having so much fun. She also looked like she didn't have a care in the world. I liked the way she dressed, talked, joked and danced. I was sure she never had to worry about cooking, cleaning or pleasing someone.

Which reminded me—I had left the dirty dishes in the sink exactly as I had found them earlier. And that was about the only thing that made me feel good as I lay awake all night, dreaming of a large bird swooping down on me, claws out.

Seventeen

By 3.30 a.m. I knew there was no point in forcing myself to sleep. I was far too tense and fearful to even shut my tired eyes. I tried it all—watching television, drinking a glass of milk, reading a boring book, even lying in the classic yogic posture that guarantees relaxation.

I could hear the watchman's rhythmic tapping of the large stick he carried at night, as he did his rounds. It was reassuring to know someone else was awake in the hot, sticky stillness of the night. I had bolted myself into the bedroom and yet I feared the prospect of an intruder breaking in. I began to hear all sorts of troubling noises, mainly footsteps approaching. I also imagined I heard somebody repeatedly clearing his or her throat (the sounds were too muffled for me to be able to tell for sure whether they emanated from a male or a female).

The furniture in the room creaked noisily, while the bathroom door rattled once or twice with such force that it was as though there was a gale raging outside. I had left on the lights, the TV and my handy little transistor radio. I had hoped that the three combined would make me feel more confident and less terror-stricken. But by 4 a.m., I knew it was useless and

I gave up the struggle. I reached for a small pad I kept on 'my side' of the bed and began a letter to Nikhil:

Dear Nikhil,
It's very late in the night. Rather, it's very early in the morning. You are probably fast asleep dreaming about your next motorbike adventure. I don't know why I'm writing to you or even whether I shall let you read this. It's just that I felt I'd left our communication incomplete. Basically, I wanted to thank you. Not a polite expression of gratitude for a "very pleasant morning", but something far deeper. I do realize that in the eyes of society, I should not have spent a morning with you when my husband was not in town. In any case, as a married woman, I have no right even to talk to you privately as I do, without my husband's knowledge. This is wrong, and I feel ashamed that I am being disloyal to a man who is loyal to me (of this, I'm certain). And yet, from the first time I met you (that absurd meeting with your mother insisting on your calling me "aunty"), I felt I wanted to spend time with you and get to know you better. I should have stopped myself at that very point since I was not a free woman to pursue a friendship with a grown up man. But I couldn't be strong enough with myself. And I knew from within that our meetings were something I had to keep from my husband, or else I would have told him about you. But I felt guilty, not because I'd done anything wrong but because of the way I felt. While it is true that mine was not an arranged marriage in the strictest terms, I barely knew Ranjan when the decision was taken. I'd met him just once in

a formal gathering and I have to be honest and admit that I'd liked him. He liked me too—that's how we got married.

After we began our life together, I was keen on everything—making a new beginning in Bombay, discovering the city, meeting people, learning to keep a good house. I would say truthfully that I am still keen on all this. There is nothing wrong with my husband—your father will tell you what a good man he is. And there's nothing wrong with our marriage. Maybe there's something wrong with me that I should be feeling so restless and depressed. Maybe life in Bombay is too much for a girl from Calcutta.

It's different for you—you've grown up here. This is your city. I don't know anybody besides my in-laws and my maternal uncle. I don't have a single friend I can talk to. I miss my parents, my home, my environment, and mainly my freedom.

Somebody should have told me that this is what being married means. It means giving up everything that you've known as a carefree young girl. And for what? Maybe I'm confused. Maybe other women don't feel this way—but how would I know that? Who can I ask? Not my mother. Not your mother. Not my mother-in-law. Then who?

I don't want to fill this letter with complaints. When I said I started writing this in order to thank you, I meant it sincerely. For the first time since my arrival in your city, I felt like laughing, singing, enjoying the salty sea air on my face. I looked at the sky and felt happy. When a gulmohur blossom fell at my feet, I wanted to pick it up and kiss it. When we sped down the broad streets, I wanted to cry out with joy. It was so wonderful—but how would you know that? It's your everyday life—nothing special about it. But for me, each moment was precious. I felt my age. I felt relaxed. I felt free. And then—later—I felt sad. Because I knew this unique feeling was only for today. It was a gift of great value. I'd probably never experience it again.

And I felt bad that I had betrayed Ranjan. Maybe I should have asked his permission about such things. I felt awful about doing this behind his back. I felt like a sneak, or a thief. Other women might not feel this strongly. Maybe Bombay women will find my reaction foolish. After all, nothing happened.

But this is not true. For me, everything happened. Everything that should happen with a husband, with a man you love. And that's when I asked myself—do I love you? Am I falling in love with you, Nikhil?

If the answer to that question is 'yes', then I must stop seeing you at once. At this point, I don't really know. I'm confused and afraid to ask myself too many questions. It's possible that it isn't love at all, but a need to know you. You or anybody else could ask where is the need for that when I have a husband. And you would be one hundred per cent right. Yes, I have a husband. Just like your mother has your father. Maybe I should get to know my husband better instead of you. That might be the answer I'm looking for. If I were to ask my mother's advice, she'd tell me that it is my duty to fulfill my husband's every wish and abide by his rules. Nikhil, I've tried to, believe me, and it has been very difficult. Maybe I don't please my husband sufficiently. I feel there is something wrong with me. I should try harder to understand him and win him over. If that has not happened so far, the fault is with me. I tell myself I should have waited a little before jumping into marriage. But would that have made much of a difference? The truth is, I wanted to get out of Calcutta. I was bored. I wanted adventure. Bombay had always fascinated me. When my uncle suggested this match, I agreed immediately. Not because I fell head over heels in love with Ranjan at our first meeting but because I was keen to come here and become a part of this city. That didn't happen. Rather, it hasn't happened so far. Now I'm feeling lost and miserable. I spend most of my days wondering where you are and what you're doing. I also feel jealous that you're meeting other girls—girls your own age, pretty, modern, cheerful girls, who wear smart clothes, smoke cigarettes, dance in discos and go home late. I have never known such a life—and never will.

My college years were completely different. I had to study all the time and stay at home. Very rarely was I allowed to go out with my cousins for an outing. What I see in Bombay is all very new. Boys and girls move around freely, mix, joke, work and fight. Nobody cares. Nobody notices.

My husband, even though he studied in America and all that, is not like this. He is old-fashioned and conservative. Basically, I'm the same too. But I also feel that he's a bit too serious and hard-working. I don't know whether your father also comes home tired. But at least your mother has some outlet. She goes to her parlour, she earns money. Not like me. Maybe I should try and get a job in Bombay. That way, I'll be less depressed. Do you think that is the answer? Will that solve my problem?

Nikhil . . . I wish you were here with me just now. I like your voice, I like the way you talk, I like your teasing me. I even like it when you get angry. But best of all, I like your laughter—did you know that? Have I told you? Probably not, I'm far too shy.

You've probably guessed that I have never had a proper boyfriend, or known any man other than my father, cousins and uncles. In Bombay this would be considered abnormal and I, a freak. Not so in Calcutta—most girls from my college were in the same boat too. It was only after coming here that I realized how common it is to have two, three, even more boyfriends before marriage. Maybe I should have known someone—but where was the chance?

In the area where we lived, had I as much as been seen with a boy, it would have created a scandal that would have shamed my parents. I could never hurt them. You'd find this funny living in such a modern city where young people are so liberated but think of me in my old house in Calcutta. A boyfriend? Impossible. When I got married to Ranjan everybody was happy— and a little jealous. You know why? Because I'd be leaving Calcutta and coming to Bombay. People are so fascinated by your city—I wonder if you know that. When I was growing up and people who had visited Bombay came to our home, I would regard them as extraordinary creatures who had experienced something wonderful. Like astronauts who had come back from a moon trip.

I remember asking my maternal uncle all kinds of silly questions about Bombay, each time he visited us. And I distinctly remember telling myself I would live in this wondrous city some day. Marrying Ranjan was like marrying Bombay. I thought I was the luckiest girl in my locality. Certainly, I was the only one who had bagged a foreign-educated, Bombay-based bridegroom. I still believe I'm very lucky to have become Mrs Malik. Ranjan is not an ordinary man (your father will tell you that too). He is so humble even though he has all these degrees and comes from such an excellent background. Actually, I'm very surprised he married someone like me when he could 've got a fine girl from Bombay itself. But in many ways Ranjan is reserved and complex (unlike you!). Bombay has not spoilt him. His values are still traditional. Thank God for that. I can't imagine being married to a very modern man who would expect me to drink and smoke with him and his friends.

I know what you are thinking. That if Ranjan is so fantastic, why did I go out with you today. Right? Anybody else in your place would think the same. And I wouldn't blame you for doing so. The truth is, I'm confused and ashamed of myself. I know it's wrong— very wrong—for a married woman to go out with a man especially when her husband doesn't know about it. I have no clear-cut answer. I can only say that I was helpless and wanted to go out with you very desperately. Please don't misunderstand me or misjudge me. As you do know by now, I'm not that type of person. I am not a flirt. I've never been cheap. Maybe God will punish me for this. But in my heart of hearts, I know I didn't do anything wrong. Is it a sin to want to go out and breathe the air? I don't have an answer. If God is to punish me for what I've done, he will.

The fact is, it was one of the best days of my life. So, I'm not sorry. I have no regrets. And if you were to ask me to come out with you again, I probably would. This time with less guilt. Am I making any sense?

Love, Maya.

It was close to dawn when I finished the letter. I re-read it a few times and it sounded all right to me. Neither romantic nor cold. I was not sure whether to give it to Nikhil. I had started writing it only to keep my fear of the dark at bay. It didn't matter whether or not Nikhil read it.

I began switching off some of the lights. I didn't want any of the early risers in the building to notice them. I was sure the night watchman had seen them blazing and wondered about it. Ranjan had not phoned as he had promised. Since he had locked the direct dial facility, I had no way of reaching him either except by booking a call.

I rested my head wearily against the unruffled pillows and fell into a light sleep listening to the cawing of the boisterous crows outside and just as the first light of dawn was bathing Bombay in a pale pink glow. The sun would be up in minutes. I felt safe enough to snatch some sleep.

*

When the doorbell rang a few hours later, I thought I was dreaming and that the school fire alarm was on. I looked at my bedside clock—it was well past ten o'clock. I sprang out of bed and rushed to the door knowing it would be the first domestic of the day—the woman who came in to do the dishes.

It was Nikhil, dressed to go out, hair slicked back, shirt freshly pressed and his father's after-shave liberally splashed on. How did I know it was his father's and not his own? Because his father and Ranjan left at about the same time, often meeting at our doorstep and walking down together after exchanging exaggeratedly effusive greetings.

I had asked Ranjan once whether he liked Nikhil's father. Ranjan had said simply, 'He is my senior. I have to like him.'

Even though Ranjan didn't report directly to him, he made sure to create a good impression because Nikhil's father was at least four rungs higher. I understood that. My father had felt the same way about his seniors, an attitude my mother brusquely dismissed by saying that there was no need for a man who knew his job to 'kowtow' to his seniors. Each time she made the statement, my father would bristle and protest indignantly that there was no question of his kowtowing to anybody. But seniors had to be given due respect and that was that.

'Coming?' Nikhil asked jauntily, dangling his motorbike keys in front of my nose. I shook my head firmly.

'Impossible,' I said, not meeting his eyes.

'Why? Don't feel like it?' Nikhil asked, his sneakers tapping a tattoo on the coir doormat at the entrance.

'No,' I said, still looking down forlornly.

'Liar,' Nikhil taunted. 'Bet you're dying to. Admit it. Scared, right? Don't worry, nobody will find out. Promise.'

'It's not that,' I explained heatedly. 'I haven't slept all night and I'm tired.'

Nikhil leaned against the door frame.

'You haven't slept? Why not? Feeling bad? Lousy? Rotten? Good. Then the thing to do is to get out of this place. Quickly. Now. I'll take you to see a movie—a Hindi film. Something really stupid. How about *Coolie No. 1*? Bet you've never seen such a dumb film. Stop fussing Maya. And I'll give you the world's best dosa. Roadside place. Sensational. Wear jeans.'

'No,' I said stubbornly, adding, 'And I don't have jeans, remember? I don't wear jeans.'

Nikhil laughed. 'You remind me of my grandmother. No—not even her. She's quite a sport—I'm sure she'd wear jeans if I asked her to. How can anybody in this day and age not possess jeans? It's impossible. Why do you behave like you are two hundred years old or something? What's your problem?'

I raised my voice—not too much—just a little.

'I don't have a problem. You do. You think everybody is like the people you know. What's so strange about not owning a pair of jeans? In Calcutta—at least, if you came from the sort of background that I do—girls wear sarees, not jeans. Particularly married girls. And now, Nikhil, I suggest you go—go wherever you have fun. Go eat your dosa, watch a movie. Do what you want. I have a lot of work. My house isn't clean. And neither am I.'

Abruptly, he turned around after a brief, 'Fine. Okay. Bye,' and left.

That wasn't what I had expected. I had wanted him to coax me. Persuade me a little more. And who knows, I might have washed up, dressed and gone with him. But the truth was, I couldn't take his self-assured belief that all he had to do was show up on my doorstep and ask me to join him. It angered me to see his casualness as he extended the invitation. Also, I was scared—oh yes. I had gotten away with it yesterday. But today? I knew my mother-in-law would be phoning soon to check on how I was managing without her son.

But more than that, I was worried about the neighbours, servants and watchmen. Nothing remained private in this building. And Nikhil wasn't making the slightest effort to keep it so. It surprised me that he could be this bold, this open about our meeting. It also pained me that he could walk away so easily while I remained standing by the door gazing after his retreating figure and wondering when or even if I would see him again.

I hadn't dared to mention the letter. And now I doubted whether I would ever give it to him. I had hoped it would clear my confusion—that was how it used to be in the past. Whenever I had felt troubled about things, I had written a long letter about my feelings and felt instantly better—as if by the simple act of reducing my emotions to the written word, I had solved everything.

I thought of going back to my bedroom and writing to my mother—truthfully. But I didn't share that sort of relationship with her. And any 'confession' at this stage would only have alarmed her and given rise to a panic attack. I shut the front door and went in for my overdue bath making sure to leave the bathroom door ajar for when I'd have to rush out to let in one of the domestics.

I wasn't used to showering and this house only had showers. I never felt clean enough standing under the weak interrupted trickle of an overhead shower, watching the soap trail down my body in slow motion. In my home in Calcutta, baths were something of a ritual—prolonged and elaborate, with two buckets of water, one hot, one cold. Half the pleasure of bathing was in mixing the water to the right temperature, transferring it one lota at a time till one achieved the right degree of soothing warmth. Bombay baths were quick and functional and invariably left me feeling a little unclean, with traces of leftover soap still clinging between folds of skin.

Bombay towels were different too—less absorbent. I didn't know what it was about these towels, but they didn't dry me to my satisfaction. Perhaps the dampness in the air prevented them from drying completely. Or perhaps synthetic fibre was woven into them. I found it easier to dry myself with my old, soft sarees than with the stiff, solid coloured towels Ranjan preferred.

*

As I soaped myself that morning, I wondered about Nikhil's life outside this building. I wanted to ask him so many things. Did he have girlfriends? Had he known a lot of women? Older women? He seemed so comfortable amidst women. Too comfortable, in fact. There was no awkwardness at all, the kind one associated with young, unmarried men when they were in the presence of unknown women.

Nikhil was always perfectly at ease—confident, relaxed and interested in a way that went beyond polite curiosity. How come? Or was it that some men were born in harmony with their surroundings—no matter how lousy? I envied that trait in him almost as much as I resented his constant references to my 'lack of cool'. It was a new and puzzling term that took me a while to fathom. Nikhil considered me 'uncool'—so what? I suppose I was uptight by his relaxed standards.

Then again, had I been 'cool' would Ranjan have married me? Ranjan wasn't 'cool' either. We were well matched in that respect. Sad. So sad. Two uncool people stuck together in unholy matrimony.

Ha! Sometimes I laughed out loud thinking of my wedding ceremony. It had been almost comical with a motley group from my side and a formidably sizeable crowd from Ranjan's. How vulnerable we must have looked—probably as vulnerable as we felt, being pushed around by Ranjan's mother. She was definitely in charge, dictating the entire proceedings down to the last detail. Red was not my colour but of course I had had to wear it as a bride. The texture of the saree was stiff and the gold thread running through it had cut my skin.

The woman who had come to embellish my forehead with delicate patterns created out of sandalwood paste and kumkum had filthy nails, paan-stained teeth, greasy hair and the world's worst body odour. I had had to hold my breath or take it in short, sharp gasps while she applied the paste with a delicate applicator—rather like a miniaturized printing block.

My mother had been a nervous wreck during the wedding week, while my father had switched off so completely it was difficult to believe he was even remotely related to any of us. Only my cheerful uncle and his equally cheerful wife had rallied round and made me feel special, particularly at that crucial moment when I was presented in the marriage pandal for all to survey and comment on.

Prodipmama had beamed with visible pride as he escorted me to a low platform by Ranjan's side and whispered, 'You are the sun, the moon and all the stars in the firmament today.'

And then he had called me by the pet name I had been given as a child, 'Bulbul . . . you are the most beautiful bride I have ever seen.'

Even though I wasn't convinced, his words had made me feel good and a little more confident than when my mother had surveyed me critically and said with her usual lack of tact, 'All this unnecessary make up and lipstick and all that, doesn't suit Maya at all. It only suits fair people. Look at her complexion— dark. Today of all days. Everybody is going to say, "Why such a dark bride for Ranjan. That too all the way from Calcutta".'

I had glanced nervously at myself in the mirror and agreed with her. I certainly wasn't looking my best. Anything but. Besides, I was feeling slightly ridiculous with a gauzy red veil covering half my face and a wafer-thin salwood crown sitting awkwardly on my head. I had pleaded with my mother to dispense with the crown at least. But my mother had dismissed such an 'untraditional' move with a firm 'The issue is, either we are going in for a proper Bengali wedding, or not. If we are, then all these things must be observed. It is important. Culture is important. Mrs Malik wants everything done in the right way, and I agree with her. In any case, one cannot argue with the boy's side—it is simply not done. The mukut stays.'

And so it had stayed, perched on top of my elaborate hairstyle while my entire focus through the long and tedious ceremony remained on the wobbly object fixed to my hair with pins that were boring holes in my scalp.

Ranjan's headgear had looked less ridiculous if a bit dramatic. I thought he resembled a character straight out of the many TV 'mythologicals' that mesmerized viewers with their elaborate costumes and cardboard sets.

In fact, Ranjan had been so pleased with his own appearance that he had framed three wedding pictures which showed him at very flattering angles but which made me look like a Bangladeshi refugee—a mail-order bride from hell. Occasionally, Ranjan would cast a fond glance in the direction of the photographs and say smugly, 'Handsome, eh? Good photographs, good photographs.'

I was sure he didn't notice nor care whether or not I was in the frame. I had once pointed out to him that the photographs made me look awful, with hardly any light on my face but plenty of ugly shadows. He had picked one up and examined it carefully. Perhaps it was the first time it had even registered that there was someone else right next to him.

'Oh,' he had said. 'Hmm, I see what you mean about no light. But Maya, isn't that better? Imagine . . . with more light your face would have been seen.'

He had looked up cheerfully and caught my expression.

'What I mean is, you weren't looking your best that day. Definitely not . . . with so much make-up. Who had told you to apply it? Your mother?'

I had answered quietly, 'No. Yours.'

'Really?' Ranjan had said, 'I'm surprised. Very surprised. My mother disapproves of girls who use make-up. She thinks it looks very artificial. I don't like it myself. Hmmm. Must ask her. Maybe she thought it would make you look better—improve your appearance . . . you know? Some women look fairer— much fairer—with make-up.'

I had rushed to the window to look at the photographs more closely.

'What's wrong with my complexion? I like it,' I had said defensively.

Ranjan had looked up with a bored air and commented, 'It's okay. Not too dark. It's fine. But my mother was saying the other day that you should start applying turmeric paste on your skin if you want to lighten it. My mother uses it every day. It is also an antiseptic. When I was a young boy, I used to be massaged with fresh cream and turmeric. That's why I'm not all that hairy—see? Particularly my back. Most men have a heavy growth on the legs—look at mine. All these things make a difference, Maya. No harm in your trying it.'

I had argued hotly with him that I didn't suffer from any complex because of the colour of my skin. And that if he had wanted a milk-white bride, he should have advertised for one. That was when Ranjan had told me that he had. Several times.

'We were not satisfied with the response,' he had explained.

For a while, I had been too stunned to say anything.

'How could you do it?' I had asked finally.

'There is nothing to be ashamed of,' Ranjan had shrugged. 'Everybody advertises. What's so bad about it? You find fault with everything. Do you think all these thousands of people who advertise every day are all crazy? Newspapers make lots of money through those ads. My mother knows so many families who have found excellent partners through matrimonial columns.'

I nodded, making sure to keep my expression neutral. Ranjan had continued to gaze at his side of the photographs, a fond, proud gleam in his eyes. Then he turned to me with a worried air.

'Have I put on weight since the wedding?' he asked, patting his cheeks and pinching his waist.

'No . . . not really,' I said.

'Sure? Look carefully . . . here . . . just here at this spot.' He pointed to his gut. 'Well . . . maybe just a little. No problem. I'll cut back on tea.'

'But you only drink two cups,' I pointed out.

Ranjan had chuckled. 'That's what you think. You have no idea what goes on in the office. No idea at all.'

That was true enough. Once Ranjan left for work, the shutters in my mind came down. It wasn't that I didn't care. I had tried in the beginning to take what my mother called an 'active interest'. Initially, Ranjan had seemed flattered and then amused. Finally, I would discern a familiar look of impatience each time I asked him 'relevant' questions about his job.

I had got the message and given up. I knew very little about his day or his environment at the office. He said he preferred to leave his career worries at the office and not lug them home.

'The name of the game is relaxation,' he would insist as he pulled off his trousers and stripped down to his underwear after getting home. What did he do in the office all day, I often wondered. Now I knew he drank several cups of heavily sugared tea.

What else? I had heard him on the phone once, talking in a low voice to his mother when he thought I was busy in the kitchen. Since I didn't want him to think I was trying to listen, I had crept away slowly from the bedroom door and gone back to the gas range without retrieving the kitchen washcloth I had gone to get from the lowest drawer of the cupboard. I had caught only a few agitated sentences which to me had sounded like Ranjan was having problems with his immediate boss—an annoying smug Bihari called Sinha who always made it a point to say—'Sinha from Bihar. Not Bengal.' Sinha with his crude ways, gravelly voice and broad accent.

Since I wasn't supposed to have overheard the conversation, I couldn't ask Ranjan what the problem was. Even so, one night I had raised the topic albeit obliquely.

'You look tense these days. Anything wrong?'

Ranjan had turned down the volume of the BBC World News with John Major crowing about his victory over the other John, and smiled a huge smile.

'Me? And tense? Not at all. Not at all. What makes you think so?'

I had tried again weakly. 'Are you sure things are all right— at the office and all that?'

Ranjan had looked at me sharply. 'Things? All that? I tell you, when will women learn to talk directly? Do you ever hear me asking you such silly questions? What "things" are you talking about? And what do you mean by "all that"?'

He was sitting upright, his eyes bulging aggressively. I dared not probe further.

This trip of his was equally shrouded in secrecy. I had absolutely no idea why he was going away or even where.

Yes, he had tossed out the names of a few cities. But an STD phone call was an STD phone call. It could have come from any place—even Pune next door.

It troubled me that Ranjan refused to share a single aspect of his professional life with me. Did he think I was too dumb to understand? Or too disinterested? Either way, it wasn't so. Considering the sans-stimulus state of my own existence, I figured Ranjan was just old-fashioned in this area (as he was in so many others).

I wouldn't have minded all that much about being kept in the dark had he not excluded me so obviously. If he could confide in his mother, why couldn't he confide in me? I wasn't his adversary or rival. Didn't he trust me enough?

I had asked him that on a 'relaxed' Sunday when he was avidly watching the Monte Carlo Grand Prix and rooting for his favourite racing car driver—Schumacher. Without taking his eyes off the screen, he had said affectionately, 'Of course I trust you. But my mother is my mother. I've known her longer than I've known you. These things take time. Maybe after ten or fifteen years of marriage . . . it's still early. I have to know you better.'

He had turned to look at me and perhaps noticing my sad expression, he had held out his arm and drawn me to him.

'Last few laps,' he had said, 'I hope the bugger wins.'

Well, I had hoped the bugger would win too so that we could have our dinner on time.

Eighteen

Ranjan phoned at exactly three minutes past nine o'clock that night. I was strangely relieved to hear his voice.

'Listen . . . I'll make this short,' he said briskly. 'We have to pay for all our personal calls and you know what these five star hotels charge. So . . . I'll only speak for three minutes—okay?

'Now, tell me quickly is everything all right at home? No problems? I forgot to tell you . . . I've left some office papers in my side of the cupboard . . . in the locked drawer. They are needed urgently at the Bombay office. And my mother needs certain keys which are also with me. You'll find both in the drawer. The keys are in a sealed envelope marked "keys". And the papers are in a yellow plastic file.

'One more thing—quickly take down this number—4834910—call and ask for Mr Mehta. He's the man who handles my investments. Remind him about the transfer of shares. I need the certificates as soon as possible. And yes, I've just remembered—call the electrician and ask him to take a look at the air-conditioner in my room. I'm not happy with the cooling. Okay, I'll phone you in a day or two. Maybe from the office—free call. Bye.'

And that was it. I hung onto the receiver for a few seconds. I had wanted to talk to Ranjan. I had wanted him to talk to me—ask me how I was, whether I was missing him. I wanted him to tell me he was missing me, thinking of me. I had hoped to hear at least a little concern . . . some anxiety. All Ranjan had done was call and issue instructions. Left me a string of errands to run. Not that I minded doing them. I minded Ranjan's self-absorption.

'I have my priorities in the right place,' he would often state, clicking his fingers to indicate how smartly he dealt with life. Well, he had proved that to me with his phone call—he had let me know in no uncertain terms what his priorities were.

I felt tears welling up in my eyes and I hastily brushed them away with an impatient, angry gesture. What had I expected—a serenade over the phone? Tender words of love? An extended cooing session? From Ranjan, my husband? Ranjan?

Why not? Didn't husbands share pleasant nothings with their wives? There was nobody I could ask. Had I been closer to Nikhil's mother, I might have considered talking to her about it. I certainly wouldn't have questioned my mother (knowing my father). And I had no close girl-friend who could tell me the truth one way or the other.

On an impulse, I phoned my uncle at his office in the morning (he had recently been given a direct line). I felt a surge of happiness coursing through me when he answered promptly. He sounded pleased to hear my voice.

'Bulbul! How are you? Happy, very happy? Some good news for the family—huh? What we've all been waiting for?'

I laughed, and it felt wonderful just to be able to do so.

'Nothing like that, mamu,' I said lightly.

He waited. I paused too, uncertain what to say next. I hadn't called my uncle in a long while, and in the days when I did call, it was invariably to convey something to him from my mother (she always added a separate paragraph for him in her letters to me).

'Mamu . . .' I started off, 'I wanted to ask you a personal question . . .'

I could hear him smiling. 'Go on—ask,' he said sportingly. That stumped me. How very stupid it sounded. How could anybody phone and ask such a silly question. I went ahead and asked it anyway.

'Mamu, what do you say to your wife when you phone her?'

My uncle didn't snort. He didn't laugh. He answered carefully, 'Well, that depends. I mean . . . it depends on why I'm making the call.'

'So why do you make calls, generally?' I continued.

'Generally, it is to check something,' my uncle replied.

'Like what?' I persisted.

'Like . . . what's for dinner—or, has the electricity bill been paid? Or, is there something I have to pick up on the way home—like that.'

I uttered a lame, 'Oh.'

Prodipmama chuckled. 'What's the matter, Bulbul—has jamaibabu forgotten to phone you today? Tell me . . .'

I tried to dismiss it with a light, 'Oh no. Ranjan just phoned. From Delhi. He phones me at least thrice a day. It's nothing like that. I was just wondering.'

Prodipmama spoke gently. 'You can talk to me freely. Has he upset you? I won't tell anybody. Not even your mother.'

My words came rushing out. 'I'm feeling terrible. I don't know what to do and what to think. He only calls if there's some work. Never to hear my voice and chat.'

Prodipmama said, a little sadly I thought, 'Ah, but men—husbands—rarely phone their wives just for a chat. Jamaibabu is no exception. All that lovey-dovey talk only takes place during courtship. After marriage, everything changes. And mind you, I'm not saying this in a critical way. The man and woman become more comfortable with one another. There's no need to impress or talk big anymore. And what is married life all about? Routine. He must have phoned to remind you about some unpaid bill or a leaking tap or something—right?'

I sniffed louder than I had intended to. 'Yes. That's absolutely right. How did you guess?'

My uncle laughed knowingly. 'It's the same in marriages all over the world. It's universal, Bulbul. Don't feel bad. At least he phones. Besides, some men feel awkward about expressing their emotions. He's one of them. Shy chap. So what? The very fact that he phoned means he's thinking of you.'

I wasn't convinced at all, but had no desire to prolong the conversation.

Ranjan did care, I suppose, in his own funny way. And he was shy. That knowledge didn't make me feel any better. So now I was stuck with a shy man whose way of showing he cared was to make a call about taps, switches and bills. Why couldn't he have uttered even one loving word—I would have settled for a falsehood. I needed to listen to a soft, caring sentence—even a brotherly one, if that's what he preferred.

I sat by the phone, trying to visualize my husband in his office environment. I had asked him to take me there once and he had laughed.

'It's not a part of our office culture. Nobody brings their wives there. Besides, there are too many men there.'

I had been mystified by that last remark. I knew there were men there—but, surely, they weren't uncouth, hard-up fellows who would have raped me with their eyes or misbehaved in any way. Or did Ranjan think I didn't know how to behave in the presence of his colleagues? That I might embarrass him and thereby damage his professional chances?

I had asked him that one morning when he was concentrating on knotting his precious blue silk tie.

'Don't be silly, Maya. Some offices encourage spouses to hang around, some don't. Our bank is pretty conservative in this regard—if you don't believe me, ask that flashy beautician upstairs, she'll tell you. How many times has she come to her husband's cabin—go on, ask her?'

So, I had never been to my husband's work place and I had no idea what he did there. I found that depressing. Lunch? He didn't always take sandwiches. Did he dash out for a business meal? Did he stay at his desk and grab a snack? Did a colleague share something with him? How did he spend his lunch hour? Going to art galleries in the vicinity? Strolling aimlessly along the seafront? Attacking files piled up on his desk? Going to visit his mother, who lived ten minutes away?

Ranjan wouldn't tell me. I had asked him often enough. He always answered vaguely, 'Oh . . . on different days I do different things. It depends. Sometimes, I stay in the office, sometimes I go out. Sometimes I eat and sometimes I don't. You know, it's pretty flexible.'

I visualized him at work. In my mind, Ranjan always sat behind an enormous desk with a high-backed swivel chair upholstered in black rexine. His desk had a glass top and several important-looking files. His cabin was smart and modern with a silent air-conditioner that worked by remote control.

I remembered his mother telling me once that several of Ranjan's clients were prominent industrialists who had direct dealings with him.

'Mind you, they come to his office. He doesn't go to theirs,' she had made it a point to tell me. I could picture Dhirubhai, Nusli, Harshad—all those men in business magazines, waiting to see Ranjan. I also thought he had a personal secretary to deal with his appointments and phone calls. Plus, a peon who made sure the coffee was just right for visitors.

Ranjan stubbornly refused to buy a new briefcase for himself. I didn't like the one he had, which was heavy and clumsy.

'I'm attached to it,' he would always say, 'and I don't like new things.'

Which was also true. Ranjan was most reluctant when it came to discarding anything—a worn-out, scruffy shirt, a nibless pen, a dried up jotter, torn trousers, faded pajamas, even toothpaste tubes which couldn't be squeezed any more. He kept them all. And he would criticize me for being wasteful.

'You have very extravagant habits, Maya,' he would scold as he watched me pull out frayed blouses and toss them in a heap for the raddiwalla to cart away.

'There's no space in the house,' I would complain, to which he would bristle.

'Why? Isn't our flat big enough for the maharani? Did you live in a palace before you married me—huh?'

That was another thing. Ranjan had never shown the slightest interest in my past—where I had lived, how I had lived, my growing up years, my laughter or my tears. None of this mattered. There was no curiosity whatsoever. And though he hadn't visited Calcutta after the wedding, he had made it clear that when he did, my parents would have to go to his hotel to meet him if they so wanted since he wouldn't have the time to go over to their home.

But I knew Ranjan was making a lack of time an excuse. He just didn't think it worth his while to bother. And if my parents were keen to establish contact, it was upto them to make the effort.

Even on this tour of his, I didn't expect him to phone my parents. I hadn't told them about Ranjan's arrival in Calcutta, to spare their hurt feelings.

*

Perhaps it was traditional for Bengali sons-in-law to display slight (but unmistakable) contempt towards their wives' families. I had noticed it with my own father, meek as he was, when it came to my mother's relatives. He would stiffen and withdraw into his room, deigning to emerge only when it became far too obvious that he wanted to avoid meeting them. And they too, in their turn, maintained a formal, deferential attitude while addressing him.

These visits, rare and far between though they were, made my mother acutely jittery and visibly defensive. Had she handled my father better, he might have behaved himself. But she would start the day off by 'warning' him every half-hour about her relatives' imminent arrival and requesting him sarcastically to act politely even if the effort seemed too much. Had she left him alone and been more natural herself, I was certain he too would have greeted the visitors with the respect and hospitality expected from the host and head of the family.

I had asked my mother what he had against them after he had been particularly abrupt with my grand-aunt. My mother had snapped, 'Don't you know? This is a part of our great Bengali culture—to insult the wife's family.'

I had sort of understood and taken it less seriously after that. But I could still recall my father mocking my mother's generosity in buying half a kilo of expensive sandesh from the sweet shop nearby on the day she was expecting visitors.

'How nice,' he would say. 'Somebody with severe diabetes is going to get a stomach ache today with all the sweets in our house. So what? Who cares about the rising cost of sandesh these days? Nobody. Least of all the house who has pay for such a rich treat.'

My mother would scowl miserably as she busily arranged an old wooden tray with her best crockery and draped everything with a white crocheted covering painstakingly made by her sister during their childhood.

She would mutter under her breath, 'Such meanness. All for a few pieces of sweets. Do I mind when his relatives come and eat everything in sight? No. Like a fool I slave from dawn to dusk cooking in this hot, hellish kitchen so that they may not complain about remaining hungry. Hungry? Huh! Appetite of oxen, the lot of them. Even two kilos of mutton rum out. And a minimum of twelve loohies per head.'

The she would add, 'He's a fine one to lecture me about my people who hardly visit us, knowing his stingy nature. And unlike his brothers and their wives, my aunts do not come flapping their empty hands. They bring sweets and savouries. Plus a present for Bulbul. It is a woman's lot to hear these curses. Never mind. I believe in God. And He is hearing everything. All the taunts too. So much heartburn over half a kilo of sandesh. I'm ashamed. Have I married a pauper . . . ?'

I would pretend I hadn't heard anything and remain neutral, not daring to take sides. Once our visitors arrived, my father would summon me into his room and ask in a whisper, 'How many of them have descended on us this time? Have they also brought their noisy, ill-mannered children? If they ask about me,

say that I'm running a fever. Make up a story about the doctor—
but don't call me out to meet them.'

My mother's relatives were pleasant enough people who
spoke softly so as not to disturb my father. My mother made
sure they stayed out of his way and did a brilliant job of covering
up for him. But she never invoked the doctor's name in vain.

'The issue is, one must not take illness lightly. If anybody
makes a joke out of ill health, you can be sure he or she will fall
sick soon enough. I'm not a superstitious person as such but
some things I do believe in. Besides, why give people a chance
to spread rumours? If you lie about your father, he will pick
up some horrible infection. And relatives will gossip that he is
dying of some disease. This will create problems for you and
spoil your chances of getting a good bridegroom.'

Even though I couldn't always follow my mother's logic,
it did make some sort of sense. That was how Bengali families
functioned. Health bulletins were on everybody's lips. Each time
I eavesdropped on a conversation, it revolved around somebody
or the other's bowel movements and gas problems. My mother
could spend hours discussing the digestive tracts of distant
relatives. It was one topic of which she never seemed to tire.
Even a hint of minor indigestion would see her rushing to the
medicine chest in search of 'Isabgol'.

I had also overheard remarks that had struck me as being
particularly sadistic and which concerned grave ailments. My
mother would declare triumphantly, 'I'd sensed his condition
ten years ago at Tuktuk's wedding itself. Don't you remember
how much he was coughing? And his skin—so parched and
pale—a sure sign he was dying of cancer. Naturally, everybody
in the Ghosh family denied it at that time. But how long can you
keep such a thing a secret, tell me? They were trying to cover it

all up even as Amitda lay on his deathbed. "It's nothing. Just a small cough".

'Don't think I've forgotten Nandini's denials. If it was nothing, how come all the doctors have given up hope? Three more weeks—that's all. I heard it from one of the specialists. Three weeks if he's lucky. Probably less. Mark my words, even at his funeral they'll be saying, "Oh . . . who told you it was cancer? Not at all. The doctors couldn't diagnose it correctly. It was some rare infection—that's all. Certainly not cancer".'

Why did people lie about such things? I still didn't know. But whenever I had a fever, my mother would tell me not to tell a soul about it, not even my classmates. She would keep me indoors and fib to anybody who asked.

'Don't come out snivelling or wearing a sweater,' she would hiss, pushing me firmly back into my room. 'Someone might see you.'

I would retreat sulkily and lie on my bed in miserable silence till whoever was outside had been hastily dealt with and dismissed by my mother.

*

Ranjan behaved in a similar fashion. So did my mother-in-law. Each evening after his cups of tea, when he phoned his mother to give her the report on his day, he would start with his 'motion' in the morning.

'Yes, Ma, I had a good motion today. Yes—better than yesterday's. No, no gas at all. Just slight griping. But nothing to worry about. I'll remember not to eat stomach bloat. I'll stick to light dal and see if it makes any difference. But I'll tell Maya not to add hing to it. Yes, she loves the flavour. But it doesn't agree with me. Yes, Ma, I've told her that. She forgets. I'll also tell her not to give me leafy vegetables at night. Maybe in their family they didn't follow the same system. It's all right, Ma. Nothing serious. But without leafy vegetables, I tend to get constipated. What? Bananas at night? No, Ma. In the States I used to eat prunes. Those were just great. Maybe I should try dried figs in their place?'

I would half-listen while I busied myself preparing dinner. Sometimes, Ranjan would summon me to the phone to take staccato instructions from his mother. She would dictate a new recipe at such speed that I would invariably miss out a few key ingredients. Naturally, it never tasted like hers.

I would dread these phone calls. My mother-in-law's hostility came through clearly. Ranjan probably sensed my feelings at such times and tried to make amends without allowing it to sound as though he was being disloyal to his mother.

He would mumble, 'Men get used to eating a certain kind of food . . . their taste buds get accustomed to it. I've tried to change my eating patterns, but it's no use. I used to be miserable in America. All I did was dream of home-cooked food. Even after four years, I couldn't adjust. I had begun to hate the sight of pizzas and pita breads.

'Mind you, I had access to food from all over the world, and I tried it all. Finally, I forced myself to stick to deli food— pastrami sandwiches and salads. I couldn't eat even a mouthul of pasta even though I had made friends with an Italian who often invited me home. American Chinese food was not like Bombay's Chinese. I thought I'd like Greek kababs. Even those weren't like Indian kababs. I found them burnt and tasteless.

'As for Japanese food—God. I could vomit just thinking about it. Horrible. Sticky, lumpy rice and smelly raw fish—can you imagine? And they eat that rubbish for breakfast, lunch, tea and dinner.'

I nodded sympathetically. I understood. I was missing my mother's food too. And Calcutta Chinese. Particularly the Tangra dishes which somehow tasted far better because of the strong, overbearing stench coming from the tanneries close by.

But I couldn't tell Ranjan this. He had already specified, 'Men get used to eating a certain kind of food.'

I wanted to say, 'So do women,' but decided not to. It might have led to a long debate which I didn't want to enter into.

*

I did find myself remembering my mother at each meal—and she wasn't even a good cook. Food was not a priority in our house. Well, not in the same way as it was in most other Bengali homes. I had noticed this with our relatives—they discussed food even when they weren't consuming it. It was uppermost on their minds to the extent that I was sure if I roused any of them from deep sleep and indulged in some free association, we would end up referring to food—last eaten or to be eaten.

It used to baffle me, this total obsession with food. My mother would sniff in a superior sort of way and say, 'Only animals spend all their time running after food. The issue is, I agree human beings require to eat in order to survive, but surely there are more important things in life. Such as books. Knowledge. Beauty.'

I would half-agree, not daring to admit even to myself that I too had food on my mind most of the time—my neighbour's food. My mother was frugal, that was true. But she lacked both the interest and the ability to produce tasty meals.

If my poor father suffered because of this, he never voiced it. He ate his meals indifferently, rarely even looking at what he was putting into his mouth. He would stare ahead and soldier on, while my mother pulled faces (at her own preparations) and fussed. I would watch the two of them pushing a potol back and forth on the thali and lose my appetite. I would pick dispiritedly at the small mound of rice in the centre of my plate (I ate in a plastic one) and try not to look too unhappy about the miserable piece of fish floating in a watery yellow gravy.

My mother sometimes noticed my expression and felt apologetic, but not for long. She would swiftly try and distract my attention from the meagre fare on our table and say, 'Aah. The fragrance of the champak flower in full bloom. Maya . . . I do think you should spend a few years at Santiniketan. Acquire some culture—real culture. The essence of Bengal. When I was your age, I knew Gurudev's poetry by heart—not English translations. Original. What an imagination.'

I would try and look enthused but my focus would remain on my rumbling stomach.

But now, I missed the familiarity of her recipes, poor as they were. They were a part of my childhood. I missed biting into chunks of palm jaggery which my mother would offer indifferently while other families would treat the seasonal delicacy with the reverence it deserved. I would ask her why we never made payesh out of it like everybody else and enjoyed it with fluffy loochies.

My mother would stare at me in a puzzled way and say, 'Oh . . . payesh . . . loochies . . . yes. The issue is, I'm not very good at these things. Besides, the taste of *nutun gur* can really only be appreciated when you eat it like a chocolate after dinner. What's the point in dissolving it in milk? Frankly, I find payesh rather disgusting.'

That would end the matter. For her, not me. I would stare longingly at the thick, creamy kheer (as payesh was called in Bombay) brought to school by my classmates and defiantly crunch into my own lump of jaggery, trying not to think of the subtle aroma released by melting gur on a slow flame with the milk coming to a gradual boil and the rice grains getting plump and saturated with the delicious, nut brown syrup oozing into the velvety preparation that must have been created by God himself.

Even though my mother treated cooking as a chore that was slightly beneath her, she knew good food from bad. And was honest enough to admit that she specialized in the latter. This admission did not stop her from criticizing everybody else's culinary skills.

'That fancy Buladi—what does she think? That we've never eaten a good dalna before? Are our tastebuds defective? Do our palates match a monkey's? The potol was clearly stale—hard seeds and overripe pulp. As for the masala—I don't think she'd bothered to roast it more than a few seconds. I could actually smell the raw haldi even before putting a spoonful into my mouth. Did you notice the rice—lumpy and squishy. The issue is, if you don't want to take the trouble over your guests, why invite them in the first place?'

But her most withering comments were reserved for wedding banquets—especially the pretentious ones.

'Oh Ma! What showy people. Did you notice how they threw their money around? Nobody gets impressed with such a vulgar display—all that shiny new gold and those horribly colourful sarees. Not a single tangail or dhakai or genuine Benarasi in sight—just hideous stuff from New Market. As for the menu, there has to be some limit in this day and age. We all know the girl's father has made money. But it was in the last ten years—and by what means?

'The issue is, there's nothing wrong with displaying your newly-acquired wealth—but at least show a little restraint. In today's times, this attitude is simply no good, I tell you. It attracts too much attention. You know how jealous people are of prosperity? Wealth is fine, but ill-gotten wealth?'

My father would interrupt her monologue at this point and ask quietly, 'How do you know it's ill-gotten? What proof, I ask, what proof?'

My mother would throw him an exasperated look and snap. 'Does everything in life come with proof? Are there documents for all matters? Where is the proof of our marriage—show me? Do you have a certificate?'

My father would fill in an impossibly difficult word in his daily crossword and chuckle at her agitated state.

'In our days, nobody registered marriages or bothered with certificates. But when a serious charge is made against someone like this, it has to be backed up by solid evidence. Loose talk can be highly dangerous, woman.'

At the sound of that word—woman—my mother would bristle. It was a sure indication that my father was itching for an argument.

'It is not loose talk at all. The whole world knows how Buladi's husband committed fraud. I'm not the only one. Do you expect me to go and get police records for every crook in Calcutta before opening my mouth? I know what I'm talking about. And the real thing I wished to say is about the wedding menu. Even you criticized it. All that waste. How many pieces of fried fish can anybody eat without feeling sick—tell me? That too when the oil used is rancid. And did you see the way the mutton was prepared? Swimming in some fatty substance—clearly not refined oil. The issue is, when you are spending so much money and trying to show off, why try and save on a proper cooking medium—that's my point.'

*

My own wedding feast hadn't met with my mother's approval, since the arrangements had been left to Prodipmama and his

241

dull wife. And to be perfectly honest, the budget sanctioned by my parents must have fallen horribly short.

I remember Prodipmama protesting mildly, 'Do you have any idea about prices in Bombay? This amount will barely feed a party of ten, not the two hundred and fifty we've invited.'

My mother swiftly corrected him. 'They have invited, not us. Who do we know in this place? In any case, we had offered them train tickets to Calcutta. Traditionally, that's the way it's done—at the bride's house. But do you think these grand people wanted to come. Mrs Malik only turned up her nose and said "Sorry, but we don't have many links in Calcutta. All our friends and contacts are here in Bombay. Ranjan's colleagues are in this city too. What's the point in us travelling all that way—and a two-day journey by train at that? My asthma gets aggravated with all that soot".'

My father had pointed out that he was prepared to offer 'air-conditioned berths' that would take care of both, the soot and the comfort of the Maliks, but Ranjan's mother had remained resolute.

'The wedding will be in Bombay. We can enjoy it better here. And it isn't as if we don't have good Bengali purohits or anything. The local priests are excellent—in fact, more traditional than their Calcutta counterparts. As for the fish for the feast, that's not a problem either. Bishnou at Worli is used to taking big orders. Provided, of course, you give him sufficient notice.'

I had a feeling my parents were secretly relieved by the arrangements. A Bombay wedding eliminated our own relatives from the festivities. Unless we chose to bring them at our own expense and arrange for their lodging. Apart from my mother's widowed elder cousin and a nephew from my father's side, there was nobody my family was all that close to. Of course, a

Calcutta wedding would have entailed long lists of cousins four times removed and relatives we hadn't laid eyes on for decades. Plus neighbours, colleagues of both my father and mother and a whole host of casual acquaintances who made up our social world.

It would have been a nightmare endured by us in order to impress the Maliks. We couldn't possibly let them know that we really were nobodies in Calcutta with hardly any important friends and even fewer VIP relatives. Getting a respectable guest list together would have been tough enough (but manageable).

It was putting up the Maliks in a manner they probably expected that would have defeated us. Our house was not good enough with its primitive plumbing and uncomfortable beds. And we didn't have grand relatives who could accommodate the bridegroom's party and pamper my future in-laws in the traditional manner.

So, I was sure my parents were vastly relieved even though on our return to Calcutta, my mother had made a show of how sorry she was that she had been deprived of the privilege of fawning over her 'handsome, intelligent, successful' jamaibabu from Bombay.

As she would explain with a light laugh and slight wave of her hand, 'You know how different Bombay Bengalis are—not at all fussy like us in Calcutta. Maya's in-laws are so reasonable, so good, so understanding—they told us clearly, "Don't bother with formalities. We have no belief in such things. We have liked your daughter, our son has approved of her, that's all that matters. We are not concerned with where the wedding takes place. In fact, we prefer Bombay."

'Isn't that nice of them? Maya is a lucky girl. Imagine the Maliks insisting on having the wedding in their city. It shows how much they liked my Maya. Frankly, we Calcutta Bengalis should stop all this fussing over the boy's side. Really, it is too much. See how the Bombay Bengalis behave—that is the difference between the two cities. It's the mentality, if you ask me. That is why Calcutta will remain Calcutta—dirty and backward. No progress here, I tell you. Look at Bombay—like London. So modern, so clean. Everybody smart and well-dressed. What a time we had there. And now my Maya will make it her city. The Maliks have already invited us to visit her next year.'

That last bit was a blatant lie and I squirmed each time my mother trotted out the fib. If anything, the Maliks had made it very clear that once I became a Malik, I'd have very little to do with my own family.

As Mrs Malik had explained tersely, 'Girls can only be moulded if they stop thinking of their parents' home as their own. Maya will have to learn to live as Ranjan's wife without running to Calcutta for help all the time. And naturally, it won't be possible for you to come to Bombay—unless you live with your brother—since Ranjan's bank flat is not large enough.'

My mother had hastily interjected, 'I understand perfectly. I believe in the same thing myself. A girl has to cut the cord to her family quickly and identify with her in-laws. The sooner she does this, the better. And where am I going to get time to visit her here? Oh no—I'm far too busy running my own house in Calcutta, looking after Maya's father. I could barely take the time off for this trip.'

Recalling the conversation, I reflected that it was just as well Ranjan's mother had laid down the rules. I really couldn't picture my mother or father or both visiting me here—with or without Ranjan in the house. We just weren't accustomed to sharing such a small space. Even as a child, I had always spent time on my own outside the supervisory gaze of either parent. I wasn't used to their company. I didn't remember seeking my mother out for comfort, advice or even plain conversation. She too left me pretty much alone.

As for my father, he only spoke when he was spoken to. And it wasn't often that I felt free enough to go and talk to him. He was the solitary small and silent figure in an armchair who signed my report cards mechanically without really looking at the grades, and smiled politely when I informed him that I had done well enough to rank in the first five.

What would the two have done cooped up in my cramped Bombay flat? They would have been embarrassed with each other's proximity and then mine. I could imagine the three of us creeping carefully round each other, pretending we hadn't noticed anything. My mother's long and heart-breaking sighs, which were lost in the high-ceilinged caverns of our Calcutta house, would have sounded like muffled screams here. My father's frequent bouts of throat clearing too would have made us jump with their rasping unexpectedness.

I couldn't see Ranjan putting up with any of this for even a minute. Besides, my parents were creatures of habit. Both of them stuck to a strict regimen that never varied. With just one bathroom in the flat, how would my father use the toilet five times a night, as he was accustomed to doing? Five, never four, never six. I could practically time my little alarm clock to his toilet trips. Most Bombay flats had this inconvenient problem. One had to troop through a bedroom to access the toilet. I couldn't think of a worse scenario than my poor father knocking apologetically on our bedroom door five times a night in order to relieve himself.

My mother had her peculiarities as well. Though she was capable of displaying impressive bladder control when she chose to, something would go wrong with her weak digestion every time she veered away from her bland diet. It was easy to tell from her expression that some dish had disagreed with her and disagreed violently. Her body would tense up and her face turn into a mask of acute discomfort with all the tiny muscles twitching spasmodically just below her paper-thin skin.

She would excuse herself abruptly from the table and rush to the bathroom. She would remain in there for a long time, leaving my father and me to finish our tasteless meal quietly, clear the table and retire to our respective rooms.

These bouts of indigestion embarrassed my mother and made her feel acutely self-conscious if they ever occurred in the presence of outsiders. She would turn instantly apologetic and make half a dozen excuses for her delicate constitution.

'It's the Calcutta water,' she would sniff, 'it ruins everybody's health. How do people survive in this place with this sort of contamination? We Calcuttans have no sense of sanitation, I tell you. For years, we have been drinking polluted water without complaining. Does the government care? The issue is, we must do something ourselves to improve matters. Why blame the government for everything?'

No, all things considered, this was one time I was grateful to my mother-in-law for having taken care of the matter.

Nineteen

Nikhil's shadowy figure leaping on and off his battered bike continued to dominate my thoughts. As I replayed those hours on Malabar Hill over and over again, fleeting little incidents would enter my thoughts. Every encounter we'd ever had. I recalled how he'd turned up once unexpectedly as always, waving *The Afternoon* in my face.

'If you want my autograph, take it now,' he'd said sternly, 'before I become a super-celebrity.'

As usual, he'd caught me in the kitchen (the bai had let him in after yelling out *ooperwala baba aaya hai*). I was perched on a high wooden stool cleaning the shelves that took the load of my heavy pickle jars.

'What are you talking about?' I'd asked a little crossly (even though I was pleased to see him).

'See . . . my picture. I'm a major stud in town, man. Major stud.'

And he'd stuck the paper under my nose. There he was being featured as a 'Dude with potential' along with other young men his age.

'I'm famous, man', Nikhil had kept repeating. 'My mom . . . man . . . she's really freaking out.'

I found him particularly childish at that moment and said so. He'd looked disbelieving at first and then expressed his annoyance. 'What's with you? Man—you are so out of it. There's no hope. Don't you understand—this means I rate. I count. I'm somebody,' he'd underlined, his eyes registering hurt.

I'd wiped my hands on my dusty apron and held out the right one saying, 'Congratulations, Mr Famous.'

Nikhil had refused to shake it and stormed out banging the door behind him. It was at such times that I found him shallow and stupid, as compared to my husband. But as soon as my thoughts turned even mildly negative towards Nikhil, I would instantly start making excuses for him. I'd remind myself that he was young, impetuous, good-looking and sought-after. The bai who also did the clothes and dishes in his house often told me how the phone rang constantly for him.

'Always girls. Never boys. Girls, girls, girls. They just don't leave him alone. Memsaab is always complaining the phone is never free for her.'

Even though revelations like these wounded me. I maintained an impassive expression as the bai rattled on. Yet, I was extra careful about not showing interest. These freelance women were the worst gossips. God knows what she'd report to Nikhil's mother if I made the mistake of digging for more information. I taught myself to be grateful for whatever scraps the maid threw my way. Just the same way as I was grateful for stray sightings of Nikhil.

*

Ranjan's absence affected me in a strange way. My slow, eventless daily routine slowed down still further. I thought I would feel free of various duties—cooking being the most obvious one. It was true I had said good-bye to the kitchen the moment Ranjan left for the airport. I hadn't bothered to fix anything for myself besides a couple of toasts, and I had managed to burn even those.

With no cooking smells, the house exuded a strange antiseptic odour. I felt as though I was in a hospital ward awaiting surgery—some mysterious probe into my innards.

The house. It was funny but that was how I always referred to this place, even to myself. It was never a home. My home. Our home. Always 'the house'—impersonal, distant, cold. Home continued to be Calcutta. My parental home. And it wasn't even as if I had such warm or wonderful memories of the place.

Perhaps I was more familiar with its rhythms, smells, creaks and leaks. Somewhere at the back of my mind, was also the awareness that I was living in a rented flat. A company flat. It didn't belong to Ranjan, and it certainly had nothing to do with me. If Ranjan quit or was fired, we would have to vacate anyway and move to another dismal Bombay accommodation with shabby fittings and fixtures.

If this aspect of our life made Ranjan uncomfortable, he never mentioned it. Once, when I had brought up the topic, he had snapped, 'What does it matter? You have a roof over your head. A comfortable bed. A cushy existence . . . TV, refrigerator, air-conditioner, toaster, mixer-blender, as many gadgets as you want. Plus, servants. Isn't that enough? Don't behave like a spoilt woman—like that horrible woman upstairs.'

By the way he had said it, I knew he was referring to Nikhil's mother. It wasn't often that Ranjan criticized anybody. Not because he saw only the virtuous side of people. He simply wasn't sufficiently interested. People didn't affect him unless he had to deal with them directly.

That was why I hadn't let the remark about Pushpa Verma slide away. I had asked, 'Why did you call her horrible? What has she done?'

Ranjan had wrinkled up his nose and pulled faces, something he did a lot. There were times I would forget to listen to his words and keep staring fascinatedly at his facial contortions. He would screw up his eyes, wiggle his eyebrows, twitch his nose and do all sorts of things with his large mouth. He resembled a child when he was like that—unguarded, unselfconscious and frighteningly open.

He had been thoughtful for a while, and I saw his forehead creasing. I knew Nikhil's mother was in for it.

'That awful woman,' Ranjan had all but spat out. 'She's so obvious. So greedy. So selfish. She is going to ruin her husband's career, I tell you. Mark my words. And she'll finish off that loafer son of hers. I hate women like that. They have no culture, no feelings.'

I had been astonished at Ranjan's vehemence. He rarely came down this heavily on anybody. The words he had used to describe Nikhil were significant. Loafer-son. I was tempted to ask him why he had condemned that 'no-good boy', as he often referred to Nikhil. But something had told me to let it go.

It was Ranjan who had been reluctant to end the conversation. He had switched off the BBC News even though Niki Marx was telling the world about the latest debacle in Quebec. He had locked his hands behind his head and stared at the ceiling.

'Women like her should be controlled before it's too late . . . or else they spoil society,' he had said finally after obvious deliberation.

'How? I mean, how does she spoil society?'

Ranjan had turned to me—this time his forehead was uncreased but his mouth had stretched. 'Just look at her. Is she a good wife? No. She's a nag. That man looks miserable. He can't function properly in the office. His wife is always criticizing him . . . comparing and complaining. Which man can live with such a woman in peace?

'Then, look at how she has raised that fellow. Does he have any manners? Any goal in life? What does he do all day, I really wonder? Eat, sleep and spend his father's money. Useless chap. Show-off. Strutting around like a peacock. Behaving as if he owns this building. But why blame him? With an uncouth mother like that, he cannot progress in life. No values, you see.'

I had stared at Ranjan disbelievingly. I hadn't realized till that point how strongly he felt about Nikhil and his mother. I was tempted to defend 'that boy' and explain that he wasn't as much of a no-good as Ranjan thought him to be. I debated with myself whether to take the conversation any further. Ranjan was examining my face and obviously waiting for some sort of a reaction.

I had made sure my expression remained studiedly neutral.

'Nikhil is quite a good student . . . I'm told. And his mother was saying the other day that he is studying hard for a scholarship to the States. He can't help his looks. But then, when you see how young people dress in Bombay . . .' I had trailed off deliberately.

Ranjan had shaken his head. 'What nonsense. I'm also a Bombay boy. I grew up here. I got a scholarship. I studied in the States. Was I ever like that worthless fellow roaring all over the place on a motorbike bought with my father's money? Never. I had more pride. More self-respect. So many times I've heard his father taking his calls in the office. Always the same thing—"give me money, daddy. I need money for this and money for that". All his mother's doing. When he is not pestering his father, his mother is. I'm surprised Mr Verma hasn't had a heart attack yet with all that tension.'

He had paused a moment and then continued, 'You tell me—I was the only son. Only child. My parents could've spoilt me, couldn't they? Given in to all my demands. Firstly, I didn't make any. I told myself, "be happy with what you have". Secondly, I knew even if I had asked for big things, unreasonable things, things I didn't really need, my mother would have refused outright. Not because we didn't have the money. Oh no. Because in life one needs certain principles. One has to grow up with certain values. No wastage. No false show. I worked hard and I paid my own way through college. And you . . . you are defending that no-good. Lives off his father. Exploits his mother. Tell me—would a man of character do that? Never. It all comes down to proper upbringing. That's what my mother always said. Raise a child with correct values, and you will give the nation a good, law-abiding citizen. Raise anybody the wrong way and you'll get a criminal.'

I had suppressed a sly smile and asked seriously, 'Do you really think Nikhil is a criminal in the making?'

Ranjan had turned to look at me. Sharply, he had said, 'You're asking me like he has given you a job as his defense lawyer or something.'

I knew I had said the wrong thing. I shouldn't have brought Nikhil into the conversation at all. Now I had walked into a potential landmine that would blow up in my face in a moment unless I found some way of diverting it.

I had switched on a bright smile and asked cheerfully if I could make Ranjan a cup of coffee. He had shaken his head and continued to glare at me. He looked very belligerent when he did that, his eyes blazing and bulging with anger.

I had turned away to avoid holding onto his gaze and started tidying up our already tidy bedroom. I had prayed that Ranjan would switch on the BBC channel and let the conversation go. I strained to hear the soft click of the remote. But Ranjan had had other things on his mind.

Abruptly, he had asked, 'Have you been meeting that boy by any chance?'

I had been tempted to play dumb and ask 'which boy?', widening my eyes innocently, but something had told me to play it straight. No games. I had taken my time before replying in an exaggeratedly casual voice, 'Why should you ask me such a question? The answer should be obvious enough.'

Ranjan had continued to glare. 'That hardly clarifies anything. Yes or no. Why can't you be straight with me?'

Nervously, I had pulled out dozens of old clothes from the lower drawer of my cupboard and started sorting them out into neat piles.

'I don't meet him, meet him as such . . . but if I happen to run into him on the stairs or landing, then I do wish him, that's all. Wouldn't it be rude to ignore your colleague's son? I'm being polite, nothing more.'

With my back to Ranjan, I hadn't had to worry too much about my expression.

Ranjan had remained silent for a while. Then he had said slowly, 'The other day when I got home from work, I thought I smelt cigarette smoke in the house. That fellow smokes, doesn't he?'

I had whirled around and asked, 'How should I know? I'm not his mother.'

Ranjan had had a distant look on his face as he tugged at his earlobe. 'Then who could have been smoking here? Unless you have started doing so behind my back.'

I had glanced at him witheringly. 'What rubbish. I hate cigarette smoke. With my family's history of asthma, I'm allergic to smoke.'

Ranjan's eyebrows had shot up. 'Asthma? Funny nobody told me you come from an asthmatic background. I don't think my mother is aware of that either. Maybe your uncle "forgot" to tell us. Which makes me wonder what else he may have forgotten to mention. At our first meeting, we had clearly asked for the family's medical history. My mother is very particular about such things. In an alliance, one cannot overlook matters like diabetes, heart disease, epilepsy, lunacy. Now you tell me your family has asthma. Anything else? Better to get it out of the way right now so there are no surprises later. Think hard.'

I had felt hot tears welling up in my eyes. How dared he talk to me like this? Wasn't it only because he felt superior in some way to me and my background? I remembered his mother telling a relative at the wedding, 'If you ask me, it's always wiser to get a girl from a socially inferior background. Grief comes to a man who marries above his station. A wealthier wife spells doom. The husband loses all control over her and she ends up having the upper hand. Such a marriage can never work which is why we were so careful while selecting the right candidate for Ranjan. We definitely didn't want a fast Bombay girl. You'd be surprised how Bengali girls change once they taste Bombay life. As for those who've been brought up here—you wouldn't recognize them as proper Bengalis. They can't speak their own mother tongue, I tell you. Know nothing about our customs. Care two hoots for our traditions.'

Lowering her voice conspiratorially, she had continued, 'Mind you, I have nothing against modern educated girls. But these anglicized specimens—my God, they'll finish off our boys given half the chance. My Ranjan has lived abroad, but at heart he is very conservative. He was keen on getting a bride from Calcutta. And not from one of those rich families. Mind you, we received several offers. What proposals. What dowries.

Naturally, with his education and all that. But we said "nothing doing. He is not a bull in an auction". We wanted the right girl—educated, yes, but not one of these over-ambitious career women without a care for their homes. I think we've made the right choice in Maya.'

And now there was Ranjan sounding exactly like his mother. I had thought he would ask me to produce a doctor's certificate next. Patiently, I had explained to my husband that I wasn't suffering from asthma myself. But that I had grown up in an environment that was sensitive to smoke since my grandmother, when she had been alive, sometimes got an asthmatic attack brought on by a visitor smoking in our house.

Ranjan hadn't looked too convinced. Asthma could be a killer, he told me suspiciously. I assured him I wasn't about to die.

'Still . . . these things should not be concealed, you know. It's a matter of ethics.'

I had wanted to defend poor Prodipmama and tell Ranjan that in all probability my uncle was unaware of my grandmother's allergy to smoke since she was my father's mother and had been dead for several years. But I had kept absolutely quiet, glad that Ranjan's attention had been diverted from Nikhil to the asthma I didn't have. I had known he was thinking about my uncle's deception. Chances were he would phone his mother while I was in the kitchen and tell her about his discovery. Not that it mattered to me. One more strike against my family would hardly matter.

Just as I was leaving the room, Ranjan's voice had stopped me. 'Does he enter the house in my absence? Come in here, sit down and all that?'

Instead of replying directly, I had looked exasperated and said, 'I know exactly where that cigarette smoke must have come from. Remember the carpenter? The one who had come to fix back the doors of that cabinet outside? He was the one. He kept smoking even though I told him several times not to.'

I had held my breath, wondering whether Ranjan would accept that in place of an answer. Fortunately for me, he had done just that, nodding his head and reaching for the *Economic Times*. I had let out an enormous sigh of relief. That had been close.

Twenty

Given Ranjan's genuine lack of interest in me, I sometimes wondered whether he had ever fancied any woman. Fancied her enough to wonder about the small, insignificant but intimate areas of her life. I knew that with me, he wasn't being cruel, indifferent or sadistic. He just wasn't tuned into my wavelength. He didn't feel the need for it, obviously. Perhaps it hadn't even occurred to him that he should take an interest in his wife.

It wasn't a deliberate act of neglect. Ranjan didn't know better. But had he ever? Had there been even a single instance when a woman had captivated him? Made him curious? Aroused feelings other than those of mild toleration and ill-defined indulgence?

I doubted it. Women weren't important to Ranjan. They didn't have a validity of their own. He saw them only in context to men and family life. On some level he seemed repulsed by their 'woman thing'.

I knew, for example, that he wasn't at all comfortable with the fact that I menstruated. It made him feel queasy. He pretended he didn't know and hadn't noticed. Sometimes, when I got up in the night to change and freshen up, he would keep his eyes tightly shut and feign deep sleep just so as to avoid any reference to my 'condition' (as he called it). I wondered if he had any views about the hair on my legs, arms and elsewhere. Whether I removed it or let it grow, whether he found the sight of smooth limbs pleasing, whether the texture of my body hair affected him. Or the condition of my skin at different times of the year.

Only once had he glanced critically at my elbows and said, 'Why don't you take better care of yourself? My mother always uses vaseline on her elbows or else the skin becomes dry and scaly.'

I had been flattered by the fact that he had even noticed I had elbows. After that day, I had diligently rubbed vaseline into the discoloured skin there and monitored their improved appearance with pride.

It wasn't as if Ranjan wasn't observant. He noticed things most other people didn't. Strange things, particularly about women. Moles, for example. He was fascinated by them and could tell at a glance where they were located on a woman's face or what could be seen of her body. He would ask me later whether I had spotted them too, and I usually hadn't.

He knew the exact location of the moles on my body as well, even though he very rarely saw me without my clothes on. There were a few positioned along my lower back, whose existence I hadn't known about till Ranjan had pointed them out to me in a hand-held mirror.

'Look,' he had said triumphantly as though he had stumbled upon a secret treasure, 'here's one. And there's another, right at that spot.'

Other than the odd mole-hunt, my body remained uncharted territory. In his more affectionate moments, he would draw me towards him and pat my hair fondly, adopting a manner owners use towards their pets. I enjoyed our physical closeness, the warmth of his body, his breath on my face, his hands as they absent-mindedly caressed my shoulders, even his feet as they massaged mine. Encouraged by his demonstrativeness, I would shyly trace my fingers through his hair, or wrap my arms around him.

I longed for these moments and cherished them for days afterwards. This aspect of Ranjan was so appealing, it was a pity I didn't see more of it. I also sensed that he liked to see me emerge from a bath with a saree wrapped clumsily around me. If my hair was wet, he would stop whatever he was doing to towel it dry for me. He managed to do that most expertly with quick, efficient movements that were gentle enough not to tear the hair and yet brisk enough to get all the moisture out fast. I would see him watching me as I sat in front of the dressing table later and ran a comb through the damp strands, separating each one carefully.

Often, he would say, 'Nice hair. Are you oiling it regularly or not?'

I would nod and smile in my gratitude.

*

Only once, at a dull office party, had I seen Ranjan looking animated while talking to a woman. From the look in his eyes, it was obvious he wasn't being merely polite to a colleague after-hours. Significantly, Ranjan was leaning close enough to her for his shoulder to be within brushing distance of hers. And even more significantly, his eyes were making direct contact unlike at most times when he tended to focus on a woman's cheekbone, eyebrows, hairline or chin—anything to avoid looking straight into her eyes.

He would say to me later, 'I feel awkward to stare at anybody, especially women. It's not polite—don't you think so?'

And I would agree with him even though I didn't think so, because I found his shyness sweet.

But with this particular woman, he seemed absolutely at ease as he laughed unselfconsciously, his head thrown back, his shoulders relaxed enough for them to slide towards hers. I wondered who she was but dared not ask anyone. She didn't seem at all like Ranjan's kind of woman I told myself, before realizing I didn't really know who would qualify as Ranjan's kind of woman in the first place, apart from his mother.

And this woman bore no resemblance to Mrs Malik, at least on the surface of it. Was she attractive? Yes, I had to admit as much. She was striking in the sort of way that Bombay working women were striking—studiedly attired in carefully chosen boutique tussars, subtly made up to appear perfectly natural, and with the special air of confidence that set them apart.

It was there in the way they used their hands, extended their legs, thrust out their breasts, ran their fingers through their hair, laughed openly showing a lot of teeth. It was there in the rehearsed carelessness of their conversation, the smart, witty remarks they made so effortlessly, the manner in which they handled their drinks or the elegance employed while cupping their escorts' hands when they lit a cigarette.

I envied them their many masks—how easy they made it look. It was called 'social intercourse'. I saw a special irony in the second word. As I watched my husband rush to fetch an ashtray for the woman, I felt intensely jealous. I wondered whether he even remembered my presence at the party. Or was I that irrelevant to him?

Once or twice, he had caught my eye and I noticed how rapidly his expression altered. His face seemed to collapse and look suddenly disappointed. As if he had spotted something that was a little unpleasant . . . may be potentially embarrassing.

Was he ashamed of me, just a little? Would he have preferred to marry the kind of woman he was laughing so much with? But he had been so emphatic in his condemnation of women like her. What was I to make of that?

I thought I knew. Ranjan was scared of women like her. I was certain that had he had the opportunity to spend some time with her alone in a room, he would have regarded it as a punishment. She would have paralyzed him. And he wouldn't have been able to laugh as full-throatedly as he was doing now. I could visualize the scene. Ranjan would have fidgeted around uncomfortably and even his way of speaking would have changed. I had seen it happen. Whenever Ranjan was self-conscious, his tongue became heavier and his conversation slowed down, the words coming out thick and slurred. People who didn't know him better might have thought he had some sort of speech impediment. Even the expression in his eyes changed, and he looked moronic.

What was it about women—attractive women—that disoriented Ranjan so visibly? And did he marry me because in his eyes I was plain? It made me sad to think my husband felt comfortable with me because of my lack of good looks.

That evening at the party, I had rushed to the bathroom and examined my face closely. It had seemed all right to me. Not like that woman's but not all that bad either. I wasn't very skilful with make-up, that was true. And that woman's face was as glossy as a magazine ad. My attempts at experimenting with eyeliner, mascara and lipstick hadn't been at all successful. My own mother never used make-up. Her idea of cosmetics didn't stretch beyond dabbing talcum powder over vanishing cream—a combination women in Calcutta believed made them look fairer. In reality, it made them look ghoulish, like kabuki dancers in sarees.

My mother would insist on my applying talcum powder on my face before going out or when we were expecting visitors. I used to obey dutifully in her presence and then go to my own room and wipe it all off. What I couldn't do without was kaajal in my eyes. And, of course, the sindhoor in the parting of my hair.

I thought Ranjan appreciated my simplicity. He had always said so. But I had noticed his fascination for women he called 'fashionable'. His idea of fashionable didn't go beyond bright lipstick, excessive eyeliner and obviously rouged cheeks. But since I didn't know better I had assumed all this was part of the fashionable Bombay look.

It wasn't, of course, but who was going to tell me differently. I didn't have a single girlfriend in Bombay, someone who could guide me past the potholes of my adopted city. Someone I could giggle and gossip with, or confess my confusions to.

My feelings for Nikhil, for instance. His attitude towards me was so puzzling, and there was nobody who could tell me whether it was right or wrong for me to see him, talk to him, go out with him, or even think of him in the way I did. And what was that? Romantic? Immature? Pure fantasy?

I didn't know. Had I had a boyfriend in Calcutta, I might have recognized my feelings better. Identified them clearly. Stuck little labels on them. My complete lack of experience was unnerving me. And then I was married to a man who had turned out to be a novice in these matters too.

That evening, as I watched him looking so completely captivated by the woman at the party (her nail polish was so brown it looked like she had dipped her hands into melted chocolate), I reasoned to myself—a little foolishly perhaps—that such feelings did not constitute disloyalty. Ranjan was showing his fascination for another female quite openly—in my very presence, in fact. He wasn't hiding anything from me. So that must have meant he had nothing to be ashamed of.

By the same argument, if I felt what I did for Nikhil and showed it, Ranjan would also have to acknowledge that I was innocent. Everything was aboveboard. And yet, I felt small and rejected when I noticed him rushing to the dining table to fetch the woman a dinner plate while she stood there near a potted plant with her chocolate-tipped fingers stroking its fleshy leaves suggestively. How could a husband treat his wife like this? Didn't it occur to him that I might be hungry too? That it was ill-mannered of him to ignore me like this?

I decided to walk up to the table and help myself. As I passed the woman by the plant, I smiled and said, 'Hello—I'm Mrs Malik. Ranjan's wife.'

She turned to look at me—no, examine me, curiously. Her eyes expertly surveyed my body. She parted her lips, teeth gleaming and held out her hand.

'Oh . . . Maya . . . the girl from Calcutta,' was all she said.

But the way she said that one sentence made me understand exactly what she thought of me. I wondered what Ranjan had told her. Had they laughed about 'the girl from Calcutta'? Had they made fun of me for being so different from them?

I saw Ranjan staring at us. He looked alarmed. And then he rushed up with the woman's plate.

'Just salads, right?' he said.

She nodded and explained to me, 'I'm on this lunatic diet. Disgusting, isn't it? But why don't you go ahead and gorge? The food is always great here. I'm sure you'll find your Bengali fish too.'

She emphasized the word 'your' as though she wouldn't have touched the fish even had she not been on a 'lunatic diet'.

Ranjan gave me a push in the small of my back and said, 'Go ahead. I'll join you soon.'

So I went ahead and looked at the laden table disinterestedly. I had been hungry minutes ago. And now, as I took in all the rich food laid out on heavy silver, I felt a little sick. Perhaps I shouldn't have drunk all those colas, I told myself.

Ranjan came up and smiled a bit too warmly. 'Good food,' he said.

Yes, I could see it was good food. I nodded and helped myself to a piece of chicken. Ranjan was piling rice onto his plate and cracking a joke with some man with bulging eyes and hairs in his tunnel-like nostrils.

Ranjan nudged me and said, 'Maya, my wife.'

Bulging Eyes nodded knowingly. '. . . from Calcutta,' he muttered, his mouth already full of food.

What was this rubbish about Calcutta? It wasn't as if I was from the moon or something. Why was everybody commenting on where I came from? I was beginning to feel like a freak. Maya from Calcutta.

When Bulging Eyes moved away, I asked Ranjan, 'Why does everybody say "Maya from Calcutta"? It's so irritating.'

Ranjan shrugged. 'They don't mean it. I suppose its because everybody here is from Bombay. And . . . and . . . you look different. People can tell the difference immediately. You look like a Calcutta girl—know what I mean?'

I felt tears stinging my eyes as I spluttered, 'No, I don't know what you mean. And why should I want to look like all these women, anyway? Maybe I like looking like myself. Maybe I don't wish to look synthetic and cheap and made up like a . . . like a prostitute.'

The last word emerged from my lips without my intending it. Ranjan stared at me in shock.

'Who are you referring to? Which woman in this room looks like a prostitute to you—huh? Tell me. These are all very respectable people. Highly qualified. My colleagues—you understand. Don't you dare call them cheap and all that.'

I made a valiant effort to hold back my tears. The last thing I wanted was to attract attention. Ranjan was breathing heavily. His plate was empty. I tried to change the subject by asking, 'Aren't you going to eat something? You must be hungry.'

Ranjan glared at me and snapped back, 'No, I'm not. Not anymore. You've ruined my appetite. Forget it. Let's go home.'

He placed his plate down heavily and walked away. I felt wretched. And guilty. I could see that woman watching me. She had finished with the leaves in her plate and was licking each finger delicately. Her lipstick was still intact, her saree immaculate. I knew she had seen me making a fool of myself with my husband. Now I didn't want her to see me leave the party hungry.

I took a few sips of water and walked around the table heaping things on my plate that I didn't want at all. She was still watching. I ate as I walked round and round the dinner table, greedily replenishing what was over and stuffing it down my gullet. Once or twice I glanced in her direction. She looked stricken. Horrified. I ate more than I had ever eaten in my life. I wanted to prove to her that Maya from Calcutta had a healthy appetite. And she didn't have to starve to stay slim.

Twenty-one

Ranjan returned from his trip in an exaggeratedly elated state. I decided after some hesitation to go to the airport to greet him, not at all sure whether he would be pleased to see me there. Since he was travelling on an Indian Airlines flight, I waited at the new terminal—the one Bombay people were so proud of. I often felt tempted to tell them about the even newer one at Calcutta, but didn't. I had soon realized it was pointless talking to people here about cities they didn't have the slightest interest in or curiosity about.

Once, I had met a man and his wife from New York and I had noticed the same thing about them. They couldn't stop talking about New York, making it appear that it was the centre of the universe. Though they were in India, they weren't really here. Their minds were still in New York. And I remembered thinking to myself what a waste their trip was. They had spent all that money to travel all those many miles, and it would have been the same thing had they remained in Manhattan and looked at travel books from the comfort of their luxury home on the East River.

Bombay people were equally smug about their city. They complained about it all the time and discussed its myriad problems threadbare. So long as it was them doing all the nit-picking, it was all right. But if an 'outsider'—like me—said a word against the city, they pounced on the person viciously. And of course they weren't in the least bit interested in anyone else's city.

'Calcutta?' they would ask, eyebrows raised, as though they would find it difficult to locate such a place on the map of India. After a pause, the women would smile in a kind way and say, 'Very nice sarees there. I also got a gorgeous dhoti for my husband when a cousin brought it for me. Embroidered. Very ethnic. Artistic. You Bengalis really love your own culture. That's nice. Living in Bombay, we get so cosmopolitan . . .'

And then would follow a long lecture about how liberal everybody and everything was in this city. And how narrow-minded the rest of India seemed in comparison.

'It's the spirit of the people here,' I had been told repeatedly, and I would wonder how different it really was from the 'spirit' of the people in Calcutta. Weren't we all the same under the skin?

Ranjan, too, would often be infected by this kind of talk. He would boast in the presence of his colleagues, 'I'm a pucca Bombay product. But my wife . . . well, she's from Calcutta. The life there is very different. After growing up here, I would never be able to adjust there. Calcutta is a dying city, you know.'

That was another stupid cliche that got on my nerves. What did people mean by that? Did they even think about it? If Calcutta was dying, what about Bombay? It was dead and decomposing, going by the stink and piles of uncleared garbage.

Ranjan would smile his crooked smile, and pat my hand in front of people. 'She's very proud of the Calcutta metro,' he would explain, making me feel like a stupid child showing off a doodle.

Then he would add, 'The metro-shetro is all very well . . .
but do phones ever work in Calcutta?'

He would shake his head from side to side and say, 'I tell
you, that place is impossible. How do people function there? It's
definitely not a city for hard-core professionals.'

I would smile weakly and look down at my interlocked
fingers. Once, I had managed to counter, 'At least women don't
get pinched, pushed, teased and molested on the streets like in
Bombay.'

Ranjan had shot me a warning look before covering up the
indiscretion with a brusque, 'Oh come on, Maya . . . it's not all
that bad. How many times have you been molested after coming
to Bombay—huh?'

I had blushed at the bluntness of that remark and kept
quiet. Back at home, I had asked him why he had shut me up.

'It doesn't look nice for a wife to criticize her husband's
city,' he had said.

'But it's okay for a husband to criticize his wife's—is that
it?' I had murmured.

'You argue too much,' Ranjan had replied crossly and
banged the bathroom door shut behind him.

*

I saw him before he could see me. Ranjan was coming down on
the escalator with his overnight case tucked under his arm and
a plastic parcel in his hand. He looked rather sweet, his hair
ruffled and his tie (the maroon one he was partial to) askew. He
was talking animatedly to his colleague and nearly lost his step
at the bottom of the escalator. I began waving out uncertainly
to attract his attention. Maybe my presence would annoy him.
Or maybe Bombay wives were not supposed to wave to their
husbands.

His colleague saw me first and informed Ranjan whose eyes immediately lit up. Encouraged by that, I moved forward, unsure of what to do next. I had seen women peck their men lightly on the cheek and place an arm around the waist.

That wouldn't have come naturally to me at all. So, when Ranjan walked up to me briskly, all we did was stand face to face awkwardly and smile. I felt quite silly and was sure people were laughing at our awkwardness.

Ranjan handed me the plastic bag. 'It's for you—a saree. Your mother sent it,' he said.

I felt disappointed. I wished it had come from him. I took the bag shyly and said a very formal 'thank you' (his colleague was listening and I didn't want to make any mistakes).

We walked out of the terminal and Ranjan looked up at the sky with irritation.

'What, no rain? We've had it. There will be a severe water shortage this year, just see.'

I had already seen. The kitchen and bathroom were filled with buckets of stored water.

'How's Mummy?' he asked, adding, 'I did speak to her, of course. I phoned three or four times. She was complaining that her leg was giving her trouble again. I hope you found the time to go and see her.'

I nodded. I had gone to visit my mother-in-law. Not once, but twice. That I had come back miserable and depressed was besides the point. Anything else would have been surprising.

'You look all right,' Ranjan said in the car.

All right? What did he mean? Or was that his way of paying me a compliment? I kept quiet and wondered whether I should reach for his hand which was tapping a tattoo on the briefcase between us.

269

'So, what did you do in my absence? Were you upto any tricks?' he asked casually.

My heart skipped a beat. 'Nothing,' I said a trifle too hastily. 'I did nothing really.'

'No?' Ranjan said slowly. 'My mother told me you were very busy . . . that often the phone would keep ringing—nobody to pick it up.'

I said carefully, 'Maybe I was having my bath or something.'

'Not at those hours. I found it quite strange, I must say. Are you sure you haven't started those pottery classes? Or that weaving nonsense?'

So that was it. Relief swept over me. 'No way. No, no, no,' I assured Ranjan, my voice stronger. 'Where is the time for all that? I was busy cleaning out all the cupboards . . . organizing the kitchen shelves. Oh yes . . . I went to the market a few times. And I've started going for evening walks. I need some exercise. I've become so lazy after coming to Bombay.'

Ranjan continued to look absorbed in thought. 'Shall we stop at my mother's on the way home? She's asked me to see her. Poor thing, her leg is really acting up. And she was saying her blood pressure is bothering her again.'

'Fine,' I said, relieved that Ranjan had changed the topic. 'How was your trip—successful?'

Ranjan brightened up. 'Excellent. I'd say highly successful. Even Calcutta wasn't too bad. Hot, of course. And the usual power cuts. But that nightclub we all went to wasn't bad.'

'Nightclub?'

Ranjan nodded. 'Incognito—at the Taj Bengal. I went for the music. Their sound system is supposed to be very good.'

'And . . . was it?'

'What?'

'The sound system?'

'Yes . . . I told you.'

'How come you didn't tell me about going to Incognito when you phoned?'

'Don't be idiotic, Maya. What's so great about it? I didn't think it was important enough to waste precious money on.'

That didn't sound like Ranjan at all—not his comment about the wasted money but his visit to the nightclub. Bombay had several such places—I read about them all the time. Discos, pubs, restaurants, clubs. We never went to any of them. And now, when he was in Calcutta, off he went on his own.

But this wasn't the right time to cross-examine him. We were near his mother's home. I said lightly, 'Why don't I drop you off here and carry on home with the luggage? That will give me time to heat up the food and get things ready. I'll send the car back for you.'

Ranjan promptly agreed. Maybe he had been wondering how to tell me not to tag along while he had his reunion. I had just made it easier for him.

*

As I struggled with Ranjan's small bag outside our building, Nikhil's arm reached out from behind me and lifted it out of my hand.

'Let me help you with your husband's luggage,' he said, and the way he said it made me wonder whether it was meant as just an innocent helpful remark.

Nikhil's proximity made me nervous. Plus, I was angry. I hadn't seen him after the day he had abruptly disappeared, leaving me wondering what had gone wrong or worse, where I had gone wrong.

In a voice filled with accusation, I whirled around and asked, 'Where have you been?'

Nikhil smiled. 'Around. Here. Wrapping up my applications. Busy.'

I was shaking with rage. 'Why didn't you come over? Or call? I was waiting for you.'

Oh God! I hated myself for uttering those awful words. But it was too late—they were out of my mouth. How degrading, and how obvious. It was exactly the sort of thing that women in TV soaps said to callous uncaring men who invariably rebuffed them. I was asking to be humiliated.

Nikhil started walking up slowly, dragging Ranjan's bag. He ignored my whining and asked conversationally, 'What on earth is in this? Does Mr Malik carry rocks on a business trip? You should see my dad's bag. Weighs nothing.'

I was still seething. 'Well?' I asked as I put the key into the keyhole.

Nikhil made a great show of wiping his brow and checking his arm for possible muscle injury.

'I told you. I've been busy. These applications . . . God . . . what a nightmare.'

I was breathing heavily and glaring. Nikhil reached over easily and held my face in both his hands which were smelling of his father's aftershave.

'Relax, Maya, relax. You're so wound up. Cool down. I told you . . . I've been running around.'

The door was open now.

'Do you want me to come in . . . or is that not allowed any more? Are you talking to me? Nicely? Come on . . . stop being angry.'

I knew how idiotic I must have appeared to him. I took a deep breath and said, 'I'm not angry. I thought you'd drop by. How long does it take to make a phone call? I was worried about you. I also thought you were upset with me. Were you?'

Nikhil laughed and started to light a cigarette.

'Oh, no. Please don't do that. Ranjan will smell it . . . and then I've had it,' I blurted out.

'What?' Nikhil exclaimed. 'Your husband goes around sniffing all over the place? Don't tell me. This is crazy, man. I'd better get out of here.'

Without thinking, I grabbed him by the wrist and pleaded, 'Don't do that. Please. Don't act like this. Come in for just a few minutes. I have something for you.'

Nikhil removed my hands from his wrist and took two steps backwards. 'No way. Look, forget it. This is getting too much. I'd better leave. I don't want your husband to come running up and complain to my dad. That will be the end for me. Right now, I need to be in his good books . . . can't afford any trouble. Sorry.'

I was desperate. I wanted to prolong the conversation somehow. I also realized what a risk I was taking. It was entirely possible that Ranjan would be back any moment.

'Okay,' I bargained with Nikhil, 'don't come in. Wait right here. I'll be back. I've written something for you. A letter. I want you to read it.'

Nikhil held up both his hands and stuck out his left hip.

'Hey, don't complicate things. Do you know, you are sounding exactly like my mother when she nags dad.'

And then Nikhil began mimicking a woman's voice, in a silly high-pitched tone.

'I don't speak like that,' I protested hotly.

'Oh yes, you do, ma'am,' he laughed.

'Fine, in that case, I'm sorry I brought it up. Thanks for helping me with the bag. Bye.'

Nikhil pulled out a freshly ironed handkerchief from his pocket and mopped his brow.

'You need a fan—the electric kind,' he smiled. 'Cool down. I'll see you around. Soon. I've got to get these aps out of the way first.'

I called after him lamely, 'What aps?'

I heard his voice from the next floor. 'Didn't I tell you? I'm leaving for the USA.' He sang it out like the Bruce Springsteen number which began with 'Born . . .'

I continued to shout, 'Why didn't you tell me earlier?'

Nikhil shouted back, 'What for? I didn't think it would be of any interest to you.'

At that precise moment, I heard the car driving up and Ranjan instructing the driver. I hastily pulled the bag (which was still outside the door) into the house and dragged it towards the bedroom. In the hurry, I missed seeing a wire lying across the living room floor where I had plugged in the iron last night (the ironing board had collapsed and the switchboard in the bedroom was damp with the rainwater that had leaked in).

My sandal caught in the wire and I fell headlong over Ranjan's bag. The front door was still ajar when he ran up the stairs and saw me sprawled across the floor. Ranjan frowned and stood outside, staring at me.

'What's going on here? Are you all right? What are you doing on the floor—and why is the front door open? Haven't I told you how dangerous it is?'

My eyes must have been pleading because he suddenly changed his expression and came towards me.

'I thought I heard your voice downstairs,' he said worriedly. 'Were you crying out for help? Poor thing . . . what did you do to land up like this?'

He looked around and spotted the wire. 'Why is the iron here? Since when have you started ironing our clothes in this room? I don't understand your methods.'

I still hadn't uttered a word. I was conscious of pain—my knee was throbbing and my elbow looked awful with an angry-looking bruise climbing up my arm. Ranjan busied himself unplugging the iron and taking it back to its original place in the bedroom. Only after he had put it where it belonged did he come up and sit next to me. He saw the bruise and his eyes softened.

'I'll get some ice,' he said and walked into the kitchen. I started to cry. Tears poured out of my eyes as I put my head between my tender-to-touch knees and howled like a child. Ranjan returned with an improvised icepack and pressed it on my elbow. I winced at the sharp pain.

'Where else?' he asked, as I gingerly lifted up my saree to show him my knees. I felt almost shy doing that. It seemed an inappropriate, incongruous and suggestive gesture. Even through my pain, I found myself wondering when it was that Ranjan had last seen my bare legs at such proximity. Our life in the bedroom had settled into a routine. We could have been brothers. Or sisters. Or flatmates. Even when Ranjan did reach out for me, it was a gesture devoid of any passion. An impersonal, friendly sort of gesture which always left me feeling like a well-trained dog being rewarded for his good behaviour.

Ranjan too was staring at my legs with a slightly embarrassed expression. Maybe he had forgotten what they looked like. Maybe he didn't like what he saw. I tried to pull my saree down to cover their bareness. He averted his gaze.

'Still hurting?' he asked, his voice full of concern.

I nodded as I rested my head against his chest. I found Ranjan's familiar smell most reassuring. I breathed it in deeply while he stroked my back and hair. My crying ceased and I started to feel intensely sorry for both of us. Yes, Ranjan too. He had married me to satisfy his mother. Or maybe something within him. (What? The need to conform?) And I had married him to get away from Calcutta and a family with whom I didn't really feel a sense of belonging.

Now here we were, locked together in a relationship that didn't satisfy either of us. He very obviously longed to be on his own, leading the life he had become so accustomed to as a student and then as a promising bank executive living by himself. And I longed for the perfect romantic companion—if such a creature existed at all outside my imagination.

*

As I sat on the floor clutching my throbbing knee, the entire hopeless emptiness of my marriage with Ranjan flashed through my mind like a ticker tape. With each passing day, I had begun to feel more doomed. My life was going to be a repeat of my mother's. A poor one at that. And I could so clearly see it coming. My mother had lived hers unknowingly perhaps. This was worse. I was walking into something immeasurably depressing. I was even more cowardly than my mother. Perhaps she hadn't had any real choice in the matter. But I did. And what was I going to do about it? Nothing. Why? Because I felt honour-bound.

I consoled myself with the thought that Ranjan and I weren't bad people. We didn't harm anybody. We minded our own business. We weren't wicked or cruel. We didn't resort to devious, manipulative means to get our way. We were quite okay as compared to so many other people. Besides, I still harboured tremendous hope about our marriage changing its pattern. I told myself these things took time. Marriages needed a great deal of effort. Even friendship in a marriage couldn't be forged instantly.

I knew I had a stubborn streak in me. That would have to go. My mother always said it would come in the way of a happy marriage.

'The issue is, Maya, marriage involves sacrifice. And all the sacrificing has to be undertaken by the woman. The sooner you accept that, the happier you'll be.'

I would have accepted it had I been more convinced. Observing the way my mother led her own life, I saw no evidence of any sacrifice on her part. Or maybe that was exactly what she was trying to open my eyes to. Perhaps she was pointing to the disaster of her own marriage and telling me how I could avoid the same pitfalls.

I often wished I had a more open relationship with my mother. I longed to ask her questions about herself, her early years, her decision to marry my father, why they hadn't had any more children, how they'd reached this state in their marriage, what their differences were. But chiefly I wanted to know from her which of the many regrets in her dry, predictable life she resented the most. Which were the compromises that continued to hurt. Which the longings she knew would never be fulfilled.

Whenever my spirits flagged, I would think of Ranjan and myself ten years later. Yes, in all probability, we would be childless. On the other hand, we would be friends—I was so sure of that. Best friends. All it needed was more of a push from my side. I was the one who could make the difference in this marriage. I would have to change, become more understanding, teach myself to read Ranjan better.

In my less angry moments, I had convinced myself that Ranjan and I could still make a go of it if I tried harder. That was it—if I tried harder. I had already reconciled myself to being the one who would have to make all the effort if my marriage was to work. Why? Because Ranjan had established that his contribution to the contract was over on the day he decided to make me his wife. That act alone had redeemed him for life. That was his effort. He had chosen me. And that was sufficient.

I wanted to shout, 'Oh no, it isn't. I'm not ready to settle for something as paltry as that.'

But it remained a silent scream stuck somewhere in my throat, unable to push its way out. At least Ranjan didn't distract me by pretending. He was what he was, take it or leave it. Maybe he had suffered during his early years. But how was I to know if he refused to talk to me about his childhood, his adolescence, his highs and lows?

Twenty-two

I struggled painfully to my feet and hobbled to the bedroom. Ranjan followed me, muttering, 'I'd better call and let Ma know about your fall. She'll know what to do. She'll tell me whether or not to call a doctor. She's very good at these things.'

I said softly, 'It's nothing serious. I don't need a doctor. I can decide these things for myself.'

Ranjan examined my face to see whether there was more to what I'd just said.

'I'm sure you are capable of judging your own condition. Even so, I'd feel better if Ma came over and saw it for herself. You don't mind, do you? It's for your own good. Besides, the driver is waiting downstairs.'

Ranjan was about to get up and summon him, when I placed a restraining hand on his arm.

'Please . . . don't. I'll be fine. I only need some more ice. We can get it from the neighbours.'

Ranjan pushed my hand away. 'I don't understand your attitude. Why are you being so obstinate? I keep telling you to spend more time with my mother so that you can learn from her. I get the feeling you don't like her . . . and let me tell you, I won't tolerate that. She's my mother and she must be shown proper respect at all times.'

I tried to defend myself by saying, 'But I do respect her. Who says I don't? And I am trying to get to know her better. The truth is, I'm a little scared of her—she's so stern.'

I was sure Ranjan would understand that and soften. He didn't.

'My mother—stern? Are you crazy? You have no idea how loving she is. Her whole day is devoted to serving others. Do you know how many charitable organizations she's connected with? People love her, adore her. She's full of kindness. It's only you who has not seen that side of her and you know why? Because you refuse to. That's the problem. Fine . . . if you don't want her to come here and help you, leave it. You'll suffer. Don't blame me later if something goes wrong.'

He strode towards the bathroom. 'Where's my towel? I hope you remembered to replace the shaving cream? This is what a man gets when he comes back from a long tour. This is the welcome. Where are my slippers? Why aren't they in the usual place? Really! Look at the state the room is in. Didn't the dhobi come this week? Why haven't you changed the bedcover?'

I held onto my throbbing knee and said plaintively, 'The dhobi did come. But since I'd hardly used the bed, I didn't think the cover needed to be changed. I'm sorry. The shaving cream is right there next to the basin. The towel is inside too.'

Ranjan threw off his clothes but kept his underwear on (he always did). Even through the pain, I couldn't help thinking how comic he looked striding angrily round the room, stomping his feet hard on the floor and all this show of rage while stripped down to his white underwear with its waistband sagging over his fattened-from-the-tour belly.

*

That night, as I lay beside my husband, I started thinking about sex and what a complicated issue it was. Or maybe that's what we made of it. In my case, what I didn't really know, I couldn't miss. I was happy enough with physical demonstrations of affection. I enjoyed being held, stroked, kissed. But I also knew that this wasn't at all what married life was meant to be.

For the past few weeks, I had watched several TV shows that dealt with the subject of sex. Some of the revelations had been startling. I wondered what made normal people agree to appear on these shows and talk about such an intimate aspect of their lives. Would I do it? Would I be able to sit primly on a panel and tell the world that my husband and I had no sex life at all? That I'd never experienced an orgasm? That I still felt ashamed and shy to be naked in my husband's presence? That I'd reconciled myself to the fact that I'd never bear children?

Could I do it? Never. I couldn't visualize Ranjan in such a situation either. This was a matter between us. We had to resolve it. Or make our peace with it. I had even considered counselling—people did go in for it these days. I'd seen an excellent programme and been very impressed by the counsellors.

But Ranjan would never have agreed. Once or twice when I had summoned the courage to broach the subject, he had snapped, 'What's your problem? You are beginning to sound like some sort of a nymphomaniac. Are you that sex-starved? Nothing else on your mind? How can sex be so important to anybody, I've never understood. If your mind is busy and you keep yourself active, where is the time to worry about sex. Really, I'm shocked.'

He had made me feel so ashamed of myself for harbouring such thoughts. I felt low and dirty. Perhaps he was right. Maybe women who led full lives didn't allow the lack of sex to bother them. Then how come all those guests on TV chat shows kept harping on it? I remembered one woman saying she couldn't do without it for even a single day. She had explained it by admitting she had a very high sex drive. Well, mine must have been very low, in that case. And Ranjan's practically non-existent.

I couldn't help feeling I was missing something even if I didn't know what that something was. I had heard Oprah Winfrey recommending masturbation to a woman on her show. I had also heard other women on the same show endorsing that suggestion. One or two of them had come up with 'exciting new ways to pleasure yourself, as they had put it. I had been fascinated but timid when it came to trying out some of the methods they had discussed.

The problem was simple—I had never learnt to be comfortable with my body. As a child, my mother had made me very self-conscious about my nakedness and changing contours. When I reached puberty, she had slapped her forehead dramatically and made me feel like a catastrophe had descended on both of us. After that 'event' (as she called it), my parents had stopped hugging or caressing me.

'You are a young lady now,' my mother had instructed. 'Please behave like one. Don't be a tomboy jumping all over your father. It is simply not done. Be conscious of your limbs and where they are going. The issue is, the event has changed your life forever. Now you have to be extra careful with any man—including your father. No more sitting in his lap or lying next to him on the bed. No more changing clothes in our presence. Go to the bathroom if you need to take off any garment. And always remember, unless you respect your own body, nobody else will.

'Another thing, don't allow anybody to come too close. Make sure no attempt is made to touch you anywhere. If someone tries to act funny or asks you to do something dirty— report the matter to me immediately.'

Her words had made a tremendous impact on me and I had withdrawn into myself totally. I shrank away physically from touch. My body became a major responsibility. I created a distance between it and my mind. If I felt aroused by a book or a film, I blamed myself for being a 'dirty girl with dirty thoughts'. I stopped looking at my breasts or lower down in the large mirror in the cupboard. When the first few pubic hairs sprouted, I hated the sight of them and wondered whether all girls had them or was I the abnormal one.

My proudest moment in these years was when I overheard my mother telling an aunt, 'I have no worries where Maya is concerned. She is not like other girls. She is very pure and unspoilt.'

But was I really? Times when I felt a stirring between my legs and squeezed a pillow held by my knees to suppress it, I knew I had been wicked. But it was the only way to experience some relief from the unbearable dull ache that distracted me from doing anything else.

I wondered what Ranjan did to satisfy his urges. Surely he must have had them . . . everybody did at some time or the other in their lives. I had heard an attractive anchor on El TV asking a male guest most matter-of-factly how often he masturbated and how? He had confessed equally matter-of-factly that it varied from between three to four times a week and that he used his hand to 'do the job', as he put it.

Ranjan seemed to do nothing at all. Yet, he didn't look either frustrated or unhappy. Sometimes I thought I should take the initiative and try my luck with him. Shyly, I had tried snuggling up to him and caressing him one night as we lay in bed, but Ranjan had recoiled—jumping back as though he had received an electric shock. He had lain trembling in bed for a long time, his breathing heavy, his eyes screwed shut.

'Stop behaving like a cheap woman. A prostitute,' he had muttered before turning around and going to sleep.

*

Well . . . tonight I wanted to behave like a cheap woman, a prostitute. I wasn't getting any sleep. My knee was still hurting and the old ache between the legs was bothering me. I reached out for Ranjan, put my arm across his chest and rested my head on his shoulder. I could feel his body stiffening, resisting. His eyes were wide open and he was staring fixedly at the ceiling.

'What's wrong?' I asked gently.

'Nothing. Who said there was anything wrong?' Ranjan replied.

'Please . . . kiss me,' I pleaded.

He turned his head and pecked me on the cheek.

'Not that way. Properly.'

Ranjan inched away from me. 'I don't know any other way . . . please, Maya, I'm tired. I've been travelling. A man needs some rest and a little peace after a hectic tour. First, you go and trip over something and create a scene. Now you've started this business. Why don't you turn your thoughts to something else? Or go read a book in the drawing room. I tell you . . . leave a woman alone for a few days and she lands up creating trouble for herself and others.'

I was determined not to give up so easily this time. I traced my index finger over his left ear and whispered, 'I missed you. I really did. It was so lonely here without you. I hated being in this empty house. I thought of you all the time. I'm so glad you're back.'

Ranjan softened a little. 'I missed you also . . . of course during the day I was busy. But in the evenings I wondered what you were doing and whether you too were thinking of me.'

I moved my body closer to his. 'Ranjan . . . I'm so happy right now. I feel so close to you. Wouldn't it be wonderful if . . .' I let my words trail away.

Ranjan shifted his weight slightly, almost imperceptibly, so that his body was no longer in touch with mine. I should have felt rejected but didn't. I was determined or should I say doomed to see this conversation through.

'Why are you moving away from me? Don't you like me? Do you hate my body . . . or just me?'

Ranjan rolled his eyes heavenwards and looked exasperated.

'Oh God, Maya, do we have to start all this nonsense now? Can't you understand—I'm tired.'

He sighed in an exaggerated way. I ran my fingers through his hair even though he jerked his head away.

'Let me give you a soothing massage. It will really relax you . . . I'm quite good at it,' I murmured, my mouth close to his ear.

Ranjan moved away some more, making me a little worried. Two more inches and he would be off the bed and on the floor. I slid my leg over his and interlinked my foot with his. He kept his leg stretched, resistant and stiff.

'Ranjan, I've been so lonely . . . all alone in a city that isn't mine. In a house I don't still feel I belong to.'

He swung around. 'Whose fault is that—huh? Mine? It's in your hands to make yourself feel at home. Other wives travel to far off places. I know girls who have gone and settled in New Zealand—you know how far that is? Canada . . . South America. What are you complaining about? And it isn't as if Bombay is a jungle . . . some underdeveloped city without any facilities. If you can't adjust to Bombay, how will you ever adjust to, say, Bangalore or Madras or Delhi in case I'm transferred there?

'And you are talking about not feeling at home in your own house. That's a big laugh, isn't it? Have you tried to make it more liveable? I'd told you right at the beginning—get Ma involved. She would have helped you to fix up this place better. But did you listen? No. You stubbornly tried to do things your way. And now look at what's happened. I don't know, Maya. You really have a very negative attitude. All this constant cribbing and cribbing upsets me. I have to concentrate on my job. How can I do that if I have your problems on my head? Not real problems, either. You've brought all this on yourself. What rubbish! Don't like this and don't like that. Don't like Bombay and don't like your home.'

I interrupted the flow by interjecting quietly, 'I didn't say I didn't like Bombay or even that I didn't like our home. Maybe I should have put it differently. Maybe I shouldn't have said anything at all. Oh Ranjan . . . let's stop arguing and fighting. Just as you are tired, I'm also tired. Forget I brought this up. I'm sorry . . . really, really sorry.'

I was about to turn around and go to sleep when Ranjan grabbed my shoulder roughly. He was sitting up in bed, his large eyes nearly falling out of their sockets.

'Wait. . . it's easy to say "sorry". What's the point in saying sorry, sorry, sorry now? You've already ruined what's left of the night. I don't understand you Maya. What's your problem? You live in a comfortable house. There's no shortage of money. I treat you well. You have all the time in the world to just loll around in bed if you want to. I hardly make any demands. I even eat whatever you give me. But still you aren't satisfied. Remember, contentment doesn't come in this way. Learn from my mother.'

I knew I shouldn't have said what I did, but I couldn't restrain myself.

'Is your mother happy? Is she content?' I murmured. Ranjan nearly flew out of the bed.

'Are you casting aspersions on her? How dare you. Of course she is happy. Very happy. If you tried to be even a little bit like her, you'd understand. She's happy with very little. My happiness is her happiness. How would you understand that? You only think of yourself.'

Ranjan was so agitated, his body quivered with anger. I felt alarmed and more than a little scared. Folding my hands, I pleaded, 'Please stop . . . let's not fight. I don't want to upset you, Ranjan.'

'Upset?' he bellowed. 'I am already upset—how much more can you upset me?'

He reached dramatically for the bedside phone.

'Who are you calling?' I asked, my voice cracking.

'Your mother,' he replied through clenched teeth.

'But why? Why involve her in this minor thing. She'll only get unnecessarily worried,' I begged.

'Unnecessarily? I like the cheek. You are worried about her state of mind. What about mine? Or doesn't that concern you? I could die of a heart attack right now, this minute. I can feel something paining inside my chest.'

He clutched the pocket of his nightshirt and shut his eyes. I didn't mind, just as long as his hand wasn't on the phone. I rushed to the kitchen to fetch cold water. When I came back to the bedroom, he had stretched himself out with his arms by his side. He seemed very still. He could have been dead. I said a small prayer and went upto him.

'Ranjan . . .' I called out softly. 'Ranjan . . .'

There was no response. I placed the palm of my hand on his forehead. He didn't resist. His breathing was even and his expression less agitated. Soon he was fast asleep.

I sat by his bed for a long time. After a while, Ranjan began to snore. Finally, I went to my side of the bed and put my head down wearily on the pillow. Just outside the window, I could hear Nikhil revving up his bike. I was tempted to rush over and try and spot him before he roared off. Just listening to him kick-starting his machine filled me with sadness. I could have been on that pillion with him. We would have zoomed off into the Bombay night. The possibilities were many . . . but wasn't that what I had thought the day I had overheard my mother's conversation with Prodipmama asking us to come to Bombay to meet a very 'promising' match?

I didn't want to blame Ranjan. Or anybody else, for that matter. It wasn't Ranjan who had made the promises. It was I who had foolishly assumed them. Ranjan had pledged nothing more than financial support, a decent house to live in and four square meals a day. As far as he was concerned, he had redeemed his pledge. It was upto me to accept or reject it.

Twenty-three

My mother-in-law rarely phoned before seven-thirty in the morning. She respected her son's rituals and never disturbed him during his bathing-shaving-praying routine. Which was why I was surprised to hear her voice at six o'clock.

Without greeting me, she whispered hoarsely, 'Give him the phone, quickly.'

I knew something had happened. Something was wrong. Ranjan was up and reading the business section of *The Times of India* (he had been following the Enron controversy with a keenness that surprised me—or maybe I had no idea as to his bank's involvement in the Dabhol project).

I called out to him, my voice louder than usual.

'Why are you shouting so early in the morning?' he grumbled.

'It's Ma,' I said, picking up his empty teacup. He put down the paper and grabbed the phone from my hand.

'Ma?' his voice was stricken. He knew immediately something was wrong even before his mother could say it. He replaced the receiver after reassuring her that he was on his way. He rushed to the room and hurriedly began to dress.

'Call the office and say there has been an emergency,' he instructed.

I fluttered around handing him his handkerchief and locating matching socks.

'What's happened?' I asked him, as he opened the cupboard and reached for a wad of notes he kept carefully hidden in the jacket pocket of his old grey suit.

'I think it's Ma's heart,' he explained briefly.

'Has she had an attack?' I asked, trying to show a concern I wasn't really feeling. Ranjan nodded as he stuffed the money into his trouser pocket. I was quite distracted by that. It was supposed to be a secret—his private funds that he didn't want me to know about. From time to time, he would dip into them when he thought I wasn't in the room. If ever I walked in inadvertently while he was slipping a few hundred rupees into his wallet, he would shut the cupboard door hastily and whirl around with a funny expression on his face.

Once or twice, I had been tempted to ask him whether he thought I was a petty thief who would rifle through his jacket pockets and run away with a couple of thousand bucks. But by some tacit signal that passed between us, I always pretended I hadn't noticed a thing, and Ranjan altered his expression after the first few embarrassed seconds to the standard half-scowl, half-smile that was specially designed to keep me in place and at the same time reassure me that I wasn't dealing with an outright enemy.

I followed him to the door where he picked up the car keys in one smooth, fluid motion.

'Do you want me to come later?' I called after him as he ran down . . . or rather hurtled down the stairs, five steps at a time.

'No need,' he yelled before leaping into the car and rushing off.

It struck me as being a little strange that men were always leaving me to jump into or onto various vehicles and roaring away. It had happened with Nikhil last night (not that he had even been aware of abandoning me). And it was happening now.

I stood by the window for a long time, unsure of what to do next. It was likely that Ranjan would keep me completely in the dark about his mother's condition. It was equally likely that he would flare up if I decided to go there on my own and offer to help. I was pretty sure Ranjan would, in fact, resent my presence, particularly if I landed up unbidden.

Ranjan didn't approve of surprises. I suddenly thought of the small gift I had bought for him once on an impulse— an attractive, leather bound, hand-crafted filofax. Seeing the package, Ranjan had stared accusingly at me.

'What's this?' he had demanded suspiciously.

'It's . . . it's . . . a present,' I mumbled.

'For whom?' he had asked, turning it around and examining it as though it was a tiny bomb that could explode in his face.

'For you . . . naturally,' I had smiled, urging him to open the smartly wrapped package.

'But why? It's not my birthday. You shouldn't waste money like this.'

I had run to my dressing table to get my nail scissors and cut the elaborate tape around the bright wrapping paper. Ranjan had finally stared at the filofax and said, 'I don't need this . . . I prefer an electronic planner which fits into my wallet. Give it to someone else. And . . . in future, Maya, ask me before you buy something. Everything costs money, you know. I hate waste.'

Crushed by his lack of grace, I had taken the offending gift from his hands, walked into the bedroom and hurled it to the back of my cupboard where it still lay. I had learnt one significant lesson—no surprises.

*

I sat by the window for more than two hours. I had never felt so useless. Nobody needed me, absolutely nobody. My parents no longer thought I belonged to them. My husband belonged to his mother. It was unlikely that I would bear children who would belong to me. And I didn't have a single true friend to call my own.

Perhaps the only human beings to whose lives I made even the slightest difference were the freelance domestics who came to ensure my house was clean, the pots and pans in the kitchen gleaming and the clothes properly washed. It was these people and the few vendors who came to the building—the idli man and the floor mop man—who made me feel wanted. As if I was in some way relevant to their lives. And even with them, I felt such a fraud. It wasn't my money that I was paying them. They didn't have to feel indebted to me. I was only the cashier dispensing Ranjan's money.

Perhaps they didn't know that. Maybe they believed I had the power to decide. I wanted them to believe that. It made me feel important. More important than I had felt in any other relationship.

I heard the doorbell ringing. Wearily, I went to answer it, clutching my crumpled caftan—the one with blue paisleys that needed to have its hem shortened by at least three inches. I caught a quick glimpse of myself in the mirror. The kaajal in my eyes was smudged and my hair looked both unwashed and uncombed.

But it was my expression that scared me. It was vacant. I looked totally blank as if behind those large eyes there was a deep void into which everything fell and disappeared.

I opened the door and turned around to go back into the bedroom without even bothering to check who the caller was, certain it was one of the bais.

'Good morning, beautiful.'

Nikhil. How dared he. How dared he just ring my doorbell and present me with his impertinence without thinking that he would be causing me great offence. I whirled around to say 'get out'. It was the sight of the flowers in his hand that stopped me.

'Happy birthday to me . . . happy birthday to me,' he sang out lustily, waving the bouquet of baby-pink carnations around. He walked in confidently, declaring, 'I know you don't know its my birthday. That's why I am here to inform you. And since I knew that you didn't know it's my birthday, I have brought my own flowers. Now . . . how shall we celebrate?'

He kicked the door shut with the heel of his shoe and before I could react to his presence in my house, he grabbed hold of my shoulders and pulled me into an embrace that left me gasping for breath.

With the flowers still in his hand, he held me at a distance and laughed, showing his square white teeth. 'Surprised?' he said.

I started to say something—anything. But Nikhil's mouth covered mine gently. His eyes were shut and his hands were in my untidy hair with the bouquet getting caught in the tangles.

It was a kiss that involved Nikhil's entire being. A kiss so focused, so complete, I surrendered to its soft urgency even though my mind was on mundanities like the washerwoman showing up earlier than usual. Or Ranjan rushing in, using his latch key, to pick up some more cash for his mother's whatever it was.

Every bit of me was suddenly alive to the feel of Nikhil's lips, hands, arms, neck, chest, knees, legs. An unknown recklessness started to sweep over me. Maybe I was going crazy.

I didn't want to think of consequences. I refused to assume responsibility. I really didn't care one way or the other. I felt free. Lunatic. Wonderful.

Nikhil's eyes were still closed as he started marching me backwards. One-two. One-two. His lips had started to travel all over my face. I could feel the pores of my skin opening up as if I was in a sauna. Dimly, I heard the doorbell and the phone as they rang simultaneously. I made a weak attempt to stretch my arm. I even tried to speak—a muffled, incoherent sound emerged from my mouth which had another mouth firmly over it, shutting out speech.

Our strange two-step dance continued backwards. Of course, I knew exactly where Nikhil was headed. What surprised me a little was how well he knew the layout of the flat. He made a steady, sure-footed progress towards the bedroom, his hand placed squarely in the small of my back, as he guided me deftly past furniture and other obstacles.

My head was starting to swim but that may have had more to do with the fact that I hadn't eaten anything since waking. Nikhil hadn't shaved for a couple of days, judging from the stubble that was scraping my cheek and neck. I was hanging onto the front of his Madras-check shirt like a child clinging to the edge of a precipice, afraid of letting go and falling down into a bottomless ravine.

I kept my eyes shut not out of passion but fear and embarrassment. I sincerely believed that if I didn't see what was happening, if I didn't look into Nikhil's eyes, if I shut everything out visually, I would be free of any responsibility. I wouldn't be an accomplice. There would be no role played by me if a conspiracy was later sought to be proved.

By blinding myself, I felt as though I had disappeared. I wasn't there. If I couldn't see anybody, nobody could see me either. My innocence was established.

I allowed myself to be pushed back on my bed—the bed I shared with Ranjan. I knew we were on Ranjan's side of it by the smell of the bed linen and pillows. I could feel Nikhil's hands under my caftan, pulling it up, up and up.

Since I wasn't seeing, there was no shame even when my legs were bared upto the thighs. The caftan climbed higher, it was now at my waist and still climbing. I knew my breasts were clearly visible (I'd removed my bra the previous night). I didn't want to think about how they must have looked to Nikhil. He was positioned alongside me, the length of his body next to mine, one leg swung over and wedged between my knees.

With a swift, smooth motion, he pushed the caftan over my head and off the bed. His lips were over mine again, as his hands moved expertly over the rest of my body, choosing where to linger before moving on again.

I heard the phone ring. And then I heard the doorbell. Nikhil whispered, 'Ignore. Ignore.'

Meekly, I obeyed. Not that I could have rushed naked to answer either. For that to happen, I would have had to open my eyes and acknowledge the fact that Nikhil and I were doing what we were doing.

At some point, he must have removed his own clothes. I still don't know how and when he did that since at least one of his hands was always touching some part of my body all the while. I could feel the hair on his legs curling against my belly. I could feel the tension in his back muscles as he lowered himself over me, making sure not to land heavily but balance his weight dexterously between his elbows and knees.

I could feel a slight bump on his hard buttocks—a mole? A boil? A bite? A scar? Nikhil's right knee was between my legs, parting them firmly but not roughly. His right hand was in my hair, massaging the base of my skull. His other hand was touching me like one would touch temple flowers—gently, almost respectfully, as though afraid to shock or hurt.

When Nikhil's tongue met mine, I knew there was no way I could open my eyes now. It was much too late for anything. I was beyond recklessness, beyond sane thinking, beyond repercussions. Had even Ranjan climbed in through the window, I was sure I wouldn't have made the slightest attempt to move out from under Nikhil or cover up my nakedness.

Nikhil was surprisingly refined. There wasn't a single awkward movement or a rough caress. As his fingers stroked my body, they made music of the sweetest kind. I lay there in a state that was physically passive but in my mind a spectacular tropical storm was in full progress complete with thunder and lightning. I could even smell the earth as its dryness disappeared and it gradually softened, moistened by the skies as they opened up to release its trapped fragrance.

Nikhil was inside me now. He'd accomplished it painlessly, smoothly, gently. As I held him prisoner within my body, I felt an overwhelming sense of power. He was my captive . . . his very being deep inside a dark, silent, mysterious tunnel that led straight to my womb. I would keep him there at my will. And with this consciousness dominating my senses, I felt my body opening up languidly. My initially rigid arms crept fluidly over Nikhil's back with an assurance I hadn't suspected I possessed. My thighs gave up their struggle to keep Nikhil out and opened up joyfully. I arched upwards so that my breasts could brush against Nikhil's chest. I threw my head back while he nuzzled my neck with his face buried in the hollow created by my shoulder blades. My hands stayed over his buttocks possessively as if to make sure he remained where he was—inside me.

I could feel him distinctly, now that the dance had begun. Nikhil moved over me adopting a strange rhythm. Half the challenge lay in trying to follow his pace even when it became frenetic in its urgency. My legs and arms had wound themselves so tightly around Nikhil's athletic frame, it was a wonder he could move at all, or breathe. I wanted to swallow Nikhil completely . . . suck him into my womb inch by inch. I wanted, oh, so, desperately, to make him mine. Make him me.

Fifteen minutes later, my eyes were still shut. Nikhil had obviously dressed and gone (I had heard the small click of the front door at some point). I didn't have the slightest idea what time it was—it could have been noon or midnight. The disorientation was total and complete. It was only the irritating chiming of Ranjan's grandfather's carriage clock that told me what I didn't want to know—the most wonderful, the most unimaginable, the most moving experience of my life had taken no more than a quarter of an hour. That was it.

I had no desire to move, get out of bed, bathe or straighten the bedcovers. I wanted to lie there for the rest of my life, savouring each micro-second of what had transpired between Nikhil and me.

My breathing was even and back to normal. My body felt like melting chocolate or liquid gold. My limbs had suddenly become far too heavy for me to try and lift. My back, which had taken Nikhil's weight in the final five minutes, had turned to concrete. My tongue, which I had never imagined would be capable of doing all the things it had done, lay resting against the inside of my cheek—exhausted by the unaccustomed activity I had subjected it to.

*

The doorbell was ringing again. This time, more insistently. I had not the slightest desire to see who it was. My limbs had turned to mushy amoebic extensions that refused to obey orders from the central nervous system.

I lay on the bed immobilized and drained, my mind dull and the rest of me reduced to a caricature in slow motion. The lifeless heap that was me lay against Ranjan's comfortable pillows, breathing in his smell which had now merged with mine and Nikhil's. It exuded a strange, sharp bouquet—a mixture of dried and dead rose petals, rancid cheese, curdled milk, butter on the boil and stale bread.

I could feel an unfamiliar, sticky fluid flowing down my inner thighs, and there was a thick, snot-like deposit on my stomach, some more on my wrists. I let it remain where it was without the slightest urge to wipe it away.

My eyes were seeing inner pictures that had nothing to do with my room, my house, my childhood or my immediate environment. I could hear music that wasn't playing anywhere, not even in my mind—discordant chords without a beginning or an end. I tried to lick my swollen lips to taste what was left of Nikhil on them, but my tongue weighed so much it couldn't move.

I gave up all effort to think or act. I fell into a deep, dark sleep. I would deal with Ranjan (and his mother) later.

*

I awoke abruptly to the sound of firecrackers. At first I thought they were bombs going off at the nearby slum colony. Perhaps fresh riots had broken out in Bombay after more than a year of uneasy peace. I was startled to find myself naked and in Ranjan's bed. I made a monumental effort and picked myself up. The temptation to collapse again was overwhelming.

I glanced at the clock and noticed it was past one o'clock. The maids had obviously rung the bell and gone. The kitchen was reasonably clean and free of too many dirty utensils. The house seemed neat enough. That left the unwashed clothes in the bathroom and the unmade bed.

I stared down at my body—nothing had changed. I was oddly disappointed. God knows what I had expected or hoped for. Maybe a garden in full bloom with multi-coloured blossoms sprouting from my breasts, my pubes, my armpits, my mouth, my eyes, ears, toes and hair.

Instead, I touched my damp skin which was drenched in perspiration, even though the fan was whirring overhead. I couldn't postpone my bath any longer. The water was cool against my skin which seemed to be glowing phosphorescently. I looked down at my limbs and they were transparent. My skin was radiating a strange, strong light. And the soap failed when it came to dealing with the stickiness which continued to gush from me and flow down my legs.

I glanced at the image in the bathroom mirror. Even my tangled hair looked like a magnificent halo. The smudged kaajal in my eyes gave them an unreal luminosity as they shone like coals. I wished Ranjan was here to see me now. I looked beautiful. Truly beautiful. Even Ranjan would have had to acknowledge that.

The thought that I would never look this beautiful again for my own husband filled me with a sudden, overpowering sadness as tears poured out of my eyes—the same ones that had seemed so luminous only moments ago, and coursed down the length of my body to join the remnants of the warm, pearly fluid that was still trickling out of me.

I stayed in the bathroom for more than an hour, unable to stop the tears and unwilling to do so. My lips had puffed up grotesquely, protesting against the sharpness of my teeth as I bit into them in a vain effort to gain control and get back to reality.

It was only the loud, aggressive banging on the door that broke the spell I had self-induced.

With a start, I dried myself with a vigour that was almost violent. The thumping increased. I could hear Ranjan's voice calling out.

'Maya . . . open the door. Maya . . . Maya.'

I rushed out from the bathroom, pulled a clean caftan out of my cupboard, flung it on and ran through the living room, flinging myself against the locked door. In my confusion and hurry, I failed to notice the discarded bouquet of rapidly wilting carnations lying on the threshold of my room—our room.

It was the first thing Ranjan spotted when he walked angrily past me muttering, 'Some people are born deaf. I've been hammering on that door for ten minutes—ten whole minutes. Even a corpse would have heard me. Just today of all days I had to go and forget my latch key, imagine.'

Before I could ask him how his mother was, he tripped over a side table and pounced on the bouquet.

'What's this? Who gave it to you? Why is it lying here on the floor? What's going on in my house—behind my back?'

Some mysterious signal from my brain ensured that I maintained a blank expression that gave nothing away even as my heart pounded heavily inside its cage.

'Those . . . those flowers, they are for your mother. I wanted to come and see her . . . and cheer her up a little. Poor thing,' I lied smoothly.

Ranjan looked unconvinced. He picked up the flowers and sniffed suspiciously as though their fragrance would provide some sort of clue.

'Then why did you throw it on the floor?'

I lied again, this time more confidently. 'I didn't throw it— it got knocked down when I ran from the bathroom to open the door. I'm sorry, I didn't hear you thumping on it—the water was running.'

Ranjan stood where he was, a puzzled expression on his face, the bouquet dangling from his hand. 'Why didn't you pick up the phone? I called several times from the nursing home. Where were you?'

This was easy.

'I'd gone to the market to get the flowers. You must have called when I left the house for about half an hour. I couldn't get a cab quickly—peak hour.'

Then I remembered he had said something about a nursing home.

'Oh, how is Ma? What happened? Where is she? You should've brought her straight to our home. I would have done everything to look after her.'

Ranjan stared at me penetratingly. I thought he was finding it hard to believe his ears.

'She's all right now. The doctors say she's out of danger. But who knows what might have happened if I hadn't reached on time? By now, I might have lost her. Anyway, thank God she's going to be all right. It's nothing serious—a flutter in the heart. But it gave her a good scare—that's all. And me too. When I saw her lying on the bed, I really thought "this is the end". She looked so frail and weak and helpless.'

I started tidying up the place busily. The idea was to keep him talking about his mother. Distract him. Divert his attention.

'We really should bring her home for a few days,' I suggested again brightly. 'Coffee for you? You're looking tired.'

Ranjan declined and went into the kitchen. I heard him calling out agitatedly, 'What's this? The sink is full of dirty dishes. Didn't that bloody woman come this morning?'

I rushed into the kitchen with an outraged expression.

'These women are so unreliable, I tell you. They keep bunking on some pretext or the other. One day it's a sick child, next day their mother dies—God knows how many times Shantibai's mother has died since she joined us. Today it must be Ganpati. Don't worry, I'll handle it. No problem. I've done it before—why don't you relax. Sit outside. The bedroom is a bit of a mess.'

Ranjan whirled around. 'Why? Don't tell me the other woman didn't turn up either? Remind me to cut their day's wages. Make a note in the diary. That's the only way these women learn. One has to teach them a solid lesson. Everyone in Bombay is taking advantage of everyone else. Well . . . all this doesn't work with me. You work and I pay. You don't work, I no pay. Simple.'

I made a few clucking sounds to demonstrate how perfectly I understood his attitude.

'Even in Calcutta, the situation is rapidly deteriorating. My mother's letters are full of complaints. I suppose servants just aren't what they used to be. It's getting harder and harder to get good people. But forget all that—tell me about Ma.'

Ranjan went into a long and boring description about how he summoned the family doctor who had recommended instant hospitalization.

'Why take chances? After all, she isn't a young woman anymore,' Ranjan added.

With the doctor's help, he had located a convenient nursing home, summoned an ambulance and moved her.

'Thank God I had taken enough cash,' he stated, his voice full of self-congratulation. 'These days people, even doctors, are so heartless. Unless you first put down some money, nobody will bother to look at you even if you're dying. I wanted the best for Ma—naturally. "A" class room, a/c and all that. Can't expect her to do without the comforts she's used to. It's going to cost me a lot of money, but so what?'

I said encouragingly, hoping I was sounding like a supportive, understanding wife, 'What is money when Ma's health is involved. She must have the best possible treatment. Have you got a good day-and-night ayah to look after her?'

Ranjan stared at me as though I had said something utterly ridiculous.

'We don't need an ayah. I'm planning to take leave—I have a lot of it accumulated as it is. And you, in any case, have nothing much to do at home. Between us, we'll manage. I can't have Ma suffering at the hands of a complete stranger. You know how these nurses and ayahs are. In the first place, most of them are from Kerala. Who understands what they are saying, even if it is in English? Ma would hate to be touched or sponged by those women. You'll have to do it. Help her to the toilet and all that. I've come to pack a small bag, shower and go straight to the nursing home. You can join me a little later.'

And with that, Ranjan disappeared into our room. I heard him switch on the air-conditioner and television. I heard the bathroom door slam. Another one slammed equally forcefully in my heart as I realized what this new development was about to do to my life. A life that had just about become worth living.

My body was still raw and shaking from having had a man inside. I had yet to savour and cherish the memory of having been joined with another. My brain, my heart, my belly, my breasts, my fingertips, every bit of me was still tingling from having been brought to life so acutely.

In my newly awakened state, I was being told to die again. To go back to being a corpse. It seemed so unfair. So cruel. Far more so than anything Ranjan's mother was going through right then.

I longed to hear Nikhil's voice. To share my feelings with him. To make him a part of my tumult—a tumult created by him and known only to him.

I was ready to make any kind of deal with God at that moment. All I wanted was time with Nikhil—an hour, no, I would have settled for half, quarter . . . even five minutes. I wanted him so badly. Wanted his arms around me, his chest to rest my head on. Nothing more. And I was certain he wanted me in exactly the same way—with the same intensity, the same passion.

As I began scrubbing the dirt from the unwashed utensils, my tears landing on caked remnants of last night's dinner, I prayed to a God I had never believed in. I prayed with every fibre of my being. Give him to me, oh God, I begged. Make Nikhil mine.

Twenty-four

The next ten days saw me in the entirely unaccustomed role of a full-time nursemaid to my mildly ailing mother-in-law. The nursing home (Pyar Mandir—Temple of Love) was run by avaricious promoters out to fleece the desperate who flocked there in the mistaken belief that a modest medical facility in suburban Bombay would be cheaper than the grand showpiece hospitals in the centre of the city that demanded a king's ransom even as patients lay on stretchers gasping their last breath while wild-eyed relatives passed the equivalent of a begging bowl around to drum up enough funds for a hefty deposit prior to admission.

Pyar Mandir was in a leafy, secluded lane in Andheri West—an area infested with immigrants from Kerala who had their own temples, eateries, shops and banks in the area. The place was comfortable enough but I was convinced my mother-in-law's heart flutter was nothing more than a petulant cry for attention.

If it was attention from her son that she sought, what she received was overwhelming filial devotion. Ranjan and I took turns to remain by her side round the clock to ensure that she remained wrapped in cotton wool, her every demand instantly met, her every wish promptly fulfilled. When I wasn't rushing out to get fresh, thin-skinned mosambi to squeeze for her two-hourly juice, I was going on wild goose chases to locate rubber bedpans since the old enamel ones hurt her.

She didn't like the food served by Pyar Mandir and insisted on home-cooked Bengali fare which naturally fell to my lot to prepare. Of course, my efforts were completely wasted since she had a low opinion about my cooking and disapproved of even the simplest dishes. She also didn't trust the nursing home to do her laundry which meant that I had to rush her clothes back and forth (ironed according to her specifications). I also had to make sure she had a pile of fresh hand towels next to her pillows and a thermos filled with boiled and filtered drinking water.

It was left to Ranjan to read out the entire *Times of India* to her, including the Classifieds and obituaries. Since she claimed she found my accent hard to understand, I was told to get her 'colourful' magazines with a large print, as she found it a strain to wear her glasses.

Between my sick-bed duties and routine domestic chores, I didn't have a single moment for myself. When I wasn't actually rushing around, I was far too tired to do anything more than sleep a deep dreamless dead sleep. If Ranjan appreciated my efforts to please the two of them, he himself was equally drained and didn't voice his feelings.

It was strange that the strain of looking after Ma got to him before it got to me. Ranjan cracked much earlier than I did. Half an hour of dealing with her constant demands and he would start complaining of severe stomach cramps or an impending migraine. This would be his signal for shuffling around restlessly before leaving for home, saying 'Don't worry, Ma, Maya is there in case you need anything. Besides, I'm only a phone call away.'

He would then turn to me sternly with a 'don't-you-dare-let-me-down' expression and say, 'Stay with Ma. Make sure she gets her juice and tablets on time.'

Once back in the house, he would jump into bed and stay there watching TV—old movies, the US Open, Channel V, even afternoon soaps on the national network. When I would get back in a state of nervous collapse, I would find him happily munching chivda on the bed and watching Andre Agassi pulp his opponent. He would barely look up, acknowledge my presence, ask perfunctorily about his mother's condition and go back to the screen.

Sometimes, I would join him on the bed, not because I particularly wanted to watch tennis but just to anaesthetisize myself against thoughts about Nikhil.

I had started missing him in a ridiculously acute way. He was there in my thoughts, a constant, challenging presence. I awoke with him in my mind's eye. I went to bed thinking of him. Each and every action of mine, even in the nursing home, involved Nikhil in some way. What would he think of my efficiency with the bedpan? How would he react to my squeezing sweet lime juice? Would his expression change along with mine at the sight of the ugly overbearing matron?

I dressed for him, knowing fully well he wouldn't see me. I felt beautiful. I wanted to look beautiful. I fantasized that I would meet him while running in and out of the building. I wrote poems and notes in my head. I carried on a silent, running conversation with him, I laughed and shared secrets. And suppressed smiles at jokes yet uncracked.

I told myself that this was just a pause—a badly-timed one in the glorious relationship to follow. Once things were back to 'normal', I would take the initiative and invite him over to discuss our status. Meanwhile, I had begun to enjoy textures, tastes and sounds that had meant nothing to me in the past. I was alive to every aspect of living because I knew I had Nikhil in my life.

I was sure he was going through exactly the same thing. And I felt sorry for him because I hadn't been able to tell him about the recent developments in my life and why I was never at home these days. Of course, he would understand once I got the chance to explain. Poor chap—how bewildered and tense he must have been. And so uncertain.

I wanted to reassure him of my love in case he was insecure. My commitment to him was total. Unwavering. True. I was sure he knew this instinctively. That's why I wasn't overly worried. We had all the time ahead of us. Our entire lives.

It wasn't going to be easy. But nothing this precious ever was. In my awakened state, even Ranjan's little eccentricities didn't bother me half as much as they used to. I felt' benevolent, tolerant and exceedingly kind. I forgave him for bullying me, pushing me around, being inconsiderate even boorish.

Formerly, I couldn't bear to watch TV with him because of the absolute power he exercised over the selection of the programmes. He would switch channels without as much as a glance in my direction, just when I was beginning to get involved. It used to infuriate me. Or, he would casually switch off the set once he had finished watching something or was leaving the room to go out. What about me, I felt like screaming. I was still there, sitting dumbly in front of a blank screen. Maybe I wanted to see something of my choice. Maybe there were programmes out there that interested me. How come he didn't realize that? How come he didn't care?

I had tried protesting a couple of times, and been crushed by his cutting response.

'Sorry,' he had snapped, 'I didn't realize you were that interested in world affairs. And in case you want to watch any of those other mindless programmes, I suggest you use your time a little better. Take more interest in the house.'

I would bite my lower lip in frustration and turn my face away so he wouldn't see my tears.

But now, I felt nothing at all. I would sit by his side, numb and passive. If a CNN anchor was going on and on about a war nobody cared about, I would listen. If Ranjan switched everything off and picked up a business magazine, I could close my eyes and pretend to be catnapping. It didn't really matter, for all I could see or hear was Nikhil everywhere and in everything— on TV, in the papers, even in the tiles of our bedroom floor.

So whether or not a programme held my interest became completely irrelevant since I wasn't watching it anyway. Or rather, every single character on the screen was Nikhil—the weather man on CNN, Barry Norman on Film '95, David Cass on the Newshour, even Niki Marx.

My obsessive preoccupation didn't bother me at all. I know it should have. But it gave me great comfort to know that I had Nikhil in my life and that it was just a matter of time before we were joined again, literally and metaphorically. There was no question in my mind that Nikhil was experiencing exactly the same syndrome and feeling equally frustrated. Being the observant sort of chap that he was, he had probably noted the change in Ranjan's schedules and decided to stay away.

Besides, the building grapevine was such, somebody must have told him about my mother-in-law. I remained calm and far from agitated even when Ranjan exasperated me. Each time my spirits dipped, I thought of what I had known, the magic of those glorious moments, and nothing else mattered.

When the time was right, every troublesome aspect of my life would fall into place. I anticipated resistance from Ranjan—but not too much of it. I was certain my decision would come as something of a relief to a man who really didn't need marriage, romance or sex.

*

We brought my mother-in-law back to our home at Ranjan's insistence.

'Ma, I will not allow you to go back there,' he said firmly. 'Maya will look after you for a few months till you're strong enough to live on your own again.'

She shook her head weakly and made small, strangled noises protesting the move. Ranjan ignored her and shouted out various instructions to me.

'Pick up her bag. Check the bathroom. Don't leave soap or hair oil behind. What about all those unused capsules and tablets? Collect the strips of vitamin supplements. That thermos belongs to us—don't forget to pack it. And the plastic glass. Ma's hand towels—count them. There should be at least six fresh ones.'

My mother-in-law leaned on her son's arm and made soft groaning noises like an animal in pain. Ranjan paid the cashier and marched his mother into the waiting car, calling out to me to follow in a cab. I didn't understand the logic of that—there was enough place in the car—but I said nothing. It was only a matter of a few more days. I had decided to live those gracefully.

I even managed a friendly smile and wave as they got into the car and drove off. Ranjan had said Ma would be with us for a 'few months'. So what? Of course, she would be watching me like a hawk but I was confident of giving her the slip once a pattern had been established. Nikhil would understand—he wasn't insensitive. We would find time together somehow. It was all a matter of smart planning.

Ranjan had two more days of leave left. When I followed them home carrying Ma's bag and at least six heavy plastic packages, I found them in the bedroom. Ranjan was plumping up the pillows for his mother and making the kind of meaningless cooin sounds one reserves for thumb-sucking infants in prams. She was moaning and muttering, 'Hey ma. Hey ma'.

Ranjan told me briskly to make tea for them, adding, 'Oh, Maya . . . I think Ma and I should use the bedroom while she's here. You don't mind, do you? The couch in the drawing room is pretty big. I'll buy extra cushions. And maybe a couple of bedcovers.'

I nodded, put the packages down and rushed into the kitchen. The arrangement suited me fine. I wanted to be on my own anyway. While the tea was brewing, I started making plans keeping in mind the fact that Ma would be monitoring my every move and phone call. Well, I would just have to beat her at the game and devise new strategies. All I really needed was one meeting with Nikhil to brief him on all the new developments.

*

It was at around eight that night when I was attempting to make a chicken soup according to my mother-in-law's croaked directions that the doorbell rang. I turned the flame down and went to see who it was. The question of Ranjan getting up from in front of the TV to answer either the telephone or the doorbell did not arise. He would just stay put and yell out to me impatiently, 'Phone, Maya, phone', or 'Someone's at the door, Maya', as though I was deaf or absent-minded enough to ignore either.

My mind was still on the chicken soup bubbling on the gas when I opened the door. It took me a second to recognize Nikhil's mother, Pushpa. For one, she was so ridiculously overdressed, it took me a while to see beyond the paint on her face, the tinsel of her gaudy clothes and the kilos of gold jewellery she had loaded onto her neck, ears and wrists.

Mrs Verma was holding a decorated earthen pot filled with sticky sweetmeats and covered with yellow cellophane.

'Hello, hello, long time, no see, Maya. Where have you been hiding, huh?' she asked cheerfully.

Still taken aback by her appearance, I mumbled something about my mother-in-law.

'Is your sweetie pie husband home? May I come in? I've got some good news for both of you.'

With that, she pushed past me and entered the drawing room where I had already made my bed.

'What's this? Visitor? Guest?' she asked, making no attempt to hide her naked curiosity. I evaded giving her a reply and called out to Ranjan.

'Look who's here,' I said, trying to bring some enthusiasm into my voice. I was sure she had come across to gloat about her husband's promotion. I had heard Ranjan talking about it to his mother and rapidly changing the subject when I came into the room.

Mrs Verma continued to stand in the middle of the room waiting for Ranjan to join us. I knew he was probably scrambling into a pair of trousers and looking for his 'holiday T-shirt'.

He was out a couple of minutes later saying, '*Mubarak ho, bhabiji.*'

I was surprised to hear him speak Hindi and to realize he had addressed her as 'bhabiji'. Since when had Pushy Pushpa become his sister-in-law? I also added my congratulations—in English.

'Thank you, thank you. This is such a proud moment for us. You know how it is for parents. That too when there is only one son in the family. Our only son.'

Even though I heard her words clearly, I didn't understand their import. Maybe she was being oblique, I thought. I didn't really see where Nikhil came into it. Okay, his father had been promoted. Great. But what did Mr Verma's promotion have to do with Nikhil being the only son?

I smiled as I took the proffered sweetmeats from her hand.

'Thank you,' I said. 'Such good news. You must be so happy.'

'Naturally,' she said, her voice smug and self-congratulatory. The jangle of her bangles distracted me for a moment. I took in her orange nail polish (to match the orange lipstick) and heavily embroidered green outfit with an orange dupatta. Her toenails were an inch-long (almost) and filed into sharp points. She wore three heavy necklaces around her neck (where she had forgotten to apply foundation). Her face resembled a mask with layers of pressed powder and shining green eyeshadow caking her eyelids.

'You look like you're going to a wedding,' I commented, unable to think of what else to say.

She laughed her false, tinkling laugh. 'Well . . . call it a dress rehearsal . . . even though the wedding won't be for four more years.'

'Whose wedding are you talking about?' I asked, as I passed Ranjan who was heading purposefully towards the kitchen with a scowl on his face.

'Nikhil's,' she said. 'Whose did you think?'

The 'what' that emerged from my constricted throat was alarmingly loud.

'Yes,' his mother continued, 'my tension is over. I was sure he wouldn't agree to the match—that too on the eve of his departure. You know how obstinate boys are these days. Who likes to get hitched? And an arranged match at that. You must meet my Anshu. She's from Delhi. Actually, she's the daughter of an old college friend of mine—can you imagine? Such a coincidence, I tell you. It all happened so quickly . . .'

Her voice echoed through my head. '. . . Just two months ago, my friend came to Bombay—you may have seen her when she visited me. Very nice. Tall. Fair. A little fat now. She saw Nikhil and *bas,* she decided to stage a dharna. She made me promise I would accept her daughter as my bahu. I told her, "*Arrey baba,* do you know my son's age? He's still a bachcha. Let him finish his education first. We are trying for a scholarship. He wants to go abroad for further studies."

'Did she listen? No way. "Meet my daughter just once", she said. I told her "What's the point in my meeting her? Nikhil has to agree first." So she said "Okay. I'll send Anshu across with her aunt. No problem."

'I was really trapped then. Nikhil—you know how he is, refused flat. I told him not to be stubborn. "What's the harm if you meet the girl?" I argued.

'Thank God he agreed. Anshu came over ten days later—and that was it. Nikhil flipped. Anshu was thrilled. We decided to finalize everything—why wait? Quickly, quickly, I made all the arrangements. Naturally, they insisted on having the engagement ceremony at the girl's place. I said "why not?"

'Nikhil still hasn't returned. I'm so worried—he has to pack. Did I tell you, he got into Rochester University? Very good place. But he's not willing to come back. Every night when I speak to him and plead, "Beta, there is so much to do. When are you getting home?", he just laughs and says, "Not now, mom.

314

Later, later." I say, "When later?" He doesn't give me a proper answer.

'I'll have to tell his Dad to speak to him. At this rate he'll miss his flight and his place in the university. But how can you argue with young people in love? I know what the feeling is. We've all gone through it. So I say, "Forget it. Let him enjoy, *yaar.*"

'Anyway, I'd better run. I still have so many flats left to distribute mithai to. In our community this sweets business never ends. You Bengalis are lucky that way.'

With those words, she was gone, leaving me holding Nikhil's engagement matka.

*

I stood motionless and unthinking . . . till Ranjan came out of the kitchen to inform me that the chicken soup had boiled over and was burnt.

'Didn't you smell it?' he asked crossly.

I shook my head.

'How come? My mother smelt it burning from the bedroom and sent me to see what was happening.'

My head was hanging low. But there were no tears.

'You women! Always gossiping and wasting time. Is this the hour to come over without calling first? You should have told that woman. But did you? You could have said frankly that you had to give Ma her dinner. Discharge your duties towards a sick person. Instead of doing that, you stood there chatting and chatting while the soup got burnt on the gas. Honestly, Maya, I sometimes wonder about you. You never pay attention. Where is your mind?'

For once, Ranjan had asked a good question. I walked slowly into the kitchen. The gas range was a mess with sticky soup all over it.

I started to laugh. I looked at the spilled liquid—thick, white, chalky mucous-like, and I just broke up. It looked so funny. And so familiar. Like a baby's puke or coagulated snot, or something I had seen before somewhere, not so long ago.

I leaned against the refrigerator to steady myself. My entire body was shaking with mirth. The more I stared at the spilled soup, the funnier I found it. I knew I would have to make it again from scratch.

So what? I had all the time in the world now.

Also by Shobhaa Dé

Sultry Days

Nisha falls in love with God in the college canteen
when she is an impressionable teenager and he a
ragged, streetwise student. God's driving ambition
leads him into journalism while Nisha lands a job in
advertising. Sycophants, court jesters, whores, dirty
old men, fixers, pretty boys and party girls drift in
and out of their lives as their careers take off with
dizzying speed and then, abruptly and harrowingly,
everything about their lives goes wrong . . .

For more information,
visit www.penguinbooksindia.com.

Also by Shobhaa Dé

Starry Nights

Aasha Rani, Bombay's no. 1 heroine, has everything she wants—fame, money, success. All except for Akshay Arora, the film star she is desperately and unhappily in love with. This is her story—from her early days as a vulnerable small-town girl, pushed by her ambitious mother into sleeping her way to the top, to getting her first break from Kishenbhai, the small-time distributor who never stops loving her, to sealing her career under the patronage of the deadly Bombay don Sheth Amirchand. Glittering, glamorous and full of unforgettable characters, *Starry Nights* is the ultimate Bollywood novel.

For more information,
visit www.penguinbooksindia.com.

Also by Shobhaa Dé

Snapshots

Six school friends come together for a reunion. As the wine and conversation begin to flow, memories start to surface—some happy, others bittersweet and some utterly poisonous. Forced to confront secrets that they thought lay buried deep in the past, the women begin to turn against one another and the mood of the happy party becomes something much, much darker . . .

For more information,
visit www.penguinbooksindia.com.

Also by Shobhaa Dé

Strange Obsession

Amrita Aggarwal, young, gorgeous and sexy, comes to Bombay from Delhi to make her career as a successful supermodel. Within months of her arrival in the glamorous city, she is the envy of its beautiful people. Then, one day, she attracts the attention of a mysterious woman called Minx, and before she knows it, Amrita is trapped in a relationship that takes over her life.

For more information,
visit www.penguinbooksindia.com.